SHALLOW RIVER

USA TODAY BESTSELLING AUTHOR

H. D. CARLTON

Cover Design: TRC Designs by Cat
Editing: Angie Hazen with Lunar Rose Editing
Interior Formatting: Chelsea Timm
Distributed by Zando

Fourth Edition: November 2024

978-1-63893-251-2 (Paperback)

10 9 8 7 6 5 4 3 2 1

Manufactured in the United States of America

Important Note:

Shallow River is a dark romance that contains *very* triggering situations such as graphic domestic violence, graphic rape (not between main love interests), all forms of abuse, manipulation, gaslighting, graphic violence, graphic language, graphic sexual scenes, murder, mention of child assault (not depicted), familial abuse, and kidnapping.

Please take these warnings seriously.
Your mental health matters.

If you or anyone you know is experiencing domestic violence and needs support, please call 1-800-799-7233, or if you are unable to speak safely, you can log onto thehotline.org or text LOVEIS to 1-866-331-9474.

YOU ARE NOT ALONE.

For the vulnerable. For the strong.
For the survivors. For the warriors.

One

River

MY FIST CONNECTS WITH THE fucker's nose. The crunch of bone is satisfying as it gives beneath my knuckles. I haven't even pulled my fist from his face yet, and I already want to do it again.

Expletives burst from his mouth as blood trickles down his nose. The flashing colored lights from the disco balls above us wash the blood in different shades of red. One hand clutches his broken nose while the other rises to backhand me. I gear up, ready to take the slap, but a hand shoots out to catch his arm. Said hand is attached to a man whose looks rival a god. I give him a once over, and I'm immediately attracted to him.

He's the dark, rugged type. The type your mom insists is bad for you even though she secretly wants to fuck him, too. Well above six feet, with dark hair and pretty eyes. I'm willing to bet the fake diamond ring on my finger that he has a wicked smirk capable of disintegrating any straight female's panties off.

I turn and walk away. I don't even say thank you.

"Girl, can we go out just *once* without you murdering a guy's nose?" my best friend, Amelia, playfully pleads from beside me. It's our freshman year of college and I managed to land the best roommate. I never had friends before her.

I snort. "Apparently not. It's not my fault he was grabbing my tit. We'd been dancing for literally thirty-eight seconds," I say with exasperation.

"Thirty-eight seconds, huh?" Amelia repeats, cocking a perfectly sculpted eyebrow. I'd kill for her eyebrows.

"I was counting to an appropriate time to move on to the next guy, but I suppose I shouldn't be so gracious next time."

She tips her head back and laughs. I grab her hand and guide her the rest of the way through the crowd and up to the bar. I shoulder-check a few on the way since saying "excuse me" politely only grants me a dirty look and silence.

I'd never been the patient type, anyway.

When I reach the bar, I lean over, showing an ample amount of cleavage, and wait for the bartender to notice me. Impatiently, might I add.

The bartender that notices me first is a chick. Honey blonde hair, hazel eyes, and a dainty nose ring. She glances down at what I'm offering. When I chose my skin-tight, emerald green dress, it was specifically for the way it makes my ass and tits look photoshopped.

One... two... and here she comes.

I return her wicked smile.

"Two Long Islands, please," I order.

"Sure thing," she says, adding a saucy smile. I like her.

"And two lemon drops!" Amelia shouts from beside me when the bartender turns to make our drinks. She acknowledges Amelia's request with a sexy wink. I lick my lips in response.

"You're determined to give me a hangover, aren't you?" I complain to Amelia, still eyeing the bartender. Her ass is cupped perfectly by her ripped jean shorts. I pull my eyes away, refusing to leer like the dirty men invading this club like cockroaches.

"Says the bitch ordering a *Long Island*. You only need two of those, and you're on your ass."

I sniff. "Whatever."

The bartender comes back with our requests, sliding them toward us. Before I can say thank you, another girl is calling her away—one with a much curvier body and gorgeous red hair.

I'd ignore me for her, too.

"River, quit eye fucking the bartender. You're not even into girls," Amelia chides. I slurp on my Long Island, ignoring the people wanting to get in to order their drinks.

She's kind of right. I've never been with a girl. But that doesn't mean I haven't thought about it. Doesn't mean I *wouldn't*.

"How are you and David doing?" I ask, changing the subject. She and her boyfriend have been together for a couple of years and were best friends for even longer. The puppy love hasn't faded even to this day, despite his parents not approving of her.

A dreamy look takes over her eyes, and just for a split second, I want to stab them with my straw. Not any reflection on her or her boyfriend. I love them both.

But I'm jealous.

I've never had that. Not with any man. And sometimes—well, sometimes it fucking hurts.

The feeling fades in plumes of smoke when a gorgeous smile spreads across her face. After all, her happiness does bring me peace. Stars twinkle in her eyes when I mention David. If I could snatch a couple from the sky and put them in her eyes, it'd only tarnish the glow. Amelia hasn't had the easiest childhood, either. She deserves someone who will love her unconditionally.

"He's amazing," she croons. "He's taking me on a surprise date tomorrow. Won't tell me what it is. I even coerced him with a blowjob."

I cock an eyebrow. "And it didn't work?"

A blush creeps into her cheeks and a guilty smile tugs at her lips. "It kind of backfired. He ended up making me completely forget about it, actually."

I laugh at her sheepishness. "That sounds like a good problem to have," I comment, gulping more of my Long Island down.

I should slow down.

"You should slow down," Amelia says, echoing my exact thoughts. I swear the bitch can read my mind sometimes.

"I should," I agree half-heartedly.

But I don't.

CALABRIA BY *ENUR* PULSES through the surround sound and into my veins. My vision is blurred, and Amelia is somewhere behind me, trailing along, just as inebriated as I am. My body threatens to move to the beat before I've fully made it to the dance floor. The crowd claps along with the beat, and I spot a few girls busting moves that would land me in a hospital.

I get lost in the crowd and finally let loose.

My hands rise as my hips seek each beat. I sway and twirl to the upbeat song, laughing as my world spins. I'm free. Unchained from life and all its expectations as my feet carry me across the dirty dance floor.

I feel the touch on my raised hands first, light and sensual. His fingers skim the ring on my finger, but it doesn't deter him. I wear it for that exact purpose, but it doesn't always work. Something tells me he knows it's fake. I don't know how, but I can feel it in the way his hands trail my body like he's daring me to say no.

I don't dare look at my next victim behind me. I begin to count as his hands trail down my arms, leaving goosebumps in their wake, down my sides and across my hips.

Eight, nine, ten…

His hands grip my hips possessively, as if he's finally caught the rare jewel in the middle of a dangerous trap. I'm pulled against a physique far bigger than mine. Heat soaks into my body as an intoxicating smell fills my senses. A spicy cologne with a hint of sweat. Absolutely divine.

Fifteen, sixteen, seventeen…

Our hips collide, and I'm pleased to find that there's *not* a hard dick digging into my back. I like a man with control.

I gyrate against him, his hips matching my movements perfectly. Surprisingly, a smile breaks across my face. Starting out small and then widening until I'm nearly laughing again. And somewhere between the end of Calabria and the middle of the next song, I stopped counting.

Still, I don't look him in the face.

His touch stays strong and confident, but never crossing a line or roaming to inappropriate territories. Soft lips travel across my neck and shoulders, but he never sinks his teeth into the apple. He never loses control.

Oh, how I want him to.

It leaves me a writhing mess. The pulsating heat between my legs grows stronger with each song that passes us by.

I'm lost in him. So lost.

I want him. I want him wrapped around my body as he loses himself inside me. I want to be wrapped around his when I ensnare him and don't let go until the morning light creeps through my windows. Only then will I show his lost soul how to leave.

I ache for all of this without even seeing his face. His body chemistry tells me he's attractive. He's confident. Smooth and languid.

And he aches for me too.

I'm snapped from my sweet fantasy when a desperate tug nearly pulls me from the universe our bodies created. My eyes snap open and Amelia's green face is before me. Without having to ask, the hands leave my body and I'm left bereft and bone-chilling cold.

I don't want to leave. My friend needs me, though. I step away without looking back. It hurts, but I don't want a face attached to that fantasy. I'd rather he remain anonymous so I don't look for him every place I go and in every face that passes me by.

ANGELS ARE FLOATING AROUND me, beckoning me to come closer. To crawl into the light—a painful blinding light that's setting off a plethora of fireworks inside my head. I'm certainly not capable of fucking standing right now.

I'll blow chunks everywhere if I do.

I groan, rolling over in my bed. The dorm room mattress is normally not the most comfortable, but right now, it feels like I'm lying on a bed of rocks. My blankets feel like wet nylon and I think the little feathers in my pillow are poking through.

I'm still in last night's dress, makeup is caked all over my face, and my mouth tastes like dead skunk.

I've never eaten dead skunk, but I'm positive this is what it tastes like.

An answering groan sounds from the other side of the room where Amelia's bed is.

"I fucking hate you," Amelia growls, her voice raspy from sleep. I look over to see her waves of golden blonde hair spilling across her face, some of the strands stuck in her mouth. Usually Amelia is always sun-kissed, but right now she looks like a pale zombie. It doesn't help that her makeup is smeared across her face. I'm sure her raccoon eyes look exactly like mine. We'd be able to walk onto a horror movie set and be instantly hired on the spot.

"I hate me, too."

Even speaking right now sends sharp pin pricks of pain through my head. I try to remember if I have any classes today, but all of my thoughts are clogged in the toxins of alcohol. I give up trying to think, deciding I couldn't care less if I have class today or not. Whatever day today is.

My head is pounding and nausea swirls in the trenches of my stomach as I attempt to sit up. Hopelessly, I look to my nightstand and find an empty bottle of water.

Ugh. Fuck drunk River. Couldn't even set herself up for success before passing out.

Those goddamn Long Islands. They're the fucking devil wrapped in a pretty bow.

"We need greasy food," Amelia says as she sips on her full bottle of water. The sight has me irrationally frustrated, nearly to the point of tears. Why is drunk Amelia so much more successful than me?

Noting my distress, Amelia caps the bottle and tosses it to me. By the grace of god, it plops next to me on my bed instead of on the floor, where I was positive it would land with that sad throw. I sip the water gratefully, resisting the urge to chug it.

The thought of food makes me want to follow those annoying angels into the light. Who needs to be alive anyway? Let the wild have the fucking planet back. Nature deserves this planet more than we do anyway.

"Whoever throws up first is buying," I say.

"Deal, bitch."

I DRAG MY FRIES THROUGH the mound of ketchup and shove them into my mouth. It takes me forever to chew considering my throat refuses to swallow. The usually salty goodness tastes like rat poison on my tongue. I force the fries down and shove a few more in.

I'm not about to waste free food.

Since I won, I chose the place. *Marty's Diner*, the best hole-in-the-wall restaurant you'll find in North Carolina. Grease is permanently etched into every surface in this place, including the cracked red booths and tables decorated with random magazine clippings. Normally the smell soothes me, but right now the chemistry between my stomach contents and the fumes of grease are causing an epic cat fight in the pit of my stomach. My addled brain wanders, conjuring up an actual fighting pit with a ball of fumes and a green acidic blob with arms slapping each other like two grade schoolgirls.

"So, River, who's going to be your plus one to the party?" Amelia asks around her food, bringing my attention away from my alcohol-induced thoughts. Pretty sure I'm still drunk.

She grimaces as she chews, turns a little green, and has to choke her food down. I look away before her nausea makes my own worse. I'm a sympathy-puker.

I shrug my shoulders noncommittally. I don't even want to go, to be honest. I'm supposed to meet my mom that day. Not that that's a good reason to miss the party. I'd rather make a Venn Diagram of the taste of dead skunk and my morning breath than meet with Barbie.

"Maybe ask Ryan?" she hedges. My eyes whip to her, turning from tarnished yellow to molten gold. I know because Amelia has graciously called me out on it endlessly. Ryan brings that reaction out of me without my permission, and it's got to be the most annoying thing to date.

"You know he's dating Alison," I grumble. I hate that she can see I'm interested in him. Being interested in the male species sucks when they've done nothing but make me want to hate them. Alas, here I am, getting wet for a taken man. A man I always *think* I'm doing a stellar job at hiding my interest in, but really, I might as well get in a costume, and dance around like the poor souls you see on the side of the road, while waving a sign that points directly to my vagina. Open for business.

The man from last night creeps into my thoughts, but I push him from my mind before I become obsessed with the faceless stranger.

Amelia waves an unconcerned hand in the air, shooting me an exasperated look.

"They broke up last weekend," she says airily.

The fries I'm gripping freeze halfway to my mouth, the ketchup dripping off and into my lap.

"They broke up?" I echo nonchalantly, turning my attention to the ketchup on my already stained sweatpants in hopes that it'll hide my piqued interest. I'm hiding from her and she knows it. In all honesty, I'm floored. Ryan and his girlfriend were high school sweethearts. They've been together forever. I'm pretty sure they were even engaged.

"Yep," she chirps, the smirk on her face falling flat due to her having to work hard not to vomit everywhere.

Again.

"What happened?" I ask, attempting to sound casual. Fuck, I failed. I don't appear as unflappable as I hoped. I don't want to flap, damn it.

She shrugs a shoulder. "Not sure," she answers. "All I know is a horde of horny bitches are already flocking around him everywhere he goes. And Cindy said there was a frat party last night and he was already making out with another girl while Alison was in the same room."

My eyes widen into saucers. Fuck trying to appear cool, I don't care anymore. "Seriously? Did she get upset?"

Amelia shakes her head slowly, a weird look passing over her face. "That's the strange thing. Cindy said she looked as if she couldn't care less."

Hope flutters in my chest. Maybe that means I won't have to deal with a crazy ex if I ever take my shot with him. Forget the fact that he hasn't looked twice at me, that can easily be changed. Guys like Ryan are easy to ensnare if you know how to set the trap.

With that thought in the back of my mind, I change the subject onto Amelia's art project—I was never the gossiping type. Anyway, I'm genuinely interested in her art. She paints like Michelangelo and damn well knows it.

Now only if I can find my own damn hobby.

"YOU'RE LATE," BARBIE SNARLS, a half-smoked cigarette dangling from the corner of her crusted mouth. I can only imagine what the fuck kind of dirty substance she has wrapped around her lips—something tasty enough to let crust, I guess.

I shrug a shoulder, unconcerned with her bitching.

"What are you going to do about it?" I ask dryly. I can't remember the last time my mother evoked any real emotion in me besides irritation and wanting her to die already.

She calls me a few choice names—and I dutifully ignore her. Her lips tighten around the cigarette and she inhales until it's nearly depleted.

Good. Maybe she'll die faster.

"I should've aborted you," she mutters, her beady little eyes glaring holes into me.

"Oh, look. We can agree on something," I answer, emotionless as ever. "Do you have the goddamn money or what?"

She reaches into her dirty nightgown pocket and pulls out a few wadded up bills.

Dollar bills, to be precise.

"Please tell me you're fucking joking."

An evil grin slides across her face. Some of the crust cracks and flutters to her lap. I can hardly feel disgust.

"That's all you deserve."

I roll my eyes. If this waste of flesh had it her way, she wouldn't even give me half a penny. Not that the woman would put any effort into sawing the penny in half anyway—not when she has to save her energy for fucking men for drugs.

"What I deserve and what you're required to do are two different things, Barbie," I retort, trying to keep my cool and failing. I'm not even angry that she doesn't have my money. I expected it actually. But *fuck*, having to be in this woman's vicinity more than what's absolutely necessary does strike irritation in my soul. Barbie not having all the money means I have to come back.

She isn't used to our new arrangement yet, but she has no choice but to get intimate with this new relationship between us.

"Where's the rest?" I ask while simultaneously begging Jesus for patience. And maybe some divine intervention. If a tree is struck by lightning and falls directly onto the house exactly where she's standing, I'd become a nun.

"In my veins," she snips, turning to open the fridge. I curl my lip when mold wafts from the old thing. The fridge was broken when I still lived here, and Lord knows she can't afford a new one when she snorts or injects all the money she's not forking over to me.

She pulls out a half empty water bottle.

I never was a half-glass-full type of chick.

I snort when I glimpse the utter emptiness in the fridge before the door swings shut behind her. Which means that mold has been there for a while, and she just never cleaned it. All cleaning ceased to exist the moment I moved out.

Figures.

"Let me guess: didn't get enough clients? Has your moneymaker finally dried up from all the STD-ridden dicks you stick inside of it?"

"Fuck you, River," she hisses, throwing the now empty bottle at me. It falls short and thuds uselessly to the ground. How poetic.

"That was just embarrassing to watch," I say, smiling at her anger. She looks tempted to charge at me, but we both know I'd knock her out easily.

I picked enough fights in my childhood to breed myself into a scrappy bitch. Not that I need to know how to fight when it comes to a half-dead wraith like her trying to hurt me. Those fights were lessons, and they wouldn't have been as vital as oxygen in my lungs if it wasn't *because* of her and her clients. It's something I'll never say thank you for, but she can thank herself if she ever has the misfortune of running into my fist.

"I should've—"

"We are both well aware of the things you *should've* done, Barbie. But alas, that doesn't change the fact that you don't have my fucking money," I snap, finally becoming fed up with this merry-go-round we constantly find ourselves on.

She opens her mouth to spew more poisonous words my way, but a knock on the front door cuts her off. Her lip curls.

"Get out, I have a client."

I throw the useless dollar bills back at her, the crumpled paper balls falling at her feet.

"Work extra hard tonight. I want my money by Tuesday."

Three days should be plenty for a whore like her.

Two

River

I SLIDE IN THE car with a bright smile on my face, my eyes already pinned to my boyfriend. Dark blonde hair swept to the side, a maroon sweater with a collared flannel peaking around his neckline and wrists, pressed khakis, loafers, and a wristwatch. He drips elegance and class.

Normally, the pretty boy get-up isn't my type. Ryan's different, though. He carries himself with such confidence and ease—in a way that suggests he's not scared of anything. It enraptured me.

If nothing could scare him, then surely the monsters hiding in my head wouldn't, either.

Ryan's eyes meet mine, the dull blue swirling with secrets and something dark that drew me in like a moth to a flame. After almost two years together, I feel like I've only scratched the surface with him.

And finally, I'm meeting his parents. For so long, he held off, claiming he didn't want to introduce another girl to his parents until he was sure it was the girl he was going to marry. The day he told me he wanted me to meet them was one of the happiest days of my life.

He says they're going to love me. I say they're going to love me, too.

Parents usually do.

"You're wearing a lot of makeup," he comments. The smile melts off my face like butter in a frying pan.

I blink.

"No more than usual," I argue gently. I don't look away as I slide my seatbelt on.

He turns away from me anyway, putting his BMW in drive and lurching ahead with ease. I tuck a strand of my curly black hair behind my ear, suddenly self-conscious. Did I go too heavy on the foundation? Does my face look like a dimpled cake? Maybe I should've gone without the eyeliner.

"Maybe it'll turn out," Ryan says after several minutes of silence. My eyes slide toward him again. Sometimes it feels like getting too close to a black hole. He sucks you in, body and soul, with no chance of escape while he destroys every last bit of you.

"How so?"

"It'll be sexy to see it running down your face after you suck my cock." He says it casually, but with just enough darkness creeping in.

My perfectly sculpted brows pull into a small V. He's still looking ahead, one hand on the wheel, another resting casually on the gearshift. The picture of sexiness and strength. A small smirk pulls at the corner of his thin lips. That's his tell. He's feeling particularly savage tonight.

"You mean after dinner?" I clarify, hoping I'm right.

He spares me a slight glance from the corner of his eye, his smirk tightening.

"Right now, River."

Hope—what a useless emotion.

He's punishing me for wearing too much makeup. He says I'm a natural beauty and makeup makes me look like a whore. But I've always loved dressing my face up with colors. I make sure not to go too heavy, but it doesn't matter to Ryan. Intensifying my beauty means intensifying stares from other men. He's possessive and gets territorial when other men hit on me. He hasn't worn me down from wearing it yet, though.

Sometimes I like it when he tries. And sometimes I don't.

His cock is already hard, straining against his khakis. He's an average guy, but he uses it like it's a weapon.

"Ryan..." His eyebrow quirks in a challenge at my hesitance, daring me to defy him. I lick my lips as a sick feeling builds in my chest. How can I get out of this without upsetting him? If I refuse, it'll disappoint him, and that's the last thing I want.

"I'm meeting your parents for the first time. I need to make a good first impression." My argument is valid. But yet, it comes out weak. Why is that? It sounds like I'm saying that my breath smells bad so I can't suck his dick right now.

Normally, I'd be all over the opportunity. There's always a healthy dose of trepidation when it comes to sex with Ryan. He has a strange appetite, and I'm still learning how to handle it. All I want is to satisfy him. Make him happy. Give him something no other woman has before me.

Striving for Ryan's approval has been my number one priority since the day I kicked a girl out of her seat next to him and replaced her. His flavor of the week didn't appreciate it, and I promptly told her to fuck off. He looked at me as if he was seeing a real woman for the first time—awe, admiration, and a whole lot of need.

It sparked something inside of me. Actually, it lit an entire inferno. From that day forward, I wanted Ryan to look at me like that every day.

Like every day is a new discovery.

Ryan liked my shamelessness at the time. But now he likes me docile. Makeup running down my face isn't a maybe—it's a promise. One that he'd no doubt go out of his way to make happen. Yet, my body betrays me, the heat between my legs growing damp.

I'm disappointed in myself. Disappointed that even though I genuinely don't want to do this, my body says the opposite.

Ryan knows it, too. I deflate. I'm not going to pull that look out of him if I refuse.

"You have ten minutes until we're there," he says icily. He doesn't even bother unbuttoning for me. He'd rather I waste time.

Anxiety infiltrates my nerves. My hands shake and fumble with his button, pulling a cruel snicker from his throat. Tears prick at my eyes, feeling embarrassed. Ryan is so experienced, and it always makes me feel like a virgin.

I do as he says. And he keeps his word, too. He pushes my head down until I'm choking and gasping. And just when I think I'll pass out, he pushes my head down harder. Tears leak out of my eyes, snot down my nose as slobber rims my mouth.

It takes the asshole nine minutes to come.

I'm heaving in air when we pull into the driveway. Pulling down the visor, I survey the damage.

I'm an absolute fucking mess.

I wipe the evidence away as best as I can, but I don't look as pretty as I did when I got in the car. I think he likes me ugly.

"Make sure you look presentable," he orders. A growl works its way up my throat and tears spring to my eyes anew, this time from frustration. Why does he need to dig the knife in deeper? He got what he wanted. And obviously, I need to look presentable for my own dignity, not his. Despite my anger, I don't say this out loud. It might make him upset with me, and I'm already exhausted.

Ryan's relaxed now, his muscles languid as he watches me clean up. Thankfully, I have spare essential makeup in my purse. I powder my face and glide a tube of red lipstick across my plump lips just to spite him. Then use a Q-tip to remove the rest of the eyeliner without messing up anything else.

Q-tips are life.

His hand gently caresses my cheek when I'm finished, though a spark of derision flashes in his eyes when he notes the red lipstick.

"I love you," he murmurs.

He looks at me like I'm a possession. I like being possessed by him. Those three words wipe away any lingering anger or embarrassment. I'm fucking pathetic.

"I love you, too," I say, that lost smile found again and adorning my face once more. I'm ready to meet his parents now. Maybe one day, they'll become my in-laws. They'll be the first parents I've ever had.

Ryan met my mother three weeks ago. It was everything you could expect when walking into a viper's pit. She sneered at him with disdain. He tipped his chin and looked down upon her in equal measure, while I shifted nervously from foot to foot. When he ordered me to keep still, asserting his dominance over me, I listened. Barbie snarled and called me weak. Part of me had to agree with her.

Growing up in a shitty town, in a shitty house with an even shittier mother, teaches you to be independent. Shallow Hill is a breeding ground for gangs, prostitutes, and the homeless. I've learned to survive. But I'm bereft of human connection. Sometimes it feels like Ryan takes that pathetic need inside of me and wields it to his advantage.

While Barbie lives amongst the cockroaches, the Fitzgerald's live in comfort and style. Ryan's childhood home is a three-story gray house with accented stone walls and a stone entrance. Cute light posts line the walkway leading up to the bright red front door. Warm glowing light breeches the windows, inviting anyone into its warmth.

And there's grass. Green grass, to be precise. With a white picket fence surrounding it. My house never had grass that green—just overgrown tufts of brown, brittle blades, beaten down by random junk littering the yard.

The door opens right as our feet hit the first step. The first thing that assaults my senses is the smell of homemade apple pie. It smells absolutely divine, nearly causing my eyes to roll to the back of my head, much like Ryan's were just a few minutes ago. A glowing, smiling face greets us next.

Ryan's mother is stunning. Blonde hair, bright blue eyes, and subtle laugh lines that curl around a sincere smile. She radiates pure positive energy—something I've never quite experienced before. I could wrap myself around her in a warm hug, and it would feel like coming home.

Yeah.

She could be my mom.

"Welcome home, honey," she says to Ryan first, jutting her cheek out to accept a chaste kiss. Turning to me, she gushes, "Oh, aren't you beautiful. My name is Julie. Please come in."

Beautiful.

The word makes me shudder. Too many times has the word tumbled out of cracked lips, yellowed jagged teeth, and accompanied by rancid breath. I don't let the word falter my smile. Perseverance.

"It's so wonderful to meet you, Mrs. Fitzgerald. Thank you for having me," I say politely, a beaming smile chasing my words.

"Oh, please, call me Julie," she corrects, waving a hand at my greeting.

"I think I can handle that," I add with a cute wink. When she laughs, we collectively melt at each other's fingertips. Instantly, I feel a bond with her that reminds me so much of Camilla, someone who used to resemble a mother so many years ago.

Ryan surveys the interaction with a keen eye. When my golden eyes clash with his, he gives me a nod of praise. I didn't need his reassurance—I already know I have Julie's approval. But his praise sends pride through my veins like a dose of morphine.

Mr. Fitzgerald is a tall, plump man with deep laugh lines, sparkling brown eyes, and a gentle hand when he engulfs my dainty hand in his. He introduces himself as Matt. His energy is on the same wavelength as Julie's. Warm and safe.

"I'm River, it's so nice to meet you."

"What an interesting name," he comments lightly.

"It's where I was born," I shrug. His eyebrows skyrocket in question, his attention now piqued.

Not very many people are born in rivers. It's pretty unsanitary. But that word sums up the entirety of Shallow Hill.

"But that's a story for another day," I laugh, hoping—*praying*—he'll move on. He does with a tinge of reluctance, the unusual birthplace intriguing to him. I haven't even told Ryan that story yet. Not that he's ever asked.

It's not a happy story anyway. Maybe, he assumes that and doesn't want to hear about my suffering because he loves me.

Or he's just a dick, and I'm delusional.

Just as I relax, a god walks through the foyer. At first, I'm convinced that I'm the only one who can see him. Certainly, pointing out that Zeus' evil, sexier twin is walking around in the human realm would make me sound crazy.

But then Ryan tenses into solid stone next to me. Maybe he has Medusa's powers?

Julie ushers the man forward, encouraging an introduction.

Please don't.

He's tall—over six feet, but I've never been good at guessing heights. Ink black hair, a little longer on top than the sides, vivid green eyes that rival the grass outside, and tattoos. Tattoos everywhere.

"Are you his brother?" The question is out before I can stop it. I carefully arrange my face into innocent curiosity. Ryan's rigid limbs unhinge long enough to turn his head to glare at me. The approval disappears like smoke in the wind.

Strike two, River. Clearly, there's strife between the two.

The man's plump lips glide into a smirk. One that tells me he knows I never knew of his existence until now. That smirk may cause a visceral reaction inside of me that I refuse to name or acknowledge, but too bad for him. He may be hot, but I'm in love with Ryan.

"I am," he answers shortly. I'm rocked to the core when he speaks. His voice is as deep as the ocean but smooth and creamy. He's too perfect. One of the reasons why Ryan hates him. It hasn't been said aloud. After all, I didn't even know he existed until two minutes ago. But Ryan and I are attuned to each other now. I can feel what he feels. And hatred is rolling off him in waves.

A good girlfriend would hate him too, purely by association. Certainly, there's a good reason why Ryan hates him.

I hum, arranging my face into a blank expression. I won't be outwardly rude to him in front of Julie and Matt, however I won't make the mistake of being nice, either.

Julie's delicate hand lands on his boulder of a bicep, a red tinge brightening her cheeks. "River, this is my other son, Mako. Mako, this is Ryan's girlfriend, River," Julie says, noting the lack of introduction her sons offered and eyeing them both with disapproval.

I offer a polite, "Nice to meet you, Mako."

What a stupid name.

Again, he quirks that stupid brow like he knows what I'm thinking. And when he answers, it feels like he's responding to my thoughts. "Likewise."

Ryan subtly shifts his body in front of me. Stupid boy. He just gave away his insecurity.

I like that he's insecure when it comes to me.

Mako notices, and his brow quirks higher. He doesn't smirk. Or consider it a challenge. He just shakes his head and walks away.

Odd.

"You didn't tell me you had a brother," I whisper accusingly when Julie and Matt follow Mako towards the dining room.

"I don't," he clips before storming off after them.

You do, liar.

JULIE AND MATTHEW HAVE a house straight out of a Home Improvement magazine. The whole design is a rustic atmosphere, with exposed wooden beams, various stains of wood, and soft light throughout the area that brings you comfort and warmth. Everything about this place screams homey, despite its enormous size. It's hard pulling my eyes away from every detail when all I can wonder is what my life would have been like had I grown up in a house like this.

Can't imagine I would be as bitter as the two grown men sitting at the table, one is spewing hateful glares and the other ignoring his existence entirely. Mako will only look or interact with his parents, but when he does, his expression is full of warmth and respect. Whereas, Ryan picks at his dinner like a spoiled child forced to eat his greens.

How can anyone be unhappy when you have a home and parents like this?

"So, River, Ryan told me that you're graduating college this year. What did you major in?" Matt asks right before spooning a pile of broccoli in his mouth. Ryan rests his hand on my thigh and squeezes as if warning me not to say the wrong thing.

What a typical question. Why not ask me what my interests are? Where I grew up? What kind of person I am? How about the things that actually tell you about a person?

I could be a crazy bitch. Maybe I *am* a crazy bitch. Wouldn't that be important to know?

I smile serenely. "Psychology."

What a typical answer.

As if reading my mind, Ryan rolls his eyes. He never did approve of my career choice.

Why don't you want me to figure you out, sweet Ryan?

"Why psychology?" Mako asks this time, sparing me a glance from his food. I shiver when his voice rolls over me. He hasn't spoken to me since our introduction.

Hmm. Because my mother did a lot of fucked up things when I was a child, and I'm desperate to understand why? No, it can't be that. Who would care to understand a crackhead? That's all there is to her. Jagged, cracked pieces.

I shrug a shoulder. "Because I'm good at figuring people out," I answer blandly.

"Ah, you found yourself a smart one, Ryan. Make sure you're careful," Matt teases, winking at Ryan as he does. Matt talks with his mouth full and Julie lightly admonishes him for doing so. He just grins at her in return.

Something tells me not a lot bothers Matt. It makes me want to figure out what does.

Ryan scoffs lowly. "I think I can handle her."

I think I can handle you too, baby.

Dinner drags on. Every time I'm asked a question, Ryan squeezes my thigh, warning me to watch my mouth. I'm not sure what I could possibly say, but I'm beginning to feel discouraged. Do I embarrass him that much?

By the time I shove the last piece of sinful apple pie in my mouth, I can feel a bruise forming. It's almost enough to distract me from the pie, but I'm pretty sure we can get bombed by a terrorist right now, and I'd still ask for seconds. He'll kiss the bruise for me later.

"Do you need help cleaning up?" I ask Julie graciously. She smiles at me and accepts. Ryan taps my thigh twice in appreciation. I beam as giddiness floods my chest.

I collect mine and Ryan's plates first, my hands shaking at the prospect of breaking Julie's fine china. With Matt and Julie's kind of money, this china probably costs more than my college tuition. If I break it, I'll embarrass Ryan. He'd never forgive me for that.

When I circle around to collect Mako's plate, he gradually slides his gaze up to me. His eyes connect with mine, and I wish I hadn't stuck around. Julie should've taken his dishes.

I hold out an expectant hand, keeping a pleasant smile on my face. He takes his time as if I'll be standing here waiting for him no matter what. Ryan's eyes are searing into the side of my head, all previous appreciation gone.

Now I'm mad. I worked hard for that.

"Did your arm lose its motor function?" I ask with a bored tone when Mako just stares.

The slightest curl tugs on his lush lips. Without looking away, he hands the plate over. I yank it out of his grip and rush away; china be damned. My heart is racing and my stomach is fluttering. For the life of me, I can't figure out why. He hadn't even spoken to me.

"You okay?" Julie asks, noting the expression on my face. I'm not sure what it looks like, but I imagine I look flustered. Far more flustered than I should be when I just ate the best apple pie in North Carolina. Probably even the world.

"Fine," I smile, gently setting the plates in the soapy water Julie had prepared.

"I'll wash, you dry," she says.

How cliché. I smile, and listen, grabbing a dry towel and awaiting the first plate. I don't think washing dishes has ever been so stressful in my life.

"So, how did you and my son meet?"

I frown, a little surprised Ryan hadn't already told her. I assumed Ryan had at least told her all about me.

"School," I supply, forcing a smile back on my face. "We were in the same American History class together. I noticed him before he ever noticed me." Fondly, remembering all those times I'd watched Ryan walk in through the doors, laughing and talking with his friends. Sometimes even with another girl. Those moments sucked.

After he and Alison broke up, it took only a couple of months before I said fuck it and decided to kick the girl out of her seat and sit next to him. I was a little freshman and he was the big bad senior, girls dripping off his arms like water. Even after I pursued him, it wasn't until halfway through my sophomore year that he committed to only me, long after he had graduated. He'd just gotten out of a long relationship and wasn't ready for another one so soon, he had told me. He wanted to spend the rest of his college years single.

I had waited for him.

Julie hands me a plate. Anxiety taunts me as I grab the plate with the towel, careful not to smudge it with my fingers. I delicately wipe it dry and set it down with as much grace as I can muster. I'm generally not clumsy, but I'm also not usually nervous, either. I don't handle nerves well.

"He's a good kid. Both of my boys are," she says. "It seems like you two are in love."

The compliment sends warmth rushing through my veins. If his mom can see it, then he must really love me, right?

"We are," I agree.

Someone snorts from behind us. "Yeah, right."

I nearly drop the plate in my hand. That *voice*. A different warmth fills my body. It's a feeling I can't describe, but it shames me anyway. He shouldn't be making me feel *anything*.

Carefully setting the plate down, I turn and eye Mako with distaste. Instead of shooting off the mouth like I want to, I turn and give him my back. He means nothing to me.

It won't make a good impression in front of Ryan's mother if I get into an argument with her other son. I also would never want to embarrass Ryan like that.

"Oh, stop it, Mako," Julie admonishes lightly, waving a soapy hand in the air to wash away his words, sending suds flying onto my own.

"Ryan doesn't love anyone more than himself," Mako states dryly, as he reaches into the fridge and grabs a beer. I focus on the suds sizzling on my tanned skin, watching the bubbles pop and slowly disintegrate.

Don't engage, River. That's what he wants.

"She'll be gone soon. Just like the last ones. But I figure she knows that already since she's so good at figuring people out."

Three

River

MY HEAD SLAMS INTO the wall as a hand encircles my jaw. Ryan's teeth follow, ravaging my neck until I'm gritting my jaw from the mix of pain and pleasure. I arch my back, moaning while his sharp teeth draw blood to the surface.

"No hickey," I warn, pushing at his bare chest a little. He just presses into me further, growling at me in warning.

"You're mine. I'll do whatever the fuck I please," he snarls, switching his attack to the other side of my neck.

He bites down particularly hard, eliciting a sharp gasp from between my lips. It *hurts*. But I don't stop him. I want this. I really do. *I do, I do, I do.*

I dole out my own pain, clawing my nails across his chest. A thigh wedges between my own, and I shamelessly grind on it, drawing out my pleasure. More moans slip from my throat, as his hands grip my bare breasts and squeeze. I don't have enormous tits, but they still overflow Ryan's hands. He loves that.

Pinching a nipple between his fingers, he rips his mouth away from my neck—finally—and attacks my mouth, thrusting his tongue between my teeth. I swallow him greedily, sending moans circling around our tongues. I grind harder, feeling the beginnings of an orgasm start to build.

I need more, though.

"Fuck me," I beg between kisses.

He jerks back, glaring intensely at me. His blue eyes have darkened into the likes of deep ocean waters. It's a little off-putting that I can't discern if it's from lust or anger. Or perhaps a little of both.

"You want me to fuck you? Or do you wish I were Mako instead?" he growls, circling his hand back around my neck and slamming my head roughly against the wall once more. Not hard enough to hurt really, but his aggression is confusing.

I still, and my brows draw forward. Ice drenches my body, extinguishing all the heat radiating from my pores.

"What?" I ask, utterly baffled by his question. My blood chills as Ryan continues to glare. There's no longer a question if it's from lust or anger. My boyfriend is completely enraged, and I've no idea why. I hadn't thought of Mako once since we stepped through the door and he ripped my clothes off.

"Don't play fucking stupid, River."

My mouth opens and closes, not sure what the hell to say. His question blindsides me. He takes it for guilt, and pushes off me, roughly slamming me into the wall for the third time, hard enough to cause me to topple over. I hit my elbow on the floor in the process, the pain shooting up my arm.

"I fucking knew it," he growls, looking at me with accusation.

I stare up at him in shock, panic blooming. How could he possibly think that? Why can't he see how much I love him? "Ryan, I have no idea what you're talking about. I don't want Mako, I only want you," I plead, desperate for him to just see the truth. Because I *don't* want Mako. I scramble off the floor and step towards him, my hands raised with placation.

He does better and charges towards me. Instinctively, I back up into the wall. This wall and I have never been so well acquainted, and it's starting to grate on my nerves. He presses his chest into mine and leans forward until his breath is tickling my ear.

"If you're lying to me, I will hurt you, River."

The threat sends cold shivers down my spine. He's never threatened me before, not with physical violence at least. Just a minute ago, I was on top of the world, ready to get myself off on his thigh before he brutally fucked me. Now, I feel bereft.

Empty, unsatisfied, and utterly fucking bereft.

"I'm not," I say. It sounds weak. Pathetic and desperate.

The moment over, he huffs like a bull and stalks away, jeans still hanging low on his hips. I look down at my own naked body. A handprint decorates my thigh from dinner.

Tilting my head to the side, I study it.

In my psychology books, this would be considered abuse. But do I feel abused?

The tear trailing down my cheek answers my question for me. I wipe it away before Ryan sees it.

Asshole.

"SO, HOW DID MEETING the parents go?" Amelia asks, her expectant brown eyes radiating excitement. We're no longer roommates, but we never let each other go, even with us now in senior year and separate houses.

I force a wide smile. Meeting the parents went great until we got home, then everything went to shit. I'm still confused by what happened, and a cold, bottomless pit has nestled in my stomach ever since. "His parents are really nice. I think they liked me."

Amelia's grin grows, and she hops up and down a couple of times in excitement. My best friend is a good six inches shorter than me, so it's like watching a Leprechaun dance because they found the gold at the end of the rainbow. "I'm happy as fuck for you, girl. I know how important meeting the parents is."

She would. She and her husband, David, have been together for five years now, one of them married. In the beginning, David's Catholic parents didn't approve of Amelia's atheist beliefs. It took several years before they warmed up to her, and now they actually invite her over to dinner. They're a beautiful couple, inside and out. I've never met a man more genuine than David. Doesn't hurt that he looks like a lumberjack out of those erotic novels I'd sneak in the library when I was a little girl. Suppose it works considering Amelia looks like she stepped out of Vogue magazine, despite her shortness.

I shrug a shoulder. "To be honest, they're those kinds of parents that would probably love anyone as long as they aren't Satan worshippers or something. They're pretty chill people."

Amelia waves a hand. "Whatever the reason, I'm glad. Did you fuck in his childhood bed?" she asks, wiggling her brows at me suggestively. Now she looks like a Leprechaun enticing a young child to eat the lucky charms.

I chuckle. "None of that this time."

She makes a disgusted noise. "You disappoint me."

We're on our way to a local ice cream shop that sells the best ice cream in a fifty-mile radius. It's just a little shack with benches outside. Gives you that full experience—you're not truly eating ice cream unless you're racing the sun and attempting to eat it before it melts all over your hand.

"He has a brother, though. I didn't even know that until I got there," I mention casually. When Amelia stops walking and frowns at me, I bite my lip. "That's weird, isn't it?"

"Like, never, never mentioned him? Ever?"

"Never ever. He specifically said he was an only child, actually."

Her frown deepens, along with my teeth digging in my lip. I only stop when I begin to taste copper. Her blonde hair whips in the wind as she turns around and walks backward, strands sticking to her face as she seems to contemplate that. Her effortless beauty makes me want to smudge her makeup or something. I'm just waiting for her to trip, but she never does.

Graceful bitch, she is.

"You sure he's actually their son?"

I shrug my shoulders. "His mom said it on several occasions."

"Huh," she says. "Wonder why."

I snort. "Well, it was a little clear once I saw them together. They hate each other."

"Maybe they have some weird sibling rivalry going on," she says off-handedly.

We've arrived at the ice cream shop, and the menu has snagged her attention. I decide to let it go. I've heard of siblings hating each other. It happens. Normally, they don't act as if the sibling doesn't exist unless something major happens, though.

What are you hiding, sweet Ryan?

"Hey," a voice chirps from behind me. The sound makes my heart pause. I turn to find my nemesis—Ryan's ex-girlfriend.

Amelia turns and her face drops. She's never been formally introduced to Alison, but she knows exactly who she is. And she also knows the bitch tried to sabotage my relationship.

Light brown hair, hazel eyes that change colors depending on the lighting, and a bombshell body. She's beautiful, and I hated her at first sight. Even more so when I talked to her.

"Hey, Alison," I reply coolly. She has the audacity to look nervous.

"I'm sorry if I'm bothering you. I just wanted to see how you're doing?"

I try not to blanch, but I do anyway. Amelia's brows dip in confusion. I clear my throat.

"I'm fine."

Her shoulders drop, along with her voice as she whispers, "I really wish you'd listen to me."

Anger coils my innards so tightly, my throat closes. Amelia knows she's tried to sabotage my relationship, but I never told her *how*. And I don't plan to let her in on it.

"This is not the time or place," I hiss under my breath, so only she can hear.

Alison's plump, lying lips tighten into a hard line. Dimples pop out on her cheeks, and I hate her for it. My dimples are hidden in my laugh lines. Hers are cuter.

Finally, she nods her head. She spares Amelia a glance and then walks past me. Her hand touches my elbow briefly as she whispers, "Be careful."

I barely refrain from ripping my arm from her grip. Instead, I keep my gaze straight forward and let her pass.

Amelia hands my ice cream over slowly, eyeing the spot Alison disappeared from with confusion.

"She was… nice," she finishes hesitantly.

"She's a snake."

Amelia doesn't look convinced. And that breaks my heart a little.

"What did she say?"

"Nothing I haven't already heard. She's jealous and wants me to leave him."

I don't share the reasons why. Those are for me to consider.

Amelia's face morphs into disgust. "What a bitch."

She is, isn't she? I contemplate that as I lick my chocolate chip mint ice cream.

"WHERE WERE YOU?" Ryan asks right as I step through the door. I pause, and fuck, that made me look guilty. He's sitting on the couch, one foot resting on his knee as he watches ESPN. The house is spotless, and our cat, Bilby, snoozes on the headrest behind him.

"I got ice cream with Amelia after class."

"Yeah, I'm sure," he says snidely, not taking his eyes off the screen once. "She acts like a whore, so I'm sure there were guys there, too."

I sigh softly. "Babe, it was just us two, I promise. No guys. And she's happily married to David."

He rolls his tongue in his mouth. He's radiating anger. The air stinks of his bad attitude. "Let me see your phone then." I hesitate. Why does he need to see my phone?

He holds out an expectant hand. Reluctantly, I hand it over. Not because I have anything to hide, but because he doesn't trust me, and I want to fix that. Ryan's my first relationship, so it's not like I'm a notorious cheater and have a past. Don't get me wrong, I slept around with a few guys and Ryan knows that, but I was single and unattached. Ryan's done the same, so it's not fair to hold my past against me. His distrust is utterly unwarranted. I've never given Ryan any reason to think I'd want anyone else.

I watch him open my messages, scroll through them, and then open each chat and check those. Then he opens my social media, and finally, my pictures. He sets the phone down and nods his head in acceptance.

"Does this mean I get to look through your phone, too?" I say with an edge of bitterness. He looks up, and stares at me blankly. Embarrassment floods me. I'll take that as a no.

"How was work?" I try, changing the subject and attempting to sound cheerful. I hate it when he's angry.

He turns his glare to me. "My dad hired a new secretary. Same age as me. Couldn't keep her slut hands to herself."

My blood runs cold, and anxiety bursts in my stomach, swirling around like acid. Is she prettier than me? Did he fuck her? What if she's better than me?

"She better have," I snap, my increasingly dormant attitude rising to the surface.

Finally, a smile. Or rather, a smirk. His foot begins to bounce on his knee.

"Don't worry, baby. I don't want anyone but you," he assures with saccharine sweetness. Something dark unfurls in my chest, tainting any semblance of a good mood I had going. Alison had already put a damper on my day, and now Ryan's weird attitude is completely ruining it.

"Come here, baby. I just missed you, that's all. I'm pathetic and just want you around all the time," he says, patting the couch next to him. His tone seems genuine, though I still hesitate. Slowly, my fists unfurl, and my shoulders relax. Little red crescents are imprinted in my palm, and it burns. I hadn't realized I even clenched them.

At my reaction, his smile widens. "Come here. I missed you."

I walk over, grateful that he's in a better mood. I'm still a little angry about the woman, but when he looks at me with as much pride as he is now, it's hard not to forget about her.

I cuddle into his side, and he wraps an arm around me. A light kiss lands on my temple, and I'm tempted to start purring like Bilby.

A finger curls under my jaw, and gently, he raises my chin until I'm staring into his faded blue eyes. "Please don't ever leave me. I couldn't live without you."

"I would never leave you," I promise.

He shakes his head, and what looks like agony passes over his face. "Good. I don't think I would survive it. I'd probably kill myself."

A line forms between my brows. His words are sweet and unsettling, all in the same breath. "Don't say that, Ryan," I demand softly. "You wouldn't kill yourself."

"I would," he says firmly, his eyes boring into mine.

"Why?" I ask incredulously.

"I'll never find anyone that makes me as happy as you do," he says softly. "I'll never find anyone as perfect as you."

I melt. Like that fucking ice cream I ate earlier.

"I'm not. You're perfect for me."

He smiles, showcasing his beautiful smile. "Yeah?"

I bite my lip and nod. He grabs my hand and rubs it over his hard dick, straining against his shorts.

"Why don't you show me how perfect I am for you."

So, I do. He falls asleep only a minute after he comes, and I don't even have the energy to get myself off after the weird day I had.

IT'S A SUNDAY, AND Ryan and I have nothing planned. I wake with a smile on my face, excited to laze around all day with my boyfriend. He let me move into this house only a few months ago, and so far, we haven't gotten a whole day to just relax.

I stretch, enjoying all the tension being released from my muscles. Ryan's bed is absolute heaven, the perfect mixture of firmness and lying on a cloud. My body had lied on nothing but hard floors and lumpy beds up until I moved in. It had actually taken a good month before I stopped waking up incredibly sore—my body was not used to anything so luxurious. Now, I can hardly remove myself from the bed.

Ryan's side of the bed is empty. Patting the area, I find that it's cool. He's been up for a little while now. The smile slowly fades from my face as my hand wanders over the sheets he occupied all night. We used to wake up together on the weekends and snuggle in bed before getting up and attending to our responsibilities. It's been a few months since the last time he stuck around in the mornings.

Ryan's been acting weird lately. Aggressive, distrustful, distant, and flat-out mean. While Ryan's always been a bit edgy, he's never caused this amount of turmoil in our relationship before. Up until recently, he's always gone out of his way to make me feel special, loved, and cared for.

So many memories of wonderful dates that ended in passionate sex. Moments where we would just laugh together, sometimes for no reason at all. Him doting on me, professing love to me in the cutest ways, and always surprising me with sentimental gifts. I don't know when those memories started mixing with much darker ones. The sentiments and doting are nowhere to be seen. All the little things he used to do for me, like making sure I had coffee in the morning, keeping my favorite water stocked, or coming home with flowers after work, have disappeared. Now, it's just

Ryan demanding to go through my phone, calling me a whore for wearing too much make-up or revealing clothes, and now putting his hands on me in almost violent ways.

Work has been stressing him lately. Maybe that's why. He's still trying to make a name for himself that isn't attached to his father's. I can be understanding and let those little things go; they're not things I need from him anyway. As long as Ryan and I are happy, that's all that matters.

Hopping up, I quickly run my hands through my hair. I'll brush my teeth after breakfast. Though, I can't smell anything cooking yet.

When I walk down into the living room, Ryan's lounging shirtless on the couch with his laptop on his lap and his reading glasses perched on his nose. He looks so damn sexy, I want to jump his bones. Bilby is lying in his usual spot on the back of the couch, snoozing loudly.

I rescued him from the shelter a few months ago, and he's been my little shadow ever since. Ryan doesn't pay much attention to him, and often sneers at the cat hair everywhere, but otherwise doesn't complain too much. Ryan had asked me to quit my job when I moved in, so I've been lonely in the house while he works. Having a companion has eased the majority of my loneliness.

"Good morning," I chirp.

He spares me a glance but doesn't say anything.

I pause on the last step. *Uh. Okay then.*

"Do you want breakfast?" I ask.

"What do you think I've been waiting for?" he asks coldly, not looking up from his screen. My smile falls and all happiness slowly deflates.

"Fuck!" he shouts unexpectedly, slamming his laptop on the couch angrily. I jump from the sudden outburst, my hand flying to my chest as if I'm keeping it from jumping out of my ribcage.

"What's wrong?" I question breathlessly, trying to reign my heartbeat back into a normal tempo.

"Fucking internet went out again," he mutters, storming to his office where the router is. I stand there confused, staring at the space he disappeared from. He's been fighting with our cable company for the last few months about this, but he's never gotten this worked up about it before. Within seconds, he comes storming back in, plops down on the couch, and proceeds to work on his laptop again.

"Is there anything else wrong?" I ask hesitantly. Another glance, this time filled with annoyance.

"No."

Deciding to let it go, for now, I immediately start making breakfast. French toast, bacon and eggs. Maybe he's just hungry, and that's why he has an attitude. It'd be hypocritical to act like I don't get hangry sometimes, too. I pile his plate high when the food's done and even add a few fresh strawberries and cream on his French toast.

He takes the plate and digs in. In complete silence. Not even a thank you.

Of fucking course not.

Slowly, I sit down next to him and eat. Did I do something wrong? I don't want to anger him further. I look at him, watching his face for a reaction to the food. It'd only make things worse if I didn't make a good breakfast for him.

"Do you like it?" I ask anxiously. He glances at me, licking a dollop of cream from the corner of his mouth.

"I'm eating it, aren't I?"

I frown. That's not really an answer.

I can't put my finger on it, but there's a wall around him. Like if I speak, he'll snap. I keep my mouth closed. I keep it closed during breakfast, during lunch, and even during dinner. My only source of entertainment is playing with Bilby until Mary and Ava arrive.

They're the house cleaners Ryan hired to come every Sunday. Most days, I insist on helping. I'm a grown woman and perfectly capable of cleaning up after myself, so I always feel weird letting the girls clean up after us.

Mary is an older woman with salt and pepper hair, wrinkles around her eyes and mouth, and a slight hunchback. Her grandmother built their cleaning company from the ground up, and Mary, now in her sixties, has kept the business going. She's a very stern woman but has a gentleness she preserves just for Ava and me. Ava, Mary's granddaughter, follows in the family's footsteps. She's only sixteen, with sleek black hair, big doe eyes, and a shy smile. They've both always been so good to Ryan and I. And though Mary hates it when I help, she always ends up conceding since Ava focuses on cleaning better when I'm around.

Even after Mary and Ava leave, Ryan still doesn't speak to me throughout the rest of the day, and I start to get angry. He talks to a few people on the phone, and he's boisterous and laughs with them. Hands waving vigorously, more animated than a corpse awakened by a necromancer.

Why won't he talk that way to me? The moment he hangs up, the iciness settles back in, frosting the entire house with his energy. I'm generally not a petty person, but I'm on the verge of burning sage around the house to expel his negative vibes.

A few times, I tried to ask why he wouldn't talk to me. He didn't even look at me when he said, "You're not talking, either."

Yeah, because you're giving me the cold shoulder, dick.

He had nothing else to say, and if I pushed, he'd just get up and go to a different room in the house. Even Bilby couldn't cure my loneliness today. How can two people cohabitate the same house, but it feels like I'm alone? I give up trying, and by night, I'm silently fuming.

We went to bed perfectly fine last night. I woke up from the couch, and he gave me a cute sleepy smile. I helped him to bed, and he murmured how much he loved me. He cuddled me all night, up until early morning when he awoke before me.

And now this. We were fine. We were fucking fine. What happened?

I put a movie on without asking him if he wants to watch it. I could fucking care less if he does or not. I settle into the couch, the buttery black leather comforting me as I cuddle into a soft blanket. The living room is large, with three large sofa filling the space, a massive flat-screen television with Ryan's game consoles set up beneath it, and expertly placed décor and family pictures along the walls. Ryan's taste is more modern and sterile, with lots of black, gray, and white shades. It's a beautiful house, but it definitely lacks the homey, lived-in vibe that Julie and Matt's house has.

I'm halfway through the movie when Ryan closes his laptop and pokes me in the thigh playfully. The gesture irritates me, but I'd be a liar if it didn't also plant that hopeless feeling in me again. Hope. Hope is hopeless.

"Come cuddle with me," he whines good-naturedly. He even has the balls to give me puppy dog eyes.

I'm sorry, what? I look at him with a mixture of shock and anger. The audacity.

"Oh, *now* you want to talk to me?" I sass.

He scoffs and shakes his head as if *I'm* the one being unreasonable. As if *I'm* crazy and he has no idea what I'm talking about.

"Fine, then don't. I just wanted to cuddle." That cold, hard voice is back, except this time, he looks at me like he can't believe my attitude. He leans away and crosses his arms; the wall erected once again. The small amount of attention he gave me is gone, and now I feel lonely again.

Sadness hits me. He ignored me all day, and he finally gives me attention, and I'm turning it down.

"Tell me why you ignored me all day," I demand, unwilling to settle back into silence. He shoots me a weird look, as if I just asked him if he'd paint his nipples green for me.

"You weren't talking, either, River. You always do this. You make things into a big deal when it is just us sitting in comfortable silence and relaxing. Why are you trying to pick a fight with me for no reason?"

My lip trembles. Is that what I was doing? I thought he was ignoring me this whole time when really, he was just enjoying my company in comfortable silence. I feel so stupid.

"Do you want to cuddle or not?" he snaps. He's throwing me one last bone, and I snatch it up like a starved dog. Shamefully, I crawl into his lap. He smiles broadly and circles his arms around me, shifting into a comfortable position so we can both watch the movie.

He intermittently kisses the side of my head and runs his fingertips over my skin. We go to bed the same way we did the night before. He has a smile on his face, and he cuddles me all night while I lie awake berating myself for ruining the day.

Next time, I'll do better.

SHALLOW HILL IS A black hole in this state. Normally, anything that goes in never comes back out. I was one of the very few exceptions. Some days, I still don't know how I managed it. On those days, it still feels like I'm stuck here in this desolate place where innocent souls die.

I walk alongside the river I was born in. Even the river is dead. Murky, still, and devoid of life. And quite frankly, it fucking reeks. How I didn't contract some type of disease from this river is beyond me.

Broken down homes line the other side of me. The windows that aren't intact are boarded up with splintering, rotting wood. Most of the houses are missing siding panels, exposing the wooden skeletons beneath. And every house has traffic of cracked out men and women entering and leaving. Some belong there, while most don't.

Faint screaming can be heard in the distance. I keep walking until I reach Barbie's house. Her house used to be white, but now it's a pale gray color with broken panels and rust. The closer I draw, the louder the screaming becomes until it's apparent Barbie's in another fight with an addict. More than likely because she smoked and injected all their drugs after she fucked them until they passed out.

Slowly, I walk toward the back door. It's rusty and creaks as I open it up. Barbie and a greasy, skinny man come into view, both screaming so hard that they're spitting in each other's faces. They're standing in the kitchen, with yellowed, cracked linoleum flooring, a mold-infested fridge, and a kitchen table cluttered with cigarette butts, empty liquor bottles, and used needles.

Looks the exact same way it did every day for the eighteen years I was trapped inside this dump.

"You fucking bitch! Those were *mine*!" the man shouts, backhanding Barbie across the face. I don't even flinch. She grabs her cheek in shock—for the life of me, I can't understand why she's shocked—and then rears back and clocks him in the nose.

The *crunch* comes a second before the man starts howling, holding his bloody nose.

"You broke my nose!" Way to point out the obvious.

"You deserved it, you piece of fucking shit!"

"Leave," I demand. They both freeze and turn toward me. Neither of them even noticed I was here. It'd be so easy to kill them both. No one would care enough about them to find out who did it.

The man's beady eyes study me with anger and perversion, his hand still clutching his nose.

"Who the fuck are you?" he demands, his voice now nasally and stuffed with blood.

"The owner of this house. Now fucking leave."

He huffs and turns to storm out the front door, muttering obscenities and promises of revenge under his breath the entire time.

Barbie turns to me and gives me a yellow smile. "Thanks, baby."

It's honestly got to be one of the seven wonders in the world on how I came from... *that*. Barbie was once beautiful in her younger years, but you wouldn't know it by looking at her. I only figured it out when I found an old picture of Barbie and Billy in their twenties, right when Barbie started getting hooked on drugs. I'm a replica of her former self. Long, curly black hair, golden eyes and a wide smile. Now, her hair barely falls to her shoulders, the greasy strands thin and wispy. Her skin is full of pockmarks and wrinkles and cracked like cheap leather. And she's as thin as a rail, though she does retain some muscle mass from the constant scuffling she finds herself in with men and women.

I suppose that's one thing I can say about Barbie. Aside from Billy, she doesn't take *anyone's* shit. The man currently nursing his broken nose can attest to that.

"I didn't do it for you," I deadpan. Her fake smile washes off, revealing her true face.

"Bitch," she mutters. Nothing I haven't heard before. "Why are you here, anyway?"

"You know exactly why, Barbie. Came to collect rent."

Her shoulders tense. She doesn't need to say it—I already know. She doesn't have the money. She smoked, injected, or snorted it all. Probably drank it, too.

"What did you steal this time?" I ask casually, referring to the man with a broken nose.

She snarls, her dilated eyes simmering as she rages, "I didn't steal nothin'! I fucked him nice and hard for that shit. I earned that, and it was *mine*."

I sigh and pinch the bridge of my nose. "If you're going to sell your body, at least get cash for it. How are you going to eat and pay rent otherwise?" It's like talking to a brick wall. Not sure why the words even left my mouth. They won't ever penetrate her drug-addled brain anyway.

She plops down on the chair and lights up a cigarette, not bothering to respond. Typical. She'd prefer to act like I never said anything than acknowledge the fact that she owes me money.

"I own this house. I can evict you anytime I want. All I need to do is go to the courthouse and serve you the papers, and your ass is out in a month tops," I threaten, sitting down in the chair across from her.

I take care not to touch any of the surfaces if I can help it. I don't know what kind of diseases I could pick up. Ryan would kill me if that happened.

"You think because you're dating a rich man that you can get away with whatever you want," she spits, her glazed eyes narrowed into slits. "Shallow Hill is in your bones, little girl. You'll never be better than me, so quit acting like it."

"You sound bitter, Barbie," I state with boredom. "Doesn't change the fact that I own this house, and you owe me rent."

This house was foreclosed when I was a freshman in college. By that point, I had busted my ass since I was sixteen, working in fast food the next town over and then working part-time in a call center when I turned eighteen. I saved every penny, got a credit card, and built my credit from the bottom up. When the house foreclosed, I bought it from the bank for an insanely low price. It was almost insulting. That money went down the hole. I'll obviously never profit from it by reselling—no one wants to live in Shallow Hill—but it was worth it. Keeping my mother under my thumb is worth every. Fucking. Penny.

Her hands tremble as she pulls from the cigarette.

"I'll tell Billy," she threatens around a cloud of smoke. I raise an eyebrow. She says this every time she's late on rent. Which is every single month, mind you.

"Billy doesn't give a shit about you, Barbie."

"He does when he's balls deep inside me," she snaps back. I roll my eyes at her immaturity. Billy doesn't care about anyone, even when he's balls deep inside them.

Barbie and I have both seen firsthand what happens when Billy gets angry with someone. We've also seen what happens when he grows bored with them, too. Equally terrifying prospects. Neither of us seeks him out if we can help it.

"He'll tell you whatever you want to hear, and the second he comes, he's already forgotten about you."

A hand thumps on the table in anger. I've no idea what she was attempting to accomplish there. Scare me? I never feared her to begin with. Not when her clients always did so much worse than she could ever do.

Billy was always the worst one, and the one that hung around most frequently. He keeps my mother doped up on drugs, and she gives him information and lousy sex in return.

He's a drug lord and has insane connections. And Barbie fucks everyone. Men and women. With that, comes dirt on everyone in town. Barbie wraps the noose around their balls, and Billy strings them up. He owns this entire shitty town.

I'll never admit it to her, but Billy scares me to death. He's capable of making anyone disappear without a trace. Barbie knows that deep down, but I think there's a minuscule part of her that isn't willing to turn over her daughter to Satan himself. Besides, Billy always liked me better, and Barbie knows that, too.

He's caused enough damage to carry over to my next three lifetimes, at least. He took my innocence and my entire childhood. Both irreplaceable. Both I'll never get back.

"I want the money by next week. Fuck extra hard, and I'm sure you can make it."

I walk out the door, her screaming and curses following me long after I've left.

Four

Mako

"TIME OF DEATH WAS a little over two days ago based on the decomposition of his body. Looking at the blood spatter, he was shot from about ten feet away," the criminalist, Redd, observes while snapping a few more pictures of the dead body.

There's a small hole in his head. Looks like an entry wound from a .22 caliber. Carved into his bare chest is the word 'Ghost.'

"Carvings have the consistency of a hunting knife. You can tell by the patterns that whoever did this took their time. Doesn't look sloppy or rushed," Redd continues.

"Was he alive when it was carved into his chest?" I ask, observing the jagged letters closely. The blood has already dried and crusted on his chest.

"Yep," Redd says. "Very alive. There are signs of struggle, but it's not consistent with this type of torture—it's too subtle. I assume at least two people were holding him down. There's no way he acted alone."

I shake my head. The scene before me is pretty fucking morbid. I've seen a lot of shit in my career—the Ghost Killer isn't the nastiest I've seen. Just the smartest.

My partner, Amar, stands next to me, his hands in his pockets as he studies the vic.

"Ghost Killer strikes again," he murmurs to himself.

Greg "Froggy" Barber has a rap sheet related to drug activity longer than Beethoven's last symphony and has been in and out of jail since he was thirteen years old. Kid grew up in the slums with a deadbeat mother and missing father. Slinging dope was probably his only way of survival.

His mother hasn't even reported him missing.

"And as usual, he's covered in DNA," Redd sighs, shaking his head with disappointment.

Usually, finding DNA at the crime scene is lucky. But in this case, it means nothing. Every vic we've found killed by the Ghost Killer is covered in DNA from randoms. Sex workers mostly, but we've come across DNA from murderers and rapists that have been in prison for years, pinning these crimes on people who have no relation to the victims.

No fucking clue how he does it.

He has to have a connection on the inside somewhere. Problem is that the convicts are in random prisons across the country, with no apparent connection between them. Whoever the Ghost Killer is, he's powerful.

"Let's head back to the precinct, see if we can find any connections to the vic," I say to my partner, frustrated with this fucker. I've been chasing him for a good year now, and it's been the longest three hundred sixty-five days of my life.

Amar nods his head, never one to speak more than what's required. That's what makes him a damn good partner. He sees shit I don't, while I excel in putting all the puzzle pieces together.

I glance over at him, noticing how he looks at Greg's body with sadness. This kid had an entire future ahead of him—one I'd hope would be full of redemption. Maybe Greg would've seen the light eventually and worked to get himself out of a bad situation. The fucked up part about it is that we'll never know. Poor kid suffered a gruesome death because of a sick individual.

Amar's a kind soul, probably too kind. He migrated to America from India when he was ten years old. He had a harsh welcome when his father was killed walking out of a grocery store because of the color of his skin. That's what bred Amar's need to seek justice for all the innocent souls whose lives ended way before their time.

Just as I get into my car, my phone rings.

"Hey, dad," I greet.

"I ordered lunch. Come on down, take a break. Bring Amar," he says. Dad has a knack for adopting people as his kids, much to my brother's dismay. He treats Amar like a son, and it pisses Ryan off something fierce.

I rub my hand through my hair roughly as a headache begins to pound through my skull. I am pretty hungry. Not really sure the last time I even ate, to be honest. It doesn't hurt that my presence usually ruins Ryan's entire day, and I'd be a liar if I said I don't get enjoyment out of that knowledge.

The reminder of River comes racing in with that thought, ruining the satisfaction. When Ryan has a bad day, everybody suffers for it. Especially his girlfriends. For a split second, I think of telling Ryan about her, but I roundhouse kick that idea out as soon as it enters my head. I won't use her as bait to piss him off.

Not when she'll be the one to suffer the consequences.

"Alright," I concede. "Be there in fifteen."

"WHERE'S RYAN?" I ASK nonchalantly around a bite of my BMT sandwich.

"He's holed himself in his office for the past hour," Dad answers, shrugging his shoulders. He doesn't seem concerned. Typical life of a lawyer, I suppose. I'm no stranger to Dad locking himself away in his office when dealing with a particularly brutal case. Those days, the light in his eyes was always dimmer, but somehow, he managed to push through and smile for Ryan and me. Even when he was up to his ears in stress, he'd still take the time to toss a ball outside with us or teach us how to ride a bike.

He's the most resilient person I know.

"So, Amar, how's Clara been?" Dad asks, his bright blue eyes sparkling and shit. He's always been a sucker for love. Hard not to be when you've been happily married to your soulmate for over thirty years.

Clara is Amar's wife. They've been married for fifteen years, and aside from my parents, I've never seen a couple more perfect for each other. Where Amar is quiet and calm, Clara is loud and bubbly. They give me real hope of finding *the one* or whatever the fuck the kids say nowadays.

I've had a lot of good role models in my life when it comes to relationships. Not sure how the fuck Ryan ended up so jaded.

I take the last bite of my sandwich as Amar answers my Dad. It's the only time I see Amar's eyes light up.

"Be right back," I mutter. Neither of them pays me any attention.

I gun straight for Ryan's office. I'm already preparing myself for some type of confrontation. I don't know why I even bother going around him.

Ryan isn't capable of treating me like anything other than shit, and it always ends in me instigating him and then him kicking me out.

It's not like I haven't tried to get close to Ryan; it's just that he's made it fucking impossible to. The asshole has done nothing but torment me our entire childhood. Not that I ever rolled over and took Ryan's shit, but no amount of ass beatings made Ryan hate me any less. His hostility has only grown stronger over the years, and I don't give enough of a shit about him to try and repair it. I tried that once years ago, and I'll never make the same mistake again.

Dude's had a chip on his shoulder since I can remember. I'm bigger and older, but Ryan never cared. He's like a fucking chihuahua, a small little shit that acts like they have a big bark and tries to lord over everyone bigger than them. For most of Ryan's life, it's worked too.

Just not with me. Never with me.

The entire front of Ryan's office is all window, except he has the blinds shut right now. I stand outside his door for a moment, debating whether I should just be an asshole and barge in or knock. Either way, he won't be expecting me. It's very rare that I visit Ryan when I have lunch with Dad.

Which is often enough that Ryan has started closing his blinds around this time. Petty fucker.

Out of the corner of my eye, I notice one of the blinds is caught in the sill, allowing a small window of space to look in his office. I walk closer, bobbing left and right until I can get a good angle. I never said I was above spying on him. I am a fucking detective, after all. Being nosey is in the job description, and my asshole of a brother commits enough crimes on a daily basis to warrant it.

A growl nearly escapes my throat when I finally get a good angle. Spread eagle on his desk is his secretary. In between her legs is his head gripped tightly in her cherry red talons. Her head is thrown back, her slender throat rippling with moans as he goes to town on her pussy.

My spine snaps straight, and I have every intention of storming the place.

He's got a beautiful girl at home that treats him far better than he deserves, and yet he still fucks around. Can't say I'm surprised. If anyone would treat a girl like shit, it's Ryan. He treated Alison like dirt for years; there's no reason he'd treat River any differently.

I can't count how many times Alison cried on my shoulder, sunglasses covering her blackened eyes and her arms stained with bruises. He gave her chlamydia, for god's sake, *after* they had been dating for two years. I wanted to put him away for domestic violence every time, but Alison always refused to press charges. She was too scared. I was willing to take it further for her and press charges anyway, but she begged and pleaded for me not to. She wasn't ready to leave Ryan yet, and if it came back to him that he was being charged for domestic violence, we were both scared that he would make her disappear. Permanently. If anyone has the connections to make it happen, I'd trust Ryan to be one of them.

So many times, I had encouraged Alison to move on from him at least, find someone better. Someone who wouldn't cheat on and abuse her. At one point, she had asked if that someone better could be me. I had said no. She was a sweet girl, but I felt nothing more towards her than genuine concern and friendship.

But the more I intervened, the worse Ryan treated her. The abuse became more violent, and bruises turned into broken bones. There was always an excuse ready on the tip of her tongue, but she only tried pulling that shit with her very concerned friends. Eventually, I learned that if I was going to help her, I couldn't do it right in his face. The day she finally escaped from him, I felt an entire weight come off my shoulders.

That is, until River came into the picture. Now it feels heavier than ever.

"Mako!" Amar calls from behind me. I whip around, rage still painted on my face. I've been standing in front of his window for a solid minute now, glaring at the glass window, seething over this fucking prick. I'm sure I look like a goddamn lunatic, but I don't care.

"You ready to jet?" Amar asks from behind me, walking up to where I'm standing. He eyes me cautiously like I'm a bear and he's the fish I'm two seconds away from mauling.

I swallow roughly and nod my head.

Probably for the best Amar caught me when he did. Once again, I'm feeling that familiar pull to help another one of Ryan's victims. But this time, it feels personal, and I don't even want to figure out why.

I'VE BEEN AT THE precinct for hours, poring over the case. My leg has been bouncing for the past hour, a clear indicator that I'm getting restless. My hands rip through my hair for the millionth time, beyond frustrated over this case. I'll be bald by forty if I keep it up.

Every lead I get leads me to another connection that doesn't add up. Solving puzzles is what I excel at. Dad always bought me those thousand-piece puzzles when I was a kid, marveling over how quickly I put them together. Brain teasers relaxed me. Connecting the dots comes naturally. But nothing is fucking connecting in this case.

The Ghost Killer is sending me on a wild goose chase, leading me to all different kinds of dead ends. He's deliberately fucking with me, stringing me along like a puppet, and I'm the dumbass that keeps falling in the trap.

I need to see this case from a different perspective. Instead of following the clues he keeps laying out for me, I need to look for the ones he's trying to cover up.

I drag my hands down to my neck, gently massaging as I go. Women have the right idea. I need to book an appointment at a spa ASAP. Couldn't care less if it freaks people out that a six-foot-five man is chilling in a mud bath, I fucking *need* it.

I glance at the clock in the corner of my computer screen, noting the time is nearly after eleven at night.

Fuck. I need sleep, too. But I can already tell my brain won't shut off. Especially not after digging into Greg's life all day with one half of my brain, and certainly not when River is possessing the other half.

I want to help her. I should, but I shouldn't.

She's different from Alison. Tougher. Meaner. Stubborn as hell. And loyal as a dog. Alison wanted my help, whereas River definitely won't. I mean, shit, during dinner, she stared at me as if *I* hurt her somehow. She's protecting Ryan when I can guarantee she has no idea what she's even protecting him from. When someone hates their brother as much as Ryan hates me, anyone would assume he has a good reason for it. In reality, he doesn't have a single reason other than the fact that he feels I stole our parents' love and affection from him.

He's a spoiled asshole that's been throwing one long temper tantrum for most of his life. Still shocks me how two of the most loving and caring people I've ever met created a sociopathic monster.

My fingers are typing in River's name before I can stop myself. After I met her, I got a little out of line and ran a background check on her. River McAllister, born and raised in shitty Shallow Hill. There's not much else on her other than the fact that she bought a house in Shallow Hill a couple of years ago. No fucking idea why she'd ever do that.

I stopped my research there, feeling ten different kinds of creepy. And here I am again, looking into her life when I have no business doing so. But I can't watch another innocent girl suffer at the hands of that prick. I don't consider myself a good guy, but I'm not a monster either. I don't abuse girls. I don't rape girls. I don't do anything to them that they don't want me to. Ask for consent, and I shall receive. It's basic fucking morals.

After a few minutes of searching, I find out that she's attending the university. She has three classes a week, one of them on the south side of the campus. That area is tucked into a private little nook with little traffic. A perfect spot to strike a conversation with someone without many prying eyes around.

Fuck. I bang my fist against my desk, frustrated with my own damn self. Meddling with another one of Ryan's relationships can—and probably will—end in complete disaster. At the end of the day, I can't force any girl to leave Ryan. I can't force them to see the truth in Ryan. It's something they need to face themselves. But fuck, if I'm going to stand by and watch a girl suffer through domestic violence without at least *trying* to help her.

Showing up at the university has got to be the worst, best idea I've ever had. Yet, I still lift my head and see what class it is.

Professor Trumbling's Psychology 101 class.

Funny, she said she was good at reading people, but yet she's gone blind to the devil directly in front of her.

I'VE RESORTED TO FUCKING stalking. I guess I could say stalking is in the job description too, but River isn't a criminal—that I know of—and this isn't a stake-out. There's no justifying this. Fuck it, it's for the greater good and all that if I can convince her stubborn ass to see the light. Or rather the darkness in Ryan.

It's just after two o'clock in the afternoon when she emerges from the building wearing black Chucks and cuffed jeans that hug her ass in ways that should be fucking illegal. Not to mention her white shirt with tiny buttons at the chest—buttons that are completely undone, teasing wandering eyes of her ample cleavage that's nearly gobbling up the gold chain hanging between her breasts.

Her long, black hair absorbs all light, the curls bouncing as she walks across the parking lot. River has a striking beauty, unlike anything I've seen. Her golden eyes and tanned skin are ethereal, but it's not just the features of her face but the manner in which she holds herself. She walks with her spine straight and her chin high. She speaks with her head slightly tilted down, looking up at you through angled brows and long lashes, making you feel like she's looking into you instead of at you.

She's beautiful. And altogether, utterly, abso-fucking-lutely tempting.

Goddamn it. I run a hand over my face, already frustrated with how this is going. I shake my head, ripping my hand through my hair and willing myself to get it together. Last thing I need is for her to think I'm trying to make a move on her. I shouldn't be looking at her like that—thinking of her in such a way. But the surge of jealousy coating my veins like oil is hard to ignore. A beautiful girl reduced to a goddamn punching bag by a psychotic piece of shit, what a goddamn shame.

She can't see me yet. I'm hiding behind a pine tree, watching her ass swing as she walks towards her car, remembering her sweet cinnamon smell from when she met my parents. She walks like there's someone hot on her heels but is stubbornly refusing to run. Rushed and tense but confident with her chin raised high with pride.

Her hometown is bred into every move she makes. It shows that she grew up in a volatile and dangerous environment, but with every step, she beats down her past with a vengeance.

She will not cower from her roots, yet she bends like a rose bush for my brother. Her thorns may bite, but ultimately, he will clip them off until she's left with a weak backbone that will easily snap beneath his hands. Everything that once made her vibrant and beautiful will wilt, and eventually, he'll toss her aside when there's nothing left of her.

I take a step in her direction, but I'm stopped short when a tiny girl with blonde hair bounds up to River, hooking her arm with River's and dragging her away from her car.

The girl says something to River, causing her to throw her head back with laughter. Something in my chest tightens and twists viciously. Something I honestly don't want to put a fucking name to. I need to get my damn head on straight.

If I'm fucked in the head, there's no way I'll be able to worm my way into her good graces and help her get the hell away from Ryan. Before he completely breaks her. Before he does something like kill her. There were days when I was sure Alison was dead. I'll be damned if I let another innocent girl find herself in that position—where there's even a possibility that she was murdered.

Don't know why I didn't just go into the personal bodyguard profession with how my life is turning out.

Stalking her is my only resort. What the fuck else can I do? *Text her?* That psychopath, more than likely, is synced to her Cloud and is reading every interaction she has without her knowledge.

Ryan is just giving her the illusion that she has any semblance of privacy and independence. Wouldn't surprise me if he starts giving her phone to her as a fucking privilege and taking it away from her as punishment—it's exactly what happened with Alison.

My phone buzzes in my back pocket. Distractedly, I pull it out as I watch River and her friend get farther and farther away. I decide not to continue following her today any longer. Approaching River is going to be like approaching a scared dog. She's going to bite, and she's going to bite really fucking hard. Best that I don't put her in that position in front of other people. Or rather, put *myself* through that in front of other people.

Glancing down at my phone, my heart seizes. As if I conjured her into existence, Alison's name is flashing across my phone.

She never calls me. Not anymore, at least. We parted ways the same day she and Ryan officially ended their relationship. As much of an asshole as it might make me, I only felt responsible for getting her to safety, not picking up the pieces for her.

"Mako," I answer, keeping my voice professional.

"Hey…" she trails off awkwardly. "I'm sorry to bother you. But uh, I'm a little concerned, actually. About Ryan's new girlfriend, River?" She poses her name as a question, not sure if I had already met her or not.

"Yeah, I've met her," I say. The timing and reason behind Alison's call only reinforces my determination. Feels almost like kismet.

Alison pauses and then clears her throat. "I've tried talking to her. She's… she's not a very approachable person." I crack a smile at that. Quite a fucking underwhelming statement if you ask me. She continues, "Ryan's got her under his spell, and even though I've come out from under the fog, I don't know how the hell to get someone else to."

It's nice knowing that I'm not the only one who wants to try and help River escape. Alison is kind—inherently kind. She's not the type of girl to go into a jealous rage when her high school sweetheart moves onto someone else. No, I'm pretty fucking sure there's a small part of Alison that is glad it's not her anymore. But that doesn't mean she's above letting the new girl suffer when she's more than aware of what's happening to her behind closed doors.

I wait. I already know what she wants. Little does she know I've already stuck my nose in the middle of something that probably shouldn't have my fucking nose in it.

"Can you talk to her, Mako? Maybe try to convince her that she's gotten into something pretty... pretty brutal? The only reason I survived that relationship is because of you. You got me out. You saved me. I need you to save her, too."

I sigh. I hate when she says shit like that.

"You saved yourself, Alison, not me. I just gave you the push to do it. You were the one in the relationship, and you were the only one who was able to claw your way out of it. That was all you."

The girl is tougher than she gives herself credit for. Alison has been through too much for her to give all the glory to someone else. No fucking way will I ever accept that.

She growls under her breath. My mouth quirks up, the sound cute coming from her. "You know what I mean, Mako. I would never have had the strength to leave if you weren't there to help. I—I know I did that myself. But you were still my stepping stones."

Frustrated, I pivot and start walking back to my car. I'm lingering on a campus I don't belong on, where anyone can see me. The last thing I need is someone to recognize me. Ryan may have graduated, but he left his imprint on this place. And a lot of people know who I am and exactly how he feels about me. Those same people are also really fucking loyal dogs, too.

"I was planning on helping her, Ali," I say finally, changing the subject back to the matter at hand. It makes me queasy when she gets all sentimental on me.

She sighs in her relief, which just makes the responsibility I feel even more suffocating. Now I have Alison counting on me, too.

I open the car door and slam it shut behind me after nearly throwing myself into the seat. The heat is stifling, but I haven't turned the car on yet.

"But I can't do this forever," I sigh, admitting the thought that's been haunting me since I learned what Ryan was doing to her. "I don't know if I can save all his girlfriends from him forever. Maybe River will leave eventually, but we both know there's going to be another one. Ryan isn't the type to stay alone. He needs someone to control and break, and if it's not you, or River, it's going to be another girl. How do I spend the rest of my fucking life keeping tabs on him and trying to convince his girlfriends to leave?"

It's killing me, is what I don't say. The stress from it is exhausting, but when I imagine what they're going through, my stress seems so trivial and I don't have the willpower to walk away.

Alison scoffs. "That's why we convince River to press charges. I…I was too scared. But if River comes forward, I will too. I'll testify against him or whatever. We end it with River." The conviction in her tone would be sweet, but poor Alison is also very naïve.

"Even if she does, it won't stick, Ali. He's a fucking lawyer, for Christ's sake, and I know the slimy shit has already made his connections with bad people. He's dirty. And even if that wasn't the case, Ryan is very good at manipulating people—especially our father. If Ryan doesn't get himself off, our dad will… And then River will be in more danger than she was before."

Another wave of frustration surges through me. I want to punch my fist through the steering wheel. It will never cease to amaze me how well Ryan has our parents under his thumb. They think he's the perfect son—next to me, of course, because our parents would never pick favorites. But fuck, they really should, considering one of their sons is an absolute piece of shit. Ryan will spin some story about how River is manipulative and lying, and just trying to get a portion of the family fortune. And Mom and Dad will believe it.

I know this because I've tried convincing them before that he was beating Alison. I showed them pictures of her injuries and his threatening texts, and when Ryan convinced them they were photoshopped, I went to my colleagues. I went to my *boss*. Lieutenant Sharp *did* believe me, but when he started an investigation, it was immediately shut down by his superior. Ryan's reach was too far—he made too many valuable connections. My claims were buried, and my parents told me to drop them. Alison was lying; that's all there was to it. Ryan would *never* do that to a girl—least of all a girl he's in love with.

That's probably our parent's only flaw—but it's a flaw that's endangering lives. They love Ryan too much, and Ryan is too good at manipulating people. Abusers don't only manipulate their victims, but they get off on making other's believe that they're upstanding people.

They trick them into thinking that they would never hurt a fly, so when accusations come to the surface, they're considered outrageous. These people *know* Ryan and they *know* he would never abuse a woman.

And I don't know how to fix that anymore. I don't know how to make my parents—or anyone else—see the light when they believe they're already seeing it.

Ryan will never be punished for his crimes unless one of his victims press charges. And with Ryan's connections, the likelihood of him actually suffering any consequences are low. Ryan's smart enough not to hit them in public, and he knows how to scare them into silence. He cares more about his reputation than the woman he's abusing.

I had pleaded with Alison to press charges—to *try*. It didn't matter that I promised her my protection; she was still too scared to speak against Ryan. In the end, nothing came of it, and I created a divide in the family. Mom and Dad hold nothing against me, firmly believing that I was naive and was spun into Alison's wicked web.

But there's an underlying tension in the air during family dinners. Deep down, they know I still believe Alison, and that bothers them.

"Then what do you suggest we do, Mako?" Alison snaps, bringing me back to the conversation. "Let him abuse girls as he sees fit? What if he kills someone? We would have known what he was doing and done nothing about it. That—that's so fucking wrong, and you know it!" She ends her sentence in near hysteria.

I bang my head against the headrest.

"I don't know, Ali. I really don't. Right now, I'm going to focus on River. Whatever comes after, I'll figure that out when I get there."

Five

River

"RIDDLE ME THIS, RIVER. How much force does it take before a bone breaks?" a voice says from behind me. Chills rush over my skin when that deep voice infiltrates my ears. I pause mid-step, nearly tripping over my feet when my foot comes back down clumsily. Immediately, I'm frustrated. I hate that he caught me off guard, and I hate that he now knows he did.

Reluctantly and with a massive amount of irritation, I turn to find Mako, which only heightens my bad mood when I see how sinfully delicious he looks. He's dressed in black jeans and a black t-shirt, brightening his colorful tattoos. I want to study them closer, ask why he got each and every one of them. You can learn a lot about a person just from their tattoos. But I would never ask—I have as much interest in getting to know Mako as I do getting to know a shark. They're both perfectly capable of eating me alive.

The gears in my head are turning overtime as I try to figure out how the hell he found me and *why* he found me. There's no way Mako goes to school here. He looks too old—definitely older than Ryan.

The stalker raises an eyebrow when I continue to stare dumbly. Shaking myself, I feel the blood rise to my cheeks.

"What are you doing here?" I ask, my tone accusing and harsh now that he caught me checking him out.

Who am I kidding, it would've been harsh regardless.

I had just walked out of my psych class and was heading towards my favorite donut shop. I'm only a block away. It's not good for my body, and Ryan would be pissed if I gained weight, but I'm ravenous today.

At least until Mako showed up. Now, my appetite has vanished completely. Actually, I feel a little sick.

He smiles. "Getting a donut."

Without my permission, my eyes track down his body. He doesn't look like he eats donuts.

"Right," I say doubtfully, and then turn to walk towards the donut shop. *I* eat donuts. *I'm* not a liar like he is.

He falls in step behind me, and my blood heats and chills all at once. A cold, nervous sweat breaks across my brow, even though it's eighty degrees out.

What if Ryan sees us? He could easily drive by. The donut shop is only a few blocks from his work. If Ryan spotted Mako walking next to me, there's no telling how he'd react. He loves me and doesn't want me around bad influences. One look at Mako, and it's easy to see he falls under that category.

"You can't walk next to me," I snap, rushing my steps forward. His long legs eat up the little distance I gained in a matter of seconds.

"Why not?" he asks, though it sounds like he already knows the answer. It sounds like he's testing me.

"Because I don't like you."

He hums. "So, are you going to answer me? How much force does it take before a bone breaks?"

"I don't know. You'd have to stalk someone with an anatomy degree," I answer briskly, still attempting to quicken my pace. All I'm accomplishing is getting a workout in before I gorge on sugar and calories.

"I'll tell you the answer. It's not about the force, it's about their angle of attack. If you're smart and have a good angle, you can break someone without any effort at all."

I stop, and Mako doesn't miss a beat. He stops next to me, his heat crowding in on me until I'm in danger of a heat stroke. His energy feels like I'm being attacked by a solar flare.

I turn to him, my eyes narrowing. Anger pulses through me in bright heat waves. If he looked close enough, he'd see it thrumming in my neck.

"I know what you're insinuating. Ryan loves me," I say.

Why did I sound like a child right there? Instead of smiling in triumph, he frowns.

"Do you truly believe that?" he asks seriously.

"I do," I answer with conviction.

He looks disappointed. Why would he even care? I'm disappointed I care why he cares. Slowly, he nods his head as if he's accepting something he just realized.

"He's good. I'll give him that." When I frown, he clarifies, "He's broken you so effortlessly, the pain hasn't even hit you yet."

IT'S DATE NIGHT, AND I've just spent two hours getting ready. I put on minimal makeup this time and decided to let my outfit do all the shining. I'm wearing a royal blue satin dress, with silver pumps. It makes my golden eyes shine, appearing almost unnatural. I'm quite proud of the invention I've made out of myself.

Ryan's been sitting on the couch, impatiently waiting for me. I can feel the negative energy through the walls. He's taking me to an elite restaurant two towns over. Reputation only. Because only people with high social standing get in with a reservation. Anyone off the streets is put on a list and constantly overshadowed by the people of high importance.

Ryan's father is one of the best lawyers in the country. Ryan is set to take over Matt's law firm—even though he's only twenty-five. No one would dare turn down the only person capable of getting you out of *anything*. I don't know how Matt's carefree personality translates to a fierce lawyer, but somehow, he's managed to hang onto his morality.

Ryan, not so much.

I walk down the grand staircase, veins of black and gold in the pristine marble. Ryan's waiting in the foyer, the extravagant chandelier hanging above shrouding him in shadows in the otherwise dark house. When he sees me, his eyes slowly peruse my body. A chill works its way down my spine. His stare rivals a vampire's when they get that first whiff of fresh blood.

"You look beautiful," he says softly. An emotion I can't name flickers in his eyes, gone too quickly before I can figure it out.

There's that word again. *Beautiful.*

Despite his word choice, my heart flutters, and the biggest smile breaks out across my face. He returns my smile with a sinister grin and holds out a hand for me. I take it without reservation, my excitement growing. He squeezes my hand and leads me to the car.

The ride there is silent, and a little stiff. I shift, racking my brain for something to talk about. I hate the mundane small talk, but sometimes,

I don't know what else to say. Comfortable silences between Ryan and I have been nonexistent lately. Usually, when he's silent, he's brooding or upset and fills the space with uneasiness. I know I took a little longer than I should've to get ready, but I'd hoped he'd think it was worth it after seeing how good I look.

"I hope you're hungry. This place has the best food in town," Ryan announces, though his voice is missing the upbeat excitement it had when he first told me where he was taking me two days ago.

I sigh dreamily at the mention of food. "I'm starving. The only thing I ate today was a donut," I say.

Ryan shoots me a weird look. "I hope you don't eat that stuff all the time, River. You're going to get fat."

"I'm not going to get fat," I protest, laughing and smacking his arm in an attempt at humor.

My laughter fades when he pins me with a dark look. "Why? Because you want men to lust after you? Don't act like such a whore, River."

I tighten my lips, my heart dropping into the pit of my stomach at his words. I hate when he says things like that to me. "Stop calling me a whore, Ryan. I'm dating you, aren't I?" I snap, growing irritated at his name-calling.

He chuckles without humor. "Then stop acting like one. That's why you're dressed the way you are. To show off your hot little body like it's your right."

I feel myself sinking quickly, circling into a deep hole I'm digging myself. I don't know what to say. When I try to stand up for myself, it only makes things worse. It never puts him in his place, nor does he bother apologizing. It seems it doesn't matter anymore—they'll never be the right words. Fighting with a lawyer has got to be the most frustrating thing I've ever experienced.

After a moment of silence, I ask hesitantly, "Do you want me to get fat?"

It sounds like he's almost bitter about my body. I have curves in the right places, an overly generous ass, and perky tits—I know that and have used it to my advantage during my party days before Ryan. He could say yes and expect me to gain weight. The thought sends a shot of fear in my veins. My beauty used to be a curse, attracting men long before I was old enough, but now that I'm older and feel more in control of who's allowed to touch me, I like who I am and how I look. I like myself and I don't want to change for anyone.

He scoffs. "Don't be stupid. I wouldn't date you if you were above a size five."

My mouth drops in shock. *Five?* That's an obscenely low number. Does he not realize a woman can be *any* size and still have a flat stomach? And so what if they don't? Why do men always chalk women's worth up to the shape of their body and how they look? It makes no fucking sense to me when our bodies are all going to go to hell when we get old anyways.

With effort, I snap my mouth shut and contemplate how the hell to approach this. I need to do it in a way that won't cause a fight.

"What if I am a size six?" The snarky question slips out before I can stop it. I close my eyes in resignation. That's probably going to stir him up.

He chuckles. "You're not. I will check your clothing."

Don't freak out. Don't freak out.

"Why?" I whisper.

"You affect my image, River. I can't risk that when I'm trying to earn my way to the top."

He's already graduated law school and is gaining a clientele at his father's firm. Still, I'm not sure how a woman wearing above a size five has anything to do with that. If I get into an argument about the woman's body, he'll turn us around and won't let me eat for the rest of the night. Desperately, I want to argue about how wrong it is to consider any woman above five *fat* and how obtuse he's acting, but I don't want to ruin our date before it's even started.

Furthermore, I'm fucking hungry.

I clear my throat and force a smile. "I won't gain any more weight, don't worry. I've been a size five since I was seventeen." Actually, I was a size zero because of malnourishment, but I won't mention that.

I'm not in Shallow Hill anymore. I've risen above that and am at a healthy weight. I watch my diet for the most part and exercise weekly. My time in Shallow Hill isn't something I'm willing to dwell on.

We arrive at a four Michelin star restaurant named *Rosebud*. I'd obviously never been, though I had heard the food here is absolutely divine. When we walk in, wonder seizes my entire being. The restaurant is decorated with shades of white and blue, with grand arches in each entryway and carefully styled plants and pricey art decorating the place. It's quiet in here, the customers speaking in low tones and holding their knives and forks daintily. It's a little posh for my taste, but I'm sure I could get used to it.

Hopefully.

A beautiful fountain the size of my house in Shallow Hill is in the entrance where the hostess awaits guests. When she spots us, she immediately recognizes Ryan. A bright smile stretches across her petite face, and a low heat simmers in her brown eyes. She's pretty. And she's looking at my boyfriend like she knows more about him than she should.

"Good evening Mr. Fitzgerald. Please follow me, your table is ready."

The woman leads us back to a separate room that overlooks the lake. The sun is already beginning to set, its fingers stretching across the sparkling water. Reds, purples, and pinks burst from the sun, painting the sky with cotton candy watercolors.

Ryan pulls my chair out for me before sitting on his own. The woman walks away, shooting one last lustful glance at Ryan before our waiter approaches.

If it were the other way around, Ryan would have already called me a whore for attracting attention. Maybe I should do the same.

"Would you like a bottle of wine, Mr. Fitzgerald?" the waiter asks, his tone respectful.

"Bring the Chateau Petrus Pomerol," he says. The waiter dips his head and rushes off to grab the bottle. I don't know much about wine, but I can guess it's damn expensive.

I scan over the menu; the options are limited but still overwhelming. Everything sounds good, and to my embarrassment, my stomach rumbles as I consider my options.

The waiter comes back, promptly pouring Ryan and me a glass of wine before setting the bottle in a bucket of ice to chill. He then reads off the specials.

Ryan lets me order my food first and then his own. When the waiter leaves with our order, I take a sip of the wine and nearly fall out of my chair.

"This is delicious," I rave, taking another sip. Ryan smiles, pleased by my reaction.

"I'm glad you like it, babe," he says, studying me closely as I take another sip. I set the glass down before I start guzzling it. Somehow, I doubt Ryan would appreciate it.

Since I affect his image apparently.

"I have to make an appearance at a charity event in September. You'll be my date, right, baby?"

My heart melts at his boyish tone.

"Of course. I'll start looking for a dress now."

"Don't worry about that, I'll find you a dress," he says, taking a sip of his own wine. I cover my frown with my glass.

"You don't want me to pick out my own dress?"

He sighs with impatience, seemingly becoming fed up with me. I don't know why. "Why do you always make me out to be the bad guy? Have you considered that maybe I just want to treat you? Take some stress off your shoulders, so you don't have to worry about it?"

I deflate, disappointed in myself.

"You're right, I'm sorry. I wasn't trying to seem ungrateful. You know I appreciate you."

His shoulders relax, but his eyes still glean with anger. My heart plummets and a sick feeling begins to swirl in my stomach.

I'm ruining this entire night. It seems that since the moment I got in the car, I keep saying the wrong thing.

The waiter delivers our meals while Ryan and I attempt small talk. It smells absolutely divine, the different spices wafting from our dishes and intimately mingling in my nose. Ryan ordered a caramelized beef fillet with foie gras, parsley purée and Madeira sauce, complemented by black pudding and baby beets. And I ordered the crab-stuffed filet mignon with whiskey peppercorn sauce, grilled asparagus, and a side of spinach strawberry salad. The meat is tender and falls apart in my mouth. I moan around my first bite, my eyes rolling to the back of my head.

Ryan's freezes, his fork paused midair as his eyes bore into me, flaring with ire. His face reddens, but he doesn't say anything, instead slowly bringing the fork the rest of the way to his mouth and taking a bite of his food. He chews slowly, the flames in his eyes growing stronger.

"I'm sorry," I apologize quietly, embarrassed by my reaction. "I've never had food like this before." A quick glance around confirms that no one seemed to notice. The people I can see are too consumed in their own conversations.

He smiles, though it seems tight and doesn't quite reach his eyes. "Get used to it, baby. This is your life now."

Well, that sounded fucking ominous.

"YOU KNOW THAT I love you, right?" Ryan asks, his eyes trapping mine in an intense dance of willpower. He's asserting his dominance, and I don't want to let him have it.

I close my eyes tightly, desperate to block out the scene before me. I nod my head, though it's stilted. Ryan's hand is gripping my jaw too tightly, minimalizing my movements.

"Do you know that I'm the only one who does, River? I'm all you have. No one else will ever love you like I do. And you make me do these things, and I hate it," he whispers. His hand tightens, and my jaw screams. I squeal, rising on my toes to abate the pain. He follows my movements. My cheeks are beginning to pinch in my teeth. Copper blooms in my mouth, and I don't have enough movement to swallow it.

He drops my jaw long enough to wrap his hands around my arms and shake me roughly.

"Why do you make me do this to you?" he shouts, tightening his hands around my arms.

"What did I do?" I cry, tears burning my eyes.

"You dress like a whore, moan in the restaurant like a whore. Do you *want* men to take you from me? How am I supposed to protect you if you invite men to fuck you?"

A tear slips out of my eye.

"I'm sor—" My apology is cut off from another brutal shake. He grits his teeth, bringing his demonic face close to mine.

"Sorry doesn't keep men from wanting to fuck you!" he roars. I crumple in on myself. The only thing keeping me upright is Ryan's unforgiving hands around my arms.

It hurts. It hurts so bad.

"Did you not see all those men staring at you? I bet you liked it, huh?"

I shake my head desperately.

"You did," he accuses roughly. "Look at yourself—*look at yourself now!*"

My head drops as I look down at my form-fitting dress. It stops a few inches above my knees. My ample cleavage is peeking through the slouched neckline, and the back of the dress plunges low, baring my skin completely save for a few strings crisscrossing my back.

He's right, it *is* a sexy dress. And I did catch a few men's prying eyes.

Tears blur my vision, distorting Ryan's angry face. It only accomplishes in making him more terrifying. He growls and pushes me away with all his strength. I fall backwards and land awkwardly on my hip. My head smacks against the floor, causing stars to explode in my vision.

I lie there for a minute as he storms off, wholly shocked by Ryan's visceral reaction. He's never laid his hands on me like that before. Sure, I fell that one time after I met his parents, but he didn't aggressively throw me the way he just did. I breathe heavily, afraid to move and in shock by how quickly this date went downhill. After the conversation about the charity event, I thought we were having such a good time. He smiled at me and joked with me, complimented me a few more times with that ugly word—*beautiful.* I beamed at him like the word doesn't make me feel like millions of ants are crawling under my skin and made sure to tell him how thankful I was for him taking me to such a gorgeous restaurant.

Then, we got in the car, and he forced his cock into my throat again until I couldn't breathe. I moaned and acted like I was enjoying myself, even though I wasn't. Sometimes I think that's the only thing that gets him off anymore.

Tears continue to flood my eyes until it feels like I'm drowning in them. I sob quietly and lift myself off the floor, feeling pretty fucking pathetic. I don't know where Ryan disappeared off to in this large house, but I can only pray he's not in our room.

My hip smarts when I pull myself off the ground. Limping the entire way, I drag myself up the stairs and down the long hallway. Pictures on the walls scrutinize my walk of shame, his parents taunting me with their smiling faces and stupid fucking façade of a perfect family.

With the help from the walls, I reach our bedroom and breathe a sigh of relief when Ryan is nowhere to be found. I lock myself in the bathroom and slowly slide down the door, the weight on my hip becoming too much.

After a few moments of pitiful crying, I inspect my body. Handprint bruises are already forming around both biceps. A bruise blooms across my hip, too. Luckily, my head isn't bleeding, though it does feel like a drum line is practicing inside my head.

I sniffle and pick myself up from the floor once more, and tear my dress off my body aggressively, despite my sore muscles protesting. Angrily, I glare at the offending dress.

He's right. This dress *did* make me look like a whore. Men were looking at me with hunger in their eyes. What did I expect wearing something like this? This is all my fault. I ruined a perfectly good night.

I tear at the fabric in a fit of rage. The ripping noise echoes in the bathroom as I continue to shred it to pieces. Dark blue glints in the overhead light as pieces of satin fall to the stone tile like forgotten dreams. I'm only satisfied when the dress is nothing but shredded fabric.

I pick the pieces up, ignoring the flare in my hip—I deserve that pain—and toss the pieces into the trashcan next to the toilet.

I walk back to the mirror and view my tarnished body. Mascara runs down my face, making me look like the dirty whore that I am. I can still feel all of the men's eyes that roved over my body at the restaurant. Their perversions have tainted my skin, blemishing it darker than the phantom hands wrapped around my biceps.

My fist collides with the mirror, sending spiderwebs of cracks throughout the glass, distorting my face. An imprint of blood stains the mirror and drips down, getting lost in the fissures. I inspect my still curled fist, detecting tiny shards lodged into my knuckles. Blood trails down my fingers and drips on the floor, joining the rest of the shattered glass.

I walk over to the shower, ignoring the slices of sharp pain as glass cuts into the soles of my feet. I turn the water as hot as I can handle, and I scrub at my skin, desperate to cleanse the filth from my body.

Stupid, stupid, stupid River. Fucking stupid whore.

You deserved that.

Six

River

I'M FAIRLY CERTAIN I'VE died and wandered into Hell. I don't know what I was thinking—last time I checked, I wasn't starring in Dante's fucking Inferno.

My psych class ends in five minutes, and all I can think about is how Ryan hasn't answered any of my texts yet. He came to bed late last night after our fight. It didn't matter that I rested a tentative hand on his shoulder, seeking his reassurance. He turned away and refused to touch me all night.

I cried myself to sleep. I cried myself awake. I cried myself to class.

Now, I've reached the end of class and the sunglasses haven't come off once. My puffy eyes will attract unwanted attention, and the last thing I need is a bunch of petty bitches judging my relationship. Plenty of girls in my year knew Ryan and have even gotten a taste of him. Ryan's reputation was significant, which means now mine is, too.

They watch me, waiting for any opportunity to gossip and pick apart our relationship. Fuck giving any of those bitches the satisfaction. Even if wearing sunglasses inside a building is a red flag. I have no choice, hoping they'll assume I'm hungover after partying all night or something.

Anything to avoid causing issues with Ryan. I've already done enough of that lately. If Ryan is worried about his image, surely a distraught girlfriend will tarnish that. I can't do that to him. He's worked too hard to get to where he is, despite his father's reputation.

"Class dismissed," Professor Trumbling announces. The body of students jumps up at once, rushing out of the room. I take my time, gathering my books and slowly making my way down towards the door. My hip is still sore from last night, and it takes everything in me to keep the limp out of my gait.

"Ms. McAllister, can I speak to you for a moment?" Professor Trumbling says from behind me. I pause and then sigh with resignation. This is precisely what I was trying to avoid. You'd think keeping your head down would keep the attention away.

I force a smile and make my way over to him, already dreading this conversation.

"I just wanted to touch base with you. You seemed awfully distracted today. Need I remind you finals are coming up soon? Getting an A in this class is vital to your career."

Yeah, yeah, yeah. Save yourself the energy and keep the condescension to yourself, old man.

"I'm sorry, Professor Trumbling. It won't happen again," I respond robotically. I'm pleased by how steady my voice was, even if it did make me sound insincere.

He studies me closely, and I shift under his attention, making sure to tuck my cut-up knuckles behind my back. They're superficial cuts and hardly noticeable. Unless, someone goes looking for them. His stare doesn't *feel* perverted, but it makes me uncomfortable anyway. Ryan would say he's checking me out. I'd say that he can see something is clearly wrong.

What gave it away? The dark sunglasses in a dim room? This is the picture you see in any film. If he asks me to take my glasses off, he won't find black eyes, though. Just red, puffy eyes from crying too much.

I'll tell him my dog died. That should work.

"You may go, Ms. McAllister."

Thanks for your permission, asshole.

Surely, I just made the strain in my hip worse with how fast I just rushed out of that classroom, but I find it worth it if it means escaping the professor's probing gaze.

That was my last class of the week. Amelia's been asking to grab coffee, but I don't dare face her right now. She knows me too well and would sniff out my predicament in a heartbeat.

But I don't want to go home, either. Ryan's not home yet—or at least he shouldn't be—but the empty house would just make me feel worse.

I'm standing in the quickly emptying parking lot when I feel the hairs on the back of my neck rise. I know who's standing behind me before he even utters a word. Why the hell is he following me? I chalked up the first time to a weird fluke, but now it's obvious he's seeking me out. Our first interaction, he was cold and distant. It just doesn't make sense.

"Why are you following me?" I ask, not bothering to turn around.

"Why are you standing in the middle of a parking lot?" he counters, his deep voice sliding over my battered nerve-endings.

My mental state is fragile today. Normally, I can roll with Ryan's punches—literally—but I'm just so disappointed in myself.

"Not today, Mako," I murmur. I walk forward—away from him. Now more than ever, I try to walk without the limp. He'd never let it go if he saw. He follows immediately. I already knew he would, but it makes me angry anyway. I whip around, gritting my teeth against the pain, and glare at him. "Stop following me."

He doesn't answer. Instead, his concerned gaze studies me much like Professor Trumbling's just did.

"I don't need this," I mutter, turning back around. A gentle hand stops me. I flinch away from his touch, not liking how the wrong kind of shivers race up my spine. The kind of shivers Ryan's *supposed* to make me feel. It makes my skin crawl.

"What did he do?"

"What makes you think he did anything?" I snap.

Mako doesn't answer right away. He stuffs his hands in his pockets as if he needs to physically restrain them from doing something. Like from touching me.

"Then who did?" he asks softly. I'm not fooled. Dark fury is on the precipice of his voice, threatening to overtake his gentleness. It's like a tidal wave crashing into a toy boat.

I shake my head, and once again, turn to walk away. He lets me this time, but he still follows.

Damn it.

I painstakingly make my way out of campus and down the busy street. I'll come back for my car later. All I need right now is to walk off the restless energy polluting my body.

I'm sweating in a matter of minutes, but it's good to focus on something else aside from my hip.

We walk in silence. Five minutes pass. And then ten. I take back roads, avoiding any areas Ryan could possibly drive by on. The entire walk, I replay last night in my head, going over every single detail and obsessing over what I could've said or done differently. There are so many things I wish I could change, starting from wearing a more conservative dress to not arguing with him so much when he said something I didn't like. I always have to argue with everything he says instead of just picking my battles. Not everything is worth fighting over.

Eventually, I make my way up a small hill and towards an abandoned library. Graffiti taints the brick walls, vulgar words and pictures are colored across the surface. The door is hanging off the hinges. I push it away slightly and walk through the opening.

The library may be creepy to most, but it's home to me.

I spent a lot of time here when I was younger and was able to escape Shallow Hill. It closed a few years ago, and it took my heart with it. I've never been able to let it go, even as mongrels slowly started destroying it.

Mako dutifully follows me. For some unknown reason, he's intent on stalking me, and I'm too exhausted to fight it right now.

"Where are we?" His voice shatters the fragile film of silence that blanketed over us. Ryan doesn't even know about this place. It makes me itchy that Mako is witnessing such an intimate part of my life. Truthfully, I hadn't even realized this was where I was heading until I arrived. My body seemed to know where to go naturally—a place that soothes something inside of me that nothing else can.

"Home," I answer shortly.

Surprisingly, he doesn't question me further. Just follows in silence as I make my way down the empty rows where books once slept. I run my fingers across the dusty surfaces, trailing wavy lines across the shelves and coating them with a thick film of dust. If I close my eyes, I can feel the phantom binders brushing across my fingertips.

And if I keep them closed, I can remember the feeling of opening a book and watching the pages awaken from their slumber to show me their story. I'd get so lost in them when I was younger, and I'd stay long after the library closed.

The librarian, and my mentor growing up, Camilla, would let me stay for as long as she could before she had to get home to her own family. She never asked, and I never told her, but I think she knew I had a crappy home life. Which is why I think she worked so hard to give me something good to hold onto. Every day, I'd walk into the library and find enough snacks to keep my belly full for the rest of the night. Sometimes she'd even buy me a new outfit and shoes when I'd start growing out of my clothes. Barbie never noticed long enough to question where I got them from.

Camilla is the one who taught me about periods and bought me my first pads. She taught me about sex and the reproductive system. I'll never forget that day—learning that sex is supposed to be between two people who respect each other, and it's supposed to be *consensual*. That was also when I realized that the men taking advantage of my body could get me pregnant. At only thirteen years old, I begged Camilla to help me get on birth control. She probed and asked if I was being touched, but I just lied and said the cramping from my periods was awful—which it was.

The old librarian took care of me and loved me in a way that I had never experienced before. That year, when I was only thirteen, she looked into adopting me. It had been the happiest I had ever been. I was sure Barbie would've loved to hand me over. But before she could, she suffered from a severe stroke and passed away.

That was the saddest I had ever been. It's also when I started prostituting myself for basic needs to keep me alive.

My body sways as memories rush over me. I'm so lost in them; I don't register the soft touch of a hand on my hip at first.

I still, and reality comes rushing back. I jerk away from his touch and hiss in pain when the pain in my hip flares hot.

"It's purple."

I don't ask, and he doesn't explain. We both know what he means. My university t-shirt rode up, exposing the deep purple bruise on my hip. I knew I should've worn an oversized shirt today. This one is loose-fitting and up to my neck, but it's not big enough to fall past my hips. I fix it hastily, my cheeks running hot from embarrassment. The last thing I need is judgment from Mako. He has no idea what he's talking about when it comes to my and Ryan's relationship.

"I fell."

His face flattens.

It's not a lie.

"I know. Typical answer. But it's true, honestly."

"You fell," he repeats dryly. "But were you pushed?"

"No."

Now I'm a liar, liar.

I don't know why I'm trying to convince him. Mako's eyes drop back down to my hip. Now that he knows it's there, he stares as if he has x-ray vision and can see through the soft cotton. The silence grows uncomfortable.

"Can I show you something?" My voice raises his darkened green eyes back to mine. They're nearly black with rage. His large hands are curled tightly into fists, and the muscle in his jaw is pulsing like a wild horse trapped in a cage.

He nods once, sharply. I'll never know what possessed me, but I grab his hand and lead him to my favorite spot in the far corner of the library. It's not a big building, but it had a lot of gem alcoves.

Camilla trusted me with the library's biggest secret.

The rare books, so old, they would crumble if they hadn't been taken care of so well.

They're no longer here, but the room is. The door is triggered by a trap on one of the shelves. A book didn't trigger the lock but a shelf. If lifted just high enough to engage the mechanism and unlock the door.

It's one room that's been kept safe from the squatters and shitty teenagers. I lift the shelf and open the bookcase.

No amount of dust could keep my lungs from inhaling deeply. The room is small and smells of mothballs and must, but it brings me peace anyway. There are two small windows in here, allowing sunlight to stream through. Dust mites dance in the rays as I make my way in.

To get through, Mako has to hunch down a little, and I have the insane urge to giggle at watching him finesse his body through the opening. I turn away before I give in to that urge.

"Where are we?" Mako questions, wonderment in his voice as he looks around the small room.

"Where childhood dreams live," I reply cryptically.

This is where I made my plans on how to get out of Shallow Hill. I was twelve years old with a pack of crayons and a piece of paper and a shoddy outline of my future. I did the math on what my paychecks would look like making minimum wage, planned my savings, and adjusted accordingly at what age I'd be eligible for a better job and a credit card. Camilla would help me with a lot of it, explaining all the adult things like credit and how important it is.

I didn't have typical childhood dreams of becoming an astronaut or discovering the cure for cancer, and definitely not meeting Prince Charming and falling in love.

I just wanted out of Shallow Hill. Everything after that would come later when I accomplished my goal—one that seemed so impossible at the time.

"Do yours still live here?" he asks, wandering around the room.

"No, they've come true already." His eyes slide to mine. I feel pinned to the spot like invisible hands are holding me in place. He looks away, and I can breathe again.

"What were they?"

I shrug a shoulder, attempting to appear casual. "Survival."

Another glance. "That's all?"

"Pretty much," I quip, turning away. I don't want to talk about that anymore. Frankly, I don't want to talk about *me*. "What about you? What were your dreams?"

"To be a race car driver," he deadpans. I snort and then slap my hand over my mouth in embarrassment. That wasn't very lady-like. Ryan hates when I snort.

It doesn't feel so bad when he gives me a full smile in return, though. In fact, it makes me want to start snorting like a pig. He's got beautiful white teeth and sharp canines. Staring at his mouth makes me wonder what it's capable of.

God, I'm being weird. I turn away quickly. That smile is a fucking weapon capable of complete annihilation on my resolve. I *still* don't like him, nor do I want to start.

"What about when you got older?" I push.

"A detective."

"And how'd that work out for you?"

"I succeeded."

I pause and turn back to him. "You're a detective?" I ask incredulously. He nods and turns back to a dusty shelf. There's nothing to see there.

I'd like to think I'm much more interesting to look at than a dusty shelf.

I don't know why I'm shocked by his career. Considering he found what class I'm in. And when... it makes complete sense.

"Is that how you found out where I go to college? And what class I'm taking?"

He has the nerve to look a little sheepish. "I may have utilized my position for nefarious purposes," he admits, flashing me a sinful smile.

Fuck. Stop that.

"Why did you seek me out?"

"If I say I'm concerned about you, would you believe me?"

I scoff. "Absolutely not. You don't even know me. And you were pretty rude the first time we met."

He stuffs his hands into his pockets again. "I don't know you. But I know my brother. And that's enough." He scuffs the thinly carpeted floor with the tip of his worn black boot, staring down as he contemplates something else. "As for the way I treated you, you took Ryan's side and treated me with hostility after saying two words to me. I reacted accordingly." He glances up at me, those emerald green eyes pinning me to the spot. The corner of his eyes crinkles as a smirk slides across his face.

"You're still hostile," he tacks on. I cross my arms, unimpressed with his assessment—and only proving his point. I *am* hostile. "I hope Ryan didn't say too many horrible things about me. I'm curious what kind of story he spun this time to make him out to be the victim."

"I don't want to talk about him," I bite out, annoyed with the fact that Ryan didn't even bother to spin a story for me. I came in here to be peaceful. This isn't peaceful.

He nods and walks over to a corner with a dusty bench. He plops down on it, not giving a single shit about the dust coating the wood. Ryan would never. As a matter of fact, I don't think he would've even stepped foot inside this building.

Hesitantly, I sit next to him, as far away from him on the bench as it allows, which is admittedly not very much space when his body takes up three-quarters of it.

Fucking mammoth.

A slow smirk slides across his face, but he doesn't comment. Can't be sure if he can tell what I'm thinking, but sometimes it feels like it. I want to do something with that smirk. Slap it off, or… something. I don't know what, but I know I shouldn't be feeling it.

"Are you going to arrest me for breaking and entering, Detective?" I ask mockingly.

He snickers, a wicked smile stretching across his face. He's too goddamn good-looking and I'm tempted to take a knife to his face. "If you end up in my handcuffs, it won't be because I'm arresting you."

Explosions of hot lava course through my veins and straight between my legs. I squeeze my thighs and shift uncomfortably. Asshole.

Again, I turn away.

WE'VE BEEN SITTING HERE for hours, talking about everything and nothing, all except for the obvious elephant in the room.

Ryan's going to kill me. I've avoided looking at the time but based on the angle of the sun through the windows, it's going to set in a couple of hours. Which means Ryan is home by now.

He's already texted me thirteen times and called six, but the oppositional side of me is too pissed at him to care. Maybe I need to show more anger?

Maybe he takes advantage of me because I'm weak to him. Maybe if I'm stronger, he'll start treating me like it.

What's that saying? If you want to be treated like an adult, then act like one. If I want to be treated like a strong woman, then I should act like one. I pick up my phone and skim the increasingly angry messages, asking where I am.

Delete.

Ryan can go fuck himself. I was wrong for dressing like that, but he was wrong for pushing me down. Right?

I tuck my phone in my pocket and turn towards my boyfriend's brother. "So, Mr. I-know-what-a-relationship-should-look-like, if you're so much better than Ryan, why are you single?" I don't actually know if he's single. I shouldn't care, but I find myself fishing anyway.

He gives me a droll look but relents and shrugs a shoulder. "I've been in a few long-term relationships with women. They didn't work out," he answers cryptically.

"Why?" I challenge.

A smile quirks on my face. He thinks I care. I don't. But I still wait for a response.

Another shrug. "Wasn't happy. Going opposite directions in life or wanting different things. Multiple reasons."

"Were you in love with any of them?"

"Yes and no. I had immense love for them, and what I felt was real, but I don't think I was truly in love with any of them, no. Not the way you should be when in a relationship. Not the way I wanted to be."

I frown. "The way you wanted?" I question.

"I want a love like my parents. Like my partner's. With my exes, it always felt like something was missing. That's not true love in my eyes."

I hum, mulling his response over. Am I in love with Ryan like that? Yes, I believe so. Do I feel like anything is missing?

Sometimes.

"So, what age did you finally get out of Shallow Hill?" Mako asks, drawing me away from my thoughts.

I sigh and thump my head against the wall behind me. "Eighteen, when I moved into the college dorms. By then, I had the funds to buy out Barbie's house. Not that it actually cost me much. The loan was paid off a year ago."

He flashes me a sardonic look. "I still think it's interesting you bought the house."

I shrug a shoulder. "I finally have something over her. I grew up under *her* shitty roof for eighteen years, was forced to deal with everything that came my way because of *her* shitty life choices, and that was my way of getting back. Now it's *my* shitty roof."

"Couldn't she easily find a place to shack up in, though?"

A laugh bursts out of me. "She could, yeah. But no one will let her stay for more than a night, if that. She was lucky she found places to go when the house first foreclosed. Everyone knows she answers to Billy. They'll let her around long enough to fuck her, but Barbie knows too many things. No one wants to keep her around long enough for Barbie to discover their dirty secrets."

I told him about Billy, and that he was a bad guy, but I didn't mention exactly *who* he was and *how* bad he really is. Billy isn't his real name. I'm not even sure what his real name is, to be honest. I suppose I never cared enough to ask.

"Couldn't she stay with Billy?"

"Barbie's too scared of him. Besides, Billy would never let Barbie live with him. He'd probably kill her after one night."

Sadly, I feel nothing at that prospect. If Barbie died, I'd probably sigh in relief. I don't think I ever felt anything more for Barbie than contempt. Even as a child, it took me only until I was three or four years old to realize Barbie didn't love me. Nor does she give a fuck about me.

I've always kept myself pretty unattached. By then, her clients were already having their fun with my body, and she ignored it. Every time I complained, I was just being dramatic. Or told that it was a good thing that I was learning young because that's all I'd amount to in life. Sucking dirty cock and getting flopped on like a fish would be a great skill to add to my resume.

"Aren't you technically keeping Barbie in your life that way? Why not let the house foreclose and put her on the streets?"

I've asked myself the same question a million times. And I always circle around the same answer.

"Revenge. And I don't care if that doesn't make me the bigger person. I have power over her, and she's forced to pay me rent. After everything I went through in that house, I'd say I'm being pretty fucking considerate."

"What did you go through?" he asks softly. I brushed over a lot of shit this entire time, but he caught me at a good moment. It feels good to talk about this stuff. Ryan doesn't ask—or care—and Amelia knows a lot, but she's dealing with her own shitty past. It never felt right to dump mine on top of hers.

I don't think I've ever been able to talk freely. And that's what I do with Mako. I purge everything that's been done to me as a child—the dirty men raping and molesting me since I can remember. I don't recall kisses from my mother, but from strange men.

Then I tell him about Camilla and how for a short period of time, she saved me. And right when I really thought I was going to escape Shallow

Hill far before I planned, she had been ripped away from me. Sometimes I wonder if I was a horrible person in my past life, and this life is my punishment. I'm atoning for whatever sins my soul has committed.

I tell him about the countless times I've gone hungry and had to beg for food after Camilla died. Men would only give me food if I performed sexual favors. I did it. It was my way of survival. I became what Barbie always said I would—a whore.

That's why I know Ryan isn't wrong. I *am* a whore. I had sex with men at thirteen years old so that I could eat. My only requirement was that they wear a condom. I'd rather starve than catch an STD. I was fortunate I hadn't up until that point.

"Please don't call yourself that," he pleads quietly, but gruffly. The soft tone catches me off guard. I look at him with confusion. Not only was I not expecting him to care what I called myself, I certainly wasn't expecting him to ask so... nicely. Ryan's always demanding things of me, expecting my compliance, and calling me names when he doesn't always get it.

"What?"

"You're not a whore, River. You were repeatedly raped and were forced into those situations because you were slowly dying from hunger."

Fire blazes from his eyes. I'm not sure how, but I know it's not directed *toward* me, but *for* me. And I don't know how I feel about that.

I open my mouth. I almost say the words.

Ryan thinks so.

But I already know what his response will be.

Ryan's fucking wrong.

Is he? I've been called a whore my entire life. For my actions—for what I had to do. For being pretty and dressing in clothes that compliment my body. Men have whispered in my ear countless times that if I didn't look so sexy in my pajamas, they would've been able to resist me. It's because I'm so *beautiful* that men just can't resist me.

And that's when I was a little girl.

Yesterday, I wore something sexy. And men looked at me. Which upset Ryan.

"I don't believe that."

Mako turns towards me further. The bench protests under his weight, and I get a little nervous that it'll collapse.

"You shouldn't be punished for showing the world that you're beautiful. Those men are wrong for sexualizing a little girl. That's *sick*, River. It's okay if a man looks at you—as a grown woman—and finds you attractive, but it is *not* okay if that man assumes that gives him the right to make you uncomfortable in any way. Whether it's by the way he looks at you, speaks to you, or touches you. If you want to walk out of the house in the sexiest thing you own, then that's your goddamn right because it is your choice to show off your body. Don't give any man the power to control what you do with it."

"It's mine," I whisper.

"It's yours," he repeats. "No one else's."

I dig my teeth into my bottom lip. I've never had a man give me a *choice*. It's always been take, take, take.

But the thought of Mako owning my body... God, I think I'm having a heart attack. It's too sinful. Liquid heat runs through my system and straight to my core. I clench my thighs to abate the feeling, but it only serves to tighten my nipples into sharp little points.

"What if... what if I want a man to own me?"

He leans closer, and his scent assaults my nose. Pure male with a hint of soap. My eyes want to roll, but I don't let them. I'm in control of my body, not him.

"Then give that privilege to a man who deserves it. If you want a man to own you, then let him. But that's not something he has a right to without your consent," he says, his voice so, so deep and guttural.

Licking my lips, I feel compelled to ask. "Do you want to own a woman?"

My own voice is dangerously husky. My breath is too short and choppy. I'm overheating, and I'm sure there's smoke leaking out of my mouth.

"The only way I want to own a woman is by owning her pleasure. I want her body to sing for me—a tune that only I can hear. I want her body to gravitate towards mine like a moth to a flame. And I want her to grow to dislike the feeling of being so empty when my cock isn't inside of her."

Too much. Too fast. I want to do the opposite of denying him. I want to give, give, give. Until his hands are full of me, and my body is full of him.

I need out.

"I have to go now."

Seven

River

I'VE ALWAYS HEARD THAT when a ghost is nearby, you feel an impenetrable cold so strong, it soaks into your bones. And when one passes through you, it's like inhaling ice.

The house is quiet.

There must be spirits playing dress-up with my body.

I know he's here.

"Ryan?" I call.

What's the point in dragging it out? The anticipation is killing me. Adrenaline thumps inside of me, and I'm ashamed to admit my hands are shaking a little. Bilby greets me from his perch on the couch, meowing quietly, followed up by a yawn. I walk over, petting his gray fur and trying my best to distract myself from the impending confrontation.

"Right here," he says quietly. I jump, causing Bilby to jump and run from the couch. My distraction worked too well—I wasn't expecting his voice to come from behind me. I turn and see him standing in the foyer.

I'm too startled to say anything. He takes a step forward, and I take a limp back. My hip still hurts.

"Where have you been?" he asks darkly.

"Hanging out with Amelia." He quirks a brow.

"Then why did Amelia say she hasn't seen you in a week?"

He spoke to her? Fuck.

Another step towards me. "Are you cheating on me?"

I shake my head, my heart racing. "No, of course not."

"Then why the fuck are you lying to me?" he growls through his teeth, the look on his face starting to resemble more and more like a demon's.

"I don't know. Because I'm mad at you."

His eyes widen in surprise for half a second before they narrow into thin slits. A derisive laugh trickles through his teeth.

"Mad at *me*? I've done nothing but take care of you this whole relationship. You have everything you could ask for. I've loved you and cared for you. I've only treated you how you deserved. If I've had to teach you a lesson when you got out of line, then that's not my fucking fault," he spits. Literally, too. Spittle flies out of his mouth as his anger increases.

"Do I not have free will, Ryan?"

He rears back. "Excuse me?"

"I don't need your permission to live my life. If I want to go get a donut and take a walk in the park, then I'm fucking allowed to."

His hand whips out so quickly, I don't even see it coming. The sharp pain explodes across my cheek. I cry out, clutching a hand to my stinging flesh. I don't even know why I'm shocked. Anger fills my body so potently, I'm convinced my blood evaporated into wisps of smoke.

I do better. My fist flies forward and clashes with his cheek. His head jerks to the side from the force and immediately pain flares throughout my hand. It feels like I broke it.

We both freeze. Guess I'm more like my mother than I thought. That girl from the club comes hurdling back. The fearless girl who used to dance with slimy men and break their noses when they got too comfortable. The girl who refused to take shit from *any* man.

Where'd she go?

The only thing that moves is our heavily pumping chests. Slowly, he looks over at me. Several emotions play across his eyes. Shock and fury are prominent, but there's another emotion swirling around that I can't name.

"Why did you do that?" he asks darkly.

"Because you deserved it," I breathe, feeling a tad invigorated.

"Do you feel better?"

"Only if it means you'll stop laying your hands on me. You're supposed to make me feel good, not hurt me."

He sucks in his bottom lip, that unnamed emotion coming to the forefront. It almost seems calculating, but I can't be sure. And to my surprise, he nods his head.

"I'm sorry," he says.

I need a thesaurus. How many words are there for the word *surprise*? I feel every one of them, like each synonym is a different emotion.

"You... you're sorry?" I ask, my brow bunching into a deep V. Whiplash. That's the best word to describe how I feel.

He nods and touches his hand to his cheek. "Yeah," he whispers. "I'm sorry. You didn't deserve any of that."

I narrow my eyes, skeptical of his behavior. His whole face transforms. His eyes soften, and his features relax. He looks genuinely sorry. Despite my best efforts, I feel myself softening, too.

"Then why did you do that?"

Shame clouds his eyes when he looks my way. "I just get so worried about you. So many men have taken advantage of you, and I'm terrified someone will come along and try to do that. I can't protect you if I don't know where you are, River. I can't keep the monsters away if you show them what they can take from you."

I bite my lip, and I feel just a little ashamed of myself.

"I—I can tell you where I go, and I won't dress so provocatively. But I need you to stop hitting me."

He comes to me in a rush, but not with anger this time. This time, it's nothing but love in his eyes. He curls his strong arms around me tightly and brings me close, nose to nose.

"I'm sorry, baby. I shouldn't have done any of that. I won't hit you anymore. I get so frustrated because you don't understand how men think, and I do. I just need you to listen to me, okay? I need to know where you are and what you're doing. And I need to make sure your body is covered properly, so men don't try to steal you away."

I nod, and we both deflate in each other's arms.

Mako was wrong. Ryan doesn't want to *own* my body. He just wants to protect me. Keep me safe.

And no one has ever done that for me before.

"I noticed the mirror," he says quietly. I stiffen before pulling back.

"Ryan, I am so, so sor—"

"Shh," he whispers, cutting me off. He grabs the back of my head and pulls me back into him. "It's okay. I get it. I already had someone come in and replace it."

Emotion builds up inside my chest—namely relief. I didn't want him to hit me again because I broke his mirror. I bite my lip. "You sure you're not mad?"

"No, baby, I'm not mad. I love you so much, River," he says, resting his forehead against mine. "I can't lose you. I can't live without you."

Tears burn my eyes, not from sadness but from happiness. I feel on top of the world now. I feel like we're finally moving in the direction we need to be. It feels like we're healing.

"I love you, too."

"Let me make you feel good," he whispers into my ear, nipping my ear. Shivers run through my spine. I'm nodding my head before I even realize it.

His lips touch mine in a gentle kiss. It's sweet, and soothing. Slowly, he increases the pressure until it turns hungry. He scoops me in my arms and carries me up to our bedroom, never letting his lips stray from mine.

The second my feet touch the cool wood flooring next to our bed, he's peeling my clothes from my body. Hot kisses trail from my lips down to my neck. They pause at my breast, and wet heat envelops my nipple.

My head drops back as pleasure washes over me.

This right here, is what makes me feel loved.

I can get used to this.

"I THINK I MIGHT be pregnant."

I choke on my iced coffee, inhaling some of it through my nose while the rest flies out of my mouth in a perfect arch. Good thing class is over, and we're walking towards her car. If we were in the cafeteria, I would kill her.

"Wow. That was disgusting."

I laugh, partially from disbelief. I wipe my mouth and nose with my hand, trying to clean up as best as I can. Great, now I'll be sticky.

"That was your fault. Are you fucking with me?"

"No," Amelia sighs wearily.

"Why do you think you're pregnant?"

She shrugs her shoulders. "Because I've been really horny lately."

I look at her incredulously. "That's it? You've been horny?"

"No, I also threw up at the smell of bacon. Twice."

"Oh my God, you're definitely pregnant. No one throws up at the smell of bacon."

"Right?" she says, her eyes wide.

"Are you happy?"

"Are you kidding me? I'm fucking terrified."

I laugh and pull her into a tight hug. "Well, I'm happy for you, babe. You're going to be an amazing mother."

I'm beyond happy for her. Maybe one day, it'll be Ryan and I having a baby, too. Our babies can be best friends.

She beams and hugs me back. "Thank you. I can't do this without you, though, okay? I'm probably going to cry a lot. I already cried when I was watching one of those dance competition shows. Bawled like a fucking baby."

I laugh and let her go. "I think I always cry during those shows. They're just so fucking good that the only thing I can do is cry."

She slumps her shoulders in relief. "Oh, good, I'm glad I'm not the only one. I was just going to use pregnancy as my excuse."

"Yeah, I usually use my period as an excuse. It's okay."

We giggle the rest of the walk to her car. She's already coming up with wild-ass baby names like Jupiter and Italea, pronounced *i-tall-ee-uh*.

I wonder what Ryan would want to name our kids.

"YOU SEEM BETTER."

Why does my body melt every time I hear his fucking voice? I don't want my body to melt. I want it to turn into solid, unmeltable stone. Hearing his voice feels like injecting heroin. But just because heroin feels good, doesn't mean it's not capable of killing you. Mako is bad for me. He's just like Alison—another pretty face sticking their nose where it doesn't belong and trying to sabotage my relationship. For whatever reason, they can't stand to see Ryan happy.

Mako stands there like a god, dressed in black pants again with a sage green shirt that makes his eyes pop out.

He needs to go away.

"Can you stop stalking me?"

A brow raises at my harsh tone. I don't care, though. For a second, I almost fell for his shit. I regret every single moment from the library. Talking to him, telling him all my dirty secrets about my past life. Things that Ryan doesn't even know yet.

That was three weeks ago now, and it makes me feel dirty. Like I cheated. In a sense, I suppose I did. I still haven't confessed to Ryan about that day, and I never will. That'll be something I take with me to the grave.

Mainly because he'd be the one to send me there if he found out.

And I'm glad I didn't say anything either, or that night might've gone differently. Ryan made love to me and doted on me all night. Never asked for anything in return, though I was more than happy to return the favor anyway. And ever since, we've been perfect.

We've come home to each other in high spirits, laughed and joked, had at-home movie nights where we fed each other popcorn, ending in a pillow fight and making love. He's spoiled me, cuddled me, ran me candlelit baths, and expressed his vulnerable feelings towards me. We've both opened up more to each other, and he actually listened when I told him about Shallow Hill and the men there. No judgment, and only sympathy and understanding.

He's a whole new man, and I've never been more in love.

"I want you to leave me alone," I continue. "Despite what you think you know about me, I'm happy with Ryan."

Mako purses his lips, and something akin to disappointment flashes in his eyes. It's gone before I can tell for sure.

"Did he whisper sweet nothings to you all night and promise never to hurt you again?"

I bristle at his condescending words. A wave of visceral anger is thrumming through me again. Someone shouldn't be able to make me so angry as quickly as Mako does. Clearly, that's a sign. How could I think about listening to someone who does nothing but piss me off? Mako doesn't have my best interest at heart; he only cares about satisfying his own. Which is doing everything in his power to make sure Ryan is suffering.

"You don't know anything," I hiss, my eyes flaring with undisguised hate.

"I know more than he does." I flinch, my eyes widening in shock.

"Did you just throw everything I told you back in my face?"

"No. I'm just stating facts," he responds dryly. His face is a blank mask. No emotion shines through his eyes.

I take a step toward him. "The only thing you care about is getting back at Ryan. I don't know what the hell he's ever done to deserve your hatred, but don't bring that shit to my doorstep. I don't care what you think you know, you're wrong."

Mako just stares, something akin to shock registering on his face.

"Is that what he told you? That I hate him?"

I slash a hand through the air, cutting off anything else he has to say. "I'm done talking to you. Leave me alone, Mako. Or I'll tell Ryan you're following me," I threaten.

He laughs. Actually fucking laughs.

"I wouldn't mind if you did," he says around a grin. His face lights up with a cold and merciless amusement at the threat. It makes *me* feel cold.

I walk away. There's no point in responding. He got the message loud and fucking clear.

"I SEE YOU'RE STILL a piece of shit," I observe dryly.

Barbie snarls, her greasy black hair hanging in stringy clumps. She smells fucking horrid. Like a shit stain and expired milk.

"Fuck off, River."

"Do you have rent?" I ask in place of a smart response.

Be superior, River. Though I could walk in with five-day-old clothes and without a shower for even longer, and I'd still accomplish that small feat.

She reaches into the pocket of her stained, hole-riddled sweatpants and angrily slaps crumpled dirty bills on the table. Her palm catches a syringe. It pops up, twirls in the air, and topples back on the table. The tinkling lets me know it rolled off the table and onto the floor. She doesn't bother picking it up.

And *that's* why I'll never walk through this house barefoot.

Or touch that fucking table.

Good thing I came prepared. I pull a rubber glove out of my pocket, stretch it on and pick up the bills. I drop them in a plastic Ziploc baggie.

"Are you fucking kidding me? Quit acting like this isn't where you come from, you pretentious bitch," she spits. Her eyes are dilated, and she can't stop clenching her jaw. I'm not even insulted. How can I be when she's where she is, and I'm where I am?

Her words haven't hurt me in a very long time.

"How I haven't contracted an STD is beyond me, and I'm not about to test that luck."

I don't bother counting the bills. They'll all be there. They always are when I make my threats. She goes off to find a way out, no one will take her, and she comes scurrying back to the house with a pocket full of dirty money.

The front door thumps loudly against the wall. Someone just walked in like they own the house.

And there's only one person who would dare.

Billy.

Barbie and I both freeze in place, and for a brief moment, we share a connection of mutual terror. Barbie visibly gulps, and I try my best to relax my shoulders.

If Billy decides he wants more from me, I won't be able to hide his marks. Ryan will never forgive me. He'll leave me in a heartbeat if he sees another man's bruises on my body. And he'll probably create more if he finds out another man has been inside my body.

Shit.

My bones rattle and a cold sweat blooms across the back of my neck when Billy enters the kitchen. Barbie turns to greet him, a fake smile plastered on her decrepit face.

He's impeccably dressed, as usual. Slick graying blonde hair, sharp hazel eyes, and a strong jaw. He used to be handsome in his younger years. Back then, he was a young gang member, born and raised in the slums, dressed like Barbie, but had women falling at his feet. Until he had a run-in with a thug, and they cut his face up.

Those scars crisscrossing his nose, eyes and mouth make him look utterly terrifying. And the dark, blank look in his eyes certainly doesn't help matters. Billy's the type of man you see on the streets and instantly turn to walk in the opposite direction. He's incredibly intimidating, with a permanent psychotic gleam in his eyes that warns any passerby that he'd wrap his massive hands around your skull and crush it until it pops. And *enjoy* it too.

Now he runs a drug empire and is filthy rich. The cash in his wallet drips with blood and tears from all the people he killed to obtain it.

"Well, hey, suga," Barbie sings—rather loudly, might I add. Her nervous energy is palpable. Any minute now, she's going to have a bad trip, and there's not one cell in my body that feels bad for her. "I didn't know you were stoppin' by today."

"Since when am I required to announce my arrival?" he inquires, his voice devoid of emotion. I've seen Billy in all kinds of different states of emotion, but I've known him my entire life, been around him more than my nightmares are capable of keeping up with. It takes a lot to make him stray from his calm and eerily quiet state.

I swallow thickly and meet his frightening eyes. The dark pools found mine from the moment he stepped into the kitchen. They haven't strayed once.

She laughs, another nervous sound. "You're right."

Silence. Filled with his expectations and dark promises.

"Hey, Billy," I greet finally, my own voice softer than I'd like. It shames me that he still has this effect on me. I'd love nothing more than to tell him to go fuck himself and let him know he doesn't scare me. But my soul is also very attached to its vessel.

He slowly walks over to me, his polished heels clicking on the filthy floor. The contrast between the two almost doesn't compute in my brain. The image looks tremendously off. Such nice shoes shouldn't be walking on a floor so disgusting.

I'm focusing on his shoes, so I don't have to think about why he's walking towards me. I'm thinking about how there's guck caked in the cracks of the tiles, instead of how he's stopped in front of me and waiting for me to lift my eyes.

I'm thinking about how I'm about to lose my relationship tonight, and maybe even my life.

He lifts his hands towards me and it takes everything in me not to flinch away. Slowly, his finger lifts my chin, causing shivers to run down my spine. Barbie shifts in my peripheral, nervous. That makes me nervous.

My chin rises. Our eyes meet. Anger's infused in his eyes. My breath escapes me.

"You're a ghost," he says softly.

My mouth dries, and I fight to swallow.

"You were born and raised here. You were one of us, once upon a time. And now you act like you're too good for us." Despite my best efforts, my lip trembles. God, does it tremble.

His fingers tighten around my jaw, and all I can do is whisper pleadingly, "Billy…"

"Ghost," he whispers.

My face slams into the table before I can brace myself.

Pain explodes in the side of my head. The only silver lining is my face was turned enough that it didn't break my nose.

So much for not touching the fucking table.

Keeping my head pinned to the table, he leans in closer. The unforgiving surface has my eyes widening with unconcealed pain. Tears prick my eyes and threaten to leak. I don't want to show weakness. I don't want to, but Billy has a particular way of drawing it out of you anyway.

Barbie backs up a few steps, unease etched in her wrinkles.

"Where have you been?" he whispers, his tone deceptively calm. There's a torch lit inside his bloodstream. Billy's pissed.

Anger bursts inside of me. I've gotten out of this goddamn hellhole. Why the fuck do I come back? Why did I buy this stupid ass house, and why do I continue to hold it over my mother? For revenge? I was lying to Mako and myself when I said that.

Shallow Hill is ingrained in my bones, and bones won't survive without the marrow.

"Hell is not a home, Billy," I grit out. "It's only a place I come to visit."

"It is home," he barks, his voice echoing as the reins on his temper start to slip. "You're stained, River. This place is a stain on our soul, and it won't *ever* come out."

I'm breathing heavily now. Partly from fear, partly from anger. It's not smart to talk back to Billy.

"Did you try?" I challenge, squeezing my eyes shut in pain when he presses my head down further. So badly, I want to cry out. I'm toppling on the precipice of letting go of my pride and dignity.

I don't want to show weakness. I don't want to.

"Yes," he murmurs thoughtfully. "And then I realized I was only lying to myself. The joke of a life I attempted to live was a façade. Just like yours."

Finally, god, *finally*, he releases me. I scramble away from the table as fast as I can, tipping my chair over in the process, dignity be damned. The chair clatters to the tile obnoxiously, the loud sound mimicking the sound of my and Barbie's fear.

Barbie's tripping. Literally. She's blitzed off lord knows what, and the fear is messing with her high. Wide, dilated pupils jump between Billy and me. Her breathing is heavy, and her hands tremble. Pretty soon, she'll start clawing at her skin, desperate to get out of her own body. The fear is potent and inescapable.

I don't assume it's for my benefit. She's only scared he'll turn his anger on her when he's done with me.

And he will.

He absolutely will.

Eight

River

I CAN'T GO HOME like this. To emphasize my point, Ryan's name flashes across my cracked phone screen. The tiny fissures run through his name with a heart emoji on the end.

It's symbolic, and I want to throw the fucking phone.

I press the volume button on the side of my phone. Instantly, the shrill sound stops. He'll call again. I silence the phone, so I don't have to listen to the doom of my relationship anymore.

I'm soiled again. Tainted. Dirty. *Stained.*

Billy let me know just how much he missed me right in front of Barbie. She watched on with fear and resignation in her eyes. Again, not for my sake, but her own. Thank fuck he used a condom. Billy doesn't want mini's running around, that's for sure.

After beating me black and blue, he turned to Barbie and made love to her. Laid her down on the kitchen floor and took her softly. It was a warning.

Be a good little Shallow Hill bitch, and you won't get brutally raped and beaten. You'll just get softly raped. In Billy's head, that's the better option.

With the way I feel, I'm thinking so, too.

We both knew Barbie would get it later. Billy was only giving her the illusion of safety. Barbie was smart enough to know that, though. Not for one second did she relax, though she pretended she was enjoying Billy's dick inside of her regardless. If you snub Billy like that, he'll snatch away that rare moment of tenderness and beat you till you need life support. I'd already heard yelps of pain as I drug myself out of the house and into my car.

I paid her the same courtesy she paid me and drove the fuck off.

Or rather, swerved the fuck off. I definitely have a concussion, and everything feels broken. He broke my pinky when he slammed my hands in the freezer door and held it there as he took me from behind, that I'm sure of.

But it's hard to catalog your injuries when *everything* feels broken.

Somehow, I make it out of Shallow Hill, but I'm still a good ten minutes from home.

A home you can't go to, River. What a depressing reminder that is.

All because I can't just fucking stay away. It's my own fault.

It's my fault I was in that house. It's my fault I was there when Billy showed up. It's my fault he beat the shit out of me and then raped me, too.

I put myself in that situation, so it's my own fucking fault.

Fuck.

Sloppily, I wipe away the blood from my lip. For the final time, I swerve across the road. At this point, I'm an absolute menace to society. I'm basically driving drunk right now, and I could really hurt somebody.

Misery loves company, but I've always been pretty intimate with the lonely life.

I pull the car over in a quaint neighborhood. Middle class. Nice homes with treated yards, but nothing over the top and excessive. The type of neighborhood that's safe to park on the side of the road and not have to worry about getting mugged.

I would love to live in a house like this. Ryan's house definitely falls in the 'over the top' category. But I grew up on nothing, so I don't mind the simple things.

You put no value in something, then you have nothing to hold onto. You put too much value in it, and you have everything to lose. I've already made that mistake because right now, it feels like I've lost everything.

A LOUD KNOCK JERKS me awake. Big mistake.

"Motherfuu... what the fuck?" I curse.

Pain. So much pain. I'm forced to swallow down the cry. Otherwise, it won't ever stop. My bones feel broken, my lungs crushed, and my head splitting. Another more urgent knock sounds again next to my head.

If I were capable of lifting my arms, I'd clutch my head from the sound resounding in my skull. Pretty sure there's a jackhammer jackhammering my head or... something like that. I groan and flop my head over to look out the driver's window. All I can see is the blurry image of a dark figure crouched over, looking through the glass with their hands cupped around their eyes. It'd be scary if I weren't so scatter-brained.

I passed out. Not good. Especially when I have a concussion. A tugging noise follows the knocking.

Great. Now someone is trying to break into my car. While I'm in it, no less. It takes me a moment to remember where I am. Oh yeah, that deceptively cute neighborhood. I guess I did have to worry about mugging after all. Maybe I'll just let 'em. Best case scenario, they'll kill me. Worst case, they'll drive off with my car and leave me to die slowly.

A muffled voice follows next. It sounds like—is the person saying my name?

"River!"

Yup, that was my name. And they're shouting it. I've gone delusional.

Fuck it. I unlock the door. If I die, they'd be doing me a favor. A huge fucking favor.

The door flies open and gentle hands clutch my shoulders. I groan, uselessly attempting to raise my arms to get their hands off me. It's futile.

"River, what the fuck happened?"

That voice. Ugh, not again.

"Go away," I groan—another hopeless attempt.

My seat belt unbuckles and slides across my chest. Mako has to work to get my arm out of the strap. The clanging of the metal hitting the side of the car hurts. Gently, he sits me up and I'm airborne. Only a second later, I'm cocooned in warm arms. Warm, warm arms.

I'm conscious enough to know I shouldn't nestle deeper into said arms, but I do anyway. I'll find time to regret it later when I'm not on the brink of death.

I'M NO LONGER IN warm arms, but a hospital bed. Ryan and his parents sit on one side of me. Mako is on the other side. I woke up only a minute ago to bright lights and solemn faces staring at me. The moment I saw Julie and Matt watching me with faces pinched in concern, I nearly jumped out of the bed and ran. And Mako being here just makes me want to vomit. Why couldn't he have just left? Another thing Ryan won't like—Mako finding me. It'll look like I sought him out somehow.

The tension in the room is enough to finish the job and kill me via suffocation.

"What happened?" I groan. My throat is incredibly dry. It burns to speak, let alone breathe.

"You were attacked," Ryan answers, his hand covering mine. His touch feels cold, but his voice is warm and concerned.

Attacked? It takes a few seconds, but the events of... last night? — whenever it was—comes rushing back in full force.

Billy. I was in Shallow Hill collecting rent from Barbie, and he showed up. It's been a while since Billy has beaten me to this degree. I can't say I've never been in this predicament before, but back then, my hospital bed was my twin-sized one at home. My nurse was... well, myself.

The aches and pains are familiar, but fuck, it's still a shock to the system.

Turning my head, I look into Ryan's eyes, tightened in the corners with distress. Hidden beneath is a darkness swirling in his dull blue pools.

I've no idea if it's for me or Billy.

"Oh, honey, how are you feeling? I'm calling the nurse," Julie says. She stands and pushes the red button to call the nurse. I weakly signal to the water. Julie rushes towards it before Ryan can get to it.

Not that he attempted to try, anyway.

She holds up a straw to my busted lip and orders me to drink slowly. It burns something fierce at first, but after a few swallows, it eases until the cool water is a balm to my throat.

The nurse shows up a few minutes later. I'm asked a bombardment of questions that I barely have the energy to answer. Her voice is overly sweet and grating on my last nerve. I try to be civil—she has to deal with enough shitty people in a day. The nurse is in the middle of checking my vitals when the doctor shows up.

He's younger, only in his thirties or so, with spiked hair and a killer smile. Even has a dimpled chin. He's handsome. I'm not sure why that's the first thing I latch onto.

Maybe because I don't want to hear what he has to say.

"Hello, River. My name is Dr. Forrestt," he says, smiling at me softly. He's got really pretty blue eyes. Prettier than Ryan's.

"I went over your chart, and the good news is that you'll recover. You suffered a pretty severe concussion, along with two cracked ribs and a broken pinky. Other than that, you're severely bruised. No internal bleeding and no other broken bones. I want to keep you another night or two to monitor your concussion, then you should be free to go home."

I give him a weak thumbs-up, not really caring what the damage is. They're injuries I've suffered before. Probably won't be the last time either.

He gives me a serious look. "River, due to the state we found your clothes in and the abrasions to your body, I have to ask. Would you like us to perform a rape kit?"

The blood drains from my face. "No," I whisper.

"Why the hell not?" Ryan snaps from beside me, looking at me as if I have three heads.

"Because she said no," Mako intervenes, glaring at Ryan with heat. I don't like Mako sticking up for me—it makes my insides feel weird and only pisses Ryan off more.

The doctor nods his head anyway, not pushing the matter, while Ryan splits his glare between Mako and me. There's accusation in his eyes, assumptions forming in his head at rapid speed. I'm sure he thinks I cheated with Mako somehow. Maybe he even thinks Mako is the one that did this to me. Mako finding me was a pure, unlucky coincidence. I would have preferred the devil find me himself.

"River, we did report this to the police. A couple of officers are here and want to speak with you. Is that okay?" Julie asks softly. Her face. That's true concern. I appreciate that, but I really fucking wish she wouldn't have called them. I know it'd be the obvious thing to do with ordinary families, but that's not me. I don't come from a functional family that cares about each other.

I force a smile and nod. She goes to call them in.

"Don't you worry, River, they'll figure out who did it. And when they do, I'll be sure to put them away for life," Matt says, leaning forward to pat my leg in assurance. How sweet, but not going to happen.

When they walk in, Mako stands. He obviously knows them.

"River, I'm Officer Brady and this is Officer Gonzalez. I see you already know Detective Fitzgerald."

Unfortunately.

The officer who introduced himself is a stocky man with a shining bald head and a bushy, blonde mustache. His head is red from the sun. He should put some sunblock on.

"Hi," I say shortly. Officer Gonzalez steps forward. He's attractive, with Hispanic heritage and warm chocolate eyes. I'd probably be interested in him if I lived a different life.

"Do you remember anything that took place last night?"

"Based on where I am right now, I assume I was jumped." Ryan tenses from beside me.

"Do you know who they were?"

A heartbeat passes.

"No."

"Understandable, you were hit pretty hard in the head," Officer Gonzalez concedes. "Do you remember where you were?"

Do you know, do you remember, do you this, do you that...

"Shallow Hill."

The officers shift uncomfortably. The police force mostly stays away from that area. It's only twenty-five minutes from where I live, but it might as well be a whole other state. I've always wanted to move out of state, but I got too damn attached to the college I was attending, and the people in it.

Amelia... Ryan...

Stupid, River.

"Why were you there?" Ryan asks this time.

"To see my mother," I answer shortly.

"Do you remember anything else about last night? If there were more than one. What they looked like. If they said anything?" Officer Gonzalez asks, pinning me with warm, sympathetic eyes.

His sympathy bounces off me like a basketball on the court. I've received sympathy my whole life for my situation, yet only one person cared enough to get me out of it, and she died before she could. Countless teachers and adults have crossed my path, and all of them turned a blind eye, even when I showed up to school dirty and covered in bruises. That's what all the kids looked like that came from Shallow Hill. It wasn't anything new to them.

These police officers aren't going to be much different. They'll pretend to care, ask questions, and then they'll poke around for a few clues. When they don't find anything and all their leads dry up, they'll drop the façade, and I'll be grateful for that. Because the minute these cops ask the wrong questions to the wrong people, they'll go missing without a trace.

You're welcome.

"I think it was just one person. But he came from behind me. I don't remember anything," I answer robotically.

They ask a few more probing questions without getting much of an answer from me.

Officer Brady clears his throat and steps forward, a card in hand. "We'll need to take a statement from you when you get out. If you remember anything, give us a call."

I nod and take it, and they both leave. It should go in the trash, but I hold onto it for reasons I can't name. Mako follows behind them, more than likely to tell his side of the story. Meddling fool.

Julie and Matt leave a few minutes later, wishing me well and promising to stop by again soon. Their concern warms my heart. I've never had a family before.

"RYAN!" I SHOUT FROM the couch.

No answer.

He's barely spoken to me since I was discharged from the hospital, which was only yesterday. He hasn't yelled at me or questioned me, either. He's just... silent.

"Ryan!" I try again.

I'm stuck. Every muscle in my body is sore. My skin is mottled with bruises everywhere, and I still can't move easily. It feels like a plane crash-landed directly on my body. Billy beat my entire body senseless. It's a wonder that I didn't end up with more complications than a couple of broken ribs and black and blue skin.

"RYAN!" I scream, despite my ribs screaming at me in return.

I have to pee. Like really bad.

I attempt to sit up, but the pain is blinding. The doc sent me home with painkillers, but they only took the edge off. Gritting my teeth, I manage to sit myself up. I blow out a harsh breath before I haul myself up. Dizziness immediately assaults me, and before I know it, I'm back on my ass again.

This reminds me of being small again when I was helpless and had no one to help me when I needed to pee or eat. Most days, I ended up peeing myself until I had the strength to get up. It was also a pretty good deterrent from men. Fucking a little girl isn't wrong, but when she reeks of piss? Oh no, that's gross. I promised myself I'd never go back to those days, where spoiling myself and going days on end without food was my way of life. La de da, here I am once again.

"Ryan!" I try once more, frustrated tears pricking my eyes.

I hear him moving around upstairs, and I know the bastard can hear me. There's a half-bath on the other side of the house, but with how slow I'd move, it'd take me forever to get there myself. He doesn't even need to carry me there; I just need help getting up and walking there. Giving a little assistance never fucking killed anyone the last time I checked.

The pressure in my bladder builds to the point that I'm cramping. It's painful, and when I realize that I'm not going to make it to the bathroom, the tears bloom and fall out of my eyes in rivers.

At least the couch is leather.

"Ryan!" I scream once more. The effort causes my bladder to release. A sob releases from my throat as I lose all dignity and piss myself on the couch. And when he still doesn't answer, I'm forced to lay in it, just like when I was a kid.

Promises, promises, River. Can't even keep promises to your own damn self.

The warmth is sickening, and soon, my skin grows itchy. My ass will never forget the feeling of rashes on the most sensitive areas of my body. They were almost as horrid as the injuries themselves. Bad enough that I'd use my precious money for food on rash cream instead.

Snot soon joins the salty tears tracking down my face. I wipe it away angrily, but the tears and snot keep coming, which further frustrates me.

I'm fucking soaked enough, and I don't need this shit.

After another ten minutes, I hear Ryan's footsteps. And I'm *pissed*. Fury boils in my veins. I'm trembling from the rage. How dare he leave me here by myself, completely incapacitated? It's not like he left me for a minute; he's been upstairs for over an hour.

He's the one that brought me down here, claiming a change of scenery would help pep me up. He brings me down here, and then *leaves me*?

But no, I could've dealt with that. It's the fact that I screamed for him several times, and he ignored me. He fucking ignored me.

He rounds the couch and then freezes when he sees my predicament. I'm nearly frothing at the mouth, but I keep my mouth shut. I want to see what he does first.

"You pissed all over my couch?"

I didn't think it was possible to get angrier, but here we are.

"Are you serious right now?" I spit. I could literally kill him. "I yelled for you five fucking times!"

He looks down at the mess, anger flashing in his eyes. His jaw clenches and he turns his eyes up to glare at me. "I was busy," he states.

"Doing what?!"

"None of your fucking business," he snaps.

"It's not my business? Really? What could possibly be more important than coming downstairs when your *injured* girlfriend needs you?!"

He stalks towards me and leans down in my face.

"If you want to act like a bitch, then I'll fucking leave you to stew in your piss," he threatens. It takes everything in me to keep my mouth closed. *Everything.* "If anyone has the right to be mad, it's me. You went to that fucking bitch's house and got yourself jumped. It's your own goddamn fault, and you lied to the police about who did it. If you're going to protect the people who injured you, then you can suffer."

Speechless. I'm absolutely speechless. I had already blamed myself for putting myself in that situation, but I certainly didn't *ask* for it. And I sure as hell didn't deserve it.

"You also turned down a rape kit. And you know what that tells me, River?" He doesn't give me time to answer. "It tells me you fucked someone and don't want to get caught."

I blanch, my eyes widening with disbelief.

"Is that what you believe, Ryan? You think I went out and asked for any of this?"

"So, you admit you fucked someone?" he shouts, his spine snapping straight.

"No!" I protest angrily.

"Then why not get the rape kit?"

"Because I wasn't raped!"

"How do you know? You said you don't remember."

"Because I'd be able to fucking know if someone hurt me down there!"

"Fucking liar!" he screams, right before his hand whips out backhands me across the face. The pain doesn't register at first. I'm in too much shock.

No—my boyfriend couldn't have just hit me when I'd already been beaten half to death. No—not when he loves me.

But the pain does come for me, and it hurts. Everything hurts, including the goddamn muscle inside my chest that keeps getting me in these situations.

How could he treat me like this? How could he hurt me? And why can't I be able to tell my truth to my boyfriend and be comfortable and confident that he won't blame me? That he won't *hit* me?

I had no idea Billy was even going to be there. As much as he likes to call me a ghost, he doesn't show up to that house but a few times a year. Usually, Barbie goes to him. He caught us both by surprise.

"I don't believe you," he hisses, not even a minuscule amount of remorse reflected in his darkened eyes.

"Why?" I demand pitifully.

"Because you're a liar. Mako was the one that found you and brought you in. How did that happen, River? Is he the one you fucked? Maybe you didn't go to Shallow Hill at all. Maybe you let that piece of shit fuck you, and he decided to beat you, too. It wouldn't fucking surprise me."

Hypocrite.

But there's the accusation I was waiting for. I knew he'd somehow involve Mako in this. I knew he'd assume I'm cheating on him with his brother. I knew it was coming, yet the accusation pisses me off to high heaven anyway.

"I was just driving and pulled over. I had no idea it was his house. It was… a coincidence."

A high-pitched, crazed laugh bursts out of his throat.

"Coincidence?" he repeats shrilly. "I doubt that. I knew you had a thing for him the moment you met him. You're a goddamn whore, River."

"I am not!" I screech. I'm just—I'm just so fucking tired of being called a whore!

"You are," he growls. "He likes to call himself my brother, but he's *not*.

He's a fraud pretending to play the part."

His words make no sense.

"If I find out you fucked him, I will kill you, River. Do you hear me? I will fucking slit your throat." His eyes are wild, hair a mess as if he pulled at it, and his clothes askew. He looks unhinged.

Before I can muster a reply, he storms off towards the front door. His keys are swiped off the table by the door, and he's slamming it shut behind him a second later.

"Don't leave me like this!" I scream. I scream, and scream, and scream. He doesn't come back. Not even an hour later, while I'm still stuck on the couch.

I'm wet and my skin is extremely irritated, my broken ribs are probably cracked even further based on how little I can breathe, my lip is bleeding, and I'm fucking miserable. This is what dying feels like.

Slowly, I slide off the couch, teeth gritted, and crawl over to the end table where my phone rests. It takes a few attempts, but I just stare at it once I get it in my hand.

Who the hell am I supposed to call?

There's Amelia… but I don't want her to see me like this. I don't want to tell her about what Ryan did. I couldn't call Ryan's parents—not when it's their own son that left me like this.

I have no one. Unless I do something stupid and call someone I really don't want to.

I put the phone to my ear. I'm past caring at this point.

"Officer Brady."

"Hi, this is River. I… can you give me Detective Fitzgerald's number please? I'd like to talk to him about what happened."

"Ma'am, I can take the repor—"

"I'd like to talk to Detective Fitzgerald, please."

Nine

River

MY FAVORITE STUFFED ANIMAL, *Rocky, is stuffed in my mouth. The dirty fur tastes sour on my tongue from being in so many filthy places. But I need him. I need to bite down on something to keep myself from sobbing. When I cry, it hurts. I think Billy broke my ribs again. He said as long as my lungs aren't punctured, I would be fine.*

How does he know they're not?

My ankle is sprained from when I tried to run away from him. It rolled because Billy grabbed me by the hair and pulled me back unexpectedly. My ankle gave out, along with the rest of me. My body, soul, and spirit… they're all giving up on me.

Billy said if I leave the room, then I'll be punished again.

My mom is in the next room over, her moaning and screaming a mixture of pleasure and pain. Billy does the same things to me that he does to her, but I've never had the urge to make the noises she does. It doesn't feel good. Billy said it's supposed to, but all it does is hurt. It always hurts.

With him, and with the other men, Mom brings home. When they're done with her, they come to my room at night. They hurt me. They leave bruises and scratches, and even bite marks. The last guy left a scar from him biting my thigh so hard.

"Billy, please!" Mom shouts, the thin walls doing nothing to mask her terror. Flesh hitting flesh follows her desperate pleas, along with a loud grunt. Billy always makes that noise when he's finished. I look forward to that noise because then he leaves me alone.

Billy pokes his head in the door a few minutes later, shirtless with his pants unbuttoned still. A cigarette is hanging out of his mouth, the acrid smell filtering in my room. The walls are yellow from all the smoke. I don't think I've ever seen the color white in my life. Not when anything pure is tainted in Shallow Hill.

"You still crying?" he asks, a brow raised as he sucks on his cigarette. Rocky is still in my mouth, but I don't have the urge to cry anymore. Now, I just want to curl in a ball and hide.

I pull Rocky out of my mouth and toss him to the side, the once-blue dinosaur rolling across the dirty floor.

"No," I mumble. The tears haven't dried on my cheeks yet. Billy doesn't like it when I lie, but he hates it more when I show weakness.

"You better not be," he warns. "Your mother's pussy is looser than the Grand fucking Canyon. But I don't have that problem with you."

I learned what that term meant a couple of years ago. Billy loves to say the word when he's making me dirty. He said it's the best he ever had, but I don't want to be the best. I want to be worse than Mom. If I were bigger than the ocean, maybe he wouldn't want me.

"I'm not crying," I say again. His threat was clear. He'd come to dirty me up again if I keep crying. He always says that he'll give me a reason to cry when I show weakness. And when he does, I want to die.

Billy walks into the room, crouches down to eye level, and hands me the cigarette. I take it. If I don't, he'll put it out on my skin. Pride shines in his cold, dead eyes when

I bring the stick to my mouth and inhale the smoke. I used to cough all the time when Billy made me smoke these, but I don't anymore. I got better at it.

He urges me to suck on it again. I do and get a little buzz. The pain doesn't go away, but it seems a little more tolerable now.

"Will you help me to the bathroom?" I ask quietly. Asking Billy a favor never comes free. I know this, but the urge to go is starting to deepen.

He takes the cigarette back and sticks it in his mouth. I study his lips, where they're hugging the yellow filter. Where my lips just were. It makes me feel like he's touching me.

"You're too old to need help to the bathroom, River," he admonishes.

My bottom lip threatens to tremble as the feeling gets worse. I really have to pee. But I don't want to try and get up in front of Billy. He'll see me struggle. He'll see me cry. He'll see me weak. And then he'll make those things worse.

"Okay, Billy. I don't have to go that bad," I lie. It's a lie worth saying if it means he'll believe me and leave. He looks down at me, a knowing smile tugging on his lips.

"Okay, River," he repeats, his cold voice airy. "I hope you don't, because you're grounded. You're not allowed to come out of this room until morning. You hear me?"

I suck in a painful breath, but nod my head.

Billy gives me one last smile and then walks out of the room, closing and locking the door behind him. The locks have always been on the outside, never the inside.

The second he leaves, I release myself. It's cold in here, and maybe it'll keep me warm for the night.

Ten
River

WHAT THE FUCK DID I get myself into?

"I don't want to hear any comments from you, okay?" I demand, glaring at him from my spot on the floor.

I look absolutely pathetic, I know this. But it doesn't stop me from making my demands.

Mako stares down at me with a plethora of emotions in his eyes. Sadness and disbelief are there. But the most dominant emotion is the unbridled fury.

You and me both, buddy.

"What… did he do?" he asks through barely contained anger. His fists are clenched so tightly, his knuckles are bleached white.

"Nothing, can you just help me, please?" I deflect, not wanting to get into what an asshole my boyfriend is. It's embarrassing, and I don't want to hear him say *I told you so.* After a moment, he remembers himself and scrambles over to me.

"Careful, I—I'm not clean right now," I say, stuttering over how to say that I pissed myself. He pays me no mind. Gently, he picks me up, but it doesn't matter. The searing pain in my ribs is breathtaking. I gasp from pain, and he freezes.

"I'm sorry, baby," he says. My heart drops at the endearment. Normally, the pain would distract me from his words, but instead, I focus on that so I'm distracted from the pain.

Fuck you, heart. That's what got me into this situation. Clearly, it doesn't know what it's talking about.

With great pain, he cradles me in his arms and carries me out to his car. I've never been so embarrassed in my entire life. So badly, I want to crawl out of my skin and disappear. Before I can stop it, my hands cover my face and sobs wrack my body once more. I don't care about the pain right now; I'm just so… *angry.* So hurt and embarrassed. I can't believe Ryan left me like this. I can't believe he hit me again.

"I got you," he whispers in my ear. "If you're embarrassed, I got one better. I was seventeen and just showing up for a job interview. I was so nervous that I had gas. But when I went to fart, I actually shit myself."

Something between a shocked gasp and laugh escapes my mouth. It hurts my ribs, but I'm too stunned to care.

"You did not!"

I'd rather not look at Mako and think about him shitting himself. He's too hot and that story is just weird. But it seems to work long enough to cease my pity party.

"I did. I ran out immediately but not before the manager got a good look at my retreating ass." Another laugh escapes, completely bewildered that he's not the least bit embarrassed about his story. He stares down at me with a crooked smirk and a thin layer of amusement masking his true feelings. He's distracting himself as much as he's distracting me.

He opens the door to his Jeep Wrangler and daintily sets me on the seat. As he's buckling my seatbelt, he explains, "I know you're uncomfortable, but I don't want him to come home while I'm here. If he does, I'll end up in prison for first-degree murder. I'm going to sit you in the car and run up and grab some clothes."

I don't have the energy to argue, so I nod. "Panties are in the top drawer. Pajamas are in the second drawer."

It only takes him a few moments to come back. He must've found the duffel bag in the closet since it's strapped around his broad shoulder. He gets in the car, and my cheeks redden.

I'm getting his seats wet and it stinks of stale piss.

"I'm so sorry," I choke out, staring down at my damp lap.

"Don't be, this isn't your fault," he says softly, though there's a razor-sharp edge to it. "The seats are leather and easy to clean."

"This is still humiliating despite your shitty story, but yeah, I guess that helps," I mutter, offering a small smile to take away any sting. I appreciated that story more than he'll ever know.

"Will you tell me what happened?" he asks gently, as he peels away from the curb and away from my worst nightmare.

I shake my head. "Not right now. I just want to get clean," I say quietly.

"Okay, I understand."

I'M FRESHLY SHOWERED, AND just a little high on painkillers. When Mako wasn't looking, I popped another. I'm pissed enough that I'm cool with getting high.

I'm settled on his plush couch and Shark Week is playing on low. I don't much like couches right now, but it's soft and comfortable. Mako is sitting next to me, making sure my body is positioned in a way that causes me the least amount of pain.

The attention he's giving me is… disconcerting. Ryan just plopped me on the couch, and that was that.

"Do you need any rash cream?" he asks.

Did he seriously just—I can't believe I was just asked if I need *rash cream*. By a devastatingly beautiful man, nonetheless. I didn't think I could sink any lower.

Blood rushes to my cheeks, and I cover my face with my hands.

"I'm so embarrassed," I mumble through my makeshift barrier. His fingers pick at my good hand—pulling them away one by one and shooting tiny currents through each finger. I don't like the way his skin feels on mine. It feels too… good.

I pull my hand from his grip, but I don't have the lady balls to meet his eyes.

"Hey," he murmurs, lifting my chin until I'm forced to meet his gaze. "Nothing about what happened tonight is your fault. It doesn't take a genius to know you were left alone and couldn't get up."

"That doesn't mean it's not humiliating," I grumble.

He nods his head slowly. "I get it, apparently my shitty story wasn't enough. Will it help if I tell you that the smell of pee is a fetish of mine?" he asks seriously. I rear back with disgust.

"It is not! That's repulsive."

He cracks a smile and shrugs a shoulder. When he gets up and walks towards the kitchen without defending himself, I grow worried that he wasn't joking. "Oh, my god, is it really a fetish?"

The living room and kitchen are an open floor plan. The house is pretty bare, but apparently, he just moved in. Even though it doesn't look very lived in, it's beautiful. Gray wooden floors, pale sage walls with an accented black wall, and black furniture. His coffee table looks like a large rock. His kitchen has black cabinets, a gray and white backsplash with sage accents and light gray countertops.

He's got good taste. I dig it.

Mako rummages around in the fridge with his back to me, but I can see his shoulders shaking with mirth. The light glints against his tattoos. Without permission, my mouth opens, the questions resting at the tip of my tongue. So badly, I want to ask what each of them mean. From my spot on the couch, I can see intricate details of a red blooming rose among wilted, blackened roses. The bright light shining against the ashes. Something about it draws me in. He finishes pouring himself a glass of milk—*only psychos drink milk*—and turns to me. That one look, staring at me with emotions I won't dare decipher, I chicken out.

Instead, "You're laughing at me," I deadpan.

He turns, and a beautiful smile is on his face. "If it means I get to be more humiliated than you, then no, I'm not joking."

"But... that's... that's not how that works," I finally get out. What is this feeling? I'm actually touched by the notion that he'd prefer to demean himself just to make me feel better. Even if it's obvious it's a lie, it's still kind of... cute. Oddly. I wrinkle my nose.

He pulls a serious face. "I think your pee smells like roses."

My mouth parts in a perfect O. What the hell is wrong with this man?

Another casual shoulder shrug. "A lot," he answers.

I hadn't even realized I voiced that question out loud.

"This is the weirdest conversation I've ever had."

"It only gets weirder from here, baby," he chirps, pulling out a jug of orange juice. He shakes it at me. "Want some?"

"Uhm. Sure?"

I haven't recovered yet. From anything he just said. Including that damn endearment. I'm a little too high to correct it. Maybe later.

THIS BED IS REALLY comfortable. The only thing it's missing is Bilby curled up by my feet. I miss that little dude, he always knew when I was down and would curl his soft little body into mine.

My hands slide across the warm gray duvet. It's Mako's bed, considering his spare bedroom doesn't have a bed yet. It would seem he doesn't have guests very often, and it wasn't a priority. I wonder if that's because all his 'guests' sleep in his bed with him. The thought causes my heart to sink. When I realize that, I reach down inside myself, yank that pesky muscle up and slam it back in its place where it belongs.

Mako's room is bare of any personal photos except for one on his nightstand. A picture of a man that looks identical to him, but older and weathered. He's smirking at the camera, the same smug smirk on Mako's face that I've wanted to both slap and kiss off his face.

Must be an uncle. I think I remember Ryan saying Matt had a couple of brothers. Mako doesn't look much like Julie or Matt, so he must've gotten his genes from one of Matt's brothers.

Resisting the urge to grab the frame and look closer, I turn my eyes away.

The walls are a light gray except for the rough gray stone wall his bed is pushed up against. The black hardwood flooring contrasts nicely with the walls, giving the same aura to his room the rest of the house holds.

Comfortable. Safe.

A stark contrast to Ryan's house, which was built to look modern and sterile. White everywhere save for some of the furniture and the colorful pictures hanging on the walls. Cold and sterile, just like its owner.

Mako places a bottle of water and my pills on the end table.

"Is there anything I can get you?" he asks softly, sitting down on the edge of the bed. The soft mattress compresses deeply around his weight.

"Maybe…" I lick my lips, not sure what I'm even asking. "Maybe just talk to me?" I cringe the moment the words leave my mouth. Desperately, I want to snatch them out of the air before they reach his ears, but it's too late. He's already turning his head towards me, his face softened and kind. He actually looks his age when he stares at me this way. Any other time, the stress from his job ages him.

When has he ever gotten the chance to feel young? To *be* young?

"Tell me about yourself, Mako," I say. "Tell me something meaningful."

And just like Jesus shining a light down on my biggest desires, he turns his tattooed arm towards me, showcasing the beautiful design of the blooming red rose in a bed of dead roses.

"I got this when I turned eighteen. It symbolizes my life and how I see myself. I doubt Ryan told you this, but Julie and Matt adopted me when I was thirteen."

My mouth parts. All the strange comments Ryan would make about Mako not belonging, or him not being his real brother makes perfect sense now. The picture frame on Mako's bedside table, of him and an older replica of him. That must be his father. His *real* father.

"Before that, I grew up in a shitty neighborhood with pretty shitty parents. My mother sold herself for money and my father was a drug runner." My lip trembles, completely blown away by how similar Mako's childhood was to mine. Back at the library, when I spilled my life story to Mako, he never said a thing.

"This tattoo is a reminder that despite my ugly surroundings, I was still worth something. That where I came from doesn't taint who I am in any way." He lifts his eyes to me, staring at me pointedly.

The weight of his words is too much. My eyes drop back down to the tattoo.

"It's… beautiful," I whisper. That word. I hate it. But it's the only word that does his story justice.

"I understand you more than you think I do, River," he says softly, his eyes still waiting for mine to join them once again. I gather my strength and answer his silent demand. His glittering emerald eyes are enrapturing, so much that my breath dissipates. "I know what it's like not to be your parent's first choice. But that doesn't mean you can't be your own first choice. Choose yourself, River. Put yourself first."

My lip trembles. A tear sneaks past my barriers and trails down my cheek. He doesn't shy away from the emotion, instead, lifting his hand and wiping away the drop with his thumb. His skin sliding against mine so delicately leaves a trail of fire in its wake. My breath shudders out of me, completely at a loss of what to say.

He stands and looks back at me once more. "Let me know if there's anything I can do for you."

Right before he walks out the door, I find my voice, albeit being thin and hoarse. "Are you sure I can't just take the couch? I don't want to be a hindrance. You've helped more than enough."

And I mean, way more than enough. He's helped me to the restroom, and even off the toilet at one point. He's kept me comfortable, hydrated, and fed me healthy food. The nurse said a good diet helps heal bodies. I didn't even know Mako was paying that close attention. He kept me entertained with his weird fetish talk—which I still one hundred percent believe he's fibbing about—and movies. He gave me safety and comfort, and a piece of him that I'll treasure forever. And now he's giving me his bed.

I've never been taken care of like this, and I don't know how to feel about it. Mako shouldn't be the one doing this for me, it should be Ryan—who hasn't even called or texted. Either he hasn't gone home yet, or he doesn't give a shit.

Both make me want to kill him.

"Are you trying to wake up in more pain tomorrow?" he asks, bringing me back to the conversation.

I frown. "Well, no."

"Then shut your pretty mouth and get some sleep."

The door clicks behind him before I can open my pretty mouth and tell him thank you. Maybe that's for the best. He's helping me, but there's an odd part of me that feels like I'm still supposed to hate him.

More than likely, it stems from that fucked up part of me that feels loyal to Ryan. But after what he did today, I think it's time to finally accept the fact that I'm dating a lesser version of Billy.

An absolute piece of shit.

I was so desperate for love and human connection that I fell for all his bullshit. Even when there were people literally shoving the facts down my throat. And all I did was spit them back in their face.

God, Alison. It hurts to admit she was right, but then again, that's only my pride. I was awful to her. Part of that was due to jealousy, the other part because of the things Ryan fed me about her.

Alison and Ryan grew up together, though Alison is my age. Their parents were best friends, and they fell into that cliché fairytale. The parents pushed them together. Ryan and Alison went along with it, dated throughout high school and almost a year of Alison's college career, before they split.

He insisted she was a crazy bitch that cheated on him constantly and stalked him when he left her. His claims never matched the Alison I interacted with, but I convinced myself it was all an act. That *she* was the manipulative, lying bitch when all along, it was Ryan.

She was never mean or vindictive towards me; she was just a woman trying to help another woman.

"She was right," I whisper aloud. "And I'm a fucking idiot."

"RIVER, WHAT THE HELL is going on? Why the hell didn't anyone tell me you were in the hospital? Why wouldn't Ryan call me? And if you lie to me, you're on diaper duty for a full *week*. Don't fuck with me," Amelia threatens through the phone. Her threat makes me smile. Diaper duty with a mini Amelia doesn't sound so bad compared to telling the truth.

But alas. "I was jumped in Shallow Hill. I don't know by who. And Ryan… Ryan made it worse."

Silence. It sounds deathly.

"What do you mean he made it worse, River?" She questions darkly. I've seen Amelia pissed before—it's scary. When I don't answer right away, she continues her threats. "Scratch that, I'll make it a month. And I'll wait till my six weeks are up, and then David and I will have sex in the next room the entire time."

"You're tempting me with a good time," I reply in a bored tone, though there's a small smile on my face. I inspect my nails. They're broken and jagged. I wonder how many weird looks I'd get if I walked into a nail salon right now. The thought makes me want to hide and go do it all in the same breath.

Why should I hide that I was attacked? I'm a fucking survivor, right? I always have been. Maybe I should start relishing in the attention from bruises and a broken soul. Maybe I should turn it into armor.

"...River? RIIIIVEEERR."

Amelia's impatient tone snaps me out of it. I clear my throat.

"He left me, Amelia. He was so angry that I put myself in that situation."

Even now, I'm still lightening the gravity of his actions. I'm still *protecting* him, and I've no idea why. She could ask me if Jesus is a virgin, and I'd have a better answer for her.

Amelia sighs. "I'm not happy that you still go there, either, River. It's obviously dangerous, and it does nothing but cause harm. Whether it's mental or physical. But despite that, you didn't deserve a damn thing that happened to you and he has no right to treat you like that. Why don't you come stay with us? We haven't turned the spare into a nursery yet."

I lick my dry lips. To tell the truth or continue to be a liar? Hmm, decisions.

"I... I kind of have a place to stay right now. I'm good, Amelia. Really."

"Where are you staying?" Damn her nosiness. I can't fault her. I'd ask the same. "River?" she prompts when I don't answer.

"His brother's?" I said it like a question. Fuck, I said it like a damn question. Amelia pounces.

"Explain yourself. Now."

If I didn't feel so broken, I'd be pacing the floor right now. I never was in the habit of biting my nails before, but maybe I should start. Maybe I should make them nice and stumpy before going to the nail salon.

"He's a detective actually. And coincidentally, I ended up in front of his house that night. He's been helping out ever since."

I don't tell her about his random pop-ins when I'm leaving class. That would lead to confessing about *why* he felt the need to find me. And then that'll lead to the library incident when I felt too... free. Like I could say anything or do anything with no consequence.

"Are you comfortable there?"

I know what she's really asking. Is Mako just like Ryan? Does he scare me too?

He does. Just not in the way she'd think.

"Yes," I breathe. And this time, I'm telling the complete truth.

She sighs in relief. "Okay, well, I have to go throw up now. But will you text me? Let me know if you're okay and if you need anything?"

I smile, more grateful than ever that Amelia's in my life. "Of course, babe. I love you."

"I love you too, River."

126 MISSED CALLS.

349 UNREAD MESSAGES.

40 VOICEMAILS.

RYAN: Baby, please come home. I need you. I'm losing my fucking mind without you.

RYAN: I can't fucking live like this, River. You're killing me. You're fucking killing me.

RYAN: Does this make you happy? That I want to fucking kill

myself? I'll fucking do it, River. I'll write my suicide note and tell everyone it's all your fault, that way when someone asks you what it's like to murder someone, you'll know.

RYAN: I'm staring at this gun in my hand and all I want to do is put a bullet in my brain. I don't know if I'll be able to stop myself.

RYAN: I'm just so hurt by the way you're treating me. You're acting like I never meant anything to you.

RYAN: So much for never fucking leaving me, River. You promised you'd never leave me.

RYAN: Was everything a lie? All those times you told me you loved me. That we would be together forever. Everything was a lie.

RYAN: I want to kill myself right now. The only thing keeping me alive is the hope that you'll come back to me.

RYAN: Baby PLEASE.

RYAN: Where the fuck are you, River? I'll fucking find you if you don't tell me.

RYAN: No one will ever keep me from finding you.

RYAN: FUCKING ANSWER ME!

RYAN: I'm coming for you.

EVERY TIME HIS NAME flashes across the screen, I want to break it. I just got this new phone, too, considering Billy smashed the other one. That entire week, I struggled with the push and pull. I'd go from seething mad to missing him and crying because of what he did to me. My fingers would hover over the keypad, desperate to respond to him. Desperate to plead for him not to kill himself. But I couldn't bring myself to do it, not even when he threatened to come looking for me.

That was two days ago, and he still hasn't found me. I assume the last place he ever expected me to be was his brother's. Ryan doesn't know that Mako and I have talked past the short encounter when I met their parents. It didn't keep me from constantly checking out the window in fear, waiting for his car to pull up.

It's hard to admit that the past week I've been here, this is the safest I've ever felt in… well, my entire life. I hate that. I hate that being around Ryan feels like standing next to a tornado, while his brother feels like finding safety in a storm shelter.

Another text comes through. This time it's an image. Ryan is holding a gun to his head, the look in his eyes desperate and wild. My heart drops. Is he actually going to do it? When he threatened to kill himself, I never truly believed it, though it kept me up at night praying he wouldn't. But this seems too real. Ryan's not the type to hold a gun to his head.

His name flashes across my phone for the millionth time. Another incoming call. Before I can stop myself, I snatch up the phone and click the green button.

"Hello?"

A moment of silence, and then a sniffle. "I wasn't expecting you to answer." He sounds pitiful, his voice downtrodden and full of shame.

"I wasn't expecting you to leave me in a puddle of piss, but I guess shit happens, Ryan. Why are you holding a fucking gun to your head? What is wrong with you?" *My* voice is full of anger. I didn't expect the fury to hit me so suddenly and so hard. But the moment I heard his voice through the receiver, all I felt was raw agony from his actions.

"Because I can't live without you, River! How many times do I have to say that? Look, I am so sorry, River. I miss you so much, and I'm so ashamed of the way I acted. You're injured and it wasn't the right time."

I smile, though not from humor. "When *is* the right time?"

He trips over his words. "What do you mean?"

"You said it wasn't the right time. So, tell me, Ryan, when is the right time to beat your girlfriend?"

"There is no right time. That's not what I meant," he snaps, growing defensive. Ah, so he doesn't like to be called out on hitting me? And I thought I ran from my problems.

"Then what did you mean?"

"I mean, I should've handled it better. But, River, I was angry you put yourself in that situation. I've told you to stop going there. It's dangerous and this is what happens. Can you blame me for being upset that you continue to walk into a dangerous house every month? Where you were raped and abused? This was bound to happen. And you lied to me, and you're still lying about who hurt you. You're protecting them."

"I'm not protecting them," I snap. "I'm protecting everyone else. You're right, there are dangerous people in Shallow Hill. And my ghosts caught up with me, but I'm not about to let them haunt anyone else's life."

"My dad is a lawyer, *I'm* a lawyer. I could put them away for life," he argues.

I shake my head, frustration bubbling inside me. He doesn't understand. He won't ever understand. He's a privileged boy that grew up with loving parents in a beautiful house. He has *always* gotten his way.

But he won't get his way this time.

"*I'm sorry*," he says, his voice on the edge of desperation. "I just love you so fucking much, River. More than anyone I've ever been with. I've never felt this way about any of them, so this is… this is new to me, okay? I am so fucking scared of losing you. And that night… It was like watching my worst nightmare come to life. I freaked out. I treated you horribly. I fucked everything up, and I'm so fucking sorry for that." His voice cracks at the end of his sentence, right along with my resolve.

My shoulders deflate. Why does it ache so bad hearing him in pain? He doesn't hurt when I hurt. I grit my hair and pull, so frustrated with the effect Ryan has on me. It's like a riptide—every time I think I'm going to pull myself out and get free, he's right there to pull me back under. Drowning and suffocating me. It's so exhausting fighting him. I just want to go back to where we were before I went to Shallow Hill. We were so fucking happy, and god, do I want that back again.

"River, can we just… can you please come home so we can talk?"

I feel myself starting to slip. He hit me. He hurt me. He left me. He did so many bad things to me. But I think about the picture of him holding a gun to his head, the crazed gleam in his eye. He's hurting, too. And maybe this time, he's actually fucking sorry. I've never actually left him before. Maybe this time, he took me seriously and will change.

"Please?" he begs when I still don't answer. "I just want to talk to you. See how you're doing and if you're okay. I promise we'll just talk. I won't even touch you if you don't want me to."

I sigh. We do have a lot to talk about. I've put more effort into this relationship than I ever had with anyone else. All the other men I've entertained were just that—entertainment. I never felt the things Ryan makes me feel.

It's pretty clear Ryan has issues, but maybe if he opens up to me better and we establish healthy coping mechanisms for his anger, we can fix this. That's what I've learned in my studies. Coping mechanisms. Finding what triggers him and learning how to handle it in a healthy way.

Aside from that, all my belongings are there. I've been wearing Mako's oversized clothes for the past week, and I've caught him giving me a few heated glances when he thought I wasn't looking. They sent a thrill straight through my bloodstream and disgusted me all at once.

"Come on, just a couple of weeks ago, we were so happy. The way I made you laugh. How hard I made you come—"

"Fine," I interrupt, already feeling myself weakening to those memories. I have to admit, most of the last two years together have been absolute bliss. "I'll come home. But if I start to feel scared in any way, I'll have the police on speed dial."

Somewhere in the back of my mind, I realize that's a sentence I should never have to say to my boyfriend. But I don't have fucking room to talk, though. Look at where I came from. Everyone has demons, and I love Ryan enough to try to help him fight those demons.

He sighs in relief, and I can feel his smile through the phone. "Okay, baby. I'll be here waiting." That word again. Baby. It feels different coming out of Ryan's mouth. Like familiarity and comfort. With Mako, it feels… thrilling. Like touching a live wire. I think I've had enough thrills to last me a lifetime; now's the time where I settle down and relish in comfort.

I hang up the phone and immediately open up my Uber app. Mako's at work, so I don't have to worry about sneaking out.

I dress back into my pajamas that Mako packed for me, collect the few things I had here in a grocery bag and am sliding into the back of the Uber within fifteen minutes.

The entire ride back, all I can pray for is that this doesn't turn ugly again. I might not survive it this time.

"HEY, BABY. I MISSED you," Ryan says, standing from the couch and walking towards me. I take one step back, not quite ready for his touch. Immediately he pauses, a flash of hurt skirting across his eyes. But he steps back nonetheless. That one movement comforts me.

"I'm sorry. Can I get you anything? How are you feeling?"

"How does it look like I feel?" I still haven't let go of my anger yet. Just because I'm here, doesn't mean I'm not still hurting.

His eyes track over my bruised face, a casted pinky finger and a hunched over body. Every movement hurts my ribs, and I still have a slight limp.

He looks dejected, but anger brews in his blue eyes. "It makes me angry looking at you, River. Because of what that son of a bitch did to you. I want to kill him."

And apparently me too. I keep that part to myself, though.

"Please, come sit down." I glance at the couch. Memories of lying there, helpless and in a puddle of pee assault me. Memories of crying and screaming for his help, while he yelled at me and smacked me in the face.

Maybe this was a bad idea.

I take a step back.

"You're not leaving," he says. The words send a jolt of fear through me, like an espresso shot straight into my veins. When my eyes slide back to him, his concerned mask has fallen and a darker one has replaced it.

"I...I wasn't going to," I say. I hate how weak I just sounded. I lift my phone, my fingers moving towards the SOS button. The phone is ripped from my hand and thrown across the house in a matter of seconds. I flinch at the crash and sound of breaking glass. Great, there goes another one.

"You don't need that. I just want to help you, River. You never let me help you."

His soft tone starkly contrasts with the aggressive action. It's honestly fucking terrifying. I bite my tongue to keep my words in, tempted to remind him we're in this situation because of the last time I asked him for help.

Subtly, I glance around my surroundings. I know this house like the back of my hand now. I know where all the exits are.

I know where the knives are.

I smile at him. "I'd love for you to help me." I hold out my hand—the one without the broken pinky. "Will you help me to the couch? I'm still sore."

His shoulders relax, a smile slides across his face, and he grips my hand gently.

"See, baby? That's all I want to do. Make you feel better. Make up for my past mistakes."

The second my ass hits the couch, so does the reality that I made a huge mistake coming back here.

"So, let's talk," I breathe. I grab his hands and hold them tightly in mine. They feel cold but familiar. I close my eyes briefly and brush my thumbs across his skin.

No tingles. No thrill. Just familiarity. Something I've always wanted in life. Comfort, the feeling of home, to be content. I was so tired of being touched by unfamiliar hands that I thrived off the comfort of Ryan's hands on me. But I never realized that being familiar doesn't mean being safe until now.

Billy's hands are familiar...

This was a mistake.

"I think you owe me an apology first," he says. My eyes snap open. His dull blues bore into my golden orbs. He is one hundred percent serious.

Desperately, I try to search for the man I fell in love with, but all I see staring back at me is the face of evil. He isn't even trying to hide it anymore.

I clear my throat.

"What would you like me to apologize for?"

Loving you despite your flaws? Thinking I could change you? Healthy coping mechanisms, my ass. He had me so fooled. I had kidded myself, thinking he was just a man with a few anger issues and a little too spoiled. Now I realize I was wrong. So, so wrong.

"For going to Shallow Hill, putting yourself in a dangerous situation and letting another man touch you." My hand trembles with the need to pull them from his. I don't want his skin on mine; it burns like hot coals forged from Hell.

How could I when he thinks I *let* Billy put his hands on me? As if I had the goddamn choice.

"I'm willing to forgive you, River. I know"—he clenches his jaw—"I know another man fucked you. I'm willing to still be with you. But I want an apology."

So many thoughts are racing through my head, I can't pin a single one down and focus on it.

I'm sorry for being raped, Ryan. I'm sorry I was beaten half to death while my mother watched and didn't do a damn thing to save me. I'm sorry I watched my mother being raped in return. I'm sorry that an evil man is attached to me and will do anything to hurt me. And I'm sorry you're just like him.

"I'm sorry, Ryan," I say softly. If I speak any louder, he might detect the emotion in my voice. He'll hear the anger. The disgust. The absolute shame that I'll never learn. I always come crawling back to him.

His fingers brush a stray strand of hair from my face and tuck it behind my ear. I shiver beneath his touch.

He thinks it's because he excites me. I think it's because he disgusts me.

"I forgive you, baby. We all make mistakes. But just because I forgive you, that doesn't mean I will ever forget. Do you understand that?" he asks, his voice quiet and steady. Sinister and *un*forgiving.

"I understand."

He smiles, his perfect teeth poking through. He doesn't have sharp canines as Mako does. His two front teeth aren't a tad longer than the rest. They look like veneers. What did his teeth look like before a dentist made them perfect little squares in his lying mouth?

"I'm sorry I hit you, River. I'm sorry I yelled at you. And I'm sorry that I didn't come to get you before you embarrassed yourself all over my couch." I nearly see red by the time the last words slip past his stupid fake teeth. "And I'm sorry I fucked my secretary."

The red bleeds into an icy blue as my blood runs cold. "You... you fucked someone else?"

He scoffs. "You didn't think I wouldn't after you let someone else inside you? Come on, River. It was only fair I got even. And now that I have, we can be happy again. You won't go to Shallow Hill anymore, and I'll fire that slut."

Oh, sweet Ryan, yes, you will.

"Okay," I whisper. I look into his eyes and force a brittle smile. "That's fair."

The smile he returns can only be called evil, just like him.

Good thing I can be, too.

THE SHRILL RING FROM my phone startles me. I drop the coffee mug I'm washing, and it shatters into the sink. Ryan liked that mug. Anxiety rushes through me as I try to figure out how I'm going to explain how it broke. Maybe he won't notice.

Stupid.

He uses this mug every day.

My hands shake as I quickly wipe my hands on a dishtowel and answer the phone without looking who it is. "Hello?"

Stupid, stupid, stupid.

"Where are you?"

I close my eyes and release a weighted sigh. It's only been two days since I came back to Ryan. Mako called me both days, and it's been absolute hell trying to hide them from Ryan. I also skipped class, so he couldn't find me there. I'm hiding from Mako, and he knows it. He knows exactly where I am.

"You can't just call me, Mako."

Good thing I never saved his phone number on my phone. I deleted all evidence of him. Surprisingly, Ryan hasn't asked where I stayed during the week apart. I know he went looking for me at Amelia's. She told me he showed up, and she slammed the door in his face, not confirming nor denying if I was there. I think he just assumed I was.

That's where I wish I would've gone.

"Why? Because you're back with him?"

The sound of water splashing on the tiled floor filters through my racing thoughts. I whip my head to see the sink overflowing with water.

"Shit," I mutter as I rush over to turn off the spout. I scramble for the dishtowel to mop up the water on the floor, nearly crying aloud when my ribs protest. My heart is racing, and I'm not even sure why at this point.

"River?"

"Just...just hold on, okay?" I snap. I finish soaking up the water. Thankfully, I caught it before it made a huge mess. I trap the phone between my ear and shoulder and wring out the dishtowel in the sink.

I stick my hand into the sink so I can drain it, and right as I grab onto the stopper, I feel a sharp sting on my finger. Flinching in pain, I bite my lip and rip the plug out of the sink. A shard of broken glass cut me.

"River?" Mako says again, sounding impatient.

"What? What do you want, Mako?" I return his impatience tenfold.

My finger is bleeding, my hands are still shaking, and I'm on the verge of tears.

"You left without a word and haven't answered my calls for the past two days. Did you think I wouldn't be worried?"

"Yes, actually. I did. Rest assured, I'm fine."

He sighs. I ignore it as I rush to the bathroom to find the peroxide and a band-aid. I pour peroxide on it and inspect the wound. It's pretty superficial but deep enough to cause a scar. Now I definitely won't be able to hide my mistake from Ryan.

I rinse off the blood and wrap a band-aid around it tightly.

"You don't sound fine." I pause, watching the last of my blood circle down the drain.

"I was fine until you called." Truth.

Ryan has reverted back to his old self. Loving. Sweet. Thoughtful. And my fear of him is tentatively retreating. He hasn't shown his dark side to me since the day I came home, and it's to the point where I'm questioning myself—thinking maybe I just overreacted. It's hard to picture in my head when he's being so loving now.

He bought me yet another new phone, fired the secretary he cheated on me with and brought home champagne to celebrate. I nearly drank the whole bottle and let him fuck me in the ass that night, despite my bruised and broken body. I covered my tears of shame with the symphony of his snoring.

Regardless, we're on our way back to being happy again. Or something like that. I'm still healing, and he's taken good care of me so far. He's made it clear that as long as I'm a good girl and don't fuck up, he'll continue to take care of me. He promised.

"I'm just worried about you, River," he says lowly. His deep voice resonates through me.

"Well, do us both a favor and stop." I hang up and immediately delete the call from my log.

Then, I go and grab some super glue. Maybe he'll appreciate the effort to fix my mistake.

THE MUG RESEMBLES JAGGED rocks smashed together like crooked teeth, the ragged edges held together with shitty glue that will melt in the dishwasher within seconds. It resembles me. Just a bunch of mismatched pieces barely holding it together.

This mug can never go in the dishwasher again. I should've put it in there in the first place, but cleaning helps me calm my mind. Dusting the ceiling fan blades would've been less risky, but the dust makes me sneeze, and fuck it, who cares if I sneeze because pretty soon, I'll be trying to keep the blood from coming out of my nose instead.

And worst of all, now I'm doomed to a lifetime of handwashing it. It's a guarantee that I'll break it again. The broken pieces will break into tinier pieces over and over until eventually, it'll be too far gone to piece back together again.

I might as well be staring into a crystal fucking ball.

I sigh and carefully set the mug on the dinner table. My hand shakes from the anxiety blooming inside me. Ryan's going to kill me. If he tries, I'll flick the cup and it'll fall back apart, then stab him in the jugular with his favorite mug. Poetic.

Maybe I should just let him kill me. However, the bastard will surely make me suffer first. Can't be much worse than what Billy has already done to me. And those will be my last words too. He wasn't the one to truly break me.

The door opens, and I hear Ryan's feet shuffling across the gray hardwood floors.

"Babe?" he calls from the living room.

He sounds like he's in a good mood. Maybe he won't be mad.

My body knows I'm telling myself lies, and the anxiety worsens.

"In here," I answer, the tremble in my voice prominent. Damn it.

With each footstep, my hands tremble harder and grow warmer with sweat. I sit on them to abate the shaking.

He walks into the dining room, his face pinched in confusion.

"Why are you in he—" he pauses when he sees my crime in front of me. And the murder weapons are nestled nicely under my ass cheeks.

His face blanks, straightening into a perfectly calm mask. The scariest one of all.

"What happened?" he asks, his voice devoid of emotion.

I blow out a shaky breath. "I was washing it and it slipped from my hands," I explain quietly. A wobbly, uneven smile skitters across my face. "It adds character, don't ya think?"

He stares at the mug. My heart drops when a smile spreads across his face. I don't know what that smile means.

"You went through the trouble of gluing it back together again?" he asks, his darkened eyes lifting to meet mine—a tremble rocks through my body.

"Yes."

"How long did it take you?" he asks.

Why, is that how long you'll torture me for, sweet Ryan?

I shrug a shoulder. "A couple of hours."

He walks over to me and leans over slowly. I feel his lips press against the top of my head. I hadn't realized my shoulders were to my ears until I force them to drop. I'd rather not show how nervous I am. Men like Ryan feed off fear like sharks in a tank full of blood.

His hands slide up my back and to my shoulders. He starts to massage them, and a groan releases from my throat before I can stop it.

"Hey," he whispers soothingly. "It's okay. Accidents happen. I think it's cute that you put in the effort to fix it." He ends the sentence with a short laugh and drags his fingers over the jagged edges.

"Honestly, it makes me so happy you went through the trouble. I didn't think I could love you more."

I want to cry. Here I was, building myself up for a beating, so sure he'd hit me. Instead, I was just being dramatic. If he's not mad over his favorite mug being broken, then I hadn't been giving him enough credit.

Deep down, I believe Ryan does love me. Love is something otherworldly. Something entirely potent and powerful that makes you do crazy things. Like, hit them. And stay when you're hit. It's an emotion that no one person will ever be able to define. There's no saying how love *should* be. One person thinks loving someone means accepting their flaws, while another might think loving someone means trying to help them change for the better. Who's to say who's right?

All the problems we've had have been partially my fault. He's not the only one to blame. Clearly, looking at the eyesore of a mug in front of me proves that.

"I felt so bad," I say, nestling my head into his stomach. His spine straightens as he lifts his hands from my shoulders to my head, gripping me tightly into his body.

"You should," he whispers. My throat dries. "But you tried to fix it. That's what matters."

A tear slips from my eye. I nod my head and squeeze my eyes shut, so no more mistakes slip through. I don't want him to see me so weak.

"Is dinner made?" he asks.

My eyes snap open, widening into discs. Oh my god. I spent so much time trying to fix the goddamn mug, I forgot about dinner. He always comes home to dinner. He looks forward to it every night after working at the firm all day.

I clear my throat. "I figured we could do pizza tonight since I got sidetracked."

Ryan's hand tightens in my hair, tighter and tighter until strands begin to break away. Stabbing little pinpricks bloom throughout my scalp. I bite my lip to hold in the whimper.

Just as suddenly, he releases me, leaving my head spinning and my stomach in knots. "Sounds good, baby. Let me know when it's here."

He walks away without another look back, his body moving languidly out of the kitchen as if he's going on a midnight stroll on the beach.

Another tear slips through. I wipe it away quickly and pick up my phone.

I'm ordering fucking cinnamon sticks now, too.

Eleven

Mako

"YOU WANT TO EXPLAIN to me how your hair ended up wrapped around Greg Barber's finger?" I ask, my fingers threaded together tightly as I lean towards the woman sitting before me. 'Woman' is a generous word considering she looks like a half-dead wraith.

"Who?" she snarls, shooting me a dirty look.

"Froggy." I supply. Recognition lights up in her dull brown eyes. It's sad to say that there's only a thin layer of life that separates her eyes from Greg's.

"My hair wrapped arou… is he dead?"

It takes her all of three seconds to conclude why I'm asking. I pull out the crime scene photos and lay them out in front of her as an answer. Her eyes widen and horror washes over her face. Slowly, her shaking hand picks up the picture showcasing Greg's chest with the word 'Ghost' carved into it. The picture rattles in her pale fingers while her other hand covers her open mouth. Red paint colors her nails, nearly chipped completely away.

"Do you know who would do this, Ms. Franklin?"

It seemingly takes considerable effort for her to drag her eyes away from the picture and back to mine. The picture drops to the table.

"No."

Just one word. Two letters. And a big fucking lie.

It's normal for people to be shocked, horrified, even disgusted by some of the crime scene photos.

Linda Franklin is all of those. But she's also *scared*.

It's not normal to be scared of the boogeyman if you don't think they'll ever come after you. Looks to me like the sex worker sitting across the table in our cozy little interrogation room has a reason to be scared.

Amar is standing behind me, his hands in his pockets as he observes Linda.

"Can you explain your hair, Ms. Franklin?" Amar prompts. Linda's watery eyes glance up at Amar before settling back on the photos.

"Am I goin' to get arrested if I tell you I slept with him?" she asks, a bitter edge to her voice.

"No," I promise. We already know this woman is a sex worker, but we're not here to arrest her for selling sex for money.

She sighs. "I slept with him about a month ago. He paid me. I left."

"Do you remember the date and what location?"

"I don't know," she snaps. "I don't write down in my calendar what day I fucked who."

"A guess then?" I push.

She huffs. "Maybe the last weekend of last month. Around the 25th or somethin'. At Harper's Motel."

That'd put her at a few days, give or take before he died. We'll have to make a stop at the seedy motel they had sex in and see if we can catch them on any cameras. Pinning down all of Greg's locations leading up to

153

his murder is important. Anything in that timeframe could give us a clue as to who murdered him and why.

"That's the last time you saw Froggy? Was he acting out of sorts? Seem nervous to you? Did he say anything?"

Linda starts shaking her head profusely halfway through my questioning.

"No, no, and no," she gripes with irritation. "I don't know nothin' about him or what he does. He didn't say nothin' to me except what he wanted me to do to him. That's all."

"Ms. Franklin, your hair was wrapped around Froggy's finger the day he was found dead. Based on what you just told me, you had sex with Froggy not too long before he died. Last time I checked, people don't hold onto other people's DNA. At least not without reason."

"You sayin' I killed him?" she asks incredulously, looking at me like I'm a complete idiot. It takes everything in me not to snap back at her. I take a deep breath through my nose, reigning in my frustration.

"What I'm saying, Ms. Franklin, is you were either in contact with Froggy right before he died, or you were in contact with his murderer, who somehow got ahold of your DNA," I explain slowly. "Both scenarios don't look very good for you."

She crosses her arms defiantly and snipes, "I'd like a lawyer if you're going to keep questioning me, Detective Fitzgerald."

Yeah, saw that one coming.

"FITZGERALD!"

I turn my head from my computer to see Amar coming towards me, his face set in stone.

"Yeah?"

"Man's here. Claims he witnessed Greg Barber's murder."

I stand so fast, the chair I was sitting in nearly topples to the ground. Disregarding it, Amar leads me to what could possibly be our biggest lead yet. If this man witnessed Greg's murder, then there's a good chance he'll be able to identify the Ghost Killer.

The witness is standing with his hands stuffed in his pockets and an anxious look on his weathered face. Dude looks like he's been through a war or two—ragged, dirty clothes filled with holes and reeks of stale piss and sewer water.

I note each feature on his face, my eyes lingering on his own. Something about them gives me pause. He's shifting on his feet anxiously, glancing around the precinct like he's waiting for Freddy Krueger to pop out. Usually, the case when civilians find themselves in a building full of law enforcement officers.

When he sees me, he stills and slips a hand out from his pocket and holds it out to me for a handshake. I pause. Witnesses don't usually try to shake my hand. Reluctantly, I slap my hand in his, the motion sending chills down my spine as I stare into his eyes. He squeezes my hand once before letting go.

"Benedict Davis," he introduces, his voice higher-pitched than I would've guessed.

"Detective Fitzgerald. Follow me," I say, nodding towards one of our interrogation rooms.

Benedict settles in across the table from me, linking his trembling fingers loosely. Amar resumes his position behind me, per usual. Something about sitting at the table makes him feel restless.

"Alright, Mr. Davis, I hear you witnessed a murder. Can you tell me about it?"

He clears his throat and shifts again. "I was on my way to the gas station for some cigs on 3rd street when I heard a commotion. Now I'm usually not one to stick my nose where it doesn't belong, but the screams from a kid were hard to ignore. Four men were huddled together under the train tracks. Two men were holding him down while another hooded man stood before them with a gun in one hand, a bloody knife in the other. Looked like some type of hunting knife or something.

"I couldn't see much except that the screaming man was covered in blood and pleading for mercy. The hooded man said something I couldn't hear, raised his gun and shot the young male in the head. I ran after that before they could spot me."

His shaking hands run across his head nervously, much like my own tic when I'm frustrated. His body and arms are constantly shifting, and several times he lifts his ass off the chair like he's getting up, but then just sits back down nervously. It's physically impossible for this man to sit still.

"Why did you wait so long to report this, Mr. Davis?"

He scoffs, a bead of sweat trailing down the side of his head. If he wasn't wearing a light jacket, I bet I'd see pit stains on his t-shirt. "Because I was terrified, man. I ran back to my house and basically waited for someone to come find me and kill me next. I was so paranoid; I didn't leave my house until now. I figured if they were coming for me, they would've already popped me. So, I came straight here."

I mull over his story for a second. It's consistent with where we found Greg's body, and also how he was murdered. If the witness saw Greg's body on the ground and bloodied, he must've caught them right after the Ghost Killer carved the word into Greg's chest.

"Can you tell me anything about any of the men? Features, what they were wearing, tattoos, any of the sort?"

He swipes the back of his hand against his forehead, flinging off sweat in the process. "Uh... uh, yeah. The one guy holding down the... the victim was bald with some sort of tattoo on the back of his head," he stumbles, his hands shaking. "I was too far away to see exactly what it was, but it looked like some sort of bird."

I grab the pen and pad from the table and jot down notes.

"And the hooded man? Anything about him?"

"It looked like he was wearing a silver watch. But I can't remember much else than that. He was dressed all in black and the hood covered his face."

Frustration bubbles inside me. It can never be as easy as seeing the killer and identifying them in a line-up. Being able to identify his minions is at least a start, though. Better than nothing.

"Anything else about the other men?" I ask, glaring down at my notepad until the words blur.

"The other guy was blonde and had a heavy gold chain around his neck. Like something you'd see on a gang member. He was..." he trails off as nerves seem to overwhelm him. He squeezes his eyes shut tight and runs a hand back and forth on the top of his graying hair in a panicked gesture.

"Hey, hey, Mr. Davis. Relax and take your time. You're safe here. Nothing's gonna happen to you."

He laughs without humor. "Yeah, that's what all the cops say, man. Right before you get popped."

I lean my head down further to try and catch his eyes. When I do, I look for any signs of drugs. His eyes are slightly dilated, but that could be explained by fear. It looks like he has a few sores on his face, but his face all-around looks like it's been through the wringer. He's not tweaking at the moment, but I'm not ruling out drug use altogether.

"Mr. Davis, would you be willing to testify against the murderers when caught?"

He stops fidgeting and looks up at me, his eyes dilating further.

"What if they send someone after me?"

Likely to happen.

"We'll make sure you're safe. Put you in witness protection."

The man looks down, seemingly contemplating it. "There's a serious killer on the loose, Mr. Davis. Which means he could come after *anyone* next," I say, emphasizing my point. If the Ghost Killer doesn't get put away, the man before me could be killed, too, especially, if he is involved with drugs.

"Alright," he concedes. "I'd feel more comfortable with a lawyer, though."

As much as I want to recommend my father, I know whose hands this is going to inevitably end up in. "I know someone who can help you."

That hurt coming out of my mouth.

THE GHOST KILLER'S VICTIMS primarily originate from Shallow Hill, though anybody could've fucking guessed that one. The worst of the worst reside in Shallow Hill. It's an absolute miracle someone like River was born and raised there and came out the other side as a decent human being.

Mind-blowing shit right there.

Amar and I went over the footage of Greg Barker and Linda Franklin walking into the Harper Motel together and then leaving separately about twenty minutes later.

Didn't take them very long.

When Greg left, the outside camera caught a snippet of an old blue Ford Mustang with a missing side mirror picking up the kid and then racing off. The license plate was just out of shot, but a missing side mirror on that type of car is pretty recognizable. If we can find it.

Even though it was pointless, we looked at any claims for car accidents involving a Ford Mustang within the past twenty years. Nothing matched. People from Shallow Hill don't make claims with their car insurance when getting in a wreck.

It was Greg Barker's mother, Cindy, who gave us a lead. It was the first time we could get her to help with the investigation since her son's murder—too lost in grief and anger to give a shit about finding justice for her son initially. Now, when we had asked if she recognized a Ford Mustang with a missing mirror driving around, she was all too happy to give up information. Snitching in Shallow Hill is a surefire way to end up dead, but I think the way she sees it, the drugs will kill her soon anyway now that she no longer has a child to live for.

Brian Gill, a forty-two-year-old man with an eagle tattoo covering the entire back of his shiny bald head. Asshole spent ten years locked up for burglary and second-degree murder. Got out early for good behavior.

Cindy also told us Brian's favorite hangout spot was the bar in downtown Shallow Hill. It's a seedy place with sex workers lining the street, ripe for the pickin', and at least four drug deals within a block radius happening at any given time.

Amar and I park along the street opposite the bar, in an Oldsmobile that smells like stale cigarette smoke. We borrowed the car from a friend of Amar's, considering anything newer than a '05 car would be marked as suspicious. You don't drive nice cars in this town unless you're a visitor or you own the town. Last thing we need is anyone realizing we're visitors.

A flicker of metal grinding against metal, a bright flame, and then a burst of smoke steaming off a bright cherry. "You really gotta do that now?" I complain, looking over at Amar with his cigarette hanging out of his mouth.

He shrugs a shoulder. "Figured you would've accepted the fact that you're going home smelling like smoke."

"Last time I checked, you're the one going home to someone who hates it," I grumble, mashing the control to roll down his window. I leave it cracked, and watch all the smoke begin to filter out.

"She doesn't mind so much when I'm staking out a suspect. I get stressed," he says lightly before dragging in another mouthful of cancer.

My reply is interrupted by a commotion from the bar across the street. Our suspect is being roughly pushed out of the bar by another man, the latter screaming in the former's face as if he's deaf. A scuffle breaks out, the two swinging punches like they're in grade school.

I groan, my hand drifting towards the handle to break up the damn fight. Before I can even wrap my hand around the handle, the man pushing Brian whips out a gun from the back of his pants and aims it at Brian's head.

Amar and I both spring forward simultaneously, scrambling to open our doors.

Pop. Pop.

My head snaps towards the scene, my body halfway out of the car. Amar and I both freeze, absolutely stunned from how quickly everything just went to shit.

"Did some asshole seriously just kill our biggest lead yet?" I ask breathlessly.

"Fuck. That's exactly what just happened."

I punch the steering wheel, eliciting a pathetic, airy *beep* from the car. It gets swallowed by the loud yelling going on now that a person was just murdered right there on the street.

Angrily swinging myself the rest of the way out of the car, Amar and I cross the street to assist with a very dead Brian. The top half of his head is gone, leaving bloody sightless eyes staring up at the night sky as another sex worker gets picked up for a quick blowjob.

I heave out another sigh. "Want to bet that he *wasn't* just murdered by the Ghost Killer?" I ask, sarcasm coating my words.

Amar snorts humorlessly. "I'd rather bet on what time we're going to be getting home tonight."

"Midnight," I bet.

Another snort. "One thirty A.M."

"YOU DO REALIZE WITNESSES don't actually need attorneys, right?" Ryan asks condescendingly. It takes a lot of effort to keep my fist planted on my desk and not plunged deep into Ryan's mouth.

"He requested one," I answer shortly, ignoring his tone. I didn't get to bed until late last night and fifty bucks lighter.

"It's been a year. Maybe it's time to pass this one onto someone with more skill," he says. I pinch the bridge of my nose, my frustration mounting and patience depleting at alarming levels.

"Ryan. Just introduce yourself to your fucking client and get out of my sight," I growl. Not that he'll stay that way for long. My morning is going to be spent in that interrogation room with Mr. Davis and his shiny new lawyer going over every detail of that night and arranging witness protection.

With someone like the Ghost Killer, you can never be too safe.

Ryan storms away from me, and for a few glorious seconds, I embrace the solitude. This is also a great time to pour coffee down my throat. I slept like shit last night—the little sleep I did get. With Brian being dead, the case has gone cold yet again.

A man died because a jealous boyfriend went into a fit of rage when he saw his girlfriend grinding her ass on another man's dick. Such a fucking stupid reason to die. Brian has done worse things to people for a lot less. It's not like he didn't deserve what was coming to him, but I would've much rather he spent the rest of his life locked up than murdered on the street because of a frisky girl.

Later, Amar and I will be making another trip to see Greg's mother, Cindy, to see if we can get any more information out of her. Maybe about the other man involved in Greg's murder—the man with the gold chain around his neck. Now that she's talking, she probably has a lot more information up her sleeve that she didn't divulge yet.

The police report from last night crinkles in my hand. This case isn't a dead end. I'm getting closer. But the Ghost Killer still feels just out of reach, dancing across my fingertips, taunting me.

"You alright, man?" my partner asks, jolting me out of my thoughts. Didn't even see him come up to me.

"Yeah," I sigh, rubbing my eyes with my pointer finger and thumb, hoping to wake myself up. All I succeed in doing is making my vision blurry and giving myself a headache.

Amar doesn't look much better than I do. Dark circles under his eyes, drawn face and a perpetual frown. He's as frustrated with this case as I am.

"I'm just ready for this shit to be over, man," I sigh, taking another swig of lukewarm coffee. I grimace at the bitter taste.

"He's right within our reach. I can feel it," Amar says, stuffing his hands in his pockets and staring off into the distance.

"I do, too. I just wish I knew how close."

Twelve

River

THE BRIGHT LIGHT FROM the television screen is the only source of light in the dark house. Numbness has a noise. Almost like white noise, but louder. It sounds like buzzing, a hive of bees swarming in my head until everything else is drowned out except the chaos inside me.

My eyes are vacant, staring at nothing, incapable of processing the motion picture playing in front of me. I've no idea how long I've been standing in front of the screen, actively destroying my eyes as I try to claw my way out of the fog. Someone could be stark naked and doing jumping jacks in my face, and I wouldn't notice.

Not when all I can feel, hear and see is utter numbness. It's even on my tongue, sliding down my throat and into my innards, wrapping around every organ until it feels like I'm just a hollow body bag, nothing left inside of me but emptiness.

I need… I don't know what I need. I need *something*.

Maybe to get out of this house. Oppression is a living and breathing thing when I've only been allowed to leave for class. School and straight home. I haven't been allowed to stay in the library to study, and study groups are out of the question. Who cares if my grades suffer? Being a career woman isn't in the cards for me. Not when I have…him to take care of me.

Love me. Dote on me. Fuck me.

Fuck me over.

A slow blink and the world slowly starts filtering in. The buzzing in my head calms, the bees settling down. But the numbness doesn't dissipate. It feels like tar is crusting my insides. It will never peel away.

My feet are leading me towards Ryan's office before I can process what I'm doing.

I need out.

I need out.

I need out.

I need out.

Right as I lift my hand to knock on Ryan's office door, his voice filters through. He sounds excited. Happy. I've never heard him sound so… young.

"…I fucking knew it was him. I mean, it was so fucking obvious with the way he was acting… I know I can't believe he didn't figure it out, either… No, I'm not saying anything to him yet. I'm still getting a few more things worked out first, see what benefits I can get out of it… I will, man, I'll call you as soon as I break the news. We'll grab drinks to celebrate…"

Hearing how happy Ryan sounds relaxes me and equal parts saddens me. He hasn't sounded that happy with me in what feels like ages. Not since the first year of our relationship, when we hardly ever fought.

No matter, at least I caught Ryan in a good mood.

"Baby?" I call as I lightly knock on the door a moment before opening it. He looks up from his computer with annoyance, no trace of his good mood anywhere on his face. I thought he'd still be happy, but work must still be stressing him out more than I thought. Apparently, he's been dealing with a difficult client the past few days. He doesn't talk about work with me, but I did hear him complaining to someone on the phone that he got stuck with a tweaker who can't shut the fuck up.

His dad makes him accept one pro bono case a year, and he's none too happy about working with a drug addict. Ryan despises anyone who uses drugs.

"What did I tell you about interrupting me?" he demands sharply. Anxiety washes through me, breaking through the tar long enough to make me second guess why I'm here. I squeeze the doorknob in my hand tighter to cease any trembles, the metal in my hand growing slick from sweat.

"I'm sorry," I rush to apologize. "I just wanted to let you know I was going to meet with Amelia."

I don't even know if Amelia is available. It doesn't matter. If she's not, I'll spend the night in my safe space.

He sits back in his chair and examines my body. My eyes drop, too, trying to see what he sees. A baggy t-shirt with my university displayed across the top with our team mascot—and I'm pretty sure that's a ketchup stain—down to my loose sweatpants. Not my usual style, but I figured it'd be one less fight between Ryan and me. Amelia doesn't care what I wear. Who cares if she's not impressed?

Ryan raises an eyebrow at my attire.

"You'd be going out looking like that?" he snipes derisively, looking at me as if I'm an overcooked steak on his plate. Ryan likes his meat bloody.

I shift on my feet. "Yeah? I'd just be going over to hang out at her house. We're not doing anything special." I hope that sweetens the deal. A quiet night in with my girl. No clubs, bars, or anywhere public, really. Not even Walmart.

He scoffs, crossing his arms across his chest and aiming a nasty glare my way. "You'd be going over to hang out with her and *David*. Another man."

My brow lowers in confusion. "David's her husband. Why does it matter?"

"Why does it matter?" he repeats condescendingly. "Because you'd be hanging out with another man without me around. Why does it need to be explained how disrespectful that is to me?"

My hand slides from the doorknob and grabs the end of the shirt. I look down and away from his eyes, like a coward. The bottom of my shirt slides between my fingertips as I try to formulate a response that won't upset him further.

"It doesn't. I just thought you trusted me."

A sardonic smile slides across his face. The blue in his eyes is nearly gone, in its place is a color so muddy and dark, I hardly recognize the man in front of me anymore. I don't think I've recognized him in a long time. Or maybe he's finally taking off his mask and revealing who he truly is. Who he has been hiding this whole time.

It's been six weeks since I came home to Ryan. And six weeks since I've heard from or talked to Mako. It seems he's finally given up on me, which depresses me as much as it relieves me. It's one less thing I have to worry about now. But I miss him.

"You're not going," he says after a beat.

When the fuck did I ask?

The words come close to slipping out, but I keep the comment trapped behind my clenched teeth, heavy on my tongue. If it slips through, he might try to cut it off.

After a moment of reigning in my thrashing temper, I ask, "What do you mean?"

"Amelia is a bad influence on you. I don't trust her," he says.

The shirt sifts through my fingers more aggressively as too many emotions to name rise inside me. I guess I didn't have to worry about feeling numb when Ryan is a master magician at bringing emotions out of me. Anger is most prominent, but right behind that is panic. Amelia is the last person I can lose. She's been there with me through it all—since I escaped Shallow Hill and started carving my own path in life. Amelia has been the hand to guide me throughout some of the scariest years of my life. If anyone is a bad influence, it's *me*.

"No, she's not," I deny weakly. He growls from deep in his chest, glaring at me with devil eyes. I'm standing ten feet from him, but yet I still feel the need to back away. I hate that he has that effect on me.

"Can you not argue with me for once? When will you realize that I'm just trying to do what's best for you?"

"You're making a decision for me," I argue. "You don't even know Amelia."

"I know her well enough to know she's a boy crazy whore. She doesn't make an effort to include me in anything, which just tells me she doesn't want me around. And the only reason she wouldn't want me around is so she can influence you."

My mouth drops open. Amelia has actually tried to invite Ryan to plenty of things before, but I always brushed it off. I don't really know why. The few times Ryan and Amelia hung around each other, David would be super sweet and touchy-feely while Ryan would sit stiffly beside me and look down on everything they did. It's honestly embarrassing.

But now, I suppose Amelia wouldn't want Ryan around, not after how he treated me. Amelia holds a grudge firmer than anyone I've met.

She'll never accept Ryan again, and that thought makes me incredibly sad. Inevitably, it'll put a wedge between us. Ryan is my future, I don't know how I'm going to maintain a friendship with her when they hate each other.

"And, did we forget about your little temper tantrum? When you left me for a week and Amelia refused to let me see you? I have no respect for someone like that."

You mean when you left me in a puddle of piss and then went and fucked your secretary? That temper tantrum?

He continues on, making me feel smaller and smaller. "I let you live here rent-free. You don't pay for anything, and I give you everything you ask for. The least you could do is acknowledge the fact that all I've ever done is take care of you. That's what I'm doing now. I only have your best interest in mind."

"But…" I trail off, not really knowing what to say. The more I argue, the angrier he grows. I don't want him to be mad at me. When he gets angry, he gets violent.

"I'm trying to work, River. You know so that I can pay the bills?"

Shame fills me. I don't have a job, and he *does* completely support me. I never asked him to. He demanded I leave my job so I could focus on school, and I was so wooed by someone actually taking care of me for once that I acquiesced.

Now I just feel like a mooch. He does so much for me, and I do nothing for him except give him sex whenever he asks. The least I can do is stay home when he asks me to, even if his views on Amelia are completely misguided.

"Okay, I'll stay home," I relent.

"I don't want you seeing her anymore. Never again."

I don't argue. I don't know if I can comply with that. I'm not ready to give up on Amelia yet. She's my best friend. Apparently, I'm just going to have to be sneakier about it. Sadness overwhelms me at the thought. I don't want to lie to Ryan. But I don't want to lose my friendship even more.

AMELIA CALLS ME SEVERAL days later. Ryan's out having drinks with his friends. Friends I've never met or heard of before. When I asked who, he said some guys from work and didn't offer any other information. Not wanting to push, I didn't say anything else, and he didn't bother to invite me.

"Whatcha up to?" she chirps sweetly when I answer my phone.

I stare at the TV in front of me as rich women complain about their lives and talk mad shit behind each other's backs. The glare from the television is the only beacon of light in the dim living room. I'm settled into our huge leather couch with a mountain of blankets and pillows on top of me and a glass of wine next to me.

"Just watching trash television," I say, trying to keep any somberness out of my tone. I don't want her to hear how depressed I am about being left alone in the house while my boyfriend fucks off and gets drunk with unknown friends.

And probably at a strip club, I think bitterly.

"Come over," she says. "David and I are making chicken tacos and margaritas. Well, my margarita will be a virgin because this vagina is definitely not."

I smile at her crass words. That sounds fucking amazing. My mouth nearly salivates at the thought.

Then, all hunger dries my mouth to the point of nearly choking me when the conversation from Ryan's office comes filtering back. His demands for me to stay away from Amelia. To never see her again. A cold sweat breaks out across my forehead as I concoct several excuses for leaving the house. I'm forbidden from Amelia and my mother, the only two people in my life. I have no other friends—at least not anyone I could go see, and it does not look suspicious to Ryan as to why I'm suddenly hanging out with someone I never have before.

"I don't know, Amelia. I'd have to ask Ryan," I say before trapping my bottom lip between my teeth and biting it raw.

She's silent for a moment. "Is he home? He can come," she offers sweetly, which only serves to make me feel worse. Here she is, putting in an effort to invite someone she probably loathes. I haven't asked how she feels about Ryan now, and I don't think I will. I'm not ready to hear her say how bad she thinks he is for me.

"He's out with some friends," I admit.

"Then I'm sure he wouldn't mind you hanging out with your bestest friend in the world, right?"

My mouth opens, on the verge of spewing the truth and telling her, I'm not allowed to see her anymore. The words stop, but so does my excuse that follows. Ryan's out doing lord knows what with who knows what people, and I have to stay home and do... nothing?

I look over to Bilby, resting on his spot behind me, snoozing comfortably. As if sensing my stare, he opens his golden eyes—eyes that drew me to him in the first place because they look exactly like my own—and meows at me softly, as if he is telling me one word.

Go.

"I'd only be able to stay for a few hours," I hedge. I'll just go over and come back before Ryan gets home.

He told me not to wait up for him before he kissed me goodbye. Last time he went out with his friends, he didn't come back home until two o'clock in the morning. It's only seven o'clock now. Being home by ten or eleven would give me plenty of time to settle back in my pajamas and act like nothing happened.

"O-okay, well, dinner will be ready in fifteen," she replies, tripping over her words as if she's confused. I don't think I've ever given myself a curfew before.

"Okay, on my way."

I hang up and run upstairs to change into leggings and a long-sleeved university shirt. Nothing too flashy and revealing. It's ninety degrees outside right now, but Ryan's words are stuck in my head.

You dress like a whore, so men will look at you.

Brushing my hair and putting on light makeup takes all of two minutes before I'm out the door and driving over.

My hands tremble as adrenaline surges through my veins. I'm sneaking out of the house to see my best friend. My best friend that's never done any wrong to anyone in her entire life. Someone who doesn't deserve to be ostracized from me like she's a deviant slut, when the only one that acts like that is *me*.

I frown. No wonder Ryan gets mad at me. I'm always lying and sneaking around on him. He doesn't trust me, and I'm still not giving him a reason to. Still, I don't turn the car around.

While disobeying Ryan's demands sends highly toxic doses of anxiety through my veins, I'm not going to pass up time with my best friend—and especially not chicken tacos and alcohol.

WALKING INTO AMELIA AND David's house always brings me a sense of peace and warmth that I can't find anywhere else, though Julie and Matt's house comes close. Amelia's house is smaller, homey and well-lived in.

Her art decorates the walls due to David's insistence. Amelia is too humble to display her art in her own home, but David isn't. He's always been one of her biggest supporters, right next to me, of course. If I didn't know Amelia's art so well, it'd look like a professional photograph printed and hanging in a store.

Amelia specializes in realism painting. She spends months and months on one painting, perfecting it until it looks like you're staring at an actual photograph of someone. Her talent is absolutely breathtaking.

She's already featured in some of the top art galleries in L.A. and has her art hanging in several celebrities' houses. In the art world, she's a pretty big deal, but you'd never know looking at her or her house. Growing up with nothing has humbled Amelia, and she's perfectly happy living like she's middle class. Even if millions of dollars are sitting in her bank account.

"Hi, my love!" Amelia greets loudly, rushing over to hug me. I saw her last week, but it feels like it's been months. Usually, we hang after class for a couple of hours before going our separate ways. We haven't gotten the chance to actually visit each other in far too long.

David walks over to hug me next. He's a six-foot-four, burly guy with a big beard, sky blue eyes and a gruff voice. He's also an absolute teddy bear and wouldn't hurt a fly. Unless that fly was trying to kill Amelia or something—then he'd murder the fly slowly. He's attractive in a way that grows on you the more you look at him and get to know him. You wouldn't notice someone like David right away, but once he catches your attention, he makes it hard to look away.

"Hi, River," he says quietly. Tears prick my eyes when David's arms wrap around me. He's been my friend as long as Amelia has, and he's always been such a good hugger. It feels warm and safe in his arms, and I haven't felt that in so long. David's always been good to me, even when I'd act recklessly. Instead of judging me like most people would do, he offered me a shoulder to cry on and an ear to listen.

I don't think I could've picked a better person for Amelia to spend the rest of her life with.

Before I can start bawling like a baby and embarrass myself, I squeeze him hard and remove myself from his arms. If Ryan knew I hugged David, he'd be so angry with me. My heart drops into a pool of anxiety resting in my stomach, and another frown threatens to weigh down my lips. I'm constantly defying Ryan and then wonder why he doesn't trust me.

Stupid, River. I shouldn't even be here.

Just as I turn away from David, Amelia's returning with a massive margarita in her hand.

"Watermelon?" I ask, forcing a smile onto my face. I can't let them see me upset. They'll ask questions that I don't know how to answer.

"You already know it," she says with a roll of her eyes. Watermelon is my favorite, and so is my best friend. She always remembers.

I accept the drink with a wide smile and suck a quarter of it down in one swallow.

"Pace yourself," David warns lightly, an amused glint in his eyes.

I quirk a brow and suck down another big swallow. "No can do, my friend, no can do."

He laughs and leaves me be. David knows I can hold liquor better than any man he knows. He's witnessed me shit-faced and still able to walk a straight line at the end of the night. And how Amelia always bought breakfast the next morning because she puked first.

In the back of my head, I know it'd be smart to pace myself. I can't get drunk because I have to drive home. Amelia and David would be more than willing to offer me the spare bedroom, but Ryan would flip if he came home to a missing liar of a girlfriend. With that thought in mind, I sip slower and gorge myself on the best chicken tacos I've ever had.

What Ryan doesn't know, can't hurt me.

BLARING LIGHT ASSAULTS MY senses, painting my eyelids tomato red. Slowly, I crack them open, holding a hand over my eyes to assuage the pain.

"What the hell?" I mutter. When my vision focuses, a calm, blank-faced Ryan is standing at the door, his finger locked on the light switch. I just stare at him, confused by the sudden light and cold look on his face.

It's early morning, the sun barely cresting over the horizon. Bleariness still muddles my brain, but it doesn't take a genius to figure out something is wrong.

"What?" I snap. I pull a face, smacking my lips in disgust when I realize how gross my mouth feels.

Dragging myself into a sitting position, the blanket falls from my bare breasts. A lift of the blanket reveals the rest of my naked body. A frown pulls at my lips, confused on how I got naked. I went to bed dressed in my pajamas.

A quick glance down at the floor solves that mystery. They're lying haphazardly next to the bed. The strings to my tank are snapped clean from one end. My bottoms are cut in half. Neither of them wastorn. I slowly pursue the room, taking note of the scissors lying on the end table, along with a bottle of water that has a white residue at the lip.

The more I see, the more horrified I grow. Hurriedly, I push the blankets back further to see dried semen on the inside of my thigh.

"Did we have sex?" I ask, even though the answer is currently slapping me in the fucking face. I should've asked, *did you rape me?*

Ryan's jaw ticks. "You mean you don't remember me fucking you?"

I hate when he answers my question with another question.

I glance toward the water bottle with the suspicious substance dried on the inside of it. He notes my expression. A sinister smile cracks across his otherwise cold face. There's no other emotion to the action but bitter amusement.

"I don't need to drug my girlfriend in order to sleep with her," he says bitterly, guessing my train of thought.

But you do, sweet Ryan.

"It's Alka Seltzer. I had a bad headache last night from all the drinking," he explains dryly. The urge to grab the bottle and sniff it is overwhelming, but that would only add insult to injury. He's already pissed about something. Something that doesn't have shit to do with my ravaged body or a fucking water bottle.

When I just stare at him, he finally walks towards me until he's standing at the foot of the bed. The position leaves me feeling vulnerable. I feel at a disadvantage. Naked, scramble-brained and... sore. Very sore.

If it weren't for the fire-breathing dragon staring down his nostrils at me, I'd look for bruises.

Calmly, I ask, "Is there something wrong?"

"Where were you last night?"

My heart feels like a stone dropping into a well. It falls so far down, I fear I've lost it somewhere in the acidic pit of my stomach. Yet I can feel it pumping at an alarming rate, the adrenaline leaking into my bloodstream.

"What do you mean?" I ask, my voice surprisingly even.

"Don't play fucking stupid with me, River," he snarls. He clenches the duvet in his fist and rips it from my body. My attempts to hold onto the blanket are in vain. Instinctively, I cover my naked body, curling my legs against my chest protectively.

"Tell me what the hell you're talking about, Ryan," I demand, forcing steel into my spine. It feels like I've just emptied a syringe full of jello into my spine instead.

How is it that I've faced big, scary men since the dawn of my existence, yet this man still manages to put the fear of God in me? He's much smaller than a lot of the men I've gone up against in my life.

"You went to Amelia's last night," he spits, his chest beginning to heave with increasing anger.

How the *fuck* does he know that? Anger punches through my chest. It takes all of two seconds to figure it out. The fucker *bugged* me. He's tracking my goddamn phone to see where I am.

"How would you know that, Ryan?" I ask, my voice still deceptively calm. I don't like my privacy being tampered with. I received so little of it my entire childhood—or rather, absolutely none of it. It's precious to me. Sacred.

He smirks at me, more than likely noting my growing anger. The shaking starts in the tips of my fingers, traveling up my limbs and throughout the rest of my body like lightning traveling alongside a metal pole.

How curious. He likes that I'm angry.

Do you want a fight from me, sweet Ryan?

I slide out of bed in one swoop, standing before him in all my naked, pissed-off fucking glory.

"Why would you track me?"

"You obviously give me reasons to," he answers simply. "You're deflecting your mistake. Instead of focusing on what you did, you're trying to spin it back on me. Instead of owning up to your mistake and admitting you did wrong, you'd rather try to act like *I'm* the one in the wrong."

"You are!" I shout, taking a step towards him. His eyes blacken as evil washes over his face. He takes three big steps towards me, getting directly in my face. A hand shoots out, wrapping around my throat and squeezing.

My nails claw at his hands as he grits through his teeth, "You better watch how the fuck you talk to me. You disobeyed me last night, River. I strictly told you to stay away from that whore, and you didn't listen. Bad girls get punished. And when you're done getting punished, I'm taking your phone. You can have it back when you act right."

Before I can spit in his face, he's spinning me around and pushing my face into the bed. I struggle against his unforgiving hold. The more I fight, the harder his grip tightens. He scoops both of my wrists in one hand while he uses the other to push my head into the mattress.

I open my mouth to let out a scream, but the bed muffles the sound. The pounding of my heart is strong in my ears, drowning out all the noises I need to be hearing right now. If I would've calmed down, I would've been able to listen to the rustling of clothing as he drops the basketball shorts he was wearing.

I would've been able to prepare myself for the slide of his dick against the crack of my ass. He lets go of my head long enough to spit on his hand and wet his dick. I use that time to scream at the top of my lungs.

A punch to the back of my head nearly knocks me unconscious. My screams cut off while stars explode in my vision.

There's nothing that could've prepared me for the feeling of his dick shoving inside me. Inside my ass.

Fire detonates from that area and outward to the rest of my body.

Another scream is ripped from my throat, this one involuntarily. He pays me no mind, continuing to sodomize me. His hand goes back to my head, pushing me down so far my screams are beginning to choke me.

The pain is so intense, I can't see or feel anything past it. I'm slowly suffocating, and I can't even feel the panic of it when his dick is eliciting so much pain from my backside. My vision blurs as the pain intensifies. His thrusts grow choppy as excitement takes over his body. It's permeating the air.

He's loving this.

And as he groans out loudly, shudders wracking his body as he releases inside of me, all I can contemplate is the tool I'll use to shove into *his* ass when he's least expecting it.

Thirteen

River

I FEEL HIS PRESENCE first. Strong and intoxicating. Like the smell of a sharpie when held under your nose. It's almost ironic when I see said marker whipped out in front of me, halting my steps.

With an irritated huff, I glare at his hand holding the marker. His hands are massive. Long, thick fingers and calluses dotting his knuckles. His tattoos leak to those hands, the colors fading off at his wrist.

I want to touch them. I bet they're rough. I bet they'd feel so good inside me.

"Go away," I say, pushing his hand away in the same manner I push those filthy thoughts away. Roughly and with undisguised disgust. I lift my chin and resume my walk to the car.

The sharpie stops me in my tracks again. Angrily, I rip the sharpie out of his hand and throw it at his feet. Flutters assault my insides when my eyes meet his. I hate that I'm attracted to him. I hate that I missed him.

"What do you want, Mako?" I demand, glaring at him.

"I want you to use that," he says quietly, his baritone voice getting to me. Every fucking time.

I raise an eyebrow. "Use it on what?"

He directs his eyes to my hand. "When you feel unsafe, I want you to use it to draw a dot on your hand. Most people who work customer service know what it means."

I can't help it. I laugh.

"You're kidding, right? I'm not drawing anything on my hand. I don't feel unsafe."

Liar. You were just hiding out at his house a couple of months ago because you felt unsafe.

I shift, subtly wincing at the pain in my backside, despite two weeks passing since that night. I've been ripped open in a way that a person should never be. I passed out after a few minutes. When I came to, I was left on the bed naked and my phone was gone.

For a full week, he refused to give me my phone back. It took me two days before I realized fighting him wouldn't get me access to my phone. So, I started being good. I listened. Loved on him even though I felt he didn't deserve it. And reverted back to a docile, mindless girl.

That weekend, he ran me a warm bubble bath with roses and wine. Ryan sat behind me, crying into my shoulder, asking for forgiveness.

It wasn't until the water grew cold that I told him I forgave him. He was so broken, sobbing until he couldn't breathe. It didn't take long before I was crying with him. He swore that would never happen again. He took off the tracker to my phone right in front of my eyes, gave it back to me, and promised to do better. Having my phone and privacy back is what ultimately broke my resolve. I've never seen Ryan so upset in my life, so I knew he had to be truly sorry for what he did.

Mako's eyes darken into a moss green. Just like his brother. Everything goes dark when they get angry. It's like the evil shadow dwelling inside of them comes to the surface.

He nods his head slowly, a strand of hair falling across his forehead. My fingers twitch with the urge to brush it back. Bending over, he picks up the sharpie. Then he steps closer to me, bringing his body flush with mine. With bated breath, I don't dare look away from his eyes, even as he wraps his arm behind me and slips the sharpie into my back pocket.

Heat floods through me, so hot the oxygen in my lungs evaporates. If this is what it feels like with layers of fabric separating us, what would he feel like pressed against me, skin to skin?

I'm ashamed of the thought as soon as it flashes through my head. I love Ryan. I don't even like Mako.

The familiar fingers of anxiety wrap around my chest. Without thought, I glance around my surroundings, convinced Ryan will somehow see me. Just because he took off the tracker on my phone doesn't mean there aren't people watching me. I know he doesn't trust me, not after I lied to him about Amelia.

I clearly don't deserve his trust. Look at me now. Acting like a slut and entertaining thoughts of his brother. A brother he despises, at that.

Stupid, River. Walk away before someone sees you. Ryan will never forgive you.

"When I come over for dinner tonight, I promise I'll kill him if I see a black circle on that pretty little hand."

Without thinking, I step closer and bare my teeth right in his face.

"The only reason I'll put a dot on my hand is because I want to get away from *you*."

"Then why are your tits currently pressed into my chest?" he asks, a smirk sitting prettily atop his stupid fucking face.

Scrambling backwards, I nearly trip on my feet in my pursuit to act like I wasn't just pressed up against him like saran wrap. I open my mouth to respond, but nothing comes out. I've no idea what to say now.

"You're not coming over for dinner," I state finally.

He smiles. "Dad assigned him to my case. His client is a key witness to a murder. Ryan and I will be working together until this case is solved. I'm coming over for dinner, River."

I step away from him and turn to walk away. "Fine. But I would never allow you to kill him," I say over my shoulder.

Only I would get those honors.

"I WANT DINNER TO be ready by six. Make meatloaf. Mako hates meatloaf," Ryan says through the speakers in my car. I called him the second I got in this heat box. For obvious reasons, I couldn't tell him his brother stalked me again and told me about the dinner. I had to play dumb and wait until he told me.

I can't believe he didn't fucking tell me.

"I wish you would've told me this sooner. Now I have to rush to the store," I complain, swatting a sweaty strand of hair out of my face. My car is starting to get old, which means the heat of the Carolina sun is beginning to outrank my A/C. Maybe it's time for a new one—something I can't reasonably afford right now.

"I only found out yesterday. I didn't get the chance to tell you because I've been working my ass off, something you wouldn't know about," he snaps, his words lashing at me like a whip. He always knows exactly what to say and when to say it to hurt me most.

It takes everything in me to keep my mouth closed. Working my ass off was my entire life since I was old enough to have a job—but alas, Ryan always has temporary memory loss when shoving my jobless state in my face. Something he *demanded* of me.

I bite the inside of my cheek until I taste blood, and then I swish it around my mouth as a reminder of what I'll be tasting for the next week if I talk back.

"I'm sorry. I just want this dinner to go smoothly for you. I know how much Mako stresses you out."

And me.

My A/C finally kicks in just as more sweat breaks across my forehead. I've never thought I'd have to worry about Mako saying anything to Ryan until now. What if Ryan gets under his skin and he tells Ryan I stayed at his house for a week in retaliation? If I didn't already know that it's the good people that die young, I'd bet money that Ryan would have a heart attack right then and there.

Ryan's silent for a moment. "Just make the meatloaf and have it ready by six. Don't burn it. Don't be late. Just do something right for once. Can you manage that?" he asks, his voice dark and condescending.

Swish, swish.

"Yes," I choke out.

He hangs up the phone without further comment. We're fighting again. The corners of my lips tug down as guilt assaults me. I hate when Ryan is upset with me.

First, I ogle his brother and allow him into my personal space. Then, I complain about him not informing me of tonight sooner instead of realizing Ryan is swamped with work right now.

I'd get mad at me, too.

My foot presses on the gas harder. Tonight needs to be perfect.

"DINNER IS READY," I call from the dining room. I set out the meatloaf and crisp asparagus on the ten-foot table in our outrageously formal dining room and laid out our best China. I've no idea where Ryan got it from, but it's pretty, so I don't care.

Ryan and Mako have been in the living room poring over their case. All I've heard this entire time is Mako's underhanded jabs and Ryan's condescending remarks.

They hate each other, and neither of them bothers to hide it.

They both enter the dining room, their eyebrows drawn and jawlines tense. Mako stops before his chair, staring down at the meatloaf with a blank face. An evil smirk flashes across Ryan's face.

I fight the urge to roll my eyes. Ryan's being petty.

Mako's hands tighten around the back of the chair until his knuckles turn white. If he weren't wearing a long-sleeved button-up shirt, even his tattoos wouldn't be able to cover up the veins pulsing in his arms. Calmly, Mako pulls out his chair and sits down, his eyes never straying from the apparently offending food. If I didn't know any better, the meatloaf grew a mouth and is currently talking shit to Mako.

Ryan is at the head of the table while I sit on his left, and Mako is seated on his right, directly across from me.

"Did you make this?" he asks, his voice strained as he lifts his darkened green eyes to me. My breath stalls in my chest. While his face is arranged carefully into a blank mask, his eyes are glistening emeralds, ripe with anger.

I figured being forced to eat food you don't like would annoy him, but the tension rolling off him is potent and suffocating. I don't understand his reaction, but I'd love to figure it out. The curiosity in me burns to know why meatloaf would make him so angry.

"Yes," I answer. "Homemade," I tack on as if that'll make it more appealing.

He swallows and picks up his fork. Quietly, he takes his first bite. And then another. And another. He's several bites in, before I realize Ryan and I are just watching him with morbid fascination. Well, I am, at least. Ryan is watching him with a sick sense of satisfaction.

For the first time, I want to smack Ryan for the way he's treating his brother. That feeling scares me. I love Ryan. I should be on his side no matter what.

Maybe he feels this way because Mako did something awful to Ryan when they were kids. Maybe he beat him up badly. Hurt him somehow. There has to be a good reason, and I need to remember that.

I eat my own food, proud of how good it tastes. This is the one good thing that came from having a shitty childhood strife with starvation and desperation. Once I had the means to cook, I immersed myself in it. I cooked so much; I had to donate ninety-eight percent of it to homeless shelters because there was so much food.

I perfected cooking, and it's something Ryan's always praised me for. Something I was always really proud of.

I glance up to see Mako visibly force another bite down. It leaves a sour taste in my mouth. Clearly, he just doesn't like meatloaf. But I don't like someone eating my food and *not* enjoying it. It makes me feel like I'm covered in oil.

Ryan lets out a soft moan. I look over to see him roll his eyes to the back of his head.

So it's okay when *he* does it.

"This food is amazing, baby," he compliments loudly. Just like that, I feel better. Happiness floods my chest. Making Ryan happy always does that to me.

"Thanks," I beam. Mako glances at him with barely disguised disgust.

"So, how's the case coming?" I ask, hoping to take all of our minds off this weird interaction.

"We're making progress," Mako says at the same time Ryan says, "Don't concern yourself with that, babe."

I frown at the conflicting answers. Ryan never talks about work with me. I'm sure there are a lot of things that are confidential, but he always shuts me down even on the simplest questions. I've tried to show interest in what Ryan does, but peppering him with questions only irritates him.

Ryan the boyfriend and Ryan the lawyer are two separate entities. I don't know the second person, and sometimes that bothers me. I'd love nothing more than to see Ryan in action. I know he's a fierce lawyer, and seeing it with my own eyes would be incredibly rewarding. And maybe a little hot, too.

Mako gives Ryan a look I can't name, distracting me from my thoughts.

"As long as Ryan's client cooperates, I think we'll be able to catch the killer," Mako continues.

Ryan drops his fork on the plate angrily and looks at Mako with a filthy look. I look down at his plate, inspecting it for chips or scratches.

"I don't want to talk about work at the dinner table," he snaps, drawing my eyes back up to his reddening face.

Mako doesn't even spare him a glance. He chews on a piece of asparagus slowly, as if he's contemplating his next words.

"His client witnessed a murder."

"A murder?" The question slips out of my mouth before I can stop it.

Ryan's murderous eyes snap to me. Immediately, I stuff a piece of meatloaf in my mouth and keep my eyes down on my plate. The familiar fingers of anxiety start to filter throughout my body, touching all my vital organs until every part of me is gripped with dread.

I made a mistake. Ryan's going to be so mad at me now. He doesn't want to talk about the case. Mako's ignoring his request, and I just egged it on.

Stupid, River. Stupid.

"He's dubbed the Ghost Killer. He's linked to drug trafficking as well."

As soon as the name leaves his mouth, my heart seizes in my chest. I've never heard the moniker, but it brings up the horrific memories of that night. Billy calling me a ghost as he beat and raped me. Billy—who deals heavily with drugs, arms, and probably even the skin trade. Billy— who kills people.

Lots of people.

Forcibly, I swallow the now dry meatloaf in my mouth. I nearly choke on it as it slides down my throat and settles heavily in my stomach.

This time, I don't care that I'm pushing Ryan's buttons. No amount of fear can compare to what Billy instills in me. If he's out there, publicly killing people so carelessly… That could only mean one thing.

"Why is he called the Ghost Killer?" I ask softly.

"Because he carves the word 'Ghost' into his victim's chests before he kills them."

My hand trembles. Carefully, I set down my fork and then rub my sweaty hands down my pretty pink dress. Sweat dots my forehead and slides down my spine, accompanied by cold shivers. I feel sick.

"That's enough," Ryan barks, his fist thumping loudly against the table, rattling the china. "You're upsetting her."

Mako inspects me closely, noting my obvious discomfort. I let them assume it's because murder gives me the chills when in reality, it's just the fact that I know who the murderer is.

Much to my relief, Mako listens. He continues to eat his meatloaf, this time with a little more ease. Maybe it's worth it now since Mako succeeded in pissing off Ryan as much as Ryan pissed him off with the food.

The rest of dinner passes by intense silence.

Ryan is fuming, and I… I need to go see Barbie.

I'M LOADING THE LAST dish in the dishwasher—sans Ryan's coffee mug—when I hear footfalls behind me. My shoulders tense, but I don't stop as I pop soap into the slot, close the door and start the machine.

I'm just pressing Start when Ryan's hand whips out and grips my pointer finger tightly. I freeze, my eyes snapping to his cold, dull blue eyes.

"What?" I ask, forcing innocence in my tone.

"You know what," he growls. I don't have time to formulate a reply. In one quick motion, he snaps my finger backwards.

I hear the break. I feel it. But the pain doesn't register right away. I'm too shocked, my wide eyes slow to look away from his and down at my finger.

My mouth drops when I see my finger bent completely backwards.

Then the pain hits.

I rip my hand from his and cradle it to my chest as tears flow from my eyes. My mouth forms around a scream, but all that escapes is a whimper. Before I can rage at him, he grabs me by my hair and swings me into the wall. A cry rips from my throat when my broken finger hits the wall, my attempt at protecting my face. Dizziness overtakes me from the pain.

"I'm so fucking tired of you embarrassing me, you bitch," he grits out before he slams my head into the wall.

Instincts take over. Even though I'm seeing stars, I scream and kick at him, punching with both hands, broken finger be damned. He subdues me easily, clamping a hand across my mouth in the process. Both wrists are gripped in his other hand.

"Do that again and I'll fucking kill you, do you understand?" When I don't respond, he shakes me roughly, his face contorted in pure rage. I nod my head, tears slipping from my eyes without permission. "Why don't you understand that I'm the only one who would actually love you? Yet you continue to disobey me. Do I ask a lot of you, River?" he shouts, spittle flying into my face.

Against my better judgment, I shrink away from him. If it were possible to curl myself into a little ball and disappear, I would sell my soul to do so.

"Do I?!" he yells. I shake my head with desperation. I just want him to stop yelling. I don't want him to be mad anymore.

"Then why do you disobey me, huh?" he asks, shaking me again. His hands squeeze tighter and tighter until it feels like my wrists are going to snap. "I do *everything* for you. I treat you like a queen. I provide for you. I let you waste your fucking time with college and spend my fucking money. And *this* is how you act!"

He ends his statement with a rough push. The last thing I remember is falling backwards, the bottomless feeling of falling through the air in the pit of my stomach. And then nothing.

THE SHARP PAIN IN my head assaults me first. Then the ringing in my ears follows close behind. The pain is blinding. Just the thought of opening my eyes sounds exhausting and painful.

Feet shuffle next to me. Slowly, memories start coming back. The dinner with Mako. How angry Ryan was when Mako told me about the Ghost Killer. And when Mako left, how Ryan had assaulted me.

Again.

Right as that memory hits, so does the pain in my finger. My pinky *just* healed, and now another finger is broken. Though, I've had plenty of broken bones over my childhood. If I wanted to, I could welcome the pain like an old friend. Sometimes embracing it is the only way to get through it.

Brushing off the pain in my finger, I turn my attention to the person walking around. I'm in a bed—*our* bed. And I'm completely naked. The chill air registers, and immediately goosebumps rush over my skin like a tidal wave.

Fuck. If Ryan notices, he'll know I'm awake. Nobody's skin breaks out in goosebumps when they're knocked unconscious.

I keep my breathing deep and steady. Eventually, I hear the bedroom door open and then click shut. Immediately, my eyes snap open. Fuck easing into it. I don't have time.

The light sharpens the pain in my head, but I push past it. I need to figure out what the hell is going on. I look down to confirm that I am naked. My lip trembles at the onslaught of memories of waking up exactly like this not too long ago. The things he did to me afterward will forever imprint my brain, right where the rest of my trauma resides.

My breath lodges in my throat when I see bite marks marring my stomach and thighs. My eyebrows tighten, and I try to think of when he did that. They're fresh. Some of the bites even have little dots of spit on them that haven't entirely dried yet.

The soreness between my thighs answers the question I now realize I don't want answered.

We had sex a few times in the past week, and while he had been excessively rough, he hadn't bit me. When my lip trembles again, I force it between my teeth, clamping down tightly. Did he seriously do this while I was knocked out? By *his* hands? Who *does* something like that? Who knocks out someone they're supposedly in love with, and then fucks and bites them when they're unconscious?

I can't process something like that right now. Before I can figure out what to do, the door swings open. My heart freezes. It's too late to close my eyes and feign sleep. Our eyes lock, and my heart stutters like an old engine.

"You're awake," he says, his voice calm and emotionless. He doesn't sound angry. I think I'd prefer that to the cold calculation in his tone. At least when he's furious, I know what to expect. This side of Ryan is unpredictable.

"I am," I force out, my voice broken and rough. I try to clear my throat, but the dehydration burns too badly, and only makes it worse. "Can I have some water?" I ask softly, purposely subduing my voice to sound sweet.

He inclines his head towards the nightstand next to me. I glance beside me and see a half-filled bottle of water and a couple of Tylenol. I don't like that the water has been opened, but at the moment, I don't care. He wouldn't drug me now, would he? He already has me where he wants me. When I lift my hand to grab the bottle, I see my broken finger. It's black and blue and bent unnaturally. The sight of it brings back the rush of pain. For a single moment, I had forgotten about that. Now, it's all I can feel.

Ignoring the pain, I grab the bottle with my good hand and take a few small sips of the water first before forcing the two pills down my throat. My only regret is that they're not something stronger. If I had to endure this from the man I love, at least let me be buzzed while I do it.

"How do you feel?" he asks.

I want to rage at him. Ask him the cliché questions. *How* could *you? Why would you do something like this to me? I thought you loved me...*

But I don't. I just stare at him, with eyes full of hurt and anger. I'm not even angry about my finger at the moment. No, I'm angry about the violation of my body. Like a coward, he drops his eyes to my body. To what he's done to me while I was unconscious from his own hand. He promised he wouldn't do something like this again.

He *promised*.

When his eyes lift to mine, they're blank. He shrugs a shoulder and gives me a smirk. "You're my girlfriend, River. I own you. I can fuck you whenever I want."

"Did you have to do it while I was knocked out? After *you* knocked me out?" I challenge.

Another shrug. "Why not? Your pussy was available, and it turned me on seeing you so vulnerable to me. What's the big deal?" he asks, his voice growing agitated. He acts as if I'm being *unreasonable*. As if asking why he would rape me is an absolute preposterous question.

I suck my bottom lip into my teeth. I don't want to piss him off more.

"Would you have said no to me?" he asks, his voice changing to a softer tone. He sounds a little hurt, and it pulls at me. "I've always loved that you're so open and willing to do anything that makes me happy. I didn't think having sex with my girlfriend would be so hurtful to you."

I frown. Having sex with your partner isn't hurtful; he's right about that. But that doesn't make it okay. It feels strange, knowing someone was inside me without me knowing it. Feeling it. Consenting to it. This isn't the same thing as a boyfriend waking me up to the pleasure of sex—that I'd always be okay with. There was no *waking up*. No opportunity to say yes or no. A dark feeling coats the inside of my body.

I feel used and dirty. I feel... foreign inside my own body.

"I just... I just wish I could've experienced it with you," I whisper finally. His face softens.

"I'm sorry, baby. I wanted to try something new. I wouldn't mind if you had sex with me if I was knocked out."

That *still* doesn't make it okay. But arguing with him isn't going to change anything, it will only make it worse.

"It's okay," I choke out. He walks over and sits on the bed next to me. Slowly, he swipes loose strands of hair away from my forehead and behind my ear.

"How does your head feel?"

The tears dry quickly. He had pushed me. He hurt me. My finger is broken.

"You hurt me."

He sighs. "I'm so sorry, River. My anger got the best of me again. I feel like complete shit. Please don't make me feel worse than I already do."

I glance down and force myself to stare at my broken finger. Seeing the abnormal sight sends a fresh hot wave of pain in my finger. The tears come back with a vengeance. God, it *hurts*. It hurts that he continues to break me over and over, inside *and* out.

"You said you wouldn't hurt me again," I remind him weakly.

"I know, baby, I know. And this time, I'm serious when I say I won't. I promise you. I know that I really need to work on my anger. What can I do to make you see that?" he probes, sincerity coating his voice like candy dipped in chocolate.

I sniffle, snot starting to run down my lip.

"What are you going to do when you get angry next time? How are you going to handle it?" I ask. I try to toughen up my voice, but I still feel... desolate. Like something inside of me is missing. The way he's acting is relieving and a little soothing. But I'm just having a hard time feeling it right now.

"I'll walk away until I calm down. Then we can work through the problem together. We're in this forever, baby. I don't want to lose you because of my temper."

More tears well up in my eyes until Ryan becomes a blurred image. I nod my head, accepting his apology.

I know I should feel better. Now, only if I could actually *feel* anything at all.

"LUCKILY, YOUR FINGER SNAPPED cleanly. No fragments have been broken off. You'll be healed up nicely in about four to six weeks," the nurse says. She looks older than me by only a few years. Her pin-straight brown hair is pulled back into a low ponytail, and her brown eyes watch me closely as I assess my splinted finger.

She's blunt and to the point, which I appreciate.

"How did this happen again?" she asks, eyeing my broken finger with enough pity to drown myself in.

Appreciation gone.

I technically don't have to answer, but the excuse slips from my mouth anyway.

"I smashed it in the car door." It's the first thing that came to mind. And when her brows tighten, I realize it probably wasn't the right excuse.

"Huh," she says, her voice suspicious. "Usually, fingers don't break when they're crushed like that. And especially in the manner that your finger was broken."

"Are we done here?" I ask impatiently. She takes a step back, her lips tightening, seemingly sensing my growing agitation.

"If you don't feel saf—"

"I feel fine," I snap, cutting her off. I don't want to go down this road. The last thing I need is a nosey-ass nurse asking questions and trying to pry into my life. I'm glad I didn't tell her about the head wound. Ryan said I hadn't bled, but there is a small knot forming on the back of my head. More than likely, I have a slight concussion. I had already healed from the last one, courtesy of Billy.

Ryan already promised he'd wake me every couple of hours as punishment for causing the concussion.

I wouldn't have to come to this god forbidden hellhole in the first place if I was able to fix my finger myself. Unfortunately, it was too far bent for me to set it back into place. And considering neither of us have any medical experience, it's likely we would've just made it worse.

Billy *did* have medical experience. There's no way he acquired his medical knowledge the old-fashioned way by attending college. I get the feeling that Billy dealt with many broken bones in his life, and instead of going to the hospital, he learned how to handle them himself. He had to have had someone teach him surely. His connections reach far and to people with many different occupations.

Cops. Politicians. Businessmen. Doctors. Even celebrities.

Luckily, I've only had minor broken bones. Fingers, toes, and my nose. Billy would set my bones back into place for me. I was never under the impression he did it because he cared, but because having an imperfect prostitute wouldn't sell very well.

The nurse gives me instructions on how to care for the finger. I hardly listen, too anxious to get the hell out of here. Ryan's outside the door, waiting for me. He refused to let me go alone, just in case the nurse who helped me was a male. He said he doesn't like it when another man touches me, even if it's to fix a finger he broke.

I just want to go home. I fucking hate hospitals, and I'm discovering a newfound hatred for this nurse too.

"Can I go now?" I ask, cutting her off mid-sentence. She shoots me a derisive look, and huffs.

"Yep," she says shortly.

I walk out without a thank you. Nurses deserve thank-yous, but she's just going to have to get that from another patient tonight.

Fourteen

Mako

I'M SEVERELY TEMPTED TO just kidnap the little wench.

I really thought she had made a breakthrough when she called me that night. Worst fucking night of my life. Hearing her small voice through the receiver, helpless and in pain—I had nearly lost my mind.

I think I *did* lose my mind.

And then she disappeared on me. Ran right back into his fucking arms. So badly, I wanted to drive to his house and take her back. But I've seen this before. The push and pull. The mental manipulation. How he hurts them and then woos them back into his arms.

He's a master manipulator. He convinces them that it's their fault that he beat them. How he does it, I have no idea.

I know I can't even begin to understand the spell they're put under. I had asked Alison over and over again how she kept falling for the same old shit. There were so many times in the beginning where she raged at me, screaming at me that I would never understand what it's like to be in that position. I just… didn't get it.

Finally, she tried to explain it to me. The fear that grips you when you think about turning him in. How many times he threatened to kill her, and then would nearly follow through. Not for one second did Ryan make it seem like an idle threat. And then the brainwashing. He would convince her that it's her fault he treats her like that. As if she actually fucking deserved it. Gaslight her and make her feel crazy and dramatic. He would dehumanize her, strip away her identity and make her feel like no one else could love her except for him. That he's doing her a service by loving her when no one else possibly could.

I know he's doing the same thing to River.

Although I can't personally understand it, I know it's real. I know they're in a serious situation, and they feel incredibly helpless, even when they convince themselves they're not. It took an incredible amount of strength for Alison to leave him. When she did, he had threatened her, then tried to woo her again, and eventually tried to attack her.

I had been there and stopped it.

Ryan had always hated me. I was the son that was never supposed to happen. He wanted to be the one and only and terrorized me our entire childhood together because of it. *The Good Son* looked like a Disney movie compared to Ryan. Countless times, he tried to hurt me. There were moments when I was positive he was going to go to the kitchen, grab a butcher knife, and follow through with his darkest fantasy, yet something always held him back. I could see it in his eyes, though. The desire to make me disappear for good.

That night, when I had stopped Ryan from hurting Alison—that's when his hatred truly festered. It bubbled into blisters and became permanent third-degree burns over our relationship. I think if Ryan had the opportunity now, he would kill me.

And to be perfectly fucking honest, I feel the same about him.

After that, he had no choice but to let Alison slip away. I had witnessed his volatile reaction and intervened when he tried to attack her. He accused me of fucking Alison, and I let him believe it. There wasn't any way to come back from that.

Ryan would rather roll over and die than take back a girl he thinks I fucked. After that, she's tainted. Ruined forever. Disgust twisted his features when he saw me protect her, and I knew him believing I had Alison too was the only way Ryan would truly ever let her go.

But that's not what I want for River. She's been accused of being a whore since she could talk, so the last thing River would allow anyone to think is that she had to sleep her way out of a relationship. She's too prideful, and I'd be lying if I said I didn't respect her for it.

I left her alone for nearly two months because if I had seen her, I would've kidnapped her. And several times a week, I had to look Ryan in the face and not fucking murder him. My resistance is slowly fading, and I'm no longer scared of what I feel myself preparing to do.

For now, I'll respect River and keep my mouth shut about our odd relationship. But she has another thing coming if she thinks I'll ever let her forget that we have one.

"GHOST KILLER AT IT again," I sigh, staring down at the dead body. Same fucking kill, just different bodies. It's becoming tiresome. And I feel like it's fucking personal. "And I can bet my life on the fact that there's nothing new to see with this body."

Redd grimly shakes his head, his lips tightening with disappointment.

"Same MO. Plenty of DNA samples. I'll test them, but I guarantee they will match sex workers and incarcerated criminals just like the last ten bodies."

I crouch down, getting a better look at the dead man. The word 'Ghost' is carved into his chest just like every other victim. The words are as neat as possible when carving words into a live, squirming human being. A little bullet hole decorates the middle of his forehead. Same gun as before.

"Do we know who the vic is?" I ask Redd.

"Nineteen-year-old Sage Blomberg. Heavily involved in the gang that runs his neighborhood," he answers, snapping another photo.

Being heavily involved in a gang translates to drug dealer. Kid more than likely has already been in jail for dealing and possession. Every single Ghost Killer victim has been in and out of prison for some type of drug charge. Not all of them are as young as Sage or Greg, but it's disturbing to see that the majority are.

These kids could easily be rival gang members. But my gut tells me they're not. The word carved into their chest is too personal, too telling of whatever they did to piss off the Ghost Killer.

And I can bet that the Ghost Killer's motive is insubordination. The suspect is a gang leader or drug lord. Someone that these victims answered to. I bet that he runs a very tight ship, as most gang leaders do. And if kids are anything these days, they're convinced they have life all figured out.

The victims either lied, stole, or betrayed the Ghost Killer in some way. Maybe some of them even challenged him, thinking they're tough shit. Whatever the case, they acted against the wrong person and paid the price for it.

"Let me know who the DNA links to the minute you find out. I'm going to pay them a visit, even if they're in another fucking state," I say to Redd.

I turn away from the scene, Amar following behind me. Quiet as usual.

"What are you thinking?" Amar asks after a minute of letting me stew in silence.

"I'm going to find out what gang Sage belonged to, and then we're staking out their hangout location. See who goes in and out."

Amar doesn't argue. It's a dangerous stake-out, hanging out in the streets where crime happens in broad daylight without a care in the world. But that's the point I've reached myself. I don't give a fuck if it's dangerous, I just want to catch the killer.

Whoever he is, he's a cockroach. Crimes have ramped up eight percent since he started killing his Ghosts a year ago. Overdoses increased by fourteen percent. Those are fucking massive numbers within a year.

And to leave the victims out in the public for us to find shows his arrogance. He never actually leaves the bodies in Shallow Hill, but in the neighboring town where I live. He's number one in his world. Bet he feels fucking untouchable. As if he's a god.

I squeeze my fists until my knuckles turn white.

I can't wait to show this fucker just how human he really is.

"Mako?" Amar barks, snapping me out of my violent musings. I look at him, stunned. Amar is staring back at me, his dark eyes filled with concern.

"What?"

"I've been calling your name for the past five minutes. We're just sitting here," he says, gesturing towards the windshield, indicating we're still in a very parked car.

I haven't even put the keys in the ignition.

"Sorry, man," I mumble, jamming the keys in the ignition and starting the car.

"Where's your head at?" he questions, his eyes probing and too fucking observant.

A harsh breath punches out of my mouth. "I've been chasing this fucker for a year now, and I'm not any closer to finding him," I grit out.

Saying it out loud makes me want to shove my fist through the steering wheel, rip out the airbag and wrap it around my own damn head. *Fuck*, this asshole gets me heated.

I don't care that the Ghost Killer's victims are criminals. They're young, impressionable kids that chose the wrong path to walk. But that doesn't mean they didn't have the chance to turn their lives around. That doesn't mean they couldn't have been saved.

The asshole is taunting me with them, I fucking know it. I feel it in my bones.

"You're taking it too personally," Amar observes next to me. Instead of answering, I lurch the car forward, heading back to the precinct. I have to find out who exactly Sage was involved with.

"You're right, I am," I admit.

"Maybe you should remove yourself," he suggests quietly.

I grind my teeth together. Only Amar would feel secure enough to say shit like that to me. This case feels personal because it *is* personal.

"We both know he killed your real father, Mako. I haven't told anyone else that, but I'm starting to second-guess that decision."

I slam on the breaks a tad too hard when I stop at a red light, bringing the car to a sudden stop. The car behind me blares their horn, nearly rear-ending us from my dick move. If I were in a cop car right now, the car would've stayed silent. I'm not an asshole that needs to lord my badge over anyone so I ignore his anger.

"Shit, sorry," I mutter, ripping a hand through my hair again. I'm just so fucking tired.

We fall into silence while I digest his veiled threat. It's coming from a good place, I know that. But that doesn't mean I don't want to fucking strangle him for saying it. I'm not supposed to be on this case due to my involvement with the Ghost Killer's victims.

After spending a year in the foster care system, Matt and Julie adopted me when I was thirteen years old. For the first twelve years of my life, I grew up on the streets with a drug dealer for a father and a prostitute for a mother.

Johnny Lancaster was heavily involved with a gang called the Crucibles. He was a shit father, but yet there was a small part of him that cared enough about me to keep the dealings away from me as much as he could. My mother didn't pay me the same courtesy on the nights she worked, but I'd rather have a sloppy man looking for pussy in the room next to me rather than a gang member loaded with guns and high off crack.

That is until I came home from school one night to find my father dead, in a pool of blood with 'Ghost' carved into his chest and a bullet hole in his head. This was before the Ghost Killer became the serial killer he is today. It was an MO no one had seen before and hadn't seen until recently—just a year ago.

I assume my mother either found my father dead or witnessed it and fucked off. Or she could've died, too. Daria Lancaster was never to be seen again after that day, and I'd be lying if I said it didn't bother me not knowing where she was.

And now, sixteen years later, I'm being haunted by the man that turned my father into a ghost.

I'M PRETTY FUCKING SURE I'm experiencing a heart attack for the first time in my life when I see her. I'm only twenty-eight years old, but this girl is going to send me to an early grave.

She's wearing baggy jeans and a thin strawberry red hoodie. It's eighty degrees outside, but she's dressed like it's winter in Michigan. Her hair is thrown into a messy bun and her face is bare from any makeup, showcasing her unnaturally pale face. Normally when I see River, she's done up with nice clothing and her hair down. She looks just as beautiful now as she does any other time, but something about her appearance feels so unlike her.

She looks… blank. Like a white canvas.

My eyes catch a stark white cast on her hand. Last time I checked, her pinky was the only finger broken and that one had already healed. Now there's a white cast on her pointer finger. I drop my head back and count to—fuck it, I can't even focus on numbers right now.

"That cast wasn't around your finger two nights ago," I say as I approach her from behind. Darkness is threatening to creep in my voice, but I do my best to keep it from emerging. Scaring her or doing anything to push her away would be stupid. Not when I'm trying to pull her in and *away* from him.

She pauses at my voice, her shoulders inching up towards her ears as she tenses.

"Leave. Me. Alone." Her words hurt. Not because I want her to want me, but because it means she's no closer to wanting away from Ryan.

"Only when you're safe."

"Fine, I'll go where I'm safe, *then* you leave me the fuck alone," she huffs, storming off towards the sidewalk.

Her being temporarily safe wasn't what I meant, but I don't say anything. Not when she's more than likely going to the library again—a spot where we can talk without having anyone seeing us. I follow her down the familiar route. One she took me on only a few months ago, when she was limping from a fall, she didn't cause. And now, she's still bruised and healing, just like last time. Except this time, the life is slowly seeping out of her.

Her steps are swift and angry, causing her hips to swing in a manner that's so seductive—I'm forced to adjust myself like an asshole.

She pushes open the broken door to her abandoned library with a fierce shove. She stomps into the dusty, graffiti-filled building and marches through the empty shelves. I follow her into an aisle that must have been used for little kid books. The shelves are thick, waist-high, and coated with dust.

And then she stops suddenly, forcing me to balance on the tips of my toes so as not to plow down her little body. In a flash, she's whipping around and smacking a hand straight across my face. A hand that has a hard-ass cast on it, and one she definitely shouldn't be fucking using to hit people.

I take a deep breath and look away, licking my bloody lip as I try to reign in my rising temper. I don't like being hit. I got a lot of that shit before I found myself in a nice family. It's very rare I let anyone hit me without some type of consequence. I'd never hurt River—that'd defeat my entire purpose of trying to help her—but I'd undoubtedly teach her a lesson if she weren't devoted to another man. A man I'd really like to murder with my bare hands.

My jaw ticks as she gets up in my face, her heaving chest pressed into mine. Our breaths are synced, both strife with adrenaline. Her sweet cinnamon smell invades my senses. All I want to do is take a bite out of her, just like I would a cinnamon apple. I'm distracted from my anger when I get a good look at her eyes. They're the most unique color I've ever seen, the exact color of liquid gold with little flecks of brown mixed in and an outer ring of light brown.

Those are the types of eyes you can't look away from, no matter how hard you try.

"I don't need you to save me," she snarls, snapping me away from my musings. "I'm not some damsel in fucking distress. I'm not a weak little girl that needs your rescuing. I don't need *you*, Mako. The only fucking person I need is my goddamn self. Do you understand me?"

Her face is red with rage and her golden eyes are bright with a storm of hateful emotions. I'm not looking in the face of a girl. I'm looking into the face of a fierce lioness; her fangs pulled back and ready to rip my neck out with one wrong move or word.

I've never wanted to kiss someone so badly in my life.

I nod my head, keeping quiet. I feel the urge building inside my chest. I have to tamp it down, I *need* to. Kissing her would be catastrophic.

"Do you want to fuck me, Mako?" she asks, derision coating her words. Apparently, I didn't do a good job of keeping the lust out of my eyes.

Yes. "Not what I'm after," I clip. The muscle in my jaw is going to burst with how hard I'm clenching my teeth.

She gives me a challenging look, and my heart seizes. Her chin drops as she takes a big step back and peers up at me through hooded eyes. It looks like she wants to ride my cock as she slashes my throat. I'm not sure how to feel about that, but fuck if I don't want to let her do it anyway.

She reaches her hands up and runs them down her curves. Her head tips back, exposing her slender throat. I could easily reach out and wrap my hand clear around her neck. I could squeeze until her face turns pink and she's desperate for breath. Her eyes would dilate, and she'd beg for more.

A moan releases from her mouth, and my whole body turns to steel.

"Ryan!" she gasps around another moan. My eyes narrow into thin slits as anger rises in my chest. Her hands continue to explore her body as soft, melodic moans vibrate through her throat. A growl leaves my mouth before I can stop it.

"What are you doing, River?"

Her head falls forward, her eyes dark amber and swirling with rage and lust. My favorite fucking combination.

"Is this what you want, Mako?" she taunts, her voice low and breathy. "You want to touch my body, feel how wet my pussy is?" A smirk rises on her face, and her eyes roll again. "Oh, Ryan!"

The skin around my knuckles is threatening to rip apart from how tightly I'm clenching my fists. The little bitch is mocking me. I'm three seconds from saying *fuck it* and pushing her up against one of these shelves and teaching her that lesson.

"Keep it up, River. You won't be able to moan the wrong name when your mouth is full of my cock," I threaten on a low growl.

Her hands drop from her body and mirth curls her lips up. From hot to cold in a span of seconds.

"You'll never fucking have me, Mako. You'll never get to lay a finger on me."

"Are you willing to promise me that? Because I will make a liar out of you, baby girl," I challenge, my eyebrow cocking sardonically. I step into her space, pressing our chests back together. "I think we both know Ryan doesn't satisfy you the way you need to be."

How quickly my good guy plan blew out the window, is actually comically pathetic. This girl brings something out of me no one else can. I don't want to want her, but I don't think I ever had a choice. She shouldn't be with me, but I think I need her to be.

The darkness I tried so hard to hold back slips through. River knows how to push every single one of my fucking buttons. Especially when her head falls back once more, her eyes roll, and she lets out a long moan.

"Ohhh, Ryan," she moans, dramatic but still sexy as hell. Without thinking, my hand shoots out and does exactly what I've been fantasizing about since she started this bullshit. I squeeze her throat, seeing red as she moans the *wrong fucking name*. By the time I'm done with her, she'll be begging for me to hurt her.

"Try again," I snarl. My hand is barely squeezing. My grip is firm enough to make her pause, but nowhere near how tightly I really want to be squeezing. Enough to make her face turn pink and legs quiver with need. River's face turns red from anger, and her eyes whip back toward me with wrath.

She leans into my hand. "Like I'd ever moan for *you*."

"That's what you've been doing this entire time. Don't pretend like you're not imagining *my* cock buried deep inside you." My grip tightens a bit. "You wanted to play. Now try again," I demand, my voice rising.

Her nostrils flare as she glares at me with defiance. I'm whipping her to the side, and her back is pressed against the shelves in two seconds. Her hands fling to my chest to steady herself. I don't even think she's realized that yet.

"What's wrong, River? Not so brave now, are you? You like to hide from your truths. You'd rather lie to us both and pretend you love that piece of shit rather than admit you want someone better. You think Ryan could take care of you the way I could, huh? You think he makes you feel like a queen when really he treats you like a fucking peasant."

I step into her closer, my anger rising. She whimpers as her back digs into the shelves, the wood unforgiving. And just like I predicted, her eyes dilate with lust so potent, she doesn't even understand what she's feeling yet.

"You don't like the way Ryan hurts you, River, not like you like the way I fucking do. His pain only brings you sorrow and agony, while mine brings you a desire you don't even know how to handle. Now. Try. Again."

A breath bursts out of her through her constricted airways, and with it is a sound so fucking musical, it nearly makes me moan. My name. "Mako," she pants.

She's so turned on; she doesn't even realize her pussy is humping my leg. If she weren't wearing jeans, I'd feel her juices leaking through my pants. Her entire plan backfired on her. This girl loves to ignore what's right in front of her face.

Fuck it. I don't want to save her. I want to fucking *take* her. I will steal her from my brother, right out from his tiny hands and keep her to myself. I will show her what it's like to be with a real man. A man that truly does treat her like a queen. Someone that will cater to her every desire, treat her body like it's my most prized possession, and show her a happiness she doesn't know exists yet.

"I hate that I want you," she whispers. I get the feeling she didn't mean to say it out loud.

"Really? I happen to love it." I love that I scare her. If it scares her, then it's real. What we feel for each other is fucking real.

She shakes her head as if she's shaking away my words. The queen of avoidance.

"Mako," she pleads. "We shouldn't be doing this. I don't cheat." Her body grinds against my leg once more, contradicting her words the minute they leave her mouth. A wicked grin overtakes my face.

"I promise not to kiss or touch you then," I say, smiling a little wider when disappointment flashes across her eyes. I don't call her out, though. Instead, I brush my lips lightly against her neck, the tender skin puckering into goosebumps. Her pulse vibrates against my lips. I feel the vibrations even as I slowly travel to her ear.

"But that doesn't mean I can't watch you touch yourself," I whisper. A small gasp leaves her plush lips. She stops the little circles she's been inadvertently moving her hips in. I take one step back, watching with fascination as a blush travels up to her neck.

So fucking pretty.

I wait. She's battling with herself, and I'm not going to push her into anything. That's what River doesn't understand yet. She has a choice with me. And even if it doesn't seem like it, she's the one always in control.

Her golden eyes finally rise to meet mine, twin pools of molten fire. When she lifts a hand and pops her button open, I feel another wicked smile pulling at my lips. Looks like she doesn't mind being bad after all.

With patience I don't possess, she pulls down the zipper to her jeans. Hooking her thumbs on the sides of her pants, she drags them down her smooth legs. Perfect. God, she's perfect. Creamy skin fills my vision as she chucks off her pants and leans against the bookshelf. And with a lioness's grace, she plants both hands on top of the shelf and lifts herself up, widening her legs as she settles in. Black lacy panties cover her most intimate part.

I have to bite the inside of my cheek to keep myself from tearing the fabric away with my teeth and feasting on her.

"Do I get to watch you, too, or are you a selfish lover?"

It takes monumental effort to drag my gaze away from her panties and back up to her eyes. My dick is fucking granite and pressing against my zipper, like a prisoner desperate to escape their jail cell. I grin and mimic her initial reaction by popping open the button on my jeans. Her eyes flare, and her little pink tongue darts out, wetting her lips in anticipation.

"Has someone thought about this?" I taunt, dragging down my zipper, giving me sweet relief as the pressure dissipates. She doesn't glance away from my hand, even as she denies me.

"No."

My grin widens, both of us aware of her blatant lie. I step back until I'm leaning against the bookshelf opposite her, stepping on the bottom to help stabilize it; otherwise, my weight will send me crashing through the empty shelves.

She leans back on the arm that doesn't have a broken finger and plants her feet on the edge of the shelf. Her other hand drifts over her pussy, her fingers trail across her panties, taunting me. Waiting to bare herself to me until I do. I have no problem making the first move. I pull down my jeans and briefs, just enough for my dick to spring free. There's too much pressure building. I squeeze it hard, gritting my teeth against the mix of pleasure and pain. Her eyes widen, and this time she does glance up at me.

Even if I had the strength to will the cocky smile from my face, I wouldn't. Not when she's looking at me like she can't tell if she wants to come closer or run away. She swallows thickly, and ever so gently, pushes her panties to the side.

I close my eyes as my head falls back, a groan working its way out of my throat. The sight of her nearly has me on my knees.

So pink. So pretty. And glistening from how fucking drenched she is.

I squeeze my dick again, partly to help relieve the pressure and partly to shock some control into me. My head lolls forward lazily. With hooded eyes, she parts her lips and dips her fingers inside. She drags the juices up to her clit, circling the bud slowly, a small moan escaping her lips.

My hand drags up and down my shaft in response, sharp pleasure traveling up my spine. She circles her fingers faster, occasionally plunging her fingers inside before continuing her ministrations. I can't take my eyes away from her, just like she can't take hers away from me. The soft moans grow louder and bolder. Her body comes alive as she spreads her legs wider, and circles her hips wantonly against her hand.

"Fuck, River," I growl, my hand moving quicker. Briefly, her eyes close and her head rolls, but she quickly turns her eyes back to me, like she can't stand to look away for more than a second.

"I'm going to come," she whispers, her legs shaking and her brow furrowing.

"Then fucking do it," I grit out, my own orgasm on the verge of consuming me. River goes completely still, even her voice as she reaches her crescendo. And then she's falling, and my name is a chant on her lips. The first syllable of my name is all I need to hear before I'm toppling over the cliff with her. My eyes snap shut, and my knees threaten to give out as hot cum spurts from my dick.

"Fuuuuck, River," I groan, the intense pleasure nearly blinding me. It wracks my body, battering my strength to pieces. I keep my eyes locked on River's form. Her eyes roll back in ecstasy and her movements are uncontrolled and jerky as she rides out her orgasm.

The only regret I have is that she's grinding against her hand when it should be my tongue. Even as I come down slowly, my entire body goes limp and buzzes from the most intense orgasm I've ever had. I want to lick her pussy until my tongue falls off.

Her own breathing is erratic. And she won't meet my eyes. She's sitting straight now, staring at the floor, her chest still heaving and her tiny fists clenched. I've no idea what's going through her head right now, and I'm too much of a chicken shit to ask.

She slides off the shelf daintily, slides her jeans on, and shoves her feet into her Converse, the heels of her feet sticking out. I button jeans up, steeling myself against whatever is going to come out of her mouth.

Her gold eyes slowly lift to meet mine. Something invisible but potent transfers between us. I don't know what it is. I don't know what it means. But I want more of it. Without a word, she turns away and walks out of the building.

She'll be back. As much as she wants to deny it, she's as addicted to me as I am to her.

Fifteen

River

"HEY, BABY," RYAN CHIRPS from behind me, kissing the top of my head. I'm sitting at my desk, working on a paper for my Agriculture class.

"Hey," I reply distractedly. I've been invested in writing this stupid paper for the past several hours, and I'm almost done. My shoulders ache, my head is pounding, and all I want is an entire bottle of wine to the face.

A gasp is ripped from my throat when my head snaps back. My ponytail is wrapped around Ryan's hand as he pulls my head as far back as it will go. Ryan's blank face is above me, staring down at me with cold unattachment.

"I came home in a good mood, ready to be doted on by my beautiful girlfriend. Instead, all I get is a *hey*. Now is that any way to treat your boyfriend?"

"I'm sorry," I rush out, my voice strained. His grip tightens to an excruciating level before he pushes my head forward roughly, nearly sending my forehead crashing into my computer screen.

"Get pretty for me," he demands coldly. I turn towards him cautiously, my hand absently rubbing the back of my head. That hurt.

"Where are we going?"

"Out," he answers shortly. Very informative, asshole.

"I need to know how to dress," I push. His back is to me now, and his head is dipped as he takes off his tie and begins to unbutton his shirt. The frustration rolling off him is visible. He lifts his head and sighs with barely contained anger.

"Something nice. A dress, River. One that doesn't make you look like a fucking slut."

Before I can say anything, he rips off his pristine white shirt. A white shirt that has a smudge of red at the collar.

My heart drops and my world spins. He throws the shirt in the hamper, away from my eyes. None the wiser, he disappears into our bathroom, shutting the door behind him. I hear the water turn on seconds later.

Are you washing away the scent of her pussy, sweet Ryan?

Robotically, I stand up and walk over to the hamper. I pick up the shirt and find the smudge. It's damp, as if he tried to wash off the evidence, but you can't get red lipstick out of a designer shirt with water and cheap hand soap.

I press the soft fabric into my face and sniff.

Perfume. Just a hint of it. But enough to know that Ryan is a liar. I bet he didn't fire his secretary. Even if he did, he must've hired a pretty new thing quickly and charmed her onto his cock already.

Oh, sweet Ryan, now you've really made me mad.

You've made me really, really… mad.

My knees drop to the ground, no longer capable of holding my weight. My chest heaves as something like panic seizes my heart in its cold, unforgiving claws. My face contorts as tears spring to my eyes. So hard—I try so hard to keep it in. A single sob breaks loose, destroying the fragile dam. More sobs follow suit as a sharp pain stabs at my chest.

I've given him *everything*. All of me. Everything I had in me was handed over on a silver fucking platter. My heart is in the middle of the tray, bleeding openly for him. And he took a knife and ripped it apart anyway.

I press the shirt to my face, holding the unknown perfume to my nose, forcing myself never to forget what he's just done to me. Refusing to allow myself to justify his actions, to *forgive*. I've done so much forgiving, and all for nothing. Fucking nothing.

I allow myself a solid minute of gut-wrenching sobbing before I calm, slowly but surely. My tears dry, my heart slows, and something settles deep into my chest. I'm not sure what it is, but it's cold and hard and takes all of the feelings I had for Ryan and sucks them up like a fucking Dyson vacuum cleaner. It's like they were never even there. Everything shifts, hardens, and then numbs.

Everything he's done to me, everything I've forgiven him for, are no longer forgivable. Not the hitting, the mental gymnastics, the living in fear and anxiety. All of it. No more.

And most importantly, I forgive myself. Ever since the day in the library with Mako, I've been beating myself up. Agonizing because I'm a cheater and a whore, just like Ryan has always accused me of being. I couldn't eat or sleep for the last few days.

And for no reason. Because Ryan has been cheating on me all along anyway. I don't feel so bad for betraying someone who was betraying me far before fucking Mako was even a consideration. Ryan has never deserved my loyalty. I mean, really, what has he done to deserve it?

I can't believe I actually stayed this long. I can't believe I let him treat me this way. The physical and sexual aspect isn't even the worst part; it's the fucking mind games he played. It's not *just* mental abuse, it's mental warfare and can be more dangerous than a raised hand. The gaslighting and manipulation are what convinces victims to stay and endure. They train you to protect yourself, ultimately changing every part of you until you no longer recognize yourself. You're a prisoner in your own home. There are limitations on where you can go, how long you stay out, who you're allowed to see, and god forbid you hang out with anyone without their supervision. Too scared to look nice in fear of accusations of cheating. But you're going to leave the house looking like *that?* God, you're embarrassing, put some make-up on at least. But only wear it when *I'm* around, otherwise you're trying to impress other men.

You're dressed up, who are you looking nice for?

Do you want men to look at you like that? Do you want them to fuck you?

Please, baby, I get so worried that someone better is going to come along and take you away from me.

You're too good for me. I don't deserve you.

You're going to the store? Why, to cheat on me? Are you going there to flirt with other men?

You're out with your friend? I bet you're talking about other guys. Why would you hang out with them without me, what are you hiding?

A year ago, there wouldn't be a goddamn person on this planet that could convince me I'd let myself get to this point. That I'd let a man hit me. That's what everyone always says, right? *I'd* never *let a man hit me.* You don't even realize that's what has happened until it's too late. You've already been pushed down the stairs and slapped across the face. There are already hand and fingerprint bruises marring your arms and neck. And you've already told yourself he won't ever do it again. That he's sorry. He's stressed. You were wrong. Bad, bad girl. Feel guilty for making him lay hands on you. You *deserved* that. Leave? He'll kill himself. No one will ever love you the way he does, and *you love him, too*. You don't want him to die.

Even if he wants you to.

I drop the shirt back into the hamper. If he were smart, he would've had a spare shirt on him and tossed this one in a dumpster somewhere. Or maybe he just doesn't give a fuck if I see it or not. So, what if I do? What will I do? Leave him?

Don't worry, baby, I won't leave you.

I strip off my clothes and throw them in the hamper on top of his dirty shirt. Opening the door quietly, I walk into the steam-filled room. Sweat immediately breaks out on the back of my neck as I walk towards the walk-in shower. I see the distorted image of his naked body through the frosted glass. His arms are lifted as he rinses out his hair.

Sliding open the door, I step in and close it behind me. He doesn't bother looking at me yet. So confident. He doesn't see me as a threat. I cock my head. How badly I want to change that. Make him fear my presence, tremble when I come near.

His head is tilted back as suds of soap trail down his muscular body in a stream of hot water. Ryan's body is beautiful. He takes care of himself, goes to the gym often, and eats healthy for the most part. He's lean with sinewy muscles and tanned skin.

Though he possesses a work of art, it's still nowhere near as beautiful as Mako's. Where Ryan is lean, Mako is packed with muscle. I study him closely.

I much prefer his brother.

Ryan doesn't deserve to possess such a beautiful body. Not his, and not mine.

I step into him, shivering at the clash of hot water and the chill air.

"Did I upset you?" I whisper, trailing my finger down his chest and to his abs. I stop just before I reach his dick, already at half-mast. I stare down at him. He's not small, a little above average. Before, I saw it as something I didn't mind worshipping. Now, I want to wrap my mouth around it and bite until it's detached from his body.

There's no pulling my eyes away from the tool he used to give another woman pleasure. He stuck it in another woman's body today. His mouth has been kissing her lips and whispering sweet lies into her ear. His hands trailing across her skin, probably giving her goosebumps as he pumps into her. He probably looked her right in her eyes and made her believe he actually fucking wants her.

In reality, all he really wants is me. And he hates that. He hates to want me so much. He hates to be so addicted to me that he feels the need to mold me into a tiny ball in his hands like putty. He squeezes too hard, and just like putty, I creep through the cracks of his fingers, slowly separating until I'm oozing onto the floor.

He can't contain me. And the harder he tries, the more he fails.

My eyes lift the same time his head comes down, those dull, ugly blue eyes meeting mine. My world is finally shifting the way it needs to be. I don't know why it took him cheating to wake me up. I don't understand why the physical abuse and rape weren't the catalyst. Maybe because I thought the pain was surface level. I can heal. But cheating is deep. It's a pain that imprints like wolves mating and will last forever. Knowing that I wasn't good enough to keep him wanting only me. Knowing that every time he leaves my bed, he's walking into another woman's legs.

And that just won't fucking do.

"You did. But I forgive you," he says simply, before turning away to grab the loofah.

I never asked for forgiveness.

I take it from him, squirt some of this body wash onto it, and begin to rub him down. I dote on him, just like he wanted. I crouch down and soap down his legs as the water sprays directly into my face. I keep my head down and eyes closed as I worship him at his feet.

A hand wraps around my arm and lifts me up.

Shower sex in the movies is fake. The water doesn't just roll off the body and magically avoid your eyes. No, it goes right for the fucking eyes actually. I rub at them like a little kid and look up at him, my pupils now bloodshot and dry.

He smiles down at me, like I'm a cute little child that thinks they're actually going to grow up to be an astronaut.

"You know I love you, right?" he asks. His face has melted into soft lines and sweet nothings.

"I do," I say. I really, really do.

And I can't wait to show you exactly what your love has turned me into.

RYAN TOOK ME TO a classy restaurant called *Deep Blue*. It's not as upscale as the last restaurant, but the bill is easily going to be over a hundred dollars between the two of us. I made sure to choose the most expensive meal on the menu. I'm just finishing up my food and enjoying my third glass of wine when his voice cuts through my buzz.

"You graduate next May, right?" he asks, staring at me over the rim of his own wine.

"Yes," I answer, setting my glass down. The wine beckons me to pick it back up and finish it off. Alas, appearances, appearances. Can't embarrass my successful boyfriend now. Otherwise his reputation would be ruined over a glass of wine.

"What are your plans after college?"

My hand drifts over to the stem of the glass, spinning the dainty glass between my red painted fingernails. Does his secretary have red fingernails? I bet she does. Does Ryan look down at her hands and pretend they're mine? Or does he close his eyes and pretend he's fucking her when he's balls deep inside of me because he can't stand to look in the eyes of the woman he's lying to. Then, he'd have to face the fact that *he's* the one in the wrong.

"I'll start working on getting my PhD," I answer. Or maybe I'll run off to a farm and tame wild horses and fuck a real cowboy in the stalls. Who knows?

"I'd rather you stay at home."

Just barely do I suppress the sigh building in the back of my throat.

"And do what?"

He looks at me like I'm stupid. "Raise our kids, obviously," he answers slowly, speaking to me as if I suffer from the same condition as his tone.

Nice to know abusive assholes and misogyny go hand-in-hand. Ryan and I have discussed kids before. I want them eventually, but I'm not in a hurry; Ryan is adamant I have them anyways. He has a traditional outlook on life where the wife stays home and raises his little prodigies that will one day take over the law firm, while he goes off and works and fucks whoever he wants, apparently.

We'd be the perfect cliché. Raising little spoiled assholes that he only acknowledges when he's teaching life lessons and molding them into mini Ryan's, while I get drunk and high to deal with the pain of an abusive husband and settling for a miserable life. And the more I remember that I could've had a good life if I'd only left—with someone like Mako maybe—the more intoxicated I'd get until I can't even remember my own name.

Until I no longer remember *his* name.

I don't know where his outlook came from. Julie is an interior designer and highly successful at that. Ryan always used to say that his mother only stayed home with him for the standard maternity leave time frame and then was back to work, leaving Ryan with an older nanny that he hated.

Maybe he's always resented Julie for leaving him with the nanny.

As if reading my mind, he continues, "We're never hiring a nanny for our kids. It's no else's job to raise them but yours."

Not yours, though?

"The mother should always be the one to raise the kids. I'll help, of course. I don't want them to grow up as pussies."

It takes an extreme amount of effort to curb the urge to roll my eyes. It's easier to agree with him right now than to argue while we're in public. Whatever makes the fucker happy.

I shrug my shoulders. "Okay," I agree like a good bitch.

He smiles, proud that I agree with his sexist views. I want to crack my knuckles into his nose, over and over, until I'm drenched in his blood. Even then, I wouldn't be satisfied.

Just as I'm finishing my glass of wine, he stands and adjusts his pants, his movements fidgety and stiff. My brow pulls into a deep V when he walks around the table and grabs my hand. I nearly recoil when I feel how sweaty his hand is.

Why are you so nervous, sweet Ryan?

The entire restaurant gasps, and a hush falls across the room as Ryan gets down on one knee and produces a black box from his pocket.

My eyes widen, shock stealing my breath. This is the only moment Ryan wouldn't mind me looking a fish out of water.

"River McAllister, you are the love of my life. My heart beats inside of your chest, and I can't live without that. Will you do me the honor of marrying me?"

After his corny one-liner, he opens the box, showcasing a massive, gaudy ring. It's a band of diamonds with one sizable circular diamond in the middle, encrusted by a circle of yellow stones. I hate circular diamonds. I also hate colored diamonds. Especially yellow. Who wants a *yellow* diamond?

I make a show of covering my mouth, which curls into a snarl beneath the hand that still has a cast on my pointer finger. A cast caused by *him*. I widen my eyes dramatically and think about how much time I wasted on this piece of shit. He's proposing to me the same day he fucked another woman.

How poetic of you, sweet Ryan.

Tears prick at my eyes, except in mirth instead of pure elation.

It's not wise to say no to him here. He'll be embarrassed. Absolutely mortified. And he'll kill me before I have the chance to escape. The bastard already knows I'll say yes.

It takes extreme discipline that I didn't know I possessed not to laugh in his face. There's only one way I can think of to get through this shitshow. Shamefully, I picture Mako. Mako on his knee before me, grinning at me with that cocky smirk and grass green eyes glistening with love.

Mako—the incredibly infuriating man who has done nothing but stick his neck out for me and try to help me. And though most times I want to wring his neck, I can't deny the underlying, intense connection to him. Especially not after the library, where I bared myself to Mako and fingerfucked myself while he watched and got off.

That reminder brings a genuine smile to my face. That's all I need to say for what I need to say next.

"Yes!" I exclaim, casting a mask of happiness on my face. In reality, it only took me a few seconds to reply. His shoulder drops in relief, and his face breaks out into a blinding smile, showing off his perfect white teeth. Teeth that I'd love nothing more than to see decorating our pristine floors.

He slips the ugly ring on my finger, the ring complimenting my white cast mockingly. I spread my hand out wide, smiling on the outside and raging on the inside. This is what my life has come to. An ugly engagement ring and a broken finger.

At least he was considerate enough not to break my ring finger.

We both stand, the metal contraption burning my finger with a fiery vengeance. I want to rip it off; I hate the way it feels. His lips touch mine, quick and passionless. Ryan doesn't do PDA well. I'd like to fuck someone in a dirty public restroom just to spite him.

The restaurant cheers respectfully, phones flash, and a complimentary bottle of wine is sent to our table. I drink three-fourths of it while Ryan stares at my hand like he's finally caught the exotic animal in his sadistic trap. I stare at him and wonder why he thought I would want to be proposed to in a goddamn restaurant.

"FUCK, I LOVE YOU so much," Ryan moans against my neck. We're in the same position we were in after I met his parents for the first time. Except this time, I want him to get the fuck off me. I'm stiff and unresponsive, my face curling with discomfort.

"I love you, too, but babe, I don't want to do this right now," I say, pushing his bare chest back a bit. He stops cold, dragging his soulless eyes up to mine.

"Why wouldn't you want to?" His voice is devoid of emotion. A spark of anxiety ignites inside me, like the first spark of fire on a cold winter night.

"I've been having cramps all day. I think my period is starting soon," I lie. If he knew me at all, he'd know I don't have a period with my birth control.

"I don't mind a little blood," he says. My nose inadvertently curls in disgust. I'd probably fuck someone on my period if I wanted them badly enough, but that person will never be Ryan again. Not when he's a cheating asshole.

Yet *I'm* somehow the whore.

"Babe, that's gross," I say, adding a smile he will hopefully find cute.

"You think me wanting you is fucking gross?" he asks, rage creeping into his voice. His hands squeeze my arms as his eyes darken into something dangerous. This conversation is quickly going downhill, and I think I'm strong enough to keep it rolling. I don't want to have sex with him. I shouldn't fucking have to.

"No," I say slowly. "The fact that I'm telling you no and you're not accepting it is gross."

My head is whipping to the side as an explosion of pain blooms across my cheek. My ears are ringing as Ryan gets in my face. The fucker slapped me.

"You don't get to tell me no. I'm your fiancé, which means I get to touch you and fuck you whenever the hell I please."

My cheek is on fire. Tears prick at my eyes, and it only angers me. I swear this man gets off on my tears and pain.

He steps back, his arms spread out with an aghast expression on his face.

"We just got engaged. I thought you'd be excited, River. Most girls would be ripping their fiancé's clothes off right now. I don't get it."

Cue the manipulation. How have I never seen it before? Anytime I'd get angry enough to realize I'm dating the biggest asshole next to Hitler, and he'd find a way to pull me back in with his manipulation and sweet words.

"You said you'd stop hitting me," I say instead. His face contorts into anger.

"Really, River? I think I'm the victim here. I just put myself out there, made myself vulnerable to you, and did something I've *never* done for any other girl, and you have the nerve to reject me."

"I didn't reject you, Ryan. I said yes," I say calmly. He looks at me like I'm stupid.

"You're rejecting me right now," he speaks through gritted teeth. This is a losing battle, and I can feel the helplessness crawling in. Is this what made me so compliant? Maybe if I went along with things, I wouldn't get yelled at or hit?

No one can deny that Ryan's love is safer than his anger. But what he tries to hide is that there's no such thing as loving you without him being angry at you for it.

I nod once. "I am."

His face turns red, his wrath becoming an entirely different entity.

"Do you enjoy pissing me off, River? You know what happens when I get pissed."

There are so many ways I can answer that question. You hit, you rage, you rape...

In that moment, Bilby skitters by, sensing the growing tension in the room. It happens in slow motion. I watch Ryan's eyes drop to my cat and witness the moment the idea strikes him. His eyes turn glacial, and an evil smirk slides across his face. I lurch forward as Ryan picks Bilby up by the scruff of his neck, eliciting a pained cry from him.

"Let him go!" I shout, charging towards him.

No, no. *Not* my cat. Anything but my cat.

He swings Bilby out of my reach, ignoring the innocent little cat's hissing and loud cries.

"Apparently I need to teach you a lesson. If you disobey me, then you don't get to have nice things. Including your filthy fucking animal. I'll fucking kill him, River," he screams, shaking my baby in his grips.

"Stop!" I cry hysterically, once more reaching for my cat. "I'll do whatever you want, Ryan. Please, just let him go. Please, please, please!" I beg hysterically, panic taking over. I can't look away from Bilby. Tears stream down my face as complete and utter desperation takes over.

I've never felt desperation like this before. Not when I was being raped as a little girl. Not as I was being beaten within an inch of my life. Not by Billy or Ryan.

He stares at me for a solid ten seconds before he drops Bilby. In tandem, my sigh of relief releases along with my cat from Ryan's harsh grip. I cry harder, now from sheer relief that he didn't seriously hurt my baby. Bilby skitters off, his angry hissing in his wake.

Just as I step forward, ready to crush his goddamn skull in, he's seizing me by the arms and dragging me up the stairs while I fight and scream. When I manage to dislodge myself from his grip and try to run back down them, he pushes me hard. My knees give, and I go flying down the stairs.

A cry escapes me, my arms taking the brunt of my fall. I flip over, ass overhead, my tailbone landing painfully on the edge of the step. A pained yelp bursts from the throat, my eyes widening from the excruciating pain.

His hand is in my hair the next second, curling it around his fist and using it as a rope to drag me up the stairs. The strands are ripping out of my scalp with each step. I buck against him, trying to find purchase with my feet on the steps to stop him, but he only yanks harder. When he goes to grab for more hair for a better grip, I give up with that tactic, grab his wrist and lift myself, trying my best to alleviate some of the pain.

Finally, we reach the bedroom. He tosses me on the ground forcefully, causing my forehead to slam into the wooden floor. In the midst, I wish for carpet in the bedroom. I'd take rug burn over bumps and bruises from the unforgiving floor.

He grabs the front of my dress, and with one swoop, he rips the dress completely down the middle, leaving me in nothing but my thong. Another tug and those are torn from my battered body as well.

It doesn't take long before he's forcefully pushing himself inside me. It feels like I'm tearing from the inside out. I rage at him and use my nails to scratch everywhere. He pushes my hands away and then slaps me across the face so hard, I nearly blackout. Stars dot my vision as he continues to use my body for his own pleasure.

My heart is pounding, my body is aching, and my mind is in full-blown panic as he rapes me.

I never stop fighting, though. Even after the moment he finishes inside of me.

When he pulls out, I drag myself up on the edge of the bed and curl into a pathetic little ball. All I can do is cry. Cry, and cry, and cry. Cry for Bilby. Cry for myself.

This is all your fault, River. You should've just let him fuck you. Bilby would've never gotten hurt if you had.

"Just so you know, I've been spiking your drinks with antibiotics. You should be pregnant by now," he says casually. My eyes pop open in horror, a different kind of panic nearly choking me.

He's lying. He has to be. God, please tell me he's fucking lying.

"And if you ever try to leave, especially with my baby, I *will* find you. No amount of police will ever keep me from finding you, River. And when I do, I will kill you."

Sixteen

River

"DO YOU NEED ME to come get you?" the baritone voice says as a greeting through the speaker on my phone. I close my eyes, the temptation taking over.

Say yes, River. Say yes.

"No," I sigh. My lip finds itself between my teeth as I gear myself up for what I'm about to ask of him. "I need you to take Bilby."

Mako's silent on the other end, ramping up my heart faster. What if he says no? Where would Bilby go? Amelia's severely allergic to cats, and there's absolutely no way I'm keeping him in the same house as Ryan anymore. Not after last night. I refuse to put my cat in danger. He means everything to me, and I would never forgive myself if he ended up dead because of my bad choices.

"Bilby?" he repeats finally, confused.

"My cat."

More silence.

"Did Ryan hurt the cat?"

My eyes close again, embarrassed by the words about to come out of my mouth. "Yes. I can't endanger his life."

"But you can endanger your own?" I grit my teeth. It doesn't matter that I had prepared myself for that before he even said it; it still pisses me off.

"Mako, please," I say instead, the same desperation from last night creeping in. "I'm not calling you to talk about me. I… I just need Bilby safe right now. Please."

His low sigh filters through. "Do I need to come get him?"

"No. No, I'll drop him off before class today."

"I'll be there." My lips curl as tears burn my eyes. I'm not even sure why exactly I'm crying, but the urge is becoming overwhelming. Maybe because I have to give up my cat—temporarily—because he's no longer safe in the home I brought him into. I feel so ashamed. This is something I'll *never* forgive myself for.

"Mako?"

"Yeah, River?"

"Thank you. So much."

TWO BEADY EYES INSPECT me from head to toe.

"Looks like you're finally getting what you deserve," Barbie comments before curling her wrinkled lips around a cigarette. I ignore her comment, considering I'd already wrapped myself in armor to deflect her nasty words and smugness. Only Barbie would be smug that her daughter is being abused. Especially when this is the life she's always wanted for me, and I was stupid enough to believe I was getting something she never did—safety.

I glance at the near-empty pack resting on the table. Right now, I don't give a fuck about germs.

"Give me one," I say instead, nodding my head towards the cigarettes. Surprisingly, she pushes the pack over, along with the lighter. From one abused woman to another, sometimes all we need is a cigarette.

I slide out a cancer stick, light it up and suck greedily.

I've no idea if Ryan actually did spike my drinks. Maybe I am pregnant, but I hurt too badly to stop puffing on the cigarette right now. It's been a week since he proposed, nearly killed my cat, and then promptly beat the shit out of me—again—and he hasn't let me out of his sight once, until tonight. Thankfully, I've shown no signs of pregnancy yet, so I'm beginning to doubt his threat.

"Did you know Billy was killing people all across the city?" I start. Barbie half-laughs, half-scoffs, the sound filled with phlegm.

"Whatever gave you the impression that he wasn't killing people?" she asks with condescension.

I shake my head. "This is different. Billy is smart enough to cover up his murders. He's deliberately leaving them across town, apparently for the last year. He's considered a serial killer—they've even dubbed him the Ghost Killer."

Barbie outright laughs, delight shining in her lifeless eyes. Barbie's been exposed to several dead bodies across her lifetime. Mostly from overdosing, but I can bet she's witnessed murders, too. Probably from cracked-out drug addicts having mental breakdowns and going into psychotic rages. And I'm positive Billy has made an example of a couple of people to make sure Barbie stayed in her place.

"That's too funny," she says around her laugh, ashing her cigarette in an empty beer can. She used to keep glass ashtrays around until she broke all of them over her clients' heads. Now it's just simpler to use trash. There's a fuck ton of it lying around, after all.

I roll my eyes at her classiness.

"You know that's not normal for Billy. He's under the radar, Barbie, and you know it. Why would he be leaving bodies around town?"

Her eyes shift, and something like fear flashes in her eyes. It's gone before I can tell for sure.

"He's been getting hooked on meth again," she says casually. But it's not casual at all, we both know this. It's been over fifteen years since Billy got hooked on his own product and started killing off all of his men. He'd storm the house, raging that he had no one left that he could trust because all of them were dead.

Barbie was smart enough not to ask questions. The woman couldn't tell you what eight times nine is, but she hasn't lived this long dealing with someone like Billy just by dumb luck. She's incredibly street smart, even when she's high off her rocker. So many times, I've wondered if Barbie is much wiser than she lets on.

So, Barbie would keep her trap shut, I'd listen through the door, and Billy would vent his frustrations on how all his men kept fucking the little girls he traffics and ruining their value. Or they'd be stealing his drugs or money for themselves. Or they'd give him a look he didn't like.

Whatever the case, he killed them all. That got Billy in quite the predicament when he had essentially no one to do his bidding. He quit the drugs, rebuilt his empire, and stayed clean since.

"I don't understand. He knows what happened last time."

Barbie tightens her lips, shrugs a thin shoulder, and lights another cigarette. I do the same. I'm gonna need it for this conversation. Billy on meth is... evil incarnate. It's the reckoning. He's the third Antichrist Nostradamus predicted.

"I don't know what happened," she finally says. "Explains why he popped up out of the blue and beat us both silly."

Both of our wounds from that night have healed, only to be replaced by more. She may cackle and laugh at the sight of me, but she doesn't look any better. Only difference is, Barbie has never *not* sported any bruises. That's her normal. At this point, every part of me has endured some sort of trauma that I'm not sure I know how to feel pain anymore. Guess we're turning out to be two peas in a fucking pod.

I look down at my hand with an ugly cast and an uglier ring. I don't even know why I'm still wearing the damn thing.

"He could come back around at any time," she continues, snapping me out of my dark thoughts. Her eyes narrow towards me with a clear warning. Barbie never warns me about anything except Billy. Especially Billy on drugs. I don't let it go to my head and think it's because she actually gives a shit about me. But if I die, this house will be auctioned off, and we all know Barbie doesn't have the funds to buy it back.

As much as she hates it, I'm keeping her safe from the streets. If anyone could survive it, it would be Barbie. She's like a goddamn cockroach, the bitch could survive the apocalypse. Doesn't mean she wants to, though.

"Has he been coming around often?" I ask, though I can feel my heart kickstart. I'm under no illusion that I'm safe here. That Billy coming around won't ever happen again. But I'd hoped he'd be too busy killing off his men rather than coming to see Barbie's washed-up ass.

She sucks on her cigarette, delaying an answer I'd really like to know. If he's coming around often, then I'm in more danger than I'd realized.

Finally, she answers. "About once a week. He was just here last night."

The sudden urge to run from this house nearly cripples me. I got my answers. Or at least as much of an answer as I'm going to get when it comes to the devil. Time to go.

"Then I guess it's time for me to leave."

Barbie smirks. I said it casually, but again, this isn't a casual conversation. She enjoys the fact that Billy scares me. The only good thing about Billy beating me half to death is it's less time he's beating Barbie. As long as he refrains from ultimately killing me, Barbie couldn't care less.

"Have fun with your Billy 2.0 at home," she says, cackling around her cigarette. I stand up and look down at her. She looks and smells like expired milk. How could her words ever hurt me?

Yet they stir something in me anyway. Not hurt. But something like determination.

"Oh, I will."

"WHAT IN THE EVER-LOVING fuck happened to you?" Amelia roars, her face the perfect picture of rage and shock. I could photograph that picture and it'd sell for millions. The amount of emotion conveyed on her face is actually quite beautiful.

"Would you believe me if I said I fell?"

"He's hitting you?!" she screeches, her little hands reaching up to cup my face. I'm a good few inches taller than Amelia, but her motherly instincts have always made her seem bigger than me. She's going to be an amazing mother.

"What brought you to that conclusion?" I deflect, deftly removing my face from her warm hands and turning to walk towards my car.

"Oh, no, you don't," she says, running past me and stopping right in my path. She puts her hands on her hips, her protruding stomach emphasized by her tiny hands, and stares at me with impatience and barely contained rage. Can't honestly blame her. I'd *kill* anyone that did this to Amelia.

I sigh, my shoulders dropping in defeat. "You can't say anything, Amelia. I... I got him handled."

Her eyes widen like balloons overflowing with helium. Soon they're going to pop. That can't be good for the baby.

"Please don't take this the wrong way, River, but it sure as hell looks like you're the only one being handled," she replies, her voice significantly gentler. I nod my head because she's right. It doesn't look like I have Ryan handled at all.

"I have to play this smart," I say. She bites her lip, seeming to contemplate something.

"I want you to stay with me. You can't go back to that house."

I've been pretty good at avoiding Ryan since the night he proposed, threatened to kill my cat, and raped me within hours of each other. What was supposed to be the happiest day of my life, turned to the darkest far before Ryan got down on one knee.

I bet he's fucking his secretary as we speak.

"And I plan on doing that... eventually," I tack on with a pained look. "It's a delicate situation that needs to be handled as such. I don't want to drag you into this, Amelia. I would rather die than involve you and your unborn baby in any type of danger."

Amelia chews on her lips some more, looking even more distraught by the second.

She shakes her head. "No. I'm sorry, but I'm not allowing this. There's no way in fucking hell that I will let you continue to put your life in danger.

If you go back, he'll kill you. And then I'll be pregnant in prison."

I crack a small smile.

"He won't kill me," I whisper. I won't let him. Ryan had to wear a turtleneck to work last week from how deep and red my marks were from when he raped me. Once they fade, he'll just spin it to a night of wild sex and orgasms I clearly couldn't handle.

"Of course, he won't. I'll kill him first," a deep voice says from behind me. I freeze, which just makes every ache and pain in my body flare to life. My breath shortens, and I swear it's only because it's hotter outside than an athlete's balls after practice.

Amelia's brows plummet, and she bends her torso to the side to see Mako better. "Who are you?" she asks, her voice pitched high. If I didn't feel like such shit, I'd almost laugh.

Mako steps around me, his massive body dwarfing Amelia's. She looks up at him in awe, her little mouth open in a perfect O. Her eyes slowly peruse his incredibly fit body, the tattoos coloring both arms down to his wrists and the pure sexual tension he radiates. I'd be jealous if I knew she wasn't madly in love with David and carrying his child. I also am not keen on admitting that I'd be jealous.

I glare at Mako's back as he sticks out a massive hand. My cheeks redden when I think about what those hands could do to me. With him, he'd use them for things that would only excite me, *that's* a promise.

"I'm Mako. I'm the nice brother," he greets. Amelia shakes his hand as if she's the queen of England and he's a lowly peasant. Despite my frustration with Mako popping up once again, I smile at Amelia's sass.

"Uh huh," she murmurs, unconvinced. Amelia only knows that I stayed at his house when Ryan was being a shit after Billy beat me within an inch of my life. I hadn't told her that Mako was the one that came and picked me up after Ryan left me on the couch helpless and took care of me in ways Ryan never has, or about how he's been keeping Bilby at his house for the past week. I've also never told her about all the times Mako has shown up after my classes to convince me to leave Ryan. Certainly didn't tell her about the library incidents and how I lost all common sense and let Mako get too close. Whatever voodoo that library has on me, it's dangerous when Mako's around.

But worst of all, I never told her how sinfully delicious of a man Mako is. Amelia eyes him up and down, both hands now cocked on her rounded hip like a mother scolding her child. She really is going to be an incredible mother.

I pray I'm around to witness it.

When Amelia's distrustful eyes slide over to me, I feel like that scorned child. Words don't need to come out of her mouth in order for me to know she's hurt. I've been lying to her. By omission, but keeping secrets is still lying.

I give her a sheepish smile. "You's got some s'plainin' to do," she sings with a look that says you're-so-in-trouble.

Mako looks back at me, a sinful smirk on his face. The way he looks at me can only be described as dirty—with his salacious smirk and heated eyes. And with Amelia watching the interaction very intently, it makes me want to wipe the look off his face with a Clorox wipe and then spray him in the eyes with Lysol for good measure.

I clear my throat and look back at Amelia with the most innocent smile I can muster. Which isn't saying much when nothing about me has ever been innocent.

"Mako here has enlisted himself as my personal knight in shining armor, no matter how much I've tried to show him *I'm* the dragon," I explain. Amelia cocks an eyebrow.

"Yeah? And how long has he been trying and failing to save you?" she asks, her tone almost condescending. Amelia knows as well as I do that I've never been one to accept help. Doesn't matter if you're a six-foot-five beast with bear paws for hands, I will dropkick you in the balls if it means you'll stop trying to save me. Seems I always end up just wanting to fondle him, but the message has at least been said.

"Too long," I mutter. I've yelled in Mako's face and even slapped the damn sexy work of art, and alas, he still persists. So, it looks like I'm just going to have to dropkick him in the balls next... and then maybe fondle them.

"River has made it perfectly clear she can take care of herself. Despite her badass abilities, what *I've* made perfectly clear is that I'm not going anywhere until I know she's safe. And if you take a look at Exhibit A"—he points to my bruised face— "that hasn't happened yet."

I open my mouth to show him the exhibit my foot is about to disappear into, when Amelia cuts me off. "Okay, children. Clearly this has been going on for a while." She shoots me a dirty look. "I think it's clear River is in a tough situation, and it's not always easy to leave right away, no matter how much we want her to."

My shoulders relax with Amelia's unexpected understanding. Sometimes I forget Amelia had a rough childhood, too. She grew up with an alcoholic, abusive father. Even after turning eighteen, she stuck around to try and take care of him until she left for college. To this day, she still struggles with her love for him.

The biggest misconception with survivors of abuse is that they're choosing to stay. Anyone in our situation would leave if it were that easy. But when someone is threatening your life daily, sometimes staying seems like the safer choice. Even if you know, it'll kill you one day.

The unpredictable abuse is still predictable, and that can be a little less scary than trying to rebuild a life on your own with the constant fear that this person will come after you and snatch it away. All that hard work— gone. And sometimes your life, too.

"I'm going to leave you two to work out whatever tension you have going on here. River, I expect a phone call later," Amelia announces, still eyeing mine and Mako's odd interaction. How I could be thinking about another man when the current one in my life is using me as a punching bag is beyond both of us. But it's happening. And I'm not really sure how the hell to stop it.

Or if I want to.

Amelia hugs me goodbye, gives Mako one last once over, and walks towards her car. I pivot towards the most frustrating man I've ever met.

"What do you want now?" I whine, taking up Amelia's position and planting my hands on my hips. It takes several swallows to shove the lump back down my throat when I remember that I could *look* like Amelia in a few months too. A rounded belly to look down on and haunt me.

His eyes narrow, but nevertheless, he doesn't sass back. Instead, he stuffs his hands in his pockets and skirts his eyes over campus.

"I just want to help you, River. That's all," he says finally.

I cock an eyebrow. "You don't want to fuck me?"

Emerald green eyes piston towards me, shining like freshly polished gems. The same salacious smirk glides across his beautiful face, and fuck me, if my heart doesn't stop and speed up all in the same breath.

"I do want to fuck you, and not only do I *want* to, but I *will* fuck you," he says boldly. My heart drops at the promise. I hate that my pussy grows wet in response. But I love it even more. "But that's not why I want to help you. I can't woo you and show you what a real man is like if you're dead."

Can't help but respect someone who is as blunt as I am. I tap my foot and purse my lips, contemplating this man's intentions. Aside from the library incidents, he's never made any indication that he wants to steal me away for his own personal gain. There's no denying what he's done for me. Taking Bilby will always be something I'll be grateful for. Keeping my cat safe means more to me than I am capable of expressing.

"How's my baby?" I ask, changing the subject.

"He's still adjusting. You never said what exactly happened, but I think he's still recovering. He's very… cautious."

The fact that my loving bundle of fur is now reduced to distrust, is heartbreaking. I haven't gotten the chance to visit him yet, but the second I do, I'm going to shower him with so much love, he won't know what to do with it.

"He sleeps with me at night, though," Mako continues, sensing my plummeting mood. "He's coming around, River. He's going to be okay."

I nod my head as I chew on my lip, forever worrying about him. The guilt will never go away.

Mako glances around, my eyes following the same track.

We're out in the open, and Ryan only graduated a few years ago before he left for law school. He was very popular and never let any of his college friends completely go. Often, Ryan-the-big-shot would meet up with his college buddies on campus or show up to college parties. People know him. They know me. And whether they know Mako or not, they can easily tattle and tell Ryan I'm speaking to another man. A very large, very attractive male. One who keeps looking at me like I'm the icing he likes to lick off his cupcake.

"I need to go home," I say instead.

"Let me take you out. Somewhere that's not a library, as much as I do enjoy those."

I hate how little consideration I give my answer. "Fine."

I turn and walk away.

"When?" he calls.

Pivoting, I walk a few steps backwards and say, "You're good at stalking me. I'm sure you can work out a time and date." His smile is slow and lazy, sending all kinds of feelings straight to my core before I give him my back once more.

THE FITZGERALD FAME AND fortune could not have affected my life at the worst possible time.

The clerk behind the cash register eyes my purchases and then eyes me. She's an older, shrewd woman with salt and pepper hair, extra sag with her wrinkles and a curious gleam in her eye. She's definitely the nosy neighbor type, constantly peeking out her window to spy on people. Good thing she isn't my neighbor. I'd just open my curtains, pull down my panties, spread my legs wide, and give her a show she'd never forget. And I bet she'd never, *ever* look through my windows again.

"Aren't you dating Ryan Fitzgerald?" she asks, picking up each box and scanning it. Five of them total.

It's in my nature to be rude and tell the bat to mind her business. But that little voice in the back of my head—the one I haven't kicked to the curb yet—still demands I protect Ryan's reputation. Not for his benefit, but for mine. If I'm going to get out of this situation alive, then it'd be stupid to poke the bear before I've set the trap.

"Yep," I say with forced cheer. Hopefully, she doesn't see how fake my smile is. Looks like it was about as effective as Botox would be on her crow's feet.

"I sure hope so if you've found yourself in the situation you think you have," she comments, tapping a few buttons on the touchscreen. "$60.87."

Goddamn, these are expensive. I insert my card into the slot harder than necessary. She doesn't miss it, either. Or maybe the nerves in her saggy skin are malfunctioning, and she's not actually giving me a smug little smile.

My transaction finishes up as she bags my items. And now comes the awkward moment where she waits for the receipt to spew from the machine while I think about stabbing her in the eye with the pen clipped to her work vest. When she hands the receipt over, I give her the sugariest smile I can manage.

"Thank you so much, ma'am."

We're both rolling our eyes when I walk away.

Seventeen

River

I STARE DOWN AT THE sticks, on the verge of tears.

Not pregnant.

Utter relief fills my body, so potent that I nearly faint. I scramble to hide the sticks in one of my sneakers.

Ryan's in another mood. I'm sitting in the closet, snotting and crying as he slams around the house. I'm naked and even more bruised than before. He didn't hit me this time, just grabbed me roughly until I cried out in pain. Only then, did he squeeze harder. Guess he didn't have to hit this time when I complied like a good little girl and let him defile my body.

He doesn't like that I don't love sex with him anymore. It bothers him, cuts him deep. He wants back what we had in the beginning. When he could be as rough as he pleased, and I'd fucking beg for it. I wouldn't flinch away every time his hand got within an inch of my face. My face wouldn't curl in disgust, and my eyes wouldn't glaze over as I disassociate. Every time I show my displeasure, he shows his in violent and angry ways.

A lot has changed since the night I met his parents five months ago. It feels like that was the beginning of our downfall. Why, though? What possibly could have such a dramatic and negative effect?

Meeting Mako.

Ryan was rough, and he was manipulative. But he didn't attack me until Mako came around. What is it about his brother that he hates so much?

Is it because he's better-looking? Is it because Mako is the tall, dark and handsome type while Ryan looks like your typical frat boy? No, Ryan is too vain for that. His looks have been validated his entire life. Women have fallen at his feet, begging for his attention since girls stopped thinking boys had cooties.

If I didn't know any better, I'd think Ryan is scared of Mako. But why? Anyone with goddamn sense is afraid of spiders or snakes. The experts say they're more scared of you than you are of them, right? Well, those fuckers bite when they're afraid. And sometimes, those bites end up being very deadly.

I stumble to my feet, wiping the snot from my nose and wiping it on one of Ryan's button-up shirts. My side of the closet is chaotic. Ryan got pissed when I wore a V-neck shirt to class the other day, so now most of my clothes are ripped to shreds, still dangling from the hangers like haggard scarecrows. I walk over and finger one of my favorite dresses. A sexy emerald green dress that hugged my body like a child would their favorite toy. It reminds me of Mako's eyes.

I wore this to the club many years ago, when Ryan was just a fantasy to me. Memories from that night come filtering back in. The sexy bartender. The Long Island ice teas. The lemon drops. That man....

I hadn't forgotten about him, at least not entirely. I thought about him consistently for a long while after that. But once Ryan officially entered my life, I tucked that little memory in the far back corner of my brain, leaving it to collect cobwebs and spiders for company.

Now, I brush away the webs and uncover one of the most thrilling moments of my life. Feeling the mystery man behind me, touching me expertly, leaving me panting and needy for more. His breath tickling my ear, sending shivers down my spine and making my knees weak. I close my eyes, swaying as I reminisce about my favorite memory.

If I lose myself enough, I can feel the phantom hands curving around my hips, his broad chest pressing into my back. My body fits into his like a puzzle piece.

Ryan has never danced with me like that before. Matter of fact, he's never danced with me at all.

There was one time Ryan accompanied me to a bar. I had dragged him out to the dance floor, laughing and squealing, buzzed from a few shots of vodka. I moved my body seductively, eyes only for him, and he responded by storming off the dance floor.

Later, he told me I was dancing like a whore, and it embarrassed him.

A tear drips from my eye as I finger the shredded material. This was one of the first things he grabbed, with scissors in his hands and the eyes of a madman. He split the scissors and dragged the sharp end down the dress, over and over as I just watched silently, tears streaming down my face.

I was too scared to scream and fight back. I didn't want those scissors turned on me.

"River!" Ryan shouts from outside the closet, causing me to jump several feet. Every time I hear his voice, the survivor in me wants to reach into his throat and tear out his voice box. But the poor little girl inside me wants to curl in a ball and hide from this cruel fucking world.

Fuck, what's the goddamn point in even being alive? Maybe I should kill myself. I tip my head back and smile. The thought doesn't sound so bad. On the contrary, it sounds quite alluring, just like the siren's voice leading sailors down to their death. I could be that sailor, willingly handing over my life. Fading into blissful silence, nothing but darkness surrounding me. Not the same kind of darkness that's been my shadow my entire life, but just... *nothingness.*

I don't care if there is a heaven or hell. I don't care if I become a spirit trapped in this world. Anything is better than this life.

The door slams open, the doorknob nearly cracking against the drywall. I don't move.

"Where's Bilby?"

I almost laugh. Did he seriously just now notice the cat is missing? Suppose I shouldn't be surprised. Ryan never paid much attention to him anyway. I bring my head down and meet crazed blue eyes. What would his eyes look like, full of love and tenderness? Anytime I thought I was finding that in his eyes, it was only the reflection of what a sociopath thought those emotions should look like.

"I gave him back to the shelter," I lie. God forbid I tell Ryan the cat's at Amelia's, and he goes looking for him there. And I certainly couldn't tell the truth and admit he's at Mako's. There are several shelters around our city. It'd be easy to say Bilby already got adopted if Ryan was crazy enough to find him. I'd expect him to do something like that so that he could bring the cat back and torture me with him.

His eyes narrow into thin slits. "Why?"

"Because you almost killed him," I answer, blandly. I'm finding it hard to give him emotion, too. I'm finding it hard to feel it at all. He steps further into the closet, adopting what's supposed to be an intimidating pose. Widening his stance, he leans towards me with curled fists and looks down his nose at me.

"Did I give you permission to give him away?" he snarls.

I sniff. Dead eyes meet dead eyes. "I didn't ask."

The last thing I see before I close my eyes is shock registering on his face and then instantly morphing into a black rage.

I don't open my eyes again, even when I feel Ryan's vice grip around my biceps shaking me. I don't open them when he slams me against the wall, holds my head tightly against my white painted cage much like Billy did when I was bent over that dirty table, and takes me from behind.

He's lost all sense. He doesn't care to pretend anymore. Ryan and River are no more. Now it's just a lunatic and his prisoner.

That means if Ryan is done pretending to play nice, then so am I.

I STARE AT MY PHONE, the screen blurred from the tears in my eyes. Who do I call, who do I call? I could call Mako, but fuck, something inside me just... doesn't want him to see me like this. I'm ashamed—*so* ashamed. And Amelia's pregnant so I'll be damned if I endanger her and her unborn baby.

I wipe a shaky hand down my face. Fuck, fuck, fuck.

Ryan's going on a rampage. It's been two more weeks, and all he's done is push me around and constantly rape and sodomize me. Every time I fight back, he fucks harder. I've already decided how I want to handle my situation, but I need to be smart.

He's pissed tonight.

I burnt the casserole, so he made me grab the hot dish from the oven without mitts. Obviously, I dropped the glass casserole dish the second I touched it. It broke and the food went flying everywhere.

Tiny cuts and burns cover my hands now. The floor is clean, but Ryan's temper is still running hotter than the burnt food. I need to get the fuck out of here before he kills me. I've never seen him this angry. And I swear to God I'll kill him before he kills me if he tries tonight.

Before I came up here, I snuck into his office and cut the internet. He's been raging about it ever since, on the phone with the cable company, and still hasn't figured out the internet isn't going to come back on until the cable company sends a guy out. The security cameras are linked to the WiFi, which means the recordings won't be saved to our Cloud.

Ryan's been watching me through the cameras obsessively, even when he's home with me. I'll be doing something mundane, and Ryan will come out and point out something I did wrong while he was in the office, watching me. So, with no WiFi, he can't keep an eye on me on his phone, and as long as he can see me, there's no escaping.

I scroll through my contacts and pause on the one person I could call right now. I really don't fucking want to, but she would understand my situation better than most. I click the call button before changing my mind and bringing the shaking phone to my ear.

"Hello?"

God, Alison sounds so damn *sweet*. I cringe away from her voice.

"It's me," I choke out.

"Where are you?" she asks instantly, her voice hardening into steel.

I drop my head into my hand, not caring that any contact with the burns sends fire racing through my flesh. The fact that she knew without me having to say anything is a testament to what she's dealt with for years. There's no way I could've stuck around as long as she did. Not because I'm stronger than her, but because I'm weaker and would've offed myself.

I already want to after only two years.

"At his house. I can meet you on the corner of the street, though," I whisper.

"I'll be there in ten."

My finger smashes the red button before I can tell her not to come. Heart racing, I stand on wobbling legs, grab a bag and start stuffing clothing in it. The closet has become my safe space from Ryan, and for the most part, he's let me have it.

A cupboard slams from the kitchen below me. There's no way I can sneak out of the house without him seeing me if he's in the kitchen. It's down the hall from the foyer, and the psycho will be watching that front door like a hawk. I tried to leave a few days ago without his permission, and it ended in me getting tied up to the bed for the night.

My wrists still ache and the lesions around them haven't healed yet.

I slip on a pair of sneakers, quietly open the closet door and peek around. He's still downstairs. Each step is amplified by my racing heart as I make my way over to the window. There's a roof right outside of it, and on the side of the house is a lattice covered in vines and pretty flowers I don't know the name of. Never cared to learn.

Biting my lip, I gently raise the window. To me, it sounds like I'm clawing a chalkboard with a nail, but in reality, it hardly makes a noise. Tentatively, I step out. The first breath of fresh air is exciting and terrifying at the same time. Like if I don't hurry, I won't ever get the pleasure of experiencing fresh air again. Right when I go to close the window behind me, Ryan bursts into the room. I freeze. He freezes. We both stare at each other in shock.

In tandem, we both bust into action. He guns for the window while I run towards the edge of the house.

"River, get back here," he growls. His voice isn't raised high enough to call attention to us. There are only a few houses close by, but they're close enough to hear the loud commotion.

I make it to the edge of the house and run along the edge until I get to the terrace. Just as I step my foot down, a steel hand wraps around my bicep and pulls me back up. I scream, but it's immediately cut off by Ryan's hand.

"You fucking bitch!" he howls when I bite down on his hand. Before I can scream again, his fist slams into the side of my temple. Darkness threatens to overtake me. Stars explode in my vision as he slides me across the rough asphalt on the roof towards the window, muttering expletives under his breath.

If he takes me back in there, he's going to kill me. Eyes wide and dazed, I struggle and fight as hard as I can. I can't let him take me back in there. I can't.

We make it back to the window. My phone in my back pocket buzzes, and it makes me want to die inside. Alison is here, at the end of the street where she can't see me. I was *so* fucking close to freedom.

Ryan puts one leg in the window, slides his torso through with his arms still holding onto my struggling body, and in one rough swoop, he pulls me inside. I grapple for the sides of the window, but my fingers slip before I can fully grasp onto it. My vision teeter-totters, and I'm grappling for balance before I'm thrown on the hardwood floor. The monster before me slams the window closed. He looks at me, his face tomato red and his eyes nearly black from rage. I've never seen something so terrifying in my life.

When I was a child, those men weren't out to kill me as much as they used my body. But Ryan? Ryan wants to kill me. Even though it's useless now, I scream as loud as I can.

He charges towards me. I kick my feet, trying to gain traction so I can get away from him.

"Get the fuck back here! You thought you could run away from me, huh? You little bitch, I've given you everything!"

A hand is wrapping in my hair and dragging me up.

"I'm sorry!" I yell. I don't even know why the hell I said it. I'm not sorry. I'm not fucking sorry at all. But my survival instincts are persevering.

"Oh, you're going to be fucking sorry," he mutters, dragging me into the bathroom. I've no idea what he has planned for me, but fuck if I'm going to let it happen.

"Fuck you," I spit. My body goes completely limp, becoming dead weight on his arms. The sudden weight is unexpected, causing him to stumble. Before he can continue pulling me, I twirl around, ripping out hair in the process, and kick him in his balls. I always thought it'd be Mako on the receiving end of that one, but once again, I was proven wrong when it comes to that man.

"Bitch!" he screams, immediately hunching over and wheezing out a harsh breath. My foot snaps up, and I kick him in the forehead, snapping his head backward. He grunts and falls to the floor. Heart pounding, I scramble to my feet and run for the stairs. The adrenaline rushing through my veins is reaching toxic levels, leaving me breathless.

"Get back here!" he yells, his voice gargled and crazed. Too scared to look back, I keep running, reaching the stairs and nearly throwing myself down them. Ryan's heavy footfalls sound from behind me. He's close. Too fucking close. The kitchen is closer than the front door, and he's right on my heels. It'll take too long to open the door. Pivoting quickly, I careen towards the kitchen at full speed. As I turn into the kitchen, Ryan's hand whispers across my arm, barely missing me.

I head straight for the knives. I've been planning for this moment, just not like this. This was supposed to happen when he was sleeping, and I had the advantage. But I'm not about to fucking let this moment go to waste. Not when I can finally get my revenge.

I reach the knives right as Ryan's arms circle around my waist and yank me back. My fingers are already closed around the handle, causing the drawer to rip out of the slot and onto the ground. Silverware and knives scatter across the floor. A spike of excitement ignites inside of me when I see all of the things I could use to kill him, only an arm's length away.

So close.

The monster behind me lifts my body up, my stomach plummeting from the weightlessness, and then slams me onto the floor, the back of my head smacking off the tiled floor. Everything in me seizes. My breath, my heart, and my vision.

I'm frozen on the floor as I slowly try to regain my breath. My vision creeps back in, revealing Ryan standing over me, heaving for breath like a pissed-off bull with a rider on its back. His fists curl and uncurl, in and out, seemingly trying to reign in some semblance of control.

My eyes slide to his, and I can only imagine how I look to him. "Are you going to kill me, Ryan?" I taunt through gritted teeth, glaring at him intensely. I've never hated anyone so much in my life.

Fuck Barbie, or Billy, or any of the slimy men that took advantage of my innocent body. Those men owed me *nothing*. And at least Barbie never made me love her. At least she never gave me any semblance of hope that *she'd* love *me*.

This devil of man built me up just to destroy me. Made me love him and told me the lies of loving me back. Gave me a comfortable life where I could want for nothing. Told me he wanted a future with the rundown girl from Shallow Hill with baggage strapped to her back and a jaded attitude.

He reached his hand into my chest cavity, pulled out my heart, and ate it for dinner. This was fucking personal.

Spiders of black ink slowly bleed into his eyes until I'm staring at a man possessed by a demon. His top lip curls into a snarl, and he studies me like a lion would a gazelle.

"I haven't decided what I want to do with you yet," he says, eyeing my body up and down as if he's cataloging exactly where and how he's going to inflict pain.

I lift up on my elbows, meeting his eyes despite the fact that I'm dizzy and on the verge of blacking out. Even with everything closing in on me, I refuse to cower. "Are you mapping out where you're going to hurt me?" I push, baring my teeth. "There's not an inch of my body you haven't already damaged."

Narrowing his eyes, he bends over and heaves me up by my biceps. My body is dead weight, making it more challenging to lift me effortlessly like he planned. This only enrages him more, which in turn, gives me more satisfaction. I spit in his face, and the moment he flinches away and lifts his hands to wipe it off, I headbutt him.

I've no fucking idea how to headbutt properly, but assuming since my adrenaline has risen to dangerous levels, I hardly feel it. His head snaps back, blood spurts from his nose and across my cheek, and it feels like I've won the fucking lottery. High off his pain, I kick in his kneecap before he can regain composure.

When he falls to his knees with a grunt, a rush of calmness settles over me. It feels like my whole life has led me to this moment. All the abuse, all the men acting like they own my body, has finally come to fruition.

Ryan's pain-filled cursing and threats fade to the background, becoming white noise. I become weightless, my body floating through the air. With serenity, I bend over and flutter my hand over the assortment of knives on the ground, taunting him on which knife I'm going to pick. Finally, my hand settles over the biggest knife. When he sees the knife I chose, his eyes widen comically.

I laugh, enjoying his fright.

Scrambling to his feet, he charges towards me, assuming he'll get the upper hand. Like a movie in slow motion, I watch my hand whip out in a perfect arc, the knife sliding across his cheek. I watch as the skin breaks beneath the sharp blade, the blood blooming from the wound and down his face, and I just smile.

He yells, absolutely enraged.

Oh, no. What will he do now that his perfect face has been tarnished forever?

And all I can do is smile.

Shock has frozen him, but the delight keeps my limbs languid and free. I slash the knife once more, the tip of the blade skating across his chest, stopping him in his tracks. He looks down in disbelief, the pain not yet overshadowing the pure shock filtering through his system.

Ever so slowly, his eyes rise to meet mine while his mouth hangs open. I'm not sure I can describe the look that passes on his face. Something akin to what-have-I-gotten-myself-into.

I give him a wicked little smile. "It's my turn to be the punisher."

DRAGGING RYAN'S DEADWEIGHT UP several flights of stairs is something I never prepared for. Working out in the gym would feel like floating in water compared to this. Heaving—and quite embarrassingly—I finally get him into the attic. There are plenty of exposed beams to choose from, with this being the only part of the house unfinished.

I loop a thick rope around the rafter, tie it to Ryan's wrist and use it like a pulley system. Ryan's body lifts until the tips of his toes touch the ground. Sweat drains from my pores profusely as I tie the rope to another wooden beam five feet away. I test the strength of the rope, satisfied when it holds firmly.

I work quickly, covering the area beneath Ryan in towels. Later, I'll have to go to the store for plastic. Unfortunately, we don't keep serial killer-ready items in our house. If there's too much blood, it'll soak through and stain the wood. Removing blood from untreated wood would be... yeah, let's just not get to that point.

My teeth sink into a strip of duct tape, ripping off a few pieces and slapping each one onto the slash in Ryan's chest. I don't know much about the human body, but it doesn't look too deep. Enough that he'd need stitches, not enough to open any vital organs or veins.

Blood drips on the towels slowly. The sight makes me nervous. I wasn't prepared for this yet, but I have no choice now. It's Friday night, and I have until Monday morning to figure out what the hell I'm going to do.

Now that I got him here in front of me, helpless and hurt, there's no stopping me now.

FOR THE SECOND TIME, I'm staring at my phone and contemplating who the hell to call. Only a few short hours ago, I wondered the same exact thing, but in entirely different circumstances. It feels like a lifetime ago since Ryan attacked me, and I strung him up to die.

Once again, I run through my very short list of options. Amelia is out of the question. Mako is a goddamn detective; it'd be laughable to call a cop. I have no other friends or family. No one else to turn to. Except...

Dialing the number before I can change my mind, I repeat history. This time, I'm not sobbing pathetically on my closet floor, naked and afraid. Now I'm freshly showered, still battered but no longer defeated.

"River?! Oh my God, are you okay?" Alison's frantic voice fills my ear. I smile at her concern. *Sweet Alison.*

"I'm okay," I assure her. Though being "okay" is subjective, I suppose. Am I okay with doing what I just did? I haven't figured that out yet. I was at the time, but now that I'm coming down from the adrenaline rush, panic is starting to set in a little.

But did you die, River? No. Can't say I did.

"Where are you? Did he hurt you? Let me come get you." She's nearly hysterical, and I almost forget myself and ask why. While I know Alison endured years of abuse at the hands of Ryan, it didn't occur to me until now that she might've had to fight for her life.

Like I just did.

"How about I come to you?" I suggest instead. I don't want to spend another minute in this house right now. It's too loud in here. Sitting alone with my thoughts as I process what the hell I just did will only cause a mental breakdown. I need to decompress and step away from the situation so I can figure out what the hell I'm going to do.

She pauses, seemingly thrown off by my tranquility and having the option to leave. When with Ryan, there are no other options. No, no. There's only listening to instructions.

"Y-yeah," she stutters, after leaving the question hanging a bit too long.

"I'll be there soon," I say, hanging up before she can say or ask anything else. I've no idea what the hell I'm going to tell Alison. She's undoubtedly going to ask questions. Obviously, she's going to ask a lot of fucking questions. Last time she heard from me, I was sobbing on the phone, pleading for her to come save me.

Stupid, River.

I don't know what I was thinking.

I don't need saving. I never did.

Eighteen
River

"I'M SORRY I CALLED you a bitch."

Alison looks up at me, her brow puckered with confusion. We're sitting on her guest bed, facing each other, and stewing in awkward silence. Neither of us knew what to say.

I drove Ryan's car to an abandoned lot in Shallow Hill, then got on a bus to get back in town and walked to Alison's house. She only lives a fifteen-minute walk from home, thankfully.

I'm still not sure how I'm going to handle Ryan's disappearance, but I figured getting rid of his car immediately would be the safest option. And leaving it in Shallow Hill leaves a wide range of possibilities on what happened to him.

I met Alison at her front door, quiet and reserved but no worse for wear. I don't think she knows how to act.

Attempting to escape from Ryan isn't something you just… *walk away from*. Maybe limp or crawl, but certainly not walk. And you sure as hell aren't going to do it as if you're a model walking down the runway.

"When did you call me a bitch?"

"In my head." I pause. "Several times."

Her lush mouth curves into a smile, and she shakes her head with amusement. "It's okay, I was defensive over him too, even up until I finally got away."

I shrug a shoulder, not accepting the out she's giving me. "You were trying to help, and I convinced myself you were the villain. Worst of all, you repeatedly told me about your own pain with him, and I chose not to believe you. There's enough victim blaming in this world, and I'm sorry I became one of those people."

Something like gratitude fills Alison's eyes. I look away, not knowing how to even process that response. It makes me uncomfortable. This whole situation does, as a matter of fact. Never in my life have I ran to anyone for help—not until Ryan came into my life. I've broken the unspoken promise to myself several times. Starting with Mako when Billy nearly killed me, and now with Alison, where I... I can't think about that right now.

"So, what about Ryan?" she asks, noting my discomfort. "He doesn't let go easily. The only reason I got away was because he thought me and Mako were sleeping together."

My world pauses on its axis, and my heart stutters like a stubborn engine finally dying. "You and Mako were sleeping together?"

Her eyes widen, and she waves her hands in front of her in a *backup* motion. "No, no, not at all. Mako helped me get away from Ryan. At one point, I had wanted to... but Mako didn't return those feelings, and I'm honestly glad for it. Being removed from Ryan's life completely is exactly what I needed to heal."

What, does this man have some fucking hero savior complex?

"I'm glad he helped get you away," I say sincerely. Really, I am. There's not a lot of men in this world who would go to the lengths Mako does to get them away from an abusive relationship.

She smiles at me shyly. "And now he's helping you."

I quirk an eyebrow. "I'm not telling Ryan that I fucked his brother."

Even though I came close to doing exactly that.

Red blooms across her cheeks, her face turning into mortification.

"That wasn't what I did." She laughs nervously. "When I broke it off with Ryan, I decided to have Mako there in case Ryan tried to attack me. And that's precisely what happened. Mako stopped it and Ryan made assumptions. And well, neither of us corrected him, to be honest. It was an easy out after that. Ryan looked at me as if I was the Bubonic Plague, and just like that"—she snaps her fingers— "he no longer wanted anything to do with me. I was free."

Huh.

Maybe I could've considered that route if I hadn't done what I did already. That probably would've been a lot less messy.

"I don't think Ryan's going to be an issue for me anymore," I say distractedly, my stare far away as I picture a scene in front of me—Mako dressed in white armor and deflecting Ryan's punch with a sword. It's comically arousing, to be quite honest.

"What do you mean?" Her question draws me back to reality. It takes my brain a second to catch up and even longer to process the question. What does she mean, what do you mean? "Why wouldn't Ryan be a problem anymore?" she prompts when I stare at her with confusion.

Ah, fuck. I said that out loud.

My heart pounds as I try to figure out how the hell to answer this. Do I say Ryan left me for his secretary? No, she'd never believe that. Ryan doesn't just let go of his possessions, even when he's grown tired of them. Keeping his victims under his trap means less of a chance of us coming out and ruining his reputation.

Funny how he was so scared of *me* ruining his reputation when he set himself up for that all by himself. Scorned women don't forget.

"I killed him."

You dumb bitch, River.

I close my eyes in resignation, frustrated that I can't keep my trap shut. I need to tell her that it was a lie. I didn't mean it—I only *want* to. She'd understand that, wouldn't she? Yet, something inside of me doesn't allow my mouth to open and take it back.

I keep my eyes closed, waiting for the bombardment of questions and hysteria, maybe a few *why would you do that*-s and *you must confess*-es. The last thing I expect is to feel soft lips brush across my own. My eyes pop wide open in astonishment. And there she is. Her sweet little face—so close she looks like a cyclops—angled opposite of mine as she kisses me softly.

I don't respond right away, instead staring at her conjoined eye as I try to process that Alison is actually kissing me. She peeks open an eye— or maybe both, I can't tell—but doesn't pull away. I like that she's bold enough not to pull away. I like that she's waiting for me to register the kiss first before deciding how to react. And I like that she's kissing me.

Gently, I kiss her back, moving my lips against hers sensually. Eyes locked in a strange, intimate gaze, our lips explore slowly. Something like relief makes her eyes droop, and just like yawning after someone else, my eyes start to fall, too.

Within seconds, both of our eyes are closed tight as our mouths grow bold. The first touch of her tongue against mine feels like satin on fire. Her hands slide into my mane of curls, while one of my hands wrap around the back of her neck and beckons her closer.

It feels different. Good. Amazing, actually. Unlike anything I've felt before. I won't dare compare it to the feelings Mako elicits in my body and soul. No, not when this feels amazing in a completely different way. It doesn't feel like two souls colliding and falling in love—it feels like healing.

I make the first move, pushing it to see how far this will go. My hand grips her thigh, pausing for only a moment before slowly traveling upwards until I meet the juncture of her hip. A soft moan reaches my tongue. I almost smile in response. The notion is completely wiped from my thought process the second I feel her hand slide down my chest and cup my breast.

My nipple instantly tightens into a sharp bud, and that's all the encouragement both of us need. Everything happens quickly. Our clothes are thrown off in a rush, and my naked body is sliding atop hers. Our hands are touching everywhere, silk undulating against silk as the passion starts to overwhelm us.

She flips me over, surprising me with her dominance. Her soft body slides against mine, and I relish in the feeling of her skin against mine. The ends of her hair tickle my shoulders as she leans over me. She leans down and softly kisses my lips once more. The kiss doesn't linger. Her lips move down my chin and neck, licking and sucking as she travels further south.

She pauses long enough to lick at one of my nipples, enveloping the rose pink bud in her mouth. I moan, arching my back into her touch. With a *pop*, she lets go of my nipple and continues her path. Her pink tongue pokes out, the tip trailing along my flat stomach, dipping into my navel and finally to my pussy.

I'm not ashamed of how drenched I am. Alison is hot, there's no denying it. When she settles between my legs, I lift up on an elbow, too fascinated by her not to give myself a complete view. She peeks up at me through hooded eyes. Such innocence.

I never thought I'd use the word, but it's the only thing I can think when looking down at her, mouth poised over my pussy. *Beautiful.* I'm taking back the meaning of that word and giving it to Alison Lancaster.

Because, *fuck*, she is beautiful.

The first touch of her tongue makes my head fall back. It's tentative, warm, *wet*. It feels incredible, and I need more.

"Alison," I gasp, when her tongue flattens, and she licks the entire expanse of my center. I shudder, rolling my hips to meet her sinful mouth. When my head falls forward once more, and I give her my eyes again, she's already looking up at me with a little satisfied smirk on her face.

My lip is trapped beneath my teeth so hard, I'm close to breaking the skin. She keeps licking and sucking until the orgasm is building quickly, cresting and eventually pushing me over the edge. My legs trap her head against my pussy, happy to drown her in my juices as I ride out the wave of euphoria.

She lifts up, licking her lips like a wicked little witch. I pull her up and keep guiding her until her pussy is hovering over my face. Without hesitation, I lap her up, giving her the same treatment she gave me. It doesn't take long for her to come, screaming my name as her own juices slide down my cheeks.

We become a blur of movement afterwards. I lift up and nearly tackle her. Our kissing is revived, the desperation in our tongues palpable.

I don't even realize we've fallen into the perfect position until I feel my pussy slide against hers. We both freeze, mouths parted and eyes wide as the sensation completely overloads our system. In tandem, we both release moans. Her eyes roll as my hips do, creating a feeling so powerful and wanton, I'm not sure how I'll find my way down from it.

She lifts on her elbows just as I lean towards her, our lips finding the same sync our hips are moving in.

"River," she moans into my mouth, letting me taste my name on her tongue. It tastes sweet, just like her. Our mouths break, and her breath skitters across my nipple. The sensation of her warm mouth wrapping around the bud nearly sends me over the edge. Looking down at her, her hazel eyes look back up at me between a freckled nose. Her eyes glitter with excitement, despite the innocence on her face.

My eyes threaten to close as I moan her name in return. My hips move faster, and her mouth falls away from my breast, searching for my mouth once more. I'm all too happy to give in to her silent demand.

Sweat breaks across my forehead as I feel my second orgasm building higher and higher, the pitch in our moans following suit.

My core clenches as the coil wounds tighter and tighter until it feels like I'm going to spontaneously combust. Within seconds, our orgasms peak, and we're spiraling out of control. Our hands grapple desperately as we try to find something solid to hold onto as our bodies are completely swept away in waves of pure bliss. Wide eyes locked together while moans are ripped from our connected mouths.

It isn't until I come down that I realize we were practically screaming. The sudden silence is deafening, despite our heavy breathing piercing the stillness.

We just had sex.

Because I told her I killed Ryan.

I roll off her and onto my back, both our chests heaving. Both our eyes staring at the ceiling in shock and disbelief. And maybe a little panic. Finally, I look over and study her. I really take in her big expressive eyes, long chestnut hair, and the tiny freckles dotting her nose and cheeks.

My eyes travel down her body. A body that I got very well acquainted with. She's thin but curvy with full breasts and long legs. Freckles dot her shoulders and stomach, light brown against a tanned backdrop.

She's beautiful. And a lot more complex of a girl than I gave her credit for.

She doesn't meet my eyes, seemingly too scared to face the reality of what we have just done. It feels like a needle that pricks at my heart. Nothing major, but enough to hurt.

"Do you regret it?" she whispers, her voice hoarse. Tears well in her eyes, and I study her reaction with a morbid fascination. Is she crying because I fucked her or because I killed her ex-boyfriend?

"No," I whisper, answering both questions.

A harsh breath releases from her chest, expelling all the tension in her body with it. Just like that, she turns to putty. And just like that, my heart warms again, relieved that she isn't rejecting me. She turns on her side, facing me completely and tucking both hands under her cheek.

"Me neither," she says softly. A small tentative smile graces her swollen lips.

With my eyes locked to those lips, I ask, "Then why are you crying?"

She chuckles, wiping away a stray tear before resuming her position.

"I honestly don't know. That was... a lot to take in. And the fact that we basically celebrated you murdering our abuser by having sex is kind of fucked up." When I give her a droll look, she smiles sheepishly and corrects herself. "Okay, *really* fucked up." She shrugs a shoulder. "But it felt good. It felt like closure."

I nod, comforted that we're on the same page. What we did wasn't making love, or even simple fucking. We're certainly never going to date. While there was mutual attraction, it was honestly just moving on from a fucked-up situation we both got trapped in. Two souls connecting over something no woman should ever have to endure. It was liberation.

"Are you going to report me?" I ask quietly.

Her eyes never stray as she says, "No. You gave yourself and the future women who would've found themselves in Ryan's grip something I wasn't capable of giving. He was never going to stop. Mako tried to, but no one believed him, and Ryan knew too many powerful people. And I... I didn't try enough. But you succeeded."

"Freedom," I whisper. She slowly nods her head, understanding in her eyes.

It's been so long since I've tasted it on my tongue. It's almost enough to overpower the taste of Alison's pussy on my tongue.

THE HOUSE IS DEADLY silent.

Well. *This* part of the house is. Faint tendrils of yelling filter through the vents from the attic, but if I think loud enough, I can't hear them. Sometimes I enjoy hearing them. I don't know if that makes me a psychopath.

With my breeding, I suppose it was inevitable.

How many serial killers had fucked up childhoods? Probably more often than not. I'd fit the profile perfectly. Girl grows up in the slums, crackhead mother, absent no-name father, and raped by men, which eventually led to a life of prostitution.

But I got out, didn't I? Doesn't that count for something? Even if I did turn into a murderer. Or I will soon enough, at least.

A knock on the door seizes my heart. I tuck myself deep into the shadows, staring at the silhouette of a person standing outside the door.

I'm not expecting anyone. No one should be knocking on that door.

Another light knock taunts me. My rabid thoughts lead me down the rabbit hole. What if it's Ryan's work, looking for him? No, no. It's Saturday. He's only been in the attic since last night. Monday, though. What will I do on Monday? Ryan won't show up. His dad will wonder, call him probably.

Ryan won't answer, and then his father will come looking. How the hell am I supposed to look Matt in his face and lie to him? Guess I should've thought about that before I got myself into this clusterfuck.

Another knock pulls me away from that train of thought.

Is it the police? Did Ryan get a hold of a phone? No… I hid his phone in our bedroom already. It couldn't be that. Just a minute ago, I checked on him, ensuring his body was securely hung up around the wooden beam and the knots around his wrists were still tight. He didn't escape, and I'm confident no one can hear him yelling. We live in a mansion, for god's sake, and the attic isn't even located on the side of the house closest to the street. Surely, if someone could hear screams coming from inside the house, someone would've saved me already.

I laugh at that thought. People suck. It's entirely possible no one would've saved me.

"Hello?" a soft voice rings out. My head snaps in the direction of the front door. It sounds like the devil. It must be. Who else could it be? The devil has come to collect me, for the ultimate sin I've committed.

My breath disturbs the silence in short staccato stabs of air. I pinch my eyes shut when the knocking at my front door starts again. Maybe if my eyes are closed, the knocking will go away. Maybe the devil behind it will disappear.

Shaking my head, I rub my eyelids with my pointer finger and thumb in frustration.

The devil isn't going away.

My house is bathed in darkness and shadows, but I feel like I'm standing in a spotlight. Like an idiot, I'm standing directly in front of the door, at a loss of what to do. I thump my coiled fist into my forehead, frustrated with myself. I wasn't prepared for this. For *any* of this. I thought

I had more time. Stupid of me to think I had something as precious as time, when living with a monster.

What do I do, what do I do, what do I do?

Answer it.

No. I'll never escape if I do.

What other option do I have? Hide?

Maybe it'll work for a little while, but the devil will come back for me. Facing my demons head on, is the only way.

Breathe lodges in my throat when I hear the voice. "I know you're in there, I can see you."

Fuck. That's creepy. That's literally the last thing anyone would want to hear.

Whose idea was it to get a door that's nearly all glass? Of course, it's frosted, but the design also has clear ribbons woven in, giving the outsider a tiny peek inside.

I'm caught. There's no turning back now.

Slowly, I make my way to the door, my bare feet lightly slapping across the wooden floor. Standing in front of the door, I just stare, praying that they'll give up and leave. Another knock has me jumping out of my skin, this time loud and impatient. *Jesus, was that really fucking necessary?* My hand shakes as I raise it to the doorknob.

Just fucking open it.

So, I do. My gaze immediately drops down.

"Girl Scout cookies?"

Yup, still the fucking devil.

CRUNCH.

"You're a fucked up bitch, you know that?" Ryan pants from his spot. He's bloodied and bruised, his arms hanging from the ceiling with a rope. He's naked save for a dirty pair of boxers hanging low on his hips. Minor cuts mark his skin, most already caked with dried blood. Fresh blood trickles down his arms from the wounds around his wrists. I stare at it in fascination as I nibble on my cookie.

My other hand spins around the box cutter I've been using to slice open his skin. Each scream gives me a small thrill. Is this what he felt when he lorded his power over me? When he beat and raped me? I admit it can be quite the high.

I hold out the cookie, my arm straight with one eye closed as I position the cookie over Ryan's head. "You know, you both are the devil," I murmur, concentrating on getting the image just right. I smile when I do, so it looks like a man with a cookie for a head. "You. And these cookies."

"Hey!" he shouts, spittle flying from his lips. "Fucking listen to me!" My arm drops and my eyes travel back to his. They're wide with adrenaline, potent fear and rage swirling in his ugly blue eyes. If looks could kill...

Crunch.

Fuck. These are addicting.

"Are you going to explain to me why the fuck you're doing this? Huh? Fucking tell me, River!"

I arch a brow, unimpressed. "Last time I checked, I don't have to answer a goddamn thing if I don't want to. And oh, I almost forgot to tell you." I snap my fingers at him, shooting him the gun signal with a filthy smile. "I fucked your ex-girlfriend."

His eyes widen briefly before they shrink into slits. "You're lying."

I chuckle and shake my head. "She's got a freckle right here"—I point right above my hip— "and a freckle right here," I say, pointing to my left inner thigh next, upwards close to my center. His eyes bore holes into my hand, his lip curling in disgust as he seethes. Anyone could've seen the freckle on her hip, but the freckle on her thigh? Well, I would've had to see her naked for that one.

His whole body begins to shake as his fury begins to overwhelm him.

"She's awfully good, too," I chirp. "Came harder than I ever came with you."

"Shut the fuck up!" he roars, attempting to charge at me. Hard to do when only your toes are touching the plastic-covered floor. Which, by the way, is slick with his blood. He doesn't find purchase despite his comical attempts. In the end, he ends up flailing like one of those inflatable things outside of car dealerships.

I laugh, and he grows angrier.

"Let me go right fucking now, River!" he roars, letting his body sink with defeat, though his attitude certainly hasn't caught up yet.

"No!" I shout back, dropping the box of cookies and storming towards him. I put my face as close to his as I can that's within a safe distance. "I'm done listening to you. I don't *have* to do a fucking thing for you anymore. You have no power. Not anymore. *I* have the power and it's about time you realize that, you son of a bitch," I spit.

His chest pumps in tandem with mine. Frustrated tears fill his eyes. I cock my head, fascination once more taking over.

"You're crying," I observe. Reaching a hand up, I let one of his tears drop onto my fingertip. He jerks his head away when he realizes what I'm doing. "I've never seen something so beautiful in my life," I murmur with wonder, holding the tear up to the light.

Beautiful. I'm starting to like that word.

He ignores me, and instead tries to manipulate me. "I loved you, River," he pleads, his voice wobbly and tight. "I took care of you."

"You did love me," I concede. "But you don't know how to separate love from hate. Because you hated me, too, Ryan. You hate all women. You beat me, stripped me of any self-love and worth, and then spit in my face." His bottom lip trembles.

I get as close to his hateful eyes as possible, a burning feeling rising in me. Something like anger, or even sadness. "Do you know what the worst part is?" I ask softly, my eyes stinging with tears.

He clenches his jaw, refusing to answer.

"I *defended* you. I told them they were wrong for seeing the truth in you when all I tried to do was see the best in you."

I inch closer, a hot tear trailing down my cheek.

"It was *me* that was wrong."

"Fuck you," he spits.

I cock my head, genuinely curious. "Tell me, Ryan. Why are you the way you are? You have loving parents, a beautiful home, a great job, money, a girlfriend who would've done anything for you. Why? Why, why, why, why?"

He shakes his head frantically, "Stop it! Just… just fucking stop! I *don't* have anything. You want to know why, River? You're not the only one who was raped when they were young, okay?" My heart freezes. My breath stills.

"By who?" I choke out.

His face is nearly purple, rage potent in his face and words. In his very being. Ryan *is* rage. He's made of it.

"Daddy dearest."

I close my eyes as my heart splinters. Despite how much I loathe Ryan, tears spring to my eyes anyway. Tears of heartbreak for the little boy. I know all too well how it feels to be betrayed by your own flesh and blood.

All too well.

"Matt?" I ask, my voice hoarse. I don't know why I asked. He doesn't have another father. But Matt? Sweet, boisterous Matt? The same man who always has a smile on his face. Who's always laughing and so, so kind? It doesn't compute in my brain.

I had once said that Matt had somehow held onto his morals, despite being a notorious lawyer.

It seems I was wrong.

"Yes, *Matt*," he fumes, spitting out his name like a curse. "That vile piece of shit was sucking my dick at eight years old. And some fucked up part of me thought it was normal. And then *Mako* came along. He started beating me then. I wasn't like Mako, so I was punished for it. He was the golden child. The one Dad refused to touch because he knew Mako would tell. Mako didn't take shit from anybody, and I was the weak, little boy who got fucked every night."

Tears track down my cheeks.

I get it. I get Ryan's hatred that has consumed his heart and soul. I get his hatred for Mako. Why he feels the need to assert power over women. He has felt powerless his entire life, and his revenge was to make other people feel like he did. He wants everyone else to suffer for the shitty hand he was dealt.

It's wrong. Disgusting. But *I get it*.

"Are you sorry for how you treated me?" I inquire softly. "For making me feel like how your father made you feel?"

Right as I ask the question, I also ask myself if I will let him go if he says yes. Now that I understand Ryan for the first time, I'm scared of what I'll do.

He mulls over my question, burning rage still lit in his eyes. After a moment, Ryan speaks. "I enjoyed every single second of it, River. I will never be sorry. Women are weak and powerless. If I had to suffer for being those things, then so do all of you. I refuse to be sorry for that."

No wonder why his blue eyes were always so dull. He doesn't have a soul left in him. Matt took that from him.

He took everything from Ryan, and now he wants to take everything from me.

"You think I'm weak?" I whisper, confused by his observation—and a little hurt, too. I've been anything but weak.

His eyes turn mocking, but they no longer affect me. Neither do his empty words. "I've hit and raped you, and you keep running back to me, tail tucked between your legs like a good little bitch. You're so, so weak." His body shakes from the building rage. "You're stained, River. No one will ever love a dirty slut that came from Shallow Hill. Especially not one who's had more cocks inside her than a whore in a brothel."

I smile slowly, his words oh so similar to the ones Billy told me not so long ago.

I'm *stained*.

I'm also other things too.

Broken.

Scarred.

Traumatized.

Strong.

Fierce.

Vengeful...

Rising the knife to his chest, I press the blade down and drag, eliciting sweet, sweet moans of pain. He stays still—having already learned that thrashing about only makes the cuts worse. I don't *feel* weak right now. I imagine I feel a lot like how he felt when wringing moans of pain from my mouth.

Leaning forward, I brush my lips across his ear and croon, "Your brother will love me." I pause, the knife still lodged in his flesh when I back up enough to ensnare his eyes in mine. They're wide with shock, and my smile grows in response.

"Alison, Mako... they know what it's like to love a monster. It's much easier to love each other, don't you think?"

Hot breaths puff from his nose as his rage boils over.

"The only thing I'll be stained with is your blood, Ryan. Somehow, I don't think they'll mind that too much."

Nineteen

Mako

THE SUNDAY NEWS IS on. Same old stories. Murders, kidnappings, and more depressing shit with a little dabble of inspo to keep from downright depressing the viewer.

I'm not paying a lick of attention to it. I've been agonizing over my case, and all I've accomplished is giving myself a massive fucking headache. Tomorrow, I'll be meeting with Benedict Davis, revisiting the murder he witnessed. This is the fourth time I've spoken with him, and each time his story changes. He's inconsistent, and if it weren't for the fact that he knows specific details civilians don't have access to, I'd chalk him up to being a liar and drop him.

Even without Benedict Davis and his shoddy story, we're getting closer. Finding the Ghost Killer is just outside of my grasp, so close I can feel it.

My phone buzzes on the armrest next to me and startling me from gazing sightlessly into the TV screen. Not only am I going to be bald, but now I'm going to need bifocals by forty. I glance at it and see a number I haven't seen pop up on my phone in months.

LILY: I miss you, baby. It's been a while since you've visited me. Come over? I'm wearing your favorite outfit. ;)

I sigh. My favorite outfit on her was nothing. Preferably with her face stuffed in the mattress and ass high in the air. Serena always tried to wow me with frilly, lacy lingerie. I never cared for any of it when all I wanted was a quick fuck and to leave.

For some reason, she thought the lingerie would get me to stay rather than developing some sort of personality.

It never did.

I delete the text, and then her number, and stuff the phone in my back pocket. Serena barely held onto my attention in the first place; she has zero chance of getting even a sliver of it now.

Not when a particular woman is occupying my brain space. I knew from the moment I met River that she was going to ruin me. I just hadn't realized it would also feel like damnation.

My phone buzzes in my back pocket again, indicating an incoming call. With a frustrated growl, I fish the phone out of my pocket and answer before looking to see who it is.

"Yeah?" I grunt.

"Hey…" a familiar, hesitant voice filters through.

"Hey, Ali," I greet with a sigh. I don't mind hearing from her, but I already know what this conversation will center around.

"Have you heard from River?" she asks.

"No. Should I have?"

Silence.

"Ali?" I push. When she still doesn't answer right away, fear circulates through my system, and a pit forms in my stomach. Automatically, I fear the worst. It's a feeling I've become quite acquainted with, though we're definitely not on friendly fucking terms.

"I think you should talk to her," she says finally. I don't need to see her to know she's biting her nails. It's a habit Ryan beat her constantly for, before sending her to a nail salon to get acrylics.

"Is she okay, Ali? What happened?" I ask impatiently, my tone darkening. I sit up straight and shut off the news.

"N-nothing. Well... she's okay. She's not hurt or anything," she rushes, stumbling over her words. My brow plummets and my anxiety switches gears. Something is going on—I just have no idea what.

"Did something happen?" I ask slowly, growing aggravated by her lack of explanation. My hand is gripping my hair, on the verge of yanking out the strands.

She sighs with frustration. "Yes, but I think you should talk to her, Mako. Okay? That's all I'm saying."

"Okay," I answer right as my finger taps the red button. My impatience has crested. Being nice is the last thing on my mind when it's too busy imagining all my nightmares coming to life. My mind whirls, considering the ramifications if I just show up at Ryan's house. It's late. He'll probably freak, but I can use the excuse for needing to work on the case. I'm meeting with his witness tomorrow, and I haven't gotten the chance to talk to Ryan about it in a few days.

Mind already made up, I grab my keys and start for the door, barely giving myself enough time to tie the laces on my boots.

I pause halfway through the door, my hand still on the handle. Maybe I should call first? I dial Ryan's number as I shut the door behind me and get in the car. The line rings, and rings, before eventually going to voicemail. I give it one more try, even though I'm already pulling out of the driveway.

Fifteen minutes later, I'm pulling in their expansive, obnoxiously long driveway with the stupid fucking fountain in the middle. I wouldn't be surprised if Ryan builds a monument of himself in the middle one day.

There are a few lights on in the monstrous house. Seeing this house makes my lip curl every fucking time. It's over the top, with sleek white walls, glass, and wood making up the entirety of the house. It's modern and very fucking pretentious.

Fuck. I'm nervous. My hand is sliding through my hair, frustrated with this shit. With Ryan and the constant pain in my ass he's been since I was adopted.

Throwing myself out of the car before I end up tearing out of the driveway, I rush up the steps and knock on the door loudly a few times. Glancing at the time on my watch, I note that it's only eight-thirty. Ryan should still be awake.

When no one answers, I knock a few more times. Sometimes I wish that he'd act like every other rich asshole and hire a butler. I give it all of five seconds before I try the door handle. Locked. There are cameras recording me right now with a feed that I'm positive links to Ryan's phone. I linger for another minute, hoping he'll see that it's me, and open the door.

Yeah fucking right, Mako. Like that's going to happen.

Fuck it. I've been to Ryan's house only three times in my life, but it only took one time to catalog every exit point. I jog around to the back of the house. The backyard consists of an in-ground pool on the edge of a cliff, widening into the kitchen in an open concept. The backside of the house is all glass, the entirety of the wall capable of sliding open until the backyard and kitchen become one. Fucking stupidest thing, if you ask me. Who the fuck is okay with just anyone being able to peer inside their house? The thought sends shivers down my spine.

Quietly creeping up to the door, I peer through the glass and listen for any sounds. Any yelling, screaming. Flesh hitting flesh. There's only silence. No movement, either.

The glass glides open smoothly without a sound, and though it's good for me, I still shake my head in disappointment. So stupid to leave any door unlocked. I see too many goddamn murders for this to be acceptable, and the fact that I'm breaking and entering so easily, is going to earn this fucker an earful. I could be a burglar, and apparently, that's okay with Ryan.

The white and gray kitchen is dim, casting shadows across the pristine kitchen. It's starting to get darker earlier in the day now that fall is approaching. A drawer hangs at an odd angle, catching my attention. I peek in the drawer to see a bunch of knives and silverware haphazardly thrown into it.

I click on the flashlight on my phone and inspect them. None look bloody. It does little to calm my racing thoughts.

I angle the light over the shadows until I'm sure there's not a person hiding in them. Based on the soft gleam from down the hall, there's a lamp on in the living room. I strain my ears, listening for footsteps or voices.

"Ryan?" I call loudly, clicking off the light and stuffing the phone in my back pocket. The last thing I need is to be accused of breaking and entering by an asshole of a lawyer. Ryan would take that opportunity and eat it up like candy.

A muted voice filters through, but I can't place where. As I'm concentrating on the muffled noise, a loud bang from upstairs draws my attention away.

I swear to fucking god, if he just hit her… My body is moving before I can think, rushing through the kitchen and into the hallway. I nearly crash into the wall as I swing myself around the white marble staircase. Nearly tripping up the stairs, I come to a stumbling halt when River's face comes into view. She had just done exactly what I did—almost falling in her rush to come down the stairs.

"What are you doing here?" she yells, just as I yell, "Did he fucking hurt you again?"

"What?" she asks, bewildered. We're both immobilized on each end of the staircase, staring at each other with wild expressions.

"Is he up there? Did he hurt you?" I ask again harshly.

"No—I—he's not here," she stutters. The pounding in my chest slowly calms as my suspicions rise. She looks like she's been caught with a knife over a dead body. Guilty as fuck. Home intruders don't announce themselves. Ryan could've easily invited me over and not told her. So why the fuck does she look green in the face? And why are her eyes shifting with paranoia and nerves?

"What are you doing here?" she snaps again, crossing her arms and widening her stance into a defensive position. Her chin lifts as she stares down her nose at me. Just barely do I curb the urge to question her. I am, after all, breaking into her house. She has every right to be suspicious of me.

"Ryan invited me over," I lie, steeling my spine.

She rolls her eyes. "No, he didn't."

"How do you know?"

"Because he's not even here," she repeats. At that moment, another muffled voice sounds from somewhere. I cock my head, trying to place it.

Noticing my attention is averted, she barrels down the stairs and throws herself on me, cinnamon enveloping all my senses. Stumbling backwards, I grapple with her body and the railing to keep from falling backwards. What the fuck?

"You scared me," she says breathily. "But I'm glad you're here now. Can I come over?"

The look on my face could only be described as utterly baffled.

"What the hell are you hiding, River?" I accuse harshly. She tenses in my arms, immediately pushing me away, and then walks past me as if she didn't just dramatically throw herself at me.

This woman is a fucking... I don't even know what the hell.

"Get out," she orders stoically, all emotion from her voice gone.

Crossing my arms, I widen my stance and cock a brow, letting her know I'm not going anywhere. There's a muffled voice somewhere in the house that sounds like they're yelling, Ryan's mysteriously gone, and River is acting like she's hiding something. She's fidgety, and if I didn't know any better, River is lying. Terribly, at that.

Subtly, I catalog every single detail. Shifty eyes, trembling hands, restless feet, and a small splatter of blood on her neck. The smell of some type of cleaning solution filters through my nose, overpowering her sweet cinnamon scent.

"You know you can tell me," I assure gently, attempting to soften my trembling voice. She did something. She did something very bad.

She snorts. "I can tell a cop anything? Get real, Mako," she replies, her tone dripping with poison and condescension.

"I've already crossed a few lines for you, River."

"You're saying you're dirty?" she challenges.

"Are you saying you're going to give me a reason to be?" I shoot back. Her lips tighten into a thin line. That would be a huge fucking resounding yes. I drop my head back and heave out a harsh breath. "Tell me, River. I swear I will not arrest you or get you in any kind of trouble. You can trust me."

When I lift my head back to her, she's chewing on her bottom lip and looking at me as if she can't decide if I'm Robin Hood or the big bad wolf. I'm not really sure which I am, either. Depends who's asking.

"Alison and I had sex," she blurts. The spit I was swallowing at a very untimely moment lodges in my throat. I choke, coughing as I try not to die before her feet. The evil little sprite would probably enjoy it, too.

The gears in my brain are turning too quickly. The little dude manning my brain is desperately trying to reign them in as I attempt to process what the hell she just said. She smiles at my reaction while I feel my face go red. "Are you blushing?" she teases.

"No. Fuck. Yes. What the fuck? Did you really?" I ask harshly, mostly because I'm actively trying to keep my dick from getting rock hard, which is a really big fucking feat when I can't get the image out of my head.

She nods, and then shrugs indifferently. "Not because we're like, into each other or anything. I think... we just needed it, you know?"

Weirdly, I do. I get it. Her face is arranged into a blank mask, but something tells me she's waiting for me to get mad. She expects it, actually. But how can I be upset at someone for trying to heal? As much as it pains me some days, River's body doesn't belong to me. She can fuck whoever she wants, and I have no say in it. While I'd love nothing more than to have the privilege, I'm not going to hold anything against her when she gives that gift to someone else.

Her lioness eyes study me closely. She's still guarded and on edge, but yet staring at me with tentative hope that I've been completely distracted. It almost worked for a second, but I wouldn't be where I am today if I let the obvious slip by me.

I allow a slow nod. "But that's not what you need to tell me, River."

Her shoulders slump in defeat, disappointed that her little distraction tactic didn't work.

Later, I'll be revisiting that confession. Thoroughly.

"Ryan's upstairs. In the attic." She pauses, seemingly contemplating what else to tell me. I don't tell her I'll force my way into the attic regardless of what story she spins. I'm fully expecting her to lie to me.

"I'm torturing him," she confesses softly.

This time, I was smart enough not to swallow, or I would've choked again. The last fucking thing I was expecting to come out of her mouth was the truth. Was she saying it for shock value, expecting me to think she's lying because the premise is so outrageous? It's possible she expected me to laugh, roll my eyes, and brush it off as a joke.

As much as it pains me, I had already started putting that together, each puzzle piece sliding into place. Ryan's absence, the muffled voice yelling for what sounded like help, River's apparent paranoia... and the blood and smell of cleaning solution.

"River," I groan, rubbing my hand down my face.

"What?" she snaps, giving up all pretense and becoming defensive once again. "He deserves it!"

"It's not that he doesn't, River. But have you actually thought this through? What the fuck are you going to do when people come looking for him? When our *parents* come looking for him? If he doesn't show up for work tomorrow morning, people are going to question why. Have you considered the fact that you're going to be the number one suspect?"

Her face increasingly grows pale as I bombard her with very valid questions. Ryan's too important of a guy for people not to notice him missing.

This time when her shoulders deflate, it's with resignation.

"I have. I'm just not sure what to say yet."

Heaving out another sigh, I look in the direction of the staircase. "I'm going up there."

She takes a step toward me, her eyes bulging. "You can't let him go, Mako," she says hurriedly, her eyes turned feral with desperation.

"I'm not. I promise. But I need to see what you got us into," I explain soothingly, resting my hand on her elbow to help calm her. Her brow dips, and she shoots me a nasty look.

"I didn't get *you* into anything, Mako."

I give her a sardonic smile. "We're in this together, baby."

"WELL, YOU LOOK LIKE a giant pile of dogshit," I comment, my clinical tone matching my face as I examine Ryan's body.

"Fuck you," he spits darkly. For the first time in my life, Ryan was happy to see me when I walked in. That quickly went to shit when I smiled at him, teeth and all.

He's a goddamn bloodied mess. The only thing on his cut up and bruised body is a pair of soiled boxer briefs. Fuck, he smells like shit, too. Wrinkling my nose, I circle around him, noting all his wounds.

Looks like she used something fine and sharp to cut him, like a box cutter. The cuts aren't too deep, some of them needing stitches, especially the large slash across his chest. His entire torso is mottled with bruises— most of them still a dark purple. He hasn't been up here long enough for any of them to turn yellow and green.

His foot looks like it's set at an unnatural angle, though I don't see bone poking through. His pointer finger on his left hand is definitely broken, completely bent at an odd angle with the bone sticking out. I smile when I realize it's the same finger Ryan had broken on River's hand.

That's my girl.

I glance at her hand, noting her casted pointer finger, and then drag my eyes up to the rest of her. It looks like she's just stepped out of a boxing ring. She has fresh bruises on her arms and around her neck, a cut on her brow and a fat lip. All at the hands of someone who claimed to love her. Her ribs and concussion are healed by now, but the lingering effects in her mind will never disappear.

This woman has gone through more shit than most can even handle in their lifetime. And she's gone through it her entire life. I don't think I've met someone so resilient. So strong. What she's doing to Ryan… it's fucking insane. Certifiably insane. But considering what she's been through, fuck, I can't blame her. I can't fault her for finally snapping.

"Please, Mako. You're a cop. You're a *good* cop. Don't let this bitch get away with this shit. Please, let me go," he pleads, his voice cracking at the end.

This is the first time I've ever seen Ryan scared. Vulnerable. He's always played this tough guy act, even when he was ten and I was thirteen, newly adopted into the family. It was like he felt he had to prove himself when I came into the picture. Mommy and Daddy decided to have another son, so he thought he wasn't good enough for them. The guy was a fucking selfish narcissist since birth. There's no changing him. No saving him.

"Why should I help you? You've done nothing but go out of your way to make my life miserable since I came into the picture," I say, posting up behind him where he can't see me. He attempts to turn his head to look at me, but his binds won't allow him much leeway.

"You never belonged, Mako."

River steps forward, her brow pinched with anger. "All this time, I thought you hated him because he *did* something to you. Why would you make me—anyone—believe that?"

Ryan laughs humorlessly. "Does it fucking matter? He's my *brother*," he spits the word with disdain.

"Am I?" I question with mirth, chuckling when he tries to swing his heated glare to me. Doesn't work very well. Such an angry soul, and for what? To end up tied up and tortured because he can't help being a shitty human? And then to have the brother he bullied mercilessly refuse to help because of his actions.

Ryan is getting well acquainted with Karma, and *goddamn*, is she a bitch.

I come around to face him once more and crouch down, the smile never leaving my face as I say, "Never treated me like one. I was excited to get a brother when our parents adopted me. But you always took it as an insult."

"Because it was!" he shouts, shaking in his binds. "They were never going to have another kid. They said I was *enough* for them. We were perfectly fucking happy without you, but then Dad handled your father's murder case, and he just had to grow a soft spot for you. He just couldn't let you stay in the system like every other fucking kid in this country. What's so special about you, huh? You're a mediocre detective that can't even figure out who the Ghost Killer is. *You're* not good enough for *us*."

His words bounce off me like rubber on wood. I can't be hurt by someone that I never truly cared about. I tried at one point. I tried so hard to build a relationship with him and create an unbreakable bond between brothers.

But he just wanted to hate me. It didn't take long before I stopped caring enough to stop him. He tortured me, hurt me, and made my childhood miserable.

He didn't want me as brother before, and he's certainly not going to fucking get one now.

"I HAVE A CONFESSION," River blurts. I stare at her, filled with trepidation and unease. I can't take anymore confessions from her. I've had enough to last several fucking lifetimes—that's if I'm not burning in hell for what we're doing. We're in the living room, sitting on the same couch that River was stuck on not so long ago, humiliated with tears streaking down her face. When this is all over, I'm going to burn this fucking couch.

"Matt raped Ryan," she forges on before I can voice any protests.

My world stops on its axis, causing everything to come to a crashing halt. There's no fucking way I heard that right. There's just no way she said… No. No, no, no. No way.

"The fuck did you just say?" I ask darkly. She heaves a weighted sigh. Her face is pinched with regret. Her blood-stained fingers fidget, her stare pinned to the twirling digits. She can't even look at me.

Matt saved me. He's my father. I *love* him. And that's being ripped away from me right now.

"Ryan told me. I asked him why he turned out the way he did when he had everything in life. And Mako… I don't think he was lying. It honestly didn't feel like he was."

I rub a shaking hand fiercely down my face, trying to rub away the words she's spoken. My hand glides into my hair and grips tightly. My chest tightens painfully, making it hard to breathe. My vision swims, and it takes everything in me to hold onto reality. I'm losing my shit. I'm losing a lot more than that.

"I'm really sorry, Mako," she whispers. I nod my head distractedly, not actually hearing her. It feels like water is rushing through my ears, drowning more softly spoken apologies that don't mean shit right now. It's not River's fault, but I almost hate her for telling me. Now I have to live with this new reality.

My father is a fucking rapist.

He never laid a hand on me. Never gave any indication he felt that way towards me. A slew of memories flash through my mind. How much Ryan hated me. The world. How angry he was. And how anytime Dad would try to hug Ryan or show any affection, Ryan rejected it like he was being stung by a nest of hornets. Little things that never made sense are adding up.

I close my eyes.

I guess I'm not as good at putting together puzzle pieces as I had originally thought. My brother was the biggest piece of all, right in my face. And I never suspected a thing. Guilt slams into my chest.

"Let's focus on the matter at hand right now. I—I'll worry about that later," I rasp.

River bites her lip and nods her head, reluctantly agreeing.

"Ryan's cheating on you," I start.

Disdain crosses her face as she asks harshly, "You knew?"

I couldn't keep the shame off my face if I tried. Telling her Ryan's cheating on her wasn't said as a confession, but more as the beginning of the story we're going to spin, yet she caught me before I could finish.

"You didn't tell me?" she accuses, her eyes flaring with fury. Her cheeks flush strawberry red, and all I can manage is flapping my mouth like a fucking fish, at a loss of what to say.

"It wasn't my place, River. I thought the hitting part was a little more concerning than Ryan being a player," I defend.

"When?" she demands sharply. "How long ago did you find out?"

"I saw him cheating not too long after you met our parents," I confess on a weighted sigh. This is not where I was trying to go with this, but I won't lie to her, either. "But River... he's always cheated, and I don't mean with just you. He gave Alison chlamydia after a couple of years together. I should've told you, but as I said, I was more concerned about your safety."

She looks away, hurt radiating in her eyes. It bothers me that I caused that.

"So, why tell me now?" she asks, her tone having dropped several degrees and is now ice cold.

I scratch the back of my head, a sheepish look on my face. "I wasn't, really. I was trying to get our story together, and Ryan being a cheater is going to play a big role in our cover-up."

This time when her cheeks turn red, it's from embarrassment.

"Oh."

"I'm sorry, River," I start, feeling worse by the second that I didn't tell her the truth about Ryan cheating from the beginning.

"That was what made me want to leave him," she says abruptly, glancing at me sideways. "Just like every cliché, I found lipstick on his collar and it smelled like perfume. He had tried to wash it off. Realizing that he was fucking someone else is what finally made me want to leave."

I'm not sure if she's telling me this to make me feel worse, but it fucking works. My head thumps against the back of the couch, and I sigh with defeat. If I would've told her sooner… maybe she wouldn't have felt like she had to do what she did. She would already be gone, living her life away from him. But Ryan would still be here, already searching for his next victim.

"I'm sorry," I repeat.

"So, this cover-up story?" she prompts, swiftly changing the subject.

Reluctantly, I allow it. "He said he had a work-related trip in the next town over. That was the last you've seen of him."

She nods her head once. "What happens when they figure out he didn't?"

"That's where his cheating comes in. He could've easily left to see another woman. You're none the wiser of his cheating ways and completely believed him when he said he had to leave for work. If you know he's cheating, that can be seen as motive. If you fought and he stormed out on you, that makes you look guilty. As far as you're concerned, you two were a happy little couple with no problems."

"Okay," she agrees. I shake my head, already feeling a weight slamming down on top of the other fifty pounds on my shoulders.

"He was leaving to meet with his mistress. The Ghost Killer got to him first."

River stills, her entire body becoming stone. It reminds me of her reaction when I first told her about the Ghost Killer, the day I came over to hash out the case with Ryan and ended up eating meatloaf.

My mother used to make me meatloaf. She cooked it horribly, but it was the only thing she knew how to make, really. That's all I ate for twelve years. I haven't been able to eat it since. Of course, my asshole of a brother knew that and decided to shove it right back into my face.

"How did you get that idea?" she asks softly, bringing my attention back to her. I'm not sure what it is precisely about the Ghost Killer that makes her uneasy, but I can't exactly blame her. His reputation has gained enough attention now that it's national news. Being in the same town as a serial killer would make anyone uncomfortable.

"Friday morning, Ryan called me and said he knew who the Ghost Killer is and already built his case against him. He claimed he found evidence and would have the killer in jail by Monday. He didn't share what the information was, but he was confident he caught him. He spent ten minutes rubbing in my face that he figured out who the Ghost Killer was before I did."

River's face pales, her frown deepening as I share something I can't help but be ashamed about. That my brother caught the Ghost Killer before I did. He knew, and the only way I can think of is because he was doing something seedy. The Ghost Killer has law enforcement and lawyers in his pocket. I just don't think anyone ever knew his face until Ryan.

The memory of that phone call pisses me off all over again. The second Ryan hung up the phone, I nearly broke my knuckles on the metal table in the interrogation room. I wanted the Ghost Killer found, no matter what the cost was, but fuck if it didn't sting that Ryan was the one to solve the case. His confidence was so unwavering that I believed him.

"We're going to spin it to where the Ghost Killer knew Ryan had evidence against him and got rid of him," I continue.

River shifts, curling her knees to her chest and wrapping her arms around them tightly. She rests her chin on her knees and stares at me with sadness.

"We'll get him to talk," she assures softly.

I shake my head, sliding my hand through my hair. I'm not holding out hope that Ryan will talk. If I know anything about my brother, it's that he's a hateful, evil person. Not telling me who the man is that I've been chasing for a year now will be his only victory.

I go over the rest of the plan with her, making sure she understands the part she will have to play really soon. As much as it kills me, River can never be seen as the abused girlfriend, at least not until there's a sufficient amount of evidence to show the Ghost Killer got to Ryan. Anything to keep the motive off of River is a top priority right now, even if it means Ryan's golden boy reputation won't burn in flames with him.

"He needs to disappear, River," I say hesitantly. She knows exactly what I mean.

She nods her head, not looking the least bit perturbed by murdering him. Something doesn't sit right with allowing her to.

"I don't think I can let you do it."

Her head snaps towards me.

"The fuck you can't. This is for me. Don't you dare come storming in acting like my knight. When are you going to realize I don't need you to save me?" she grits through her teeth, her eyes sharp with anger.

"You're right. You don't need me to save you. But if I can help save you from going down that hole, then I will."

She shakes her head, staring off into the distance. She's supposed to expect him home tonight, according to our made-up story. When he doesn't come home, she's going to call my parents, asking if they've heard from him.

They'll assure her he's fine, just probably running late. She'll go to bed worried. Come morning when he's still not home, she'll report him missing. That's when shit is going to get real. Really fucking real.

Anxiety filters through my nerves. My arms twitch as my adrenaline pulsates. I'll do everything in my power to keep the scrutiny away from River. I'll become fucking mud for this girl. And fuck, I won't regret a goddamn second of it. Not when this girl has me trapped in her dark little spell.

After this is all said and done, I'm still determined to show her what a real relationship looks like. I'm not even worried if she wants me back. I know she does.

"This is my kill, Mako," she says softly, tuning me back into the conversation. "I got myself—you—into this. And I will be the one to take him out."

"Tonight?"

"Tonight."

Twenty
River

MAKO STANDS BESIDE ME, despite me asking him to stay downstairs. He refused and followed me up just to look at pathetic ol' Ryan, hanging by a rope from the ceiling. It's only been two days, and he's dehydrated and suffering from blood loss. His arms are turning gray with a slight blue tint, all blood having drained from his limbs some time ago. Part of me wants to let them down so he can feel the sharp burning pain.

"I promised myself I'd shove something up his ass," I state calmly. Mako's head snaps towards me much faster than the slow lift of Ryan's head. He glares at me with the heat of a hot poker in a bonfire.

"Why?"

"For the times he shoved his dick up my ass and brutally raped me," I reply, my voice calm and even. I rub my lips together, pop them and tack on, "Twice."

Mako's reaction, however, is the opposite of mine. He nearly explodes, his body jerking with shock and then bristling when the familiar wrath that Ryan provokes in him takes over.

He stalks over to Ryan in two big steps, brings his fist back, and powers it forward straight into Ryan's face. The crunch of his nose breaking beneath Mako's fist is entirely satisfying. A loud groan slips from Ryan's mouth as blood gushes from his broken nose and down his mouth and neck. The blood drips onto the floor, joining the rest of his mess.

At this point, there's more of Ryan's blood on the floor than inside his own body. I had gone to a hole-in-the-wall hardware store down in Shallow Hill that I was sure didn't have cameras and bought rolls of plastic, using cash only. He's in the middle of the room, with no objects around, so the blood won't be too much of a hassle to clean. Aside from my poor little victim, there's only a single bulb up here. Not even a window for ventilation.

The attic is one of the few rooms in this mansion that was never finished, though it's not the typical dusty, creepy attic in most houses. Ryan would always have Mary and Ava come up here once a week and keep up the maintenance. Like any house, Ryan stored family memories up here and didn't want them compromised by nature.

I study the scene before me with delight. If Mako can get out some of his pent-up aggression from how Ryan has treated him their entire lives, I would only be happy to witness that.

Mako was abused by Ryan, too, after all. Verbally, mentally, emotionally. Maybe even physically, if I know anything about Ryan. Those are all critical aspects of a growing child, especially one born into the life Mako was born into. I've no idea what Mako went through before he met Julie and Matt, but I can guess it wasn't pleasant. Regardless, he didn't deserve Ryan's abuse any more than Alison or I did.

Ryan curses at Mako, calling him every name in the Devil's handbook.

Each insult is followed up by another hit to the face. Blood splatters across Mako's face. A droplet lands on my toe. I stare at the droplet, flesh hitting flesh and Ryan's increasingly slurred speech the backdrop to my straying thoughts.

Ryan may have suffered immeasurable pain at the hands of his father, but that was never Mako's fault. And that was never mine or any other woman's fault, either. Ryan took his anger out on the innocent, and it's unforgivable.

I refuse to feel remorse for a man who doesn't believe he did anything wrong.

I'm going to have to kill him. Murder Ryan in cold blood. This tiny droplet of blood is going to stain my skin forever. Even when it washes away, I'll still see it. I'll see it there, and I'll see it coating my hands.

Can I live with that?

Can I live with myself knowing that I was the reason a life drained from a person's eyes?

I wiggle my toes, another droplet landing on them.

Yeah, I can. I've taken back the power stolen from me, wielded it like a weapon, and slayed my demons.

Mako storms away from a limp bloodied Ryan and comes to stand behind me. He's heaving, rage still prevalent on his face. I glance down to see his bloody, shredded knuckles. I lick my lips. A darkness is spreading throughout my soul, tainting it black.

Mako covered in blood is a delicious sight. I want to be just as bloody as he is.

"Have fun with her, bro," Ryan garbles through the blood pouring into his mouth. He spits it out and licks his lips, as if that'll help. "You're dating a psychopath. Now that she's got a taste for torture and murder, what makes you think she'll stop? She's the perfect fucking formula for a serial killer. It's almost boring."

I look up at the ceiling, seriously contemplating killing another person. Maybe if they were a rapist like Ryan. A genuinely shitty person—an absolute monster that preys on the innocent and weak. But would I grab a random one off the street to torture and kill them? The thought makes me want to vomit. It doesn't matter what Ryan says, I know deep down I could never kill someone innocent.

"I don't really have much interest in covering up a bunch of dead bodies," I answer dryly. "Yours is going to be inconvenient enough."

Ryan laughs, the sound nearly reaching the same pitch as a hyena. "Good luck explaining this to my parents," he mocks, his eyes piercing Mako and me with glee.

For some reason, it bothers me that he says *my* parents. Like Mako being adopted doesn't qualify Julie and Matt as *his* parents, too. They raised him from early childhood. They're just as much Mako's parents as they are Ryan's.

Even if one of them also deserves to die.

I whip my hand out, slashing my knife across Ryan's face. The cut is superficial. It wouldn't even leave a scar. But it still stings him nonetheless.

"They're Mako's parents, too," I bite out.

Ryan doesn't acknowledge that. Beside me, Mako's eyes are burning a hole in the side of my head. I refuse to meet his eyes, not quite ready to face the emotion I'll see. Connecting with someone romantically while murdering my abusive boyfriend doesn't sit right with me. Messes with my inner peace.

"They know I'd never kill myself. You can't pass this off as a suicide. The minute I'm late for work, Dad will know something is wrong. I'm too important. You can't just explain my life away," Ryan taunts, his voice growing stronger, as does his confidence.

I tilt my head to the side and study him closely. His dirty blonde hair is stuck to his head with sticky sweat. The shady blues eyes are windows to a dark and decrepit soul. And his full lips that house too-straight teeth and a wicked tongue. His skin is drained of all color and slick with perspiration. I've never seen Ryan look so dirty and unkempt. That alone satisfies me.

He thinks we'll have no choice but to let him go. That maybe we'll try to work out a deal for his silence. He'll ask for something substantial— probably impossible, and we'll plead for him to never speak of this.

It was a mistake, I got angry, and I didn't mean to cause you so much harm.

And then he'll once again have power over me *and* his big brother. It'll make the pain he endured worth it.

Yeah.

Not going to happen.

I don't bargain with rapists and abusers. I'd rather hurt them.

I shrug a shoulder nonchalantly, causing the slow victorious smile on Ryan's face to slip. "I'm not worried about it."

Except I am. Just a little. Not that I have much of a life worth living. I'd go to prison for this for sure, especially with Matt as Ryan's father. Shit, Ryan could put me away with just himself anyway. To be honest, I'd end up just killing myself, taking the coward's way out. What would be the point in living? I've never really had one, to begin with. I'm certainly not going to find it within the confines of a dirty prison cell with my new wife undressing me with her eyes from the top bunk.

But that doesn't mean I wouldn't blast my abuse before I do. I'm sure Alison would back me up. Mako, too. Ryan's reputation will burn in the same flames I go down in.

Together forever, baby.

"You should be," he chides, tsking at me. I roll my eyes in response. He rears back in disgust at my childish response. I walk over to grab my favorite box leaning against the wall, pull out a Girl's Scout cookie and take a bite, munching on the sinful treat with a bored expression.

"Do you realize how many people are going to be looking for me? You're suspect number one. Especially if you tell people I hit you. The more you make me out to be the villain, the worse you'll look."

I frown. "Who said I'm going to make you out to be the villain?" He falters, momentarily confused by my admission. He expected me to cry wolf. "I'll act like the loving, doting girlfriend that I've been the last two years. I'll cry my little eyes out and mourn your death. But when I'm alone, I'll make myself cum every time I think about the fact that you're six feet under and I was the one who put you there."

Ryan's eyes widen gradually as I speak. By the time I'm done, he's shaking. The realization has hit that I'm not interested in kissing his little blue toes and begging for forgiveness. The asshole is rattling like a bare tree in winter winds. Any minute now, he'll be ripped from the ground and blow straight into a fucking woodchipper.

"You will fucking pay for this, River. So will you," he spits, swinging his simmering glare to Mako. Neither of us deigns him a response. Giving him any type of assurance or satisfaction would certainly keep me up at night after this is all said and done. Never mind the torture and killing— knowing that he found even the smallest thing to hold onto in his last days would have me tossing and turning all night.

I need my beauty sleep, considering I got so little of it in the duration of our relationship. He owes me that much.

"Aren't you sickened by this?" Ryan shrieks in bewilderment, staring at Mako as if he grew fins and is reverting to the fish he was named after.

Truthfully, I don't expect Mako to want me anymore. I've shown the depths of my depravity. I've made it more than clear that I'm the furthest thing from remorseful about my actions. Actually, I've made it clear that I'm enjoying it, too.

Mako's too… *good*. And the thought of losing something like that before I've ever had it hurts. But I can deal with it. I'll recover, and if I somehow get away with this, I'll live the rest of my life with Mako tucked into the back corner of my brain, only to come out when my vibrator is resting on my clit.

Said man just curls his arms across his chest and cocks a brow in boredom. "I'm a detective. I've seen worse. And I also know exactly how to cover up a murder," he reminds.

"Why would you want to help a psychopath, Mako? You know she's going to kill you next."

"I'm growing bored of your lackluster bargaining skills. How are you a lawyer?" I cut in. If I'm being honest, I don't want that seed to plant in Mako's head. I've accepted the fact that he won't want me, but that doesn't mean I want him to think I'm the same type of monster as his brother.

"Let's just get this over with, River, yeah?" Mako says. I try to pick apart his tone, finding any type of emotion in there. But it's entirely devoid of it, and I'm not sure how to interpret that.

"First," I announce. "Who's the Ghost Killer, Ryan?"

I already know who it is, but I'd prefer it coming from Ryan's mouth. I still haven't figured out how I'm going to approach that situation. Eventually, I'd have to tell Mako the truth. He won't forgive me for holding onto that secret. Even now, I'm not sure what's stopping me. What would my psychology books say?

Oh, yeah. That I'm terrified of Billy. Billy is my proverbial kidnapper. He trapped me in a house, brainwashed me to believe that if I escaped, I was going to die, and then left me in the house alone with the door wide open.

I'm too scared to walk out that door, in fear that Billy will be right there waiting for me.

Ryan tips his head back and laughs. Laughs and laughs, his voice scratchy and hoarse. "Like I'd ever fucking tell you that," he cackles, the sound manic and unhinged. "You'll never fucking know who it is, and he's been right under your nose the entire time."

Mako's tenses but doesn't say a word. Instead, he just stares Ryan down with cold indifference, committing his last moment with his brother to memory. I watch Mako closely, waiting to see if he wants to keep trying.

"I'll make your death less painful," I bargain.

Mako whips his head towards me. "No, River."

Ryan just glares at me. "Fuck you, bitch. I'm not telling him anything."

I sigh, resigned to the fact that if Mako doesn't catch him soon, the Ghost Killer's identity will be coming out of my mouth. And that thought terrifies me more than the prospect of getting caught for Ryan's murder.

"Just do it," Mako orders quietly. I catch his green eyes in mine and find nothing but assurance. He's telling me it's okay, and it breaks my heart that Ryan is still hurting Mako, even when facing death.

Calmly, I walk over to the broken broomstick, covered with double-sided tape, all except for the jagged tip. Dangling on the end of the stick is Ryan's ugly ass engagement ring. On the tape are tiny pieces of Ryan's favorite mug. When he sees me coming with it, he fights hard, ripping his body side to side, trying to dislodge the ropes, but only succeeding in dislodging his shoulders from their sockets.

Mako doesn't turn away when I pull down his shorts, grab his limp dick and begin sawing it off with the boxcutter. Instead, he grabs the roll of duct tape, rips off a piece, and slaps it over Ryan's mouth to quiet the manic screaming ripping from his throat.

I gag a little as I complete my task. I may be a tad unhinged, but fuck, this is gross. When I'm done, I take a deep breath to try and steady my churning stomach. Then, without further hesitance, I shove the broomstick up Ryan's ass.

Even duct tape can't contain Ryan's screams. And that shit can fix almost anything.

It takes a minute for Ryan to pass out from the pain. Another four before he bleeds out and dies. He was on the brink of death anyway.

Not for one single moment does Mako look away from my murder. From his murder now, too. He may not have actually done the killing, but he would be considered an accomplice in court.

My stomach is still turning. Now that I've officially killed a human being, I need a moment to gather myself. I just did some fucked up things to a live person. And though my gag reflex is working overtime right now, I can't find it in myself to regret it, either.

"You didn't have to stay for that," I say softly, covered head to toe in blood and gore. I must look like *Carrie* from Stephen King's book.

Ever so slowly—*too* slowly—his eyes rip away from the gory scene before him and slide to mine. He's as cool as a cucumber. I'm not sure if I should be relieved or worried.

"I did," he says. "I don't feel sorry for him. Not after seeing what he did to Alison, and especially not after seeing what he did to you. I've watched a monster grow into the devil from the moment I was welcomed into the family. I'm not going to mourn his death."

I don't say anything for a moment as I contemplate what he said. Ryan's words wriggle like parasitic worms through my brain, and despite constantly reminding myself that Mako will be running for the hills soon, I still have to ask. That weak part of me still seeks that assurance.

"Are you disgusted by me?"

His stare never wavers. "I'm proud of you, River."

DESPITE WEARING GLOVES, MY hands are shaking from the burn of bleach. This entire attic has been scrubbed. Even the ceiling. The fumes of bleach are overwhelming, despite the mask and safety glasses. When we're done, I boil a pot of vinegar, place it in the room and close the door. Getting rid of the bleach smell is vital. The fans are going, but that's not a quick enough solution.

Luckily, Mary and Ava are scheduled to come tomorrow morning, finishing off anything we may have missed and giving us a valid reason for the smell of cleaning solution. They usually come on Sundays, but given the situation, I rescheduled, citing that Ryan was gone for the weekend and I had the house cleaning handled. It's the only thing I've done thus far that will look suspicious if they decided to indict me. But more than likely, it won't hold up in court, considering the girls know I always insist on cleaning up after myself.

Which is why they won't be surprised by the smell of bleach. There have been countless occasions of them catching me already cleaning by the time they arrive. And with the lack of ventilation up there, any cops or detectives aren't going to think twice when they go up and get a faint whiff of bleach.

After Ryan's life was snuffed out, we immediately got to work on disposing of him and cleaning up the attic. By the time we got back, it was close to eleven at night.

It was messy, to say the least. And I may have vomited a few times. It required trespassing on private property, but his remains were taken to a farm and fed to the pigs. It was the only sure thing that would guarantee no bones or parts of Ryan would be found. Besides, trespassing is the least of the sins we committed today.

Mako and I didn't leave until every bit of him was consumed.

The weapons I used to torture Ryan were bleached and then buried deep in the woods. The ring had come out with the broomstick when I removed it from Ryan's body. Even though it disgusts me, I ended up cleaning that, too. It will look suspicious if I'm not wearing my engagement ring while pretending that my loving boyfriend has gone missing. As soon as I deem it appropriate, I'll burn the ring.

There's no trace of him anymore, save for all those memories frozen in time and hung up around the house. Eventually, those will be shipped off to Matt and Julie as they mourn his death, destined for teardrops on the glass frames.

That's the only part that truly hurts. His mother doesn't deserve to lose a child. It's not her fault Ryan turned out to be a demon. She did everything in her power to give her boys the best life, but you can't control it if your husband is a pedophile and turns your son into a sociopath.

"We need to figure out something with the cameras," Mako says tiredly. It's after one in the morning now, having spent several hours cleaning. His knees are spread, elbows resting on each leg, head bowed, and his hands clasped around the back of his neck. Getting rid of Ryan's body took a lot of emotional and physical energy. He's drained. We both are.

I offer a soft smile. "Already taken care of."

Mako's hands drop, and his head slowly rises. When our eyes clash, I'm thrown back by the look on his face. Sure, he looks just as tired as I do, but I've never seen Mako look so resolute.

"How?"

I shrug a shoulder, feigning nonchalance when I feel anything but. "I tried to escape. Ryan was watching me constantly through the cameras, keeping tabs on me. So, I cut the WiFi. We'd already been having issues with it going out, and as long as the WiFi was out, he couldn't watch me on his phone.

"He caught me, and we got into a massive fight. I managed to overpower him when I slashed his chest open and then knocked him out. I drugged him with Rohypnol, dragged him to the attic, and the rest is history. The internet is still out, even now. None of that will have been recorded and saved to the Cloud. Though, before I went to Alison's house, I drove his car to Shallow Hill and abandoned it. The traffic cams might need to be taken care of."

Mako stares at me with disbelief. When he processes my words, his eyes slowly turn to a darker moss color.

"Why the fuck was there Rohypnol in the house?" he asks slowly, his deep voice dropping an octave lower.

My lip slides between my teeth, and I look away. It's not my fault my boyfriend drugged and raped me, but I feel so much shame anyway. The memory of waking up with semen dried on my thigh, my body sore and battered, and no memory of any of it happening still sends shudders down my spine.

I should probably find myself a therapist. An expensive one, at that.

"He used it on me before."

I refuse to meet his burning eyes. Sensing I don't want to talk about it, he sighs and changes the subject. "I'll take care of the traffic cams tomorrow before the story breaks. Call Dad," he says, his voice hollow and tired. It matches nicely with the way I look. My shoulders drop in relief, and I'm more grateful than I'll ever say that he let it go.

Ryan's already dead. Getting angry right now will only be exhausting at this point.

"I don't want you involved in this anymore, Mako. Really. All your morals just went down the drain because of me. I'm not risking you getting caught, and I refuse to ruin your life like that," I say sternly.

"No fucking way are you doing this by yourself, River. Not happening."

My shoulders tense, hiking to my ears. Venom is injected in my tone when I say, "I don't need—"

"—me to save you, yeah I got it the first ten times you said it, sweetheart." I bristle, heat rising into my cheeks with indignation. Right as my mouth opens, he cuts me off again. "To be frank, River, I'm not asking. The truth is, you did us both a favor by getting rid of Ryan. So, I'm going to do you a favor and make sure your pretty little ass stays out of prison. Now, please, for the love of god, call my dad." By the time he reaches the end of his sentence, his tone turns stern and impatient, and he looks at me with pleading eyes.

All I can do is stare at him in shock, eyes wide and mouth parted. For reasons I'm not ready to face yet, I pull my phone out of my pocket and dial Matt's number without another word. Mako resumes his previous position, though I get the feeling it's because he wants to hide from this conversation.

I have to call a rapist—someone who hurt a little boy repeatedly. And act like nothing is wrong. Like he's not a piece of shit pedophile, and I didn't just murder his son.

"Fitzgerald," Matt answers sleepily. I picture him flipping on the light on his nightstand, while Julie blearily lifts her head up, wondering why her husband is getting a late-night call. The greeting makes my lip tremble.

Hearing his voice makes my entire body seize with disgust.

Swallowing, I open my mouth and do the hardest thing I ever had to do. Mourn Ryan's disappearance. "Hey, Matt, it's River," I say, my voice trembling.

There's a brief pause, filled with confusion and trepidation, before Matt bounces back, sounding more alert. "River! So nice to hear from you. Is everything okay?"

My eyes close when I hear the question. It's a simple question really, but yet has the most complicated answer.

"Uhh, I'm not sure actually, Matt," I reply, keeping my worried tone. "Look, I'm really sorry to call you so late, but Friday night, Ryan said he had to go out of town for work. He didn't say where he was going, but"—I break off, letting tears accumulate and bleed into my voice— "he was supposed to be home already. H-he's not answering my texts or calls. I'm just really worried about him." I end the tone with a sniffle, real tears tracking down my face.

By now, Mako's head has already lifted, and he's staring at me with something between surprise and awe. All I had to do was allow myself to feel. Let myself face the fact that the man I thought I was in love with turned out to be nothing more than Satan himself. Apple doesn't fall too far from the fucking tree.

"Uh—well, a work meeting, huh? Well, honey, I'm sure he just stopped for the night at a hotel or something. I'll see if I can get a hold of him. If we don't hear anything from him by tomorrow morning, I'll make some calls, okay? Just try not to worry. I'm sure Ryan is safe and sound."

Mako grimaces while I bite the inside of my cheek hard. I sniffle and make myself sound extra pathetic when I say, "Okay, Matt. Thank you so much. Let me know if you hear anything."

"Okay, honey, I will. Goodnight now."

I hang up the phone and let loose a harsh breath. Speaking to Matt was especially hard.

A lot harder than murdering my own boyfriend.

Twenty-One
River

THE HOUSE IS COMPLETELY dark save the blaring light from the TV in front of me. I stand in front of it, watching the woman reporter drone on in a monotone voice. She's wearing too much makeup.

I correct myself. Ryan always said I wore too much makeup.

She looks pretty. *Beautiful.*

"Police officials are still investigating the disappearance of Ryan Fitzgerald, a twenty-five-year-old local from North Carolina, who was reported missing on September 8th. If anyone has seen or heard from him, please contact your local police station—"

Contact your local police station? Where do they think he's run off to? Out of state? Why, he was only in an attic, my dear. Now, there's nothing left of him to find. Not even if you go looking in pig shit.

A shrill ring snaps my gaze to my blaring cell phone, vibrating on the end table next to me. *Julie.* I still haven't spoken to her.

I ignore it and look back to the television. Ryan's picture is displayed on the screen.

I pinch the skin on the inside of my wrist until I'm hissing in pain. Tears well in my eyes. I sniffle.

"I've been a mess, Julie," I whimper. "I haven't heard from him, and I'm so scared."

A tear spills over. I fight the urge to wipe it away.

"What if he's hurting? Or in pain? And I'm not there to help him?!"

Tsk. Too dramatic. I try again.

"I miss him so much, and I just want him home," I whisper brokenly, my eyes boring into the picture of Ryan on the screen. I sniffle, allowing a few more tears to trail down my pale cheeks.

"I know, Julie, I know. I love him, too. I love him, too…"

"I CAN'T DO THIS, I can't do this, I can't do this…"

"River, listen to me—"

"They're camping outside of the fucking house, Mako," I say shakily, my voice ready to fall off its foundation from the tremors. I run a hand through my hair, squeezing at the scalp until I feel sharp prickles of pain dancing across my nerve-endings.

This was not something I anticipated.

Reporters, paparazzi, vans, and cameras, constantly in my fucking face every time I leave the house. Matt tried to report Ryan missing Monday morning, but they told him he had to wait up to 72 hours before making a missing person's report. Thursday morning on the dot, he filed. It's been almost two weeks of them searching for his body, and in that time, the media has blown the story up.

Ryan wasn't a celebrity, for fuck's sake. But he's the son of a notorious lawyer, who's put away more criminals than the number of years he's been alive. He might as well be a celebrity in our town. *Fuck.*

Bilby brushes up against my legs, offering a sweet little meow. Sometimes I'm positive he can sense when I'm upset or agitated.

I plop down on the couch, settling my head in my hands. Bilby jumps up next to me and headbutts me. I remove one hand from my head to curl my fingers against the side of his mouth. He uses my fingers as a brush and rubs up against me repeatedly.

"Come to me tonight," Mako demands tightly. I sigh, weary and drained. It's a Tuesday night, and I have classes tomorrow. But I think I'm going to be skipping them for the foreseeable future, just as I have since Ryan went missing. I don't think I can handle the stares from people who are wondering where my boyfriend is.

Ryan deserved every single thing that came his way. I don't regret doing what I did. I don't regret liberating myself from an abusive relationship that was surely going to fucking kill me one day. I don't regret standing up for myself, and I don't regret getting revenge for all the bullshit I've gone through.

But the after-effect is draining. I'm still a person of interest in Ryan's murder as of right now, but they are considering other options. Mako has told his truth—the truth that will ultimately lead to Ryan's murderer. Ryan figured out who the Ghost Killer was. While he didn't get the chance to tell Mako who it was, I know for a fact Ryan told somebody.

I remember standing outside Ryan's office, gearing myself up to ask permission to go to Amelia's. The phone call I overheard. The utter excitement in his voice as he claims he figured something out. I hadn't put much thought into it at the time, but now I know that he was talking to someone about the Ghost Killer.

I had relayed that memory to Mako already, which only solidified his story. They're going through Ryan's phone records to pin down who he talked to.

There's also another theory they're looking into, one that makes me a little nauseous. With Matt's record of putting criminals away, it's only logical they look into the fact that *he* has enemies. Which I'm sure he does. He's put countless criminals away.

Furthermore, Matt isn't the man I had believed he was. Who's to say he doesn't have his own dealings in the black market? I'm sure the asshole is sitting with his head slumped, believing that there's a possibility that his career has killed his own son.

"I don't know, Mako…" I trail off. What if they follow me? Being caught going to Ryan's brother's house in the middle of the night looks incredibly suspect. The supposed heartbroken girlfriend running off with the brother? Yeah, that doesn't make me look fucking suspicious or anything.

"Yeah, you're right," Mako sighs. "I just hate the thought of you going through this alone."

Mako and I have to tread very carefully for now. We can't say what we really want to say over the phone. Mako doesn't trust anyone not to hack my phone conversations. Highly illegal, but when has the government ever had morals?

"I appreciate that," I say softly. It feels weird being nice to Mako. I conditioned myself to hate him for so many months, convincing myself that Ryan's hatred towards Mako was justified. That there was a reason of some sort. Or simply because I pledged loyalty to someone who didn't deserve it.

But Mako never gave up on me. This godsend of a man is helping me get away with murder. Literally. He's helping me cover up his own brother's death because... well because Ryan was the fucking devil incarnate. He abused both of us.

And Mako is dealing with his own shit. Not only did he do those things for me, but he's also facing the reality that his father is a rapist and how to navigate that. Through little snippets of conversation, he did decide to tell his mother the truth. I just don't think he's decided on how and when yet.

There's just no way I can mistreat Mako anymore. Regardless if we get away with it or not, I owe him my life. He's risking *everything* for me. His career, reputation, his *life*. Cops don't last long in prison. Mako has the highest catch rate out of the entire department. His enemies would be waiting for him in prison, ready to exact their own version of revenge.

"Meet me at the library tonight," I say. Meeting someone in a semi-public setting feels safer than going to his house. Or him coming here. I need to get out and away from this cold, sterile box. It's a pretty box, but one that's held nothing but haunting memories. One that I plan on moving out of as soon as possible.

I don't have a whole lot in my savings, but I have enough to get my own place and restart my life. If I get that privilege.

"I'll be there." His low answering reply sends shivers down my spine. The warm kind that travels in between my legs and settles there. Whatever has been building between Mako and I is indescribable. I don't know where it's going, but fuck if I can stop it. I don't *want* to.

I want to make this merry-go-round go faster.

THIS LIBRARY IS A haven to me, my own ghost running down the aisles—a young, broken girl with big ambitions. I see myself inside every room, every nook and cranny, all the places I escaped to when I had nowhere else to go. Camilla, looking after me, taking care of me, loving me.

My god, I miss her. Sometimes I forget just how much I miss her until I walk into this building and see her ghost alongside mine.

"It's creepy in here." The deep voice behind me makes me jump, a high-pitched squeal escaping my throat. Immediately, I'm embarrassed. Really fucking embarrassed. I've never made a noise like that in my life—and I've been scared my entire life. "Sorry," Mako whispers, an impish grin sliding across his gorgeous face.

It's nightfall, so it's dark as hell in here. Our only light source is the moon shining through the windows and the soft light from the phone in my hand. Mako's green eyes are shadowed, darkening them to a deep moss green.

My hand is on my chest, holding in my racing heart, as my wide eyes stay locked on his. I can only imagine how I look to him right now.

"You're beautiful," he whispers as if he read my mind. I hate when he does that. I hate that he knows what I'm thinking.

That word—*beautiful*—sends ice down my back and fire in my veins all in one breath. Mako calling me beautiful is debilitating. I want to hate it and cherish it.

"I hate that word," I say back, straightening myself into a somewhat normal position a human being should be in.

"Why?" he asks, his voice still low and quiet. Like if we talk any louder, we'll be caught by the snarling librarian that demands silence at all times. I wish there was one here. Being bad with Mako sounds like so much fun.

"I've heard it all my life from the wrong people," I admit. A cold rage settles in his eyes, but he doesn't unleash it. So calm and collected. So unlike his brother.

"Does it feel better when you hear it coming from the right person?"

he questions, his body still.

"I don't know," I whisper. I take a small step towards him. Shortening the little bit of distance between us feels like inching your hand towards a tiger's mouth. At any moment, it's going to snap. "Say it again."

Mako doesn't react immediately. Instead, he roves his half-lidded eyes over me. The icy fire in his eyes is slowly swirling into liquid heat. My heart kickstarts once again, racing nearly as hard as it did when he scared me. I hold my breath as my anticipation for one little word builds, electricity dancing through the air, setting the dust motes aflame.

"You're beautiful," he says again. My breath releases and I close my eyes, relishing the word coming from his mouth. It sounds deliciously sinful when he says it. It sounds like something I can get used to. Only when it's coming from his mouth with the low pitch of his deep voice.

I keep my eyes closed, even as I confess, "I liked that."

A gasp nearly escapes when I feel his body press into mine, his front molding to my back. His warm breath stirs the fine hairs around my ears. His hand slides in my hair, setting fire to my skin. Goosebumps prickle my entire body, causing me to shiver in his hold. His fingers whisper across my flesh as he slowly brushes my hair to drape across my shoulder. Another shiver races down my spine from the tickling sensation he leaves in his wake.

"Do you know what love looks like?" he asks softly. I close my eyes and release a deep sigh.

"Yes," I whisper.

"What does it look like?"

"I've seen love in the eyes of a broken woman every time she had drugs in front of her. I've seen it in the eyes of a young boy when he took his first drink of alcohol to escape his shitty life. I've seen it in a grown man exploring the body of a little girl for the first time." I suck in a sharp breath. "I've seen that in many different eyes."

A low growl rumbles from Mako's chest, the vibrations traveling across my back. I ignore it.

"The face of love is ever changing, yet it looks the same every time."

"That's not the face of love, that's the art of escape," he answers quietly.

I don't respond. I don't know how to.

"Take me to the secret place," he demands gently. Finally, I open my eyes.

I nod my head once, slowly extract myself from his hand and lead the way. It feels like the devil is nipping at my heels. The type of devil you should stay away from but only want to get closer to. Willpower and force are the only two things keeping me from running to the room. From discovering exactly what Mako plans on doing once we get there. I'm terrified to find out, but I'm nearly shaking with the need to know.

I lift the secret shelf, and the room is presented to me. My home away from hell. Where I spent the majority of time away from Shallow Hill. I walk into the room, my eyes taking in every detail of this room except the one I should be looking at.

Mako's demanding presence is right behind me, and when the door shuts, it feels like my fate has been sealed. I don't know what it is yet, but I think I'm going to like it.

I'm nervous. I'm not sure if I've ever felt this type of anxiousness before. This isn't the type of feeling I got when Billy came around. Or when a man would sneak into my room at night. Or even when I would make Ryan angry.

This is the jittery nervousness you get when you're in a room alone with your crush. My confidence was something I always held onto tightly. It was my armor, and it prevented me from feeling anything but sure of myself when in the same room with a man I wanted.

That confidence is lingering right outside my reach. Still there, but impossible to grasp onto right now.

"Do you remember when we first met?" Mako asks, breaking the silence.

"Of course. When I met your parents," I answer, my voice deceptively smooth.

Mako slowly shakes his head. "That's not the first time we've met, River."

His words silence the nerves. My brow creases with confusion as I try to recall meeting Mako before that.

"I... I don't remember," I say. An almost despondent smile slides on his face. How could we have met before Ryan? How could I not remember him? Mako has features you don't forget.

"You were drinking, so I can't say I'm surprised." Weariness replaces the confusion. I drank a lot during my freshman and sophomore years of college. It was only after Ryan and I started getting serious that I stopped. He said it made him look bad having a sloppy girlfriend.

"What'd I do?" I ask hesitantly. He chuckles.

"You changed my life, is what you did." The V between my brow deepens as I frown. I don't know what he could possibly mean by that.

"You punched a man in the nose for touching you in a way you didn't like. He was getting ready to hit you, and I intervened."

My eyes widen as the memory comes rushing back, slamming through my brain like a tidal wave. That was Mako. The man who stopped the drunk asshole from bitch slapping me after I broke his nose. I walked away from him without saying thank you, even though I was tempted to show my thanks in more nefarious ways.

"Holy shit," I gasp. "I do remember that. I hadn't... I don't know why I didn't realize that was you."

He shrugs a shoulder, taking a step towards me. The anticipation from earlier starts to creep back in as the temperature in the room begins to rise.

"You also didn't realize it was me that danced with you later that night," he says—calmly—as if he didn't just unload a massive fucking bomb on me.

"That was you?" I ask incredulously, my body rearing back in shock. Mako has been my mystery man this entire time? The man that would haunt the back corner of my brain, only to be let out in rare, weak moments.

A satisfied smirk crooks the corner of his lips.

"That was me," he confirms. He's staring at me now as if he's finally caught me. It's sexy as hell, and my body responds in kind. My pussy grows wet, beginning to pulsate as I inhale the sinful look Mako is giving me now.

As I take in the fact that Mako is who I should've been with all along. The fact that I was so close to having him is almost devastating. What would've happened if I had just turned around? If I had discovered the man making me feel things, no man has ever made me feel. What would've happened if Amelia didn't get sick that night, pulling me away from Mako's arms? I would've let him take me home that night. I would've let him ravage my body and soul until the sun peeked through the morning clouds. And I would've given him my number and asked for seconds. Thirds, fourths, fifths, and so on until I had him forever.

"Why didn't you tell me sooner?" I ask with bewilderment.

"Because you were firmly under my brother's spell. Telling you that wouldn't have changed anything. And to be honest, I didn't want that memory tainted. You hated me up until recently. If I had told you then, you would've spit it back in my face. I don't think I could've handled that."

Shame has me dropping my eyes to my feet. He's right. And I hate that he is.

"I'm sorry," I say. I release a harsh breath. "I'm sorry for the way I treated you, Mako. You were incredibly kind to me, and I threw everything back in your face. I treated you horribly, fuck, I even slapped you. And I'm sorry it took me so long to say it. I'm just… sorry."

"Don't be," he says, taking another step towards me. I eye the distance, greedily wanting it to be eradicated. "That was what made me fall in love with you, River."

Time stills. His words don't register right away. My mouth falls open and my eyes snap to his. He forges on before I can even stutter out a response.

"I don't want you to say it back. But it's the truth. You're so strong, River. You're fierce and independent. And despite the fact that someone was actively kicking you down, you kept getting back up on your feet. I admired you for that. It pissed me off, too, sure. But fuck, did it make me fall in love with you."

Hot tears burn my eyes, lining the bottom of my lids. Waves of emotion storm through me, so many I don't even know how to pick apart what I'm feeling. Shock, absolutely. But anything else I can't decide. Am I happy? Excited? Sad? I don't know.

What I do know is that everything I felt before Mako was a lie. Falling in love with Mako feels like stepping into a fire with his hand clasped firmly in mine. It burns, but I'm not alone.

"Come here, Mako."

Twenty-Two

Mako

I DIDN'T PLAN ON THIS moment happening, at least not now of all fucking times. Admitting to River that I'm in love with her just came out. But it's really fucking hard to regret it when she's staring at me like she's getting ready to eat me alive. The heady demand slipping from her lips has me instantly reacting, listening to her command like a trained K-9.

I reach her in two big steps, or maybe it's one, and she took the other step. My hand is sliding into her soft curls and her even softer mouth is crushing into mine in one swoop. River McAllister's lips feel like fucking heaven on earth.

A shaky exhale escapes her mouth, swirling into mine as our mouths open and our tongues meet. Fuck, she tastes sweeter than I imagined. Countless nights, I fantasized about those lips on mine. On my body, and especially on my cock as I got myself off to thoughts of her. Too many nights of doing the same thing, from the moment I laid eyes on River knocking the daylights out of the handsy asshole at the club. The moment her golden eyes landed on me, she trapped me in and made me hers. I didn't know it at the time, but she never let me go.

A soft moan vibrates through my mouth as my tongue spears into her. I can't get enough of her. I can't stop tasting her. Her mouth is soft and pliable, letting me take the lead for a few moments before snatching the control away and commanding the kiss. Back and forth, we push and pull for dominance, never letting the other have it for too long.

River's nails claw at my chest, drawing a growl that makes me sound like a hungry bear. The sound only spurs her on, her movements becoming desperate and needy. I snatch her wrists and pull them tightly behind her back, just like I do when I arrest a criminal.

Kissing this woman *is* criminal.

So many things I could do to her. I could handcuff her now, letting her endure the sweet torture of what my tongue could do to her body and not be able to stop me. She wouldn't want to, but she'd try when the pleasure becomes too much for her to handle.

"Mako." The soft plea is murmured against my tongue, alighting an inferno deep inside of me. I snap. Or maybe I'm just answering her plea.

I pause, my hands grasping either side of her face, and I gently pull her away.

"Is there any place I shouldn't touch? Or anything you don't want me to do? I can be gentle, I can be whatever you need." By the time I'm done, I'm positive I sound like a desperate fuck.

Her golden eyes glitter and a small smile pulls at her bruised-kissed lips.

"I'm… not ready for anal play, yet," she says gently. The *why* on why she's not ready threatens to boil my blood. River had already admitted aloud what Ryan did to her. I close my eyes, coercing my dangerously rising temperature to drop back down before I boil over. Now is *not* the time to lose my shit.

"Okay," I breathe, opening my eyes again. "Anything else?"

She gives one shake of her head. "The only thing I ask is that you don't treat me like I'm glass. I'm not weak. I'll never be weak. I just want you to be you."

Now that I can do.

Before I press my lips against hers once more, I whisper, "Not for one second have I ever thought you were weak."

Her clothes are stripped off her body in a matter of seconds. Claws and hands attack my clothes as she rips the fabric from my body with just as much urgency. Our mouths only part long enough to get the clothes off before gluing back to each other once more.

This room is dusty and dirty, not an ideal place to have sex. But I'd sell my soul to the devil if it meant I never had to stop.

I pick her up, her long smooth legs wrapping around my waist. My knees nearly collapse when I feel her wet heat settle against my cock. A groan follows when her hips roll once, twice— "River," I grit out. "You're killing me."

She grins against my mouth and rolls her hips again, my eyes copying the motion of her hips. Before I embarrass myself and either fall and drop her, or come right here and now, I storm over to the bench we sat on just months ago. The same bench she relayed her life story to me while I stewed in a fury, wanting to kill every bastard that laid hands on her. Graphic images filled my head of all the things I could do to them— fantasies that still simmer every time I'm reminded of the abuse River has endured in her life.

I spin and ease down onto the bench, more than wary of the protesting wood the last time we were here. Just like clockwork, the bench groans beneath my weight, but it holds true for now.

My hand slides up the back of River's head, plunging in her soft curls. Just as she dips her sweet little tongue in my mouth again, I curl my hand and firmly wrench her head back until her mouth is suspended a few inches away from mine. She mewls at the loss of my mouth, and I can't help but smirk at the sound. I love how much she needs me.

"Mako," she groans, her voice breathy and desperate. I take the time to pursue her body slowly. *Fuck*, bad idea. I'm too on edge and she's too fucking perfect. Beautiful breasts, the perfect size for my hands, with little rose-pink nipples budded and waiting for my mouth. Deep curves with a flat stomach. A brow raises when I catch sight of the simple jewel plunged through her belly button—something I'll have to explore later.

"You're so fucking perfect," I breathe, my eyes landing on her pussy spread across my cock. I have to squeeze my eyes shut to keep myself from shooting my load prematurely, my hand tightening in her hair involuntarily. She moans from the prick of pain, only making my willpower slip further away. Seeing her connected to me is incredibly erotic and something I intend to see every goddamn day for the rest of my life.

"Mako, please," she begs.

Fuck, fuck, fuck! This woman will be the death of me.

"What do you need from me?" I choke out, wrenching my eyes back to her molten golden orbs. They're on fire, liquid gold simmering over a fire raging only for me. Her hands splay across my chest for a moment before dragging down slowly. Right before they reach my cock, I snap her wrists up and away.

Soon, I'll let her do whatever she pleases to my body. But not tonight.

"Mako!" she protests, attempting to wrench her arms away.

"Tell me what you want with *words*, River," I grit out.

"I... I need *you*."

A firm shake of my head. "Not good enough, baby girl. What do you want me to do to you?" I ask as I transfer both wrists to one hand and use my other to lightly brush across her clit. Her eyes nearly roll, and I've decided it's my life's mission to see that sight any chance I can get.

When she just breathes out a moan, I lean forward and trail my tongue across her pert nipple. Her back arches, her body begging for more. I evade her wishes, determined to hear what she wants.

Has she ever been asked? Has no one ever given her the option to choose? Of course not. Those assholes have only just taken from her, disregarding her wants and desires. Disregarding her secret fantasies. I want to see every one of them come to life. With just a simple demand from her lips, I'll be a slave to every one of her desires.

"River," I prompt, when she begins to grow impatient, going as far as leaning her body into mine in an attempt to get me to suck on her nipple. "Use your words."

She groans with frustration. "Suck me," she says, almost shyly. Never in my life would I think River to ever be shy, but fuck if it doesn't do something to me. Heeding her demand, my lips close around the bud, sucking sharply as I lave my tongue all over her sensitive nipple.

The loud moan that escapes her mouth sounds like sweet relief. I switch to the other breast, never one to neglect both.

"What else?" I murmur, peeking up at her. Her mouth is open in a perfect O, and a deep line crinkles between her brow as she stares down at me. I quirk a brow, waiting for her response.

"T-touch my clit. Rub it," she says, her voice only a tad more confident than before. My thumb brushes across her little bud, engorged with desire.

More moans follow suit, and the louder they grow, the firmer I press. I don't stop either ministration—my tongue against her nipple and my thumb on her clit—determined to bring her to orgasm this way if that's how she wants it.

"More!" she demands.

"More what?"

"Fuck me with your fingers," she growls, all shyness absent from her sharp demand.

There's my girl.

She lifts up just enough for my hand to slide across her slit and find her opening. I groan with her when I insert a finger into her tight center. She's too goddamn perfect. Another finger joins the first, curving into a come hither motion. My thumb finds her clit again just as my finger locates the little spot inside her that instantly makes her legs quiver.

"Mako!" she gasps, her hips circling against my hand. Her orgasm rips through her entire body, suspending it completely still for a brief moment before she completely loses control. Her hips grind against my hand with fervor, and both of her hands grab my hair and tighten into a death grip, my mouth firmly attached to her breast. I don't stop working her, and she doesn't stop screaming.

She comes completely undone against me, and it's the sweetest sight I ever did see.

Finally, when she falls limp, I take back control. I'm seconds away from losing it myself, so it takes everything in me to keep it together when I grab her hips, lift her body up and then impale her directly onto my cock.

Fuuuuuuck.

Her half-lidded eyes widen into discs and a garbled scream shoots from her throat. Neither of us moves. I allow her to adjust to my size while I try not to come. Her tight, wet heat completely envelops me, squeezing the life out of me.

My head clashes with the cement wall behind me, my teeth gritted until I'm nearly grinding them to dust.

"Are you okay?" I ask hoarsely, not proud of the way my voice trembles.

"I… Is it normal to have a fucking horse dick?" she finally gasps, her round eyes traveling to where we're connected. She's seen my dick before, how big it was, but I imagine feeling it inside of her is a whole new prospect.

I can't fucking help it. A huge satisfied grin stretches across my face, earning me a little eye roll when she spots it. I know I'm bigger than most, *far* bigger than most. But I don't care what anyone says, no man can deny the ultimate satisfaction when a girl fawns over it. Especially the girl you're madly fucking in love with.

"Did I hurt you?" I ask, lifting my hips just slightly. Her mouth parts and her eyes fall back to their half-lidded state.

"I like the way you hurt me," she whispers. Something primal erupts inside my chest. It's a living, breathing beast that River has just awoken from its slumber. My hands tighten on her hips until I'm sure she'll sport bruises of my handprints for a day or two. She leans forward and brushes her plump lips across mine.

My discarded jeans are next to the bench. I slip out my handcuffs with practiced ease and have them slapped around her wrists, pinning them behind her back within seconds. She stills, my actions catching up to her as she realizes what I did.

"Am I your prisoner?" she asks seductively.

I bite my lip, quite liking the way her chest pops out and her body curves to accommodate the cuffs.

"For as long as you're willing to be," I murmur.

"You'll let me out the second I tell you to," she tells me, her voice soft but stern. I meet her gaze, making sure she can see the truth in my words.

"They'll be gone before you can finish the sentence," I promise. She nods her head once, rotating her wrists gently, testing out the cuffs. I keep them relatively loose, so they don't rub her delicate skin raw.

When I see her acceptance, I don't give her the chance to make any more demands. I spread my thighs further, slide my hands down below her ass cheeks, brace her against my body and fuck the absolute shit out of her. For the second time, River's eyes widen into round discs.

"Oh my God!" she gasps, her face tucking into the curve of my neck as the pitches of her moans increase. My mouth travels across her shoulder and up the soft skin of her neck, nipping a path as I go. I grab a fistful of her luscious hair and yank her head back, eliciting another sharp moan from her throat. When I reach the spot right behind her ear, I sink my teeth into the soft flesh, my hips relentlessly pumping into her.

"Mako!" She writhes against me, the cuffs tinkling loudly from the jostle of our bodies. Sweat beads across my forehead and chest as I fight to keep control. I've never felt anything so fucking incredible in my life. She molds to my cock like wet clay.

"Is this what you needed?" I grit out, enunciating my words with a sharp thrust, producing a little squeak from her throat. "You needed me to fuck this sweet little pussy, didn't you?"

"Ungg, yes!" she pants, nodding her head like a bobblehead.

"Is this what you fantasized about every time you touched your pussy, wishing it was me?"

Another garbled 'yes' comes from her throat. "But it feels so much better," she gasps, the whites of her eyes nearly taking over.

"You feel so fucking perfect, baby," I groan, grinding my hips against hers a few times when she's seated completely on my cock. I know her clit is sliding against my pelvis just from the high-pitched gasps every time I grind against her.

She's getting close, I can feel it. I wrap my arm entirely around her waist, careful of her constrained arms, and prop her further up, once more pistoning my hips with sharp thrusts. The only thing keeping me grounded is my need to make her come first. I refuse to come a second before she does.

As if reading my thoughts, she gasps out, "Mako, fuck, I'm gonna come!" Her legs tighten against mine and her head begins to tip back. Curses slip from my tongue as the intensity our bodies are creating reaches its peak. My tempo increases as I pound and pound, the wet slap from our bodies connecting rivaling the sounds coming from mine and River's throats.

River stills—something she seems to do right before she comes—before her pussy ripples across my cock, and she once more loses it. She contracts around me. My name falls from her lips like a desperate prayer, finally snapping my control.

"Fuck!" The hoarse shout booms from deep in my chest as I empty myself inside her, her pussy milking every last drop out of me. My name continues to fill the room as her entire body convulses and shakes against mine, riding our highs together before we inevitably come down.

I slump further into the bench as her body becomes dead weight on top of me, her face tucked in my neck. We're both shaking and completely wiped out. Tiny twitches overtake her limbs, pulling a grin from me. I grab the keys and quickly unlock the cuffs from her wrists. I laugh when her hands just fall, thumping against my sides.

"I never knew it was supposed to be like that," she whispers. I close my eyes tightly, equally proud that I could be the first one to give that to her and angry that every man before me had the nerve to give her less than what she deserves.

Though they feel like two dead logs, I lift my arms and wrap them around her body, bringing her as close to me as humanly possible.

"It will always be like that with us," I promise. "Communication is important to me, River. I'll test your limits and introduce you to new things, but I will never do anything to truly hurt you. And the moment you don't like something, I'll stop, and it will never happen again. I want to show you what sex between two people is *supposed* to be like. Two people who respect and understand each other."

She's deathly silent long enough for me to question everything that just came out of my mouth. But then a sob wracks her body, and tears begin to pool in the divot of my neck and shoulder. Panic blooms in my chest.

"Did I say something wrong?" I ask, rushing to pull her body away from mine so I can look her in the eyes. She protests, curling deeper into my body and wrapping her arms around me tightly.

"No," she says weakly. "You said everything right. You're perfect." The anxiety lessens but doesn't completely let me go.

"Why are you crying?"

She sniffles. "Because I've waited my whole life for someone like you. And now that I finally found it, I'm fucking terrified of losing it."

I close my eyes, a harsh exhale releasing the lingering panic. I grab either side of her head and softly lift her head until her wet, red-rimmed eyes are looking back at me. My heart seizes and contracts. She's so goddamn beautiful it hurts.

"I get it. That's how I've felt for months now. But if I have anything to do with it, River, that won't ever happen."

Her eyes close, her long black lashes clumped together with tears splaying across her reddened cheeks. She relents and nods her head.

"Okay. I can accept that."

"I HATE TO RUIN our little high, but… I need to go see Barbie."
Not *we*, but *I*.

Can't lie and say those words don't deflate my high like a fucking balloon.

"Right now?" I ask.

"Yes."

"Why?" I question, sliding my foot into my boot and lacing it up. Her scent is all over me now, and if I was a lesser man, I'd never want to shower again.

She sighs. "I need to collect rent."

My brow furrows. I thought she was done going there for something so trivial. I highly doubt Barbie pays River very much in rent. But maybe she's worried about money. I suppose without Ryan, she figures she'll need to start supporting herself again.

"We both know that's not safe, River," I say calmly, resting my elbows on my spread knees and lacing my fingers together. I look over at her, studying her blank face. She's sitting on the edge of the bench, her spine straight and her own fingers clasped tightly together. She looks like she's on the verge of running.

"I know," she agrees. Her downcast eyes lift to mine. Something is lurking in the depths of her honey orbs—an emotion I can't pinpoint. A rock settles in my chest and my stomach curdles like I drank spoiled milk.

"You know," I echo slowly. "What if Billy is there?" I prod, recalling the boogeyman from her childhood and the man who beat her to a bloody pulp. The man I'm dying to get my hands on to conduct my own torture. If I weren't studying her like an archaeologist studies hieroglyphics, I would've missed the slight flinch at the mention of his name. The reaction stirs all kinds of feelings inside of me. It doesn't matter how much River tries to hide it—she's terrified of Billy.

All the more reason to get acquainted with him.

"He won't be," she states firmly, sure of herself. I don't know how she could possibly know that, but if I know anything about this stubborn woman is that it doesn't matter what I say, she's going.

"I'm coming with you then." Her eyes widen and whip to me. A protest forms on her tongue, but I tighten my lips and give her a sharp warning look, shaking my head once. Her shoulders deflate in defeat. If she knows anything about me, it doesn't matter what she says, I'm going.

Twenty-Three
River

I FUCKED UP.

The moment those words left my mouth, I knew I fucked up. I should've known better than to tell Mako I was going to see Barbie. But I didn't know how to leave after we just did… well, *that*, and it not be awkward. You don't just leave with a 'see you later' when someone fucks you the way Mako fucked me.

My stomach tightens with heady desire and a sharp thrill for the millionth time when I recall what we did only twenty minutes ago. It's fucking pathetic of me to already want to do it again. And again. And a-fucking-gain.

I need to see Barbie, though. I've waited far too long already, too busy cocooning myself in the house and away from prying eyes. The Ghost Killer—or *Billy*—is still out there. I was hoping to gain more information from Barbie as I try to figure out how the hell I'm supposed to tell Mako who the Ghost Killer is. He's going to hate me; I already know it. He's put so much time and energy into finding him, and I've known from the moment he told me about the killings, and I haven't said a damn thing.

But now, Mako wants to come. So, the only thing I can do is collect the much-needed rent and find another time to talk to Barbie. If anyone would know anything, it's her. She didn't know about Billy's killings before, but now that it's been brought to her attention, she's going to weasel out any information she can get. If Barbie is good for anything besides selling her body, it's getting information.

Dread settles in my chest as Mako opens his car door for me, waiting for me to slide in. Bringing Mako is such a bad idea.

"Maybe we should just not go," I say, cringing as the words come out of my mouth, awkward and very fucking suspicious. His eyes narrow on me. I shift, uncomfortable with the way he's scrutinizing me.

"I'd feel better doing this while I'm with you," he says finally. Goddamn it. He knows me too well. Well enough to know that I want to go by myself. And there's no way Mako's going to let that happen. Not after I had already opened my big mouth and divulged some of the things Billy put me through, and *especially* not after Billy nearly beat me to death.

Fuck, fuck, fuck. There's no getting out of this, and the only person I can be angry with is myself—stupid sex-induced brain. Sex with Mako is dangerous if it completely halts the ability to think properly.

Don't freak, River. Just go in, get the money, and leave. Simple.

Nothing with Shallow Hill is ever simple.

The entire time I'm giving Mako directions, I'm tempted just to make him drive to a random, empty house and claim she's not home. There are plenty of abandoned places in Shallow Hill. It would be easy. But something feels wrong about lying to Mako even more than I already am.

He pulls into the driveway of my decrepit childhood home. Like every other house in this sad town, the white panels are hardly white and hanging on by a thread. Boarded up windows from explosive fights between Barbie and her clients. A rickety wooden porch with a collapsed step and a hole in it from when someone fell through.

It's fucking embarrassing, to say the least.

"You don't have to come in, Mako."

He's already opening the door and rounding the car to open mine for me. My heart drops when I see Barbie's beady little eyes peeking through the tattered curtains.

The dread cements inside my chest. I'm going to need a jackhammer to clear it out when this is all said and done.

I drag my feet walking into the house, Mako on my heels. His presence is overpowering and suffocating when all I want to do is remove him from this house.

"Well, who the fuck do we have here?" Barbie says from the kitchen entrance, her arms crossed over her frail body. Her eyes are eating Mako up, clearly enjoying the view based on the unfiltered excitement in her eyes. "Oh, this is an upgrade, dear. Much better than the last one you brought home. That one looked like he fucked himself with a stick for pleasure."

I can't help it. I snort in response. Sometimes I can appreciate the honesty from Barbie's mouth, even if the venom she spews is mostly directed towards me.

"Barbie, this is Mako. Don't scare him away," I warn.

A sinful smirk stretches across her face. This is Barbie in action, even though she knows Mako will never give her the time of day. Mako, ever the gentleman, gives a curt, "Hello, Barbie." Her eyes widen when she gets a taste of his voice. Deep—so fucking deep, especially when he's saying the dirtiest things in your ear while at *least* nine inches deep inside you. I shiver at the memory.

Even when Mako realizes that he's going to hate me instead of loving me, I will cherish that memory until the day I die.

"What do you want?" Barbie says, forcing her eyes away from the magnetic man behind me. It takes serious effort on her part, I know this from experience. The usual venom in her voice is absent. Probably too enthralled by Mako.

"Rent time," I chirp. Her face falls, rolling her eyes dramatically and turning to walk into the kitchen. When Barbie isn't in her room fucking, she's smoking, injecting, or snorting in the kitchen. It took four cigarettes to keep me in that kitchen—the same place Billy granted me with new nightmares— last time I was here. Smoking in front of Mako just feels wrong.

The only thing that unsticks my feet from the ground is the reminder that I have Mako here with me. His strength silently bleeds into me, giving me the courage I need to revisit my personal hell.

The kitchen is in the same state it was last time I was here. And every time before that since I can remember. I watch Mako's eyes take in every detail. The overwhelming urge to blindfold him is almost too much to bear. I hate him seeing the place I grew up in. I didn't like Ryan seeing it, either, but something about Mako discovering where I came from feels different.

With Ryan, I felt like I had to impress him. Prove something to him. And this dingy house doesn't exist on any lists to impress your boyfriend with. Ryan sneered and looked down on this house and Barbie. The whole experience left me embarrassed and with a bad taste in my mouth, and I'm almost sure it made Ryan look at me with a little less awe.

With Mako, I just want to protect him from this life. Not because I feel the need to impress him, but because I'm terrified that he'll pity me. The last thing I need is pity.

But of course, Mako always surprises me. The very thing that diminished in Ryan's eyes is the same thing shining from Mako's as he stares down at me. Awe. He doesn't need to say the words now. He's already said them before. He's… proud that I came from a hellhole like this and became the woman I am today. Even if I am a murderer, it doesn't matter to Mako. Not when the person I killed deserved every single thing I did to him.

"Do you have the money?" I ask impatiently. Barbie's sitting in her usual chair, puffing on a cigarette.

"Can't you come here to visit your mother for once? You only come here for money. You're starting to make me feel *used*."

I give her a dry look. "Cute, Barbie. Real cute."

Blackness dances on the edges of my vision. I hate being in this kitchen.

"Did River ever tell you the story of how she got her name?" Barbie prompts, looking Mako up and down like a slab of meat. I'd correct her if I weren't guilty of doing the same thing every time I'm around him.

"No." His response is short and concise. I'd say uninterested if it wasn't for the quirk of a brow that's aimed my way. I sigh, the regret from bringing Mako anywhere near this place deepening.

"I went into labor in the middle of runnin' for my life," Barbie starts, focusing her attention on the worn table. "I thought it would be harder to get caught if I was in the river out there." She nods her head towards the direction of the still, dirty river. "Figured he couldn't catch me that way. Here I am, gettin' chased by one of the scariest men alive, and *that's* when River decides she wants to make an entrance. I'm screamin' and cryin', beggin' for my life while actively trying to keep a baby from coming out of my body." A dry chuckle slithers from her cracked lips. "But River wasn't havin' it. She wanted out right then and there. So, the water is up to my chest, and Billy can't see what's goin' on. He's coming up behind me, gun in his hand already raised to my head. Then he just stops cold when I lift River up, and he hears the first cries from a little baby." She pauses, and brings her weathered, blank eyes to me. "River is what ultimately saved my life that day. As soon as Billy heard her cry, he decided he liked the sound of it. And then made it his life's mission to hear her cry until the day she escaped Shallow Hill."

An ominous silence settles over us as the last of Barbie's words ring out and then fade into the chill air. I shiver, despite it being hot as hell in this house.

I've always hated that story—the origins of my birth and how I came to be. Billy was getting ready to murder a pregnant woman and let her and her dead baby float along the river. Not surprisingly, there have been more than a few dead bodies pulled out of the river. All nobodies with no family to speak of and not a soul around that gives a shit. Barbie might've been lucky enough to gain some sympathy since she would've been pregnant when killed, but not enough to truly search for her killer.

So many nights, I wished that's what would've happened. I *hated* myself for being born because if I had only waited a minute longer, I would've never existed. I would've never endured the torture and abuse that's never really ended, even twenty-two years later. I would've been granted access to heaven without having to endure hell first. I would've been *free*.

"Your life might've been saved, but mine ended that day," I say, forcing dryness into my tone. She smirks at me as if she knows how badly that story still affects me. Mako doesn't say anything, but the edges of his eyes have softened a bit.

"Money, Barbie," I remind her, snapping my fingers obnoxiously. Being reminded of Billy has lit a new fire under my ass.

"Don't have it," she says shortly.

Mako comes to stand beside me, crossing his arms across his broad chest and staring down at Barbie with a cocked brow. He's not looking down his nose at her like he's better than her—he's looking down at her to intimidate her.

For me.

Shock slaps me in the face when I see Barbie blush from the scrutiny in Mako's stare. Never in my fucking life have I seen Barbie *blush*.

The only thing that snaps me out of my shocked state is the wad of crisp, clean bills slapping on the dirty table. Seeing the bills freezes my heart. Clean bills don't pass through Barbie's hands. It's just not something that happens. This town is dirty, and the money is even dirtier.

"Where did you get that from?" I whisper, staring down at them like they're live snakes, reared back and ready to bite.

Barbie glances down at the bills, and then back up at me with an unreadable emotion in her eyes. It almost looks like trepidation, but that word has only ever been associated with Barbie when Billy is involved.

"You know the answer to that, River."

"Why is he giving you money?" I grind out through my gritted teeth.

"Because he knows you come to collect rent each month. Says he wants to take care of his favorite girls, so he fronts me the money to give to you. He said it kills two birds with one stone."

My stomach sours, twisting and turning until I'm sure I'm going to be sick. Vomit rises in the back of my throat. I take a step away from the money.

"I don't want his money," I hiss. "What about the money *you* make?"

"That *is* my money! Who gives a shit where it comes from, River. Just take it!"

Without thought, I grab the money and whip it in her face, tens of bills smacking across her face before fluttering to the filthy tiled floor. Barbie shoots up, her chair clattering loudly behind her and gets in my face.

"What, you too scared to accept money from the Ghost Killer now? You accepted his dick inside you plenty of times. What's wrong with his money?"

All the air is suctioned out of the room, leaving nothing but stagnant, bone-chilling stillness. I cringe and close my eyes, tears already lined across my lids. One slips through when I hear Mako take a single step forward.

"What the fuck did you just say?" An hour ago, his low gravelly voice was deepened with desire and need. Now... Now it's deepened with betrayal.

A curse slips from my mouth as I turn to face Mako. He's already staring down at me, shock splayed across his beautiful face. Coupled with hurt. Deep, cutting hurt.

"I was going to tell you," I mutter shamefully. So badly, I want to drop my eyes to my feet and hide from the anger filling up Mako's eyes like an empty gas tank being pumped full of gasoline.

"You knew who the Ghost Killer was? The entire time?"

Barbie's jeering cackle sounds from behind me. My shoulders hike up to my ears, and embarrassment floods me. This is the last thing I want Barbie to witness. I brought home a man even *she* wanted, and he's breaking up with me right in front of her, not even a half-hour later.

"Yes, but—" Mako's turning and storming out of the house before I can finish my sentence—or rather, my lame excuse.

I'm whipping around, running after him, even as Barbie's heart-stopping words follow me out. "Wait till he finds out Billy's your father, too."

I *almost* stop. I almost turn back around and demand what the hell Barbie just said. But she must be lying. She's just egging on the fight to hurt me. There's no way Billy's my father. One of them would've told me that already.

"Mako, wait!" I shout, not giving a shit that there's a small party on the porch a few doors down, now quieting as they witness the Ghost of Shallow Hill chase after an unknown man. A man that clearly doesn't belong in this town.

"Just... fuck! Get in the goddamn car, River." He rips open his door, throws himself in, and slams the door shut behind him. Not wanting him to drive off without me, I scramble into the car, just barely closing the door before he's peeling out of the driveway, leaving skid marks in our wake.

Both fists are curled around the steering wheel so tightly, the leather is popping beneath his grip. White knuckles glare at me in the darkness, reminding me that I fucked up.

Again.

His arms tremble and his breathing fills the tense silence with short, staccato bursts.

"Do you have a picture of him?" he asks tightly, anger coloring his tone.

"Yes," I whisper, my mouth tasting like ash. Tears blur my vision as I pull my phone out and search for the only picture of Billy I have. I took it years ago before I left. He was particularly savage that night, brutalizing me and ripping me apart mentally and physically. I had already secured my spot at the university and knew I was leaving within a week. I still don't know why I took it, but I sneaked it in when Billy was glaring at me, still angry for whatever I did that night. The reasons for Billy's anger escape me. The only thing remaining is the abuse he inflicted because of it.

The bright light of my phone illuminates Mako's hardened face as I hand over the trembling phone. The second his eyes land on the picture, he's stomping on the brakes and whipping the car to the side of the road. My body pitches forward from the force, and even deep in the throes of his anger, Mako still cares about me enough to bar his arm across my chest and push me back into the seat.

"FUCK!" he roars.

I jump so bad, I hit my head on the glass window. Mako curls his fist and pounds it into the steering wheel so hard that the car is blaring from him hitting the horn.

"Mako, stop! What's wrong?!" I scream, my voice desperate and scared. I'm not scared *of* Mako per se, but I'm scared of what his reaction means.

He finally stops, his knuckles already bruising. His hands rip through his hair as he fumes.

"When did you figure it out?" he demands, keeping his face turned away from me and glued to the window.

Hot, steady streams of tears leak from my eyes. "When you told me about him at dinner. When Billy attacked me that night... he called me a ghost as he was... anyway, it's common in Shallow Hill because of Billy. He says that when you grow up in a place like Shallow Hill, there's no escaping it. So, when you do and then come back... you're considered a ghost. Someone that just haunts the streets when you see fit but always disappears in the end." I wipe the snot away with the bottom of my t-shirt. I forge on, my voice trembling as I confess.

"When I was six years old, Billy got hooked on meth. Real bad. He became unhinged and started killing people off pretty carelessly. It's a miracle Barbie and I survived that time. He would come to the house, raging about how all the men working for him betrayed him. Whether it was because he thought they stole from him or were fucking with the product or whatever the reason. He killed them all. Nothing came of it because he managed to dispose of all the bodies. And as sad as it is, no one really gives a shit about people who die in Shallow Hill.

"When you told me about the Ghost Killer and the way they were murdered, I knew it wasn't a coincidence. I knew it was Billy. I went over to Barbie's when I got the chance to get away from Ryan, and she confirmed Billy's hooked again. Back to killing all his men, and now labeling them Ghosts because well… that's what they are now."

Suffocating silence fills the car, nearly choking me from Mako's anger. He's trembling, shaking so hard from his rage that it looks like he's seizing. My mouth opens, ready to tell Mako what Barbie said to me as I chased him out the door, but the words die on my tongue. There's no use relaying to him something that I haven't confirmed true.

"Please tell me what's going on, Mako," I plead when the angry man beside me continues to stew. I'm shaking like a leaf in bitter winds as I watch my worst nightmare come to life. *This* is why I cried on Mako's chest in the library. Because I knew I would hurt Mako when he found out the truth. A small, stupid part of me held onto the hope that he'd understand why I did it. All the same, I'm losing him. Just like I knew I would.

He sighs harshly, slowly regaining his control. "That's the person that claimed he was a witness to a Ghost Killer murder. That was Ryan's client—Benedict *fucking* Davis. The man who killed my father and who I have been chasing for over a year was right in front of my face. Just like Ryan said."

Twenty-Four
River

THREE LONG DAYS OF grueling, radio silence from Mako. Three days of police knocking on my door, asking questions. Parasites littering the lawn, waiting for any opportunity to snap a picture of me and publish it with some half-assed article with headlines like *The Truth Behind Ryan Fitzgerald's Murder*.

It's tiresome.

Reports over the past few days have been that Ryan's true murderer was finally caught. The Ghost Killer. Who was also Ryan's client. It honestly couldn't have worked out more perfectly. It played into the story we had already spun. Ryan figured out who the Ghost Killer was, so he was silenced before he could reveal the truth. The only thing they're missing is Ryan's body, but police are figuring the Ghost Killer didn't follow his usual MO because it was a desperate, last minute kill before Ryan could reveal his identity.

In a single breath, Mako solved the case for not only his brother but one of the biggest, most notorious cases in the U.S. I don't need to be around Mako to know he's not happy about it. He technically didn't discover who the Ghost Killer was—he was told. In a pretty fucked up way to boot. There's no sense of justice or satisfaction when discovering a serial killer in that manner. When finding out that the girl you're in love with, knew who he was for months and didn't say anything. And then discovering that it was the same man who beat and raped her not too long ago.

I waited on thin ice, expecting the police to storm the house and arrest me for Ryan's murder. Surely, Mako wouldn't keep up the pretense after I lied to him for so long. Surely, he wouldn't consider me worth risking his entire life over.

And yet, he kept true to his word. He covered up Ryan's murder, blaming it on a man that committed countless heinous crimes except for the one he's going to be arrested for.

That's the scariest part. He hasn't been arrested yet. Because they can't find him. Billy has connections *everywhere*. I'm sure he knew of his arrest before it was even decided that they had probable cause.

No one knows where he is. So now, it's not a search to find who the Ghost Killer is, but *where* he is.

"You look like death." The soft voice rings out from behind me. I'm curled into a ball on the couch, facing away from the world. Amelia can't even see my face, and she's already calling me out.

I try to sniffle, but both nostrils are completely congested. "You can't even see me yet," I retort weakly.

Weight compresses the leather couch behind my legs. A soft huff escapes her mouth. She's only five months along now, but she's getting huge. When you get knocked up by a mammoth, it only makes sense that you're going to get pregnant with one.

I turn towards my best friend, confirming her presumptuous statement and settling my eyes on her basketball of a stomach.

"How's the baby?" I ask, my voice hoarse and weak. The corners of her eyes tighten, but she humors me anyways.

"I'm convinced I was abducted by aliens and injected with a baby. There's no way this thing is human. I'm five months and look like I'm ready to pop. This lady in the grocery store asked me when I'm due. And of course, when I told her, she didn't believe me! She said I must have pregnancy brain because I'm clearly about to enter into labor any day now." She huffs with annoyance when she recalls the memory. "Damn witch. I may have someone slowly consuming my body from the inside out, but I'm not *stupid*."

I laugh at her antics. "Did you decide on a name yet?"

Amelia called me yesterday to dryly inform me she's having a boy. She never cared about throwing gender reveal parties or making a big deal out of stuff like that. The technician asked if she wanted to know the gender, Amelia said yes, and there was her answer. Though she did admit that she cried when they said she was having a boy.

"I think we're going to go with Beckham."

"That is incredibly cute. You have my approval."

She smiles, though it doesn't quite reach her eyes. She's too worried about *me* and it's tainting her excitement.

"Please stop worrying about me," I whine pitifully.

"River. Your boyfriend was murdered only three weeks ago. You told me that perfectly edible man fucked the soul out of your body and then kicked you out of his car an hour later because he discovered that your abuser is also a notorious serial killer, and you knew about it and didn't tell him. *And*, that your mother told you that that notorious serial killer is also your father." She pauses for dramatic effect, earning an eye roll. "Why the hell *wouldn't* I be worried?"

"I don't know if he's *actually* my father," I mutter, ignoring the other several valid points she made.

"Whether he is or not, he's an evil man who's been terrorizing you your entire life. I get why Mako's pissed, I really do. But does he not understand the extent to which you are absolutely terrified of Billy? Does he not realize the trauma that man has inflicted on you, and in turn, gains your unwilling loyalty purely because you're fearful for your life?"

This is why I called Amelia and told her everything. Well, not *everything*. I obviously didn't tell her that I tortured and killed my boyfriend. I trust Amelia with my entire soul and being, but that doesn't mean she deserves to be burdened with a secret like that.

But I'm glad I confessed everything else to her. Not only is she a solid shoulder to cry on and an ear to listen, but she gets it. She understands what it's like to be abused. She understands the trauma and fear. We both know I should've told Mako the truth. And because I kept my mouth shut, several people were murdered because of my silence. It was never said, but I know that thought passed through Mako's head, too.

"I don't know, Amelia. I think he's too angry to rationalize it that way. It's hard for someone to do that when they don't know what it's like to have someone like that haunting your life."

She sighs and nods her head, agreeing.

"Do you think Billy is going to know that it was you and Barbie that told Mako who he really was?"

I bite my lip, debating how much I should divulge. If I should tell her the truth on how terrified I am that Billy will come for me. I glance up at her, and whatever's in my eyes must answer her question. Her lip trembles.

"Cameras working again?" she asks in place of my response. I nod once.
"Come home with me."

"And possibly put you and your unborn child's life in danger? I should
punch you for even suggesting something like that," I say, a bite in my tone.
She flinches but nods her head in acceptance. The sad truth is, Amelia
understands that there's not much I can do to get away from Billy. And
knowing that, as my best friend, is killing her inside. Just like it would do to
me if our roles were reversed.

"So aside from this Ghost Killer clusterfuck. How are you handling
everything?" she asks, forcing the conversation away from something
incredibly terrifying as she absently rubs her hand on her belly. She said
he's already started kicking. I stare at her belly intently, silently bribing baby
Beckham into kicking his mother so I can feel it.

"Everything as in my abusive boyfriend being murdered or the fact that
I think I fell in love with his brother and he hates me now?" Amelia gives
me a droll look, and I sigh. "I'm not sad about Ryan. Maybe I should be
because we were together for over two years, but any love for him went out
the window already. He hit me, raped me, and cheated on me. I feel nothing."

Amelia slumps against the couch dramatically. "I'm glad you said it. I
would've been totally willing to empathize with you if you were still in love
and missed him, but it would've hurt my soul, too."

I smile, feeling a tad lighter than I have in days. "As for Mako... I
don't know what's going on there. I finally realized that he's everything I
want in a man at the same time, he realized that I'm everything he hates
in a woman."

Amelia smacks my leg lightly, shooting me a look. "That is not true,
River. Mako's pissed, and rightly so. But he told you he loved you, and even
though I only met him for like, thirty seconds once, he doesn't seem like

the type of man to say that to just anyone. And in those thirty seconds, he looked at you like you hung the fucking moon and stars, as cheesy as that shit is, okay? He loves you, he's just hurt."

My lip trembles, and goddamn the bitch for giving me hope. I hate hope. I hate that word as much as I hate the word beautiful. Hope is hopeless. Hope is disappointment. I had no expectations for Mako to come back to me, and now I'm trashing those expectations and replacing them with hopeful ones. Gross.

"Should I reach out to him?"

She doesn't answer right away, seeming to look for the question in my penguin socks, as if the flightless birds are going to reveal the secrets of the universe. Finally, she says, "Let him come to you. He needs to cool off and think about things rationally. Right now, that's pretty hard to do when he's dealing with distraught parents that just lost their son, a manhunt for a very dangerous serial killer, and you have parasites sunbathing on your lawn."

Can't argue with that.

NIGHTTIME IS WHEN IT'S the worst. The house is enormous and empty. But it doesn't feel empty. It feels like there are all sorts of scary things lurking in the millions of shadows in this house. Even when Ryan was alive, I never liked being home alone. Scenes from horror movies would play through my mind on a reel, and my heart rate would increase until I was on the verge of hysteria.

It's so much worse now. The reality that Billy is missing has hit me full force. It's unlikely he knows that his identity reveal had anything to do with me, but that doesn't make me feel any less on edge. What if Barbie somehow warned him that Mako—a fucking detective—discovered who the Ghost Killer is?

Would I blame her for telling him? Yes and no. Barbie would warn Billy for the same reasons I didn't tell Mako who he was. Fear. Something that Billy has ingrained into Barbie and me so deeply, it's nestled deep into our bone marrow.

Without ever fully acknowledging it, I convinced myself that if I told Mako who Billy was, he'd find out. He'd know it was me, and not only would he come for me, but he'd also come after Mako, too. Barbie's pumping her system full of drugs that could quickly cause paranoia. The second we left her house, she probably convinced herself that Billy would find out and warned him.

Realizing this has me nestling deeper into the couch. I could hardly stand to look at this couch for months after I embarrassed myself all over it, and now it's the only thing offering me any shred of comfort.

I wish Mako was here.

I turn the TV up louder, some reality show on that I've hardly paid attention to. I'm hoping the privileged women complaining about their lives will help drown out the terrifying thoughts threatening to send me into a panic attack.

A SOFT NOISE FILTERS through my dreams, coaxing my brain away from my dream and back into reality. Bright flashes of light flicker across my lids before the nasal voices from the TV follow suit. Reruns of that reality show are still playing.

God, how long has it been?

My heart starts to pound as a sick feeling starts to settle in. Something woke me up. The air feels different like someone is in the room with me.

Heart in my throat, I slowly crack open my eyes until the room comes into view. Nothing immediately jumps out at me. Nothing amiss except for the feeling of eyes on me.

Light flickers across the expansive living room, casting dancing shadows across the floor and walls that bleed into the dining room. Off to the left of it is the kitchen, where one wall is all windows. Ryan had mentioned that that glass was hurricane-proof, but it doesn't mean someone can't find a creative way in if they truly set their mind to it.

I lift up on my arm, my eyes staring intensely into the darkness, praying I don't find someone in the shadows watching me. My instincts are blaring red right now, and I can't see why just yet. Just when I begin to relax a little, footsteps sound out from the dining room. I jump up, the blankets tangling in my legs and nearly tripping me as a body emerges from the shadows.

I freeze when his face comes into view. Every warning I told myself earlier has come to fruition. I knew he'd come for me. I fucking knew it.

"Hey, Billy," I greet, my voice trembling. There's no point in hiding my fear. Billy knows the taste of it well by now.

"Did you miss me?" he asks, his voice low and sinister. He's dressed in a suit, as usual. Impeccable as ever, even when he's about to conduct a kidnapping. He's thinner than the last time I saw him, his suit not as fitted as it usually is. His skin is grayer, and there are acne scabs scattered across his face.

The meth is getting to him. His body is deteriorating.

Piercing eyes penetrate me from across the room. It was always Billy's scariest quality. Never mind the massive scar on his weathered face or the intimidating nature in which Billy carries himself. It was always his eyes.

Cold, dark, and dead. Even meth can't dim the darkness in those eyes.

"I always do," I whisper, detangling my legs from the blanket and standing tall. Thank God I am dressed in sweatpants and a t-shirt. Billy would've taken great pleasure in molesting my body with his eyes if I was wearing anything remotely revealing.

My personal boogeyman stuffs his hands deep into his black slacks and stares at me with a detached expression. Shivers course down my spine, despite the warmth in the house. If I ran right now, Billy would chase me. I may know this house better than he does, but he has far more experience as the cat hunting down the mouse. He would catch me eventually.

"What are you doing here, Billy?" I ask, swallowing nervously. He takes another step forward. My eyes glance to the entrance to the foyer. I can't back up any further with the couch pressed into my legs.

"Don't play stupid, River. You know exactly why I'm here," he growls.

My heart drops. Where the fuck is my phone? Probably lodged between the cushions of the couch. Nowhere that's easily reachable. And definitely not in a spot where I could sneak it into my pocket. Billy's watching me like a hawk, waiting for me to twitch in a manner that he doesn't like before he pounces.

"What did Barbie tell you?"

"You know I'm hurt," he cuts in before the words barely finish leaving my mouth. "I raised you, River. Watched you grow into a young woman. Taught you many life lessons. I thought we had a bond." My heart speeds up when he walks closer. Closer and closer until a monster is standing directly in front of me.

His eye twitches, the only sign that Billy is angry. I don't know if he's on meth right now or not, but Billy can be pretty good at hiding when he's riding high on drugs if he needs to be. Ever the professional. Just like

Ryan, he always cared about his reputation and his image with people. He would never live it down if he looked like some tweaker from the streets.

"Billy, I don't know what Barbie tol—" The loud slap rings in my ear before the burning sensation fully sets in. I close my eyes again as the fire finally catches up, setting the nerves in my face ablaze. I glue my teeth shut, learning my lesson not to speak.

"Don't fucking lie to me," he spits, letting the blank mask slip for a few terrifying seconds before donning it once more. The switch—quickly turning from one person to the next—is unsettling to watch. Calm and collected one second, to raging mad another, and then back to calm as if I hallucinated the anger.

I don't speak again, not trusting the right words to come out of my mouth. There *are no* right words. He's angry and it doesn't matter what I say. In his eyes, there's no excusing the fact that I sold him out to the police. To a *detective*.

"Do you realize how much money it's going to cost to clear my name?" he asks, tilting his body down to eye level. His breath reeks of spearmint gum, the sharp smell invading my senses. Billy always loved to chew gum. He said it would look unprofessional to kill someone with bad breath.

I shake my head once, tightening my lips into a firm, white line. His hand snaps out, startling me as he grabs a fist full of hair and wrenches my face into his. I jump, a scream loosening from my throat. Dead eyes stare into widened eyes filled with terror.

"You betrayed me, River. Your own father."

A gasp lodges in my throat. My body freezes, and my eyes squeeze shut. From pain. Denial. Absolute rage.

I convinced myself Barbie was lying to me, just to hurt me further. Twist the knife that was already plunged in my heart when Mako found out I was lying to him. I refused to actually consider what she was saying. Refused, refused, refused.

"You're lying," I spit through gritted teeth, my body resuming its fight tenfold. Burning rage consumes me. There's no way Billy is my fucking father. "My father could be *anyone.*"

Billy's dark laugh reaches my ears and slithers down into my soul, cracking it just a little bit more.

"I had a paternity test done when you were born," he admits, shrugging a shoulder as if he isn't currently tearing my life apart. Tears burn my retinas, those words eliciting a response in me I can't quite describe. Barbie could never tell me who my father was—at least that's what she always led me to believe. Any time I asked, she'd scoff at me and ask me how many clients she fucks in a week. I could never give her an answer.

"I don't look anything like you," I argue, a last-ditch effort to catch him in a lie.

He smiles sardonically. "You're right. But you got your eyes from my mother." My eyes narrow, still not ready to believe him.

"You look so much like how Barbie did when she was your age. *Beautiful.* But those eyes, they're exactly like my mother's. Always filled with fire and brimstone. And you know what?" He pauses, waiting for my response.

"What?" I grit out.

"I *hated* my mother."

Twenty-Five
Mako

NEVER IN MY LIFE did I think I'd be sitting here consoling my mother as we bury her son—my brother. Not that I could ever technically call him that. He was never much of a brother and more of an abuser. That's what he was to many people.

Mom's head is resting on my shoulders, bawling her sad blue eyes out as we lower Ryan's casket into the ground on a chilly Saturday morning. An empty casket. Dad's on the other side of her, barely holding it together as he hugs his wife from the other side, his arm firmly wrapped around her tiny waist. It's taking everything in me not to lift my arm back and clock him. Doesn't matter that I hated Ryan, it doesn't change the fact that he raped a little boy for who knows how many years. Did he ever really stop?

That's something I'll never know.

I haven't told Mom the truth about him, yet. I tried, but it was so hard to do while she's also grieving the death of her son. I'm scared to see how she'll react when she has to grieve for her husband, too.

As many people there are that cared about Ryan, Mom and Dad insisted on a personal funeral. Immediate family only, with the obvious inclusion of his girlfriend.

She's not fucking here, though. Not sure if it's because she didn't think she could handle being able to keep up the pretense of grieving a man that hurt her in so many ways, or she didn't come because she didn't want to face me. Either way, Mom and Dad are upset she didn't make it, without a word as to why.

And me? I'm just fucking pissed.

Part of me doesn't feel I have the right to be angry. Ryan did some pretty fucked up shit to her, and if she doesn't want to show up to his funeral, then she shouldn't have to. Maybe I'm just angry because it would've given me an excuse to see her. Talk to her. Even if it would've just been an angry-filled exchange, it would've soothed something in my soul to see her again.

"No mother should ever have to bury their child," Mom whispers from beside me, dabbing her nose with her tissue daintily.

"I know, Mom," I whisper back, feeling a million different shades of guilt when I'm the one that helped put him in the ground—or rather, a bunch of pigs' stomachs. I don't feel guilty that it happened. I feel guilty that my mother is the one ultimately suffering for it.

The priest says a few prayers then Mom steps forward, Ryan's childhood teddy bear clutched in her hand. Supposedly, when he was a baby, he never let that thing go. It was his comfort when he was scared, hugging the teddy bear with tiny hands, convinced that it'd keep him safe. Mom decided to bury it with his casket in the hopes that he'd find comfort in the bear even in death.

She throws the bear, crouches down, and with a heartbreaking sob throws the first handful of dirt on the casket. Dad slowly walks up to join her, fisting the dirt like it personally wronged him, his knuckles bleeding into white, before throwing his handful on the casket as well. They asked me to do the small tradition, too, but I declined. I think I have enough bad karma built up; there's no need to rub it in by pretending I care that much.

They rejoin my side as the dirt begins to pile on, scoop by scoop.

"Where do you think she is?" Mom asks softly from beside me, her tears still freshly falling.

I sigh, not sure how to answer. "From what I know about her, she's not used to the family thing. I don't think she's the type of person that finds solace in other people. She probably just needed to be alone today, Mom."

Mom nods, accepting that answer. Always the most kind-hearted person, never judging others. "Everyone grieves differently," she says. "I hope she knows she can always find a family in us."

My heart clenches for reasons I can't even name. I can't tell if it hurts that she'd be included in the family as Ryan's girlfriend, and not mine. How would Mom even react to that? River and I falling in love with each other? Sometimes it's hard to say with her. She's understanding, but she's also never dealt with the death of a child before. She could react in ways even neither of us would expect.

Not that it matters much anymore, anyway. River lied to me repeatedly for several months. I get that we weren't on the best of terms—to no fault of my own—but she couldn't open her fucking mouth at any point when I was helping her cover up my brother's murder?

Fuck, she even tried getting the answer out of Ryan before she killed him, already knowing the answer herself. And she *still* kept her mouth shut. It hurts. It hurts that she knew how badly I wanted to solve this case, how much it was getting to me, and she didn't care enough about me to end my misery.

I'm a damn good detective, I know that. I'm on the verge of getting promoted to Sergeant, for fuck's sake. Every detective has their *one*. The one criminal that gave them absolute hell to catch. The Ghost Killer was mine, and no part of me would've been ashamed if River revealed her suspicions to me.

The only thing that pisses me off more than River lying to me is the fact that the Ghost Killer was right under my nose the entire time, attempting to fuck with the investigation in any way he could. Once his story started changing, I stopped relying on him. Stopped listening. Long-term use of meth fucks with your memory, and Billy is no stranger to tasting his own product. It started off as just a few minor details that changed and, eventually, some key details.

It makes me wonder what would've happened to the investigation if Billy would've came to me as a sober man. I loathe admitting that he probably would've succeeded in fucking with my case. I wouldn't have been chasing him this long if he wasn't a smart man. I guess I can be thankful for meth if it means I have a stone-cold killer starting to make mistakes.

The fire inside me has been raging since the moment I saw Benedict Davis on River's phone, staring at the camera with cold, dead eyes and an expression that would better suit your nightmares. And those scars. Those goddamn scars. I've been tempted to ask Benedict how he got them when interviewing him, but I always kept my mouth shut. Now, all I want to do is give him new ones. The flames are being stoked, wood thrown into the inferno now that Benedict—or *Billy*—is missing.

Now that I know who the Ghost Killer is, he has no fucking chance of escaping me now.

I PUT MOM TO bed only an hour ago, when my phone begins to buzz in my pocket. I ignore it, for now, more focused on making sure my distraught mother is okay. Couldn't give a fuck less how Dad is feeling. But the buzzing is insistent, and soon Dad is snapping at me to answer the phone already. I listen if only for the fact to get away from him.

With a sigh, I answer, "Mako."

"Mako? Oh my God, Mako. Thank God."

My brow creases, not recognizing the voice over the phone.

"Who is this?"

"It's Amelia, River's best friend."

My heart stops, and everything around me freezes. If River's friend is calling me, that means something happened. Something bad.

"Where's River?" I ask, a bite to my tone.

"That's the fucking thing, I don't know! I was just at her house yesterday, and while she was stuck on the couch crying, she was otherwise fine. And then I go back over today to drop off some comfort food, and the house is trashed! She's gone, Mako, she's fucking gone and I know it was Billy. I know he fucking took her!"

By the end of her rant, she's hysterical and I'm shaking from... fuck, from so many things. Fury is coursing through my bloodstream. That motherfucker took my girl, and now there is no hope that I'll be bringing back Billy alive. The second I get my hands around that asshole's neck... I can't think about it right now, I need to focus on finding River.

"I'm heading to her house now. Stay there."

I hang up the phone and rush out of the house, Dad's concerned questions chasing me out. I don't have the brain space to hear them, let alone give a solid answer.

I'm peeling out of the driveway and speeding towards Ryan's house, donning my sirens to get there faster. Ryan lives about fifteen minutes away from our parents. I get there in five.

Throwing the gear in park, I don't even bother turning the engine off before I'm nearly stumbling out of the car and into Ryan's house. Amelia is in the living room, pacing a hole in the carpet with steady streams of hot tears trailing down her face. Amelia chirps with relief and then throws herself at me and hugs my midsection, crying into my chest.

Shock renders me helpless, my arms splaying out with awkwardness for a moment before my brain catches up. I relax my arms and wrap them loosely around her back, listening to her garbled words while anxiously looking around the house, searching for any sign of what happened to River.

"I need you to tell me everything you know. Did River mention anything the last time you spoke? Did she seem scared or express concern that Billy was coming for her? Anything at all?"

Amelia steps back and rests her hands on her swollen stomach. Her mascara is smudged on my white t-shirt, but I couldn't give less of a shit.

"She didn't say the words, but yes, she was terrified. We had a brief conversation about it. I asked her to come live with me and she nearly bit my head off for suggesting it, knowing that it would put me and my baby in danger. I asked if the cameras were back on, and she said yes. That was about the extent of it."

Sobs crawl up her throat and wrack her body once more. She drops her head in her hands, covering her face. My own hands rip through my hair, tugging until the sharp pain rivals in the pain in my chest. I can't fucking breathe.

River knew Billy was going to come for her.

And I was too fucking selfish and stewing in my own anger to realize this. I should've fucking known. I should've known Billy wouldn't let

Barbie and River's revelation go unpunished. The man is hooked on meth and paranoid that all his men are betraying him on a good day.

Fuck!

That's the whole reason the Ghost Killer even came about. His paranoia. His complete conviction that no one can be trusted.

I swear to God, if I find River murdered with that fucking word carved in her chest…

"What are we going to do?" Amelia cries, pulling me away from my violent and very unhelpful thoughts.

I've already started carefully picking around the house. Looking at the only evidence I have. Blood spatter is on the carpet, not enough to be fatal, but enough to stall my heart in my chest. A fleece blanket is tossed on the floor, strands of curly black hair lying on top of it. It could've been from natural shedding, but I have a feeling it's from Billy yanking her around by her hair.

The more I see, the more the red haze in my vision increases. More blood on the dining room floor, this time in streaks as if a body was dragged across the blood. He made her bleed somehow, hopefully from a nosebleed rather than anything more brutal like being stabbed or cut. Then he dragged her into the dining room, more than likely by her hair considering there are a few more strands stuck in the blood. Half a footprint is stamped on the ground, likely from her kicking her feet.

The blood is consistent all the way through the kitchen and out the back door. The final nail in the coffin is the small bloody handprint on the window, the size of River's hands. Amelia cries harder when she sees the handprint, both of us imagining very vividly River's desperate attempt to get away from Billy.

The streaking of the blood and a couple more cropped footprints and fingerprints are contingent to River being taken by force.

My girl didn't leave without a fucking fight, that's for sure.

"What do you know about Billy?"

"N-nothing really. River was tight-lipped when it came to him. She said the less I knew about him, the safer I am."

I growl in frustration, storming my way into Ryan's office where his monitor is. The police have already combed through for any evidence, but all that was found was work-related information.

I sit down in the office chair and pull up the security feed. Amelia huddles behind me, peering over my shoulder as I wind the cameras back. A heavy feeling of unease settles inside my chest. I need to see this, but I already know I'm liable to punch a hole through the monitor once I see Billy lay a single finger on her. Based on the nervous energy emanating from Amelia behind me, I'm sure she's not feeling much different than I am.

With Amelia's direction from when she left the house, the feed is rewound to about ten o'clock last night, only a couple of hours after Amelia left. River is curled in a tight ball, sleeping on the couch, her black hair splayed across the couch. In her sleep, she looks so innocent. Her face softened, almost making her look like a teenager.

And then her eyes are snapping open abruptly, as if she heard a noise. She slowly sits up, propped up on one arm as she looks around the room, the only source of light being the TV. It takes a few minutes, but from the corner of the camera—right where the dining room entrance is—Billy steps out of the shadows.

My hands grow clammy watching River scramble up, tripping over the fleece blanket between her legs. I can't hear what they're saying, but River's terror is so potent, I can feel it through the camera. Adrenaline rushes into my veins, flooding my ears as I watch Billy come closer to her.

River presses her legs into the couch, her eyes rounded and wild as they exchange words. My fingers twitch with the need to reach out and touch her. Save her.

Billy raises a hand and slaps her in the face, their exchange becoming more heated. I nearly propel myself through the screen, desperate to pull Billy out of it and crush him in my fist.

There's a moment of pause, where they both look at each other, sizing the other up. And then River bolts, darting to the left towards the front door. Billy expects the move, catching hold of her by the waist before flinging her back on the couch. River doesn't stop to absorb the impact on the sofa, immediately scrambling off towards the dining room. But Billy is right there, catching her again.

She struggles and fights while I sit on the edge of the chair in suspense. I know how it ends, but yet I'm waiting for her to escape him anyways. Amelia's face closes in on the screen, her cheek nearly pressed against mine. She trembles just as I do, hating every second of watching her best friend being abducted but not being able to unglue her eyes from the scene.

River's mouth opens wide, and though I can't hear it, I feel the scream she lets loose. So loud, her body shakes from it. Billy curls a fist and punches her in the face, once, twice, three times before River's body begins to go limp. Blood pours from her nose.

Billy drags her fighting body out of the living room, past the dining room and into the kitchen. I switch camera feeds as he drags her through the house, my heart pounding as Billy gets closer to the door leading outside. Once they go through that door, I won't be able to see her anymore.

A teardrop lands on my hand as the last of River's body disappears through the door. She's gone. And I feel nothing but anger and desolation.

Amelia sniffles, more tears dripping from her face and searing into my skin. I don't move away, nor do I try to comfort her. Instead, I let the tears of River's best friend soak into me, propelling my anger. River has at least two people in her life that would die a little inside if she died. Part of mine and Amelia's soul would be lowered into the ground right alongside River's body.

"Do you have any idea where he could've taken her?" I ask in a low tone, my voice hoarse with emotion.

She sniffles again, wiping her nose. "I have no idea. From what I know, Billy didn't tell River much about his drug operations, and even if he did, she wouldn't have told me anything. If Billy would've found out I knew anything, he would've killed me."

I nod my head, already coming to the same conclusion. I lose myself in thought, staring at the feed once more, trying to find anything to go off of. *Anything.*

"Do you love her?" Amelia's soft question cuts through my concentration like a hot knife. Her question stings. Because I do love her, and I treated her badly. Now, she's gone. *Fuck.* I'm still pissed at her for keeping the Ghost Killer's identity from me. But how can I blame her for being scared when I'm watching her abduction right in front of my fucking face?

"I do," I answer.

She nods her head as if I confirmed something she already knew. "She loves you, too. I think she fell in love with you on that dance floor."

My head whips to her, surprised. She's staring forlornly at the screen. "She told you it was me?"

She shakes her head slowly. "I recognized you. Even in my drunk-addled brain that night, I remember watching you two dance. I remember watching the way you looked down at her. And I recognized that look because I see it every day when my husband looks at me. I've seen River dance with many men up until that point, but I never saw her enjoy it the way she did with you. I watched two souls connect, and even though I was incredibly sick at that point, I felt so much guilt for pulling her away. Because I know something special would've happened that night, and it's my fault it didn't. And because of that, she ran into Ryan's arms. Sometimes I feel guilty for that, too. If I would've just handled myself, she never would've dated that monster."

Another tear slips from her eyes. This time, I do wipe it away. "It's not your fault, Amelia. There's a lot of things I'd do differently that night. The first one would be getting her phone number."

A sad smile stretches across her face. "She didn't say much about you. I asked her once, and the look on her face said it all. She was plagued by you. She admitted she refused to look at your face. And when I asked why, she said she didn't want your face to haunt her every night, just as your hands do. She shut down after that, and I didn't push."

She pauses, and it seems like she's struggling with something she wants to say. "She told me what happened between you two. I get why you're mad. I really do. But this right here, is why she didn't tell you. I hope you can forgive her."

"I already have," I whisper.

Too many emotions well up inside of me. I turn my face back to the screen and watch once more as the love of my life is taken away. From me. From Amelia. From her life.

"I think we need to go pay her mother a visit."

Twenty-Six
River

THE INCESSANT POUNDING IN my skull is what pulls me out of the abysmal darkness I've lost myself in. It was comfortable there. I felt nothing. Physically, or emotionally. And now I feel *everything*. Sharp pin pricks of pain explode across my head, and if it weren't for the fact that I've woken up this way quite a few times in my life and have solid survival instincts, I'd groan aloud in pain.

Instead, I keep my face blank despite the pain and let my surroundings filter in. It's completely silent. No shuffling of feet or rustling of clothing. No breathing.

When I feel confident I'm alone, I slowly peek open my eyes. This time, I do let out a little groan when the pain intensifies.

I stare at the cement ceiling above me, not bothering to look around until my memory catches up. Everything starts coming back to me in quick, blurred images. I was home alone. Amelia had been gone for a few hours when Billy had come for me. We had fought—or at least I had—until he dragged me out of the house to his car and threw me in the trunk. The last thing I remember is Billy's fist coming towards my face before I blacked out.

Shit. Not good. I've no idea where he possibly could've taken me. And if I don't know, no one else will either.

The cold realization that I'm well and truly alone settles in. I've always been fucking alone. No one has ever saved me before.

And no one sure as fuck is going to save me now.

Mako wouldn't know the first place to look for me. And even if Barbie did, she wouldn't care enough about me to risk her life and tell anyone. Not when it comes to Billy.

Now I take the time to look around. I'm in a basement. Old and decrepit, with spiderwebs strung across every nook and cranny, accompanied by that old, musty smell. This basement has definitely seen a flood or ten in its years. Exposed wooden beams break up the basement's open concept with an exposed light bulb in the center of the room, shining bright and burning dimly. And of course, there's only one escape route—the rickety steps leading to a padlocked door.

Aside from myself and my demons, a single wooden chair, and the thin cotton mattress I'm lying on, there's nothing else down here.

Not even cameras, which surprise me. Billy's pretty old school but not enough to not keep up with the times. He's big on surveillance. His paranoia would never allow him not to keep an eye on all his operations at all times. Maybe there's one of his goonies standing outside the door upstairs. If there's any left.

Bringing me here wasn't premeditated. He chose this place last minute. Maybe he even decided to kidnap me last minute.

I settle deeper into the mattress until I'm sure I can feel the cold floor seeping into my shoulder blades and wait for Billy to show up.

TIME BECOMES DILUTED. I've fallen into a restless sleep when I hear the slam of a door. My body jolts awake. Just barely do I keep myself from bolting upright. If Billy doesn't kill me first, the onslaught of pain from doing something like that surely would.

I crack open my eyelids, only to be met with muted light. Even with the softness of the glow, it sends a sharp stabbing pain to my head.

"You're awake," he says coldly. The wooden stairs groan beneath his weight. Each creak radiates throughout my skull, followed by piercing pain so sharp, I'm sure my brain is falling into pieces. Fucker gave me a concussion.

"No shit," I groan, my throat dry and burning from dehydration. The moment the words leave my mouth, I brace myself for his trigger-happy fist. Billy never liked it when I talked back.

"Watch it," he snaps. Thankfully, he keeps his hands to himself this time. When I muster the courage to look at him, he's standing over me, legs spread and hands in his pockets. Blank-faced and well-dressed as ever, as if he's used to kidnapping girls in a three-piece Armani suit.

That's right. *He is.*

"What are you going to do with me?" I ask with a resigned sigh. It's not that the prospect of how Billy is going to kill me doesn't absolutely terrify me, it's that I've resigned myself to this fate long ago, and now that it's here, it's almost a relief. No more do I have to look over my shoulder, hoping not to see the devil standing behind me.

I've grown tired and weary of this life. I'm not entirely sad that it's getting cut short.

"I haven't decided yet," he murmurs, almost to himself. He sighs, plops the wooden chair directly in front of me, and sits, the rickety wood groaning dangerously under his weight. I hate that I flinch away when he lifts his hand to my face, wiping a stray piece of hair out of my eyes. He picks up the errant curl and tugs on it until it's straight. His eyes pick over the strand, fascinated with my natural curls.

Billy always loved my curly hair.

"Do you know why I've always loved your hair?" he asks, picking up on my thoughts.

I don't genuinely care why. But I'd rather have Billy talking to me rather than him torturing or raping me.

"Why?" I croak, wincing from the dryness in my throat. He doesn't make a move to fix my problem.

"Your hair has always been a symbol of your tenacity. You bounce back. It didn't matter what I did to you. I stretched you thin, and no matter how hard I did it—you always bounced back from it. It was fascinating watching you grow up. It made me want to try harder to break you, but I never really could."

Didn't he, though? I almost argue that point. I suppose Billy's version of breaking someone is pushing them to the point where they off themselves. I refused to kill myself, though I've always contemplated the idea like I'm deciding what I'm going to eat for dinner.

I don't say anything. I'm sure the psychopath expects me to feel praised and offer him a thank-you, but I might be liable to spit on him instead if I open my mouth.

He sighs and drops the curl like burning coal, seemingly disappointed in my lack of response. A narcissist doesn't like their compliments to go unappreciated. His hand travels back to my face, petting my skin softly. Shivers of revulsion travel down my spine, and I don't bother to hide the reaction.

"I should've killed you when you were young," he muses softly.

"You should've," I agree.

He pauses, and when he does, it feels like the world does, too. Earth stops spinning on its axis, and for a moment, time stills. His hand whips to my hair in the next second, yanking me off the cot roughly. A startled scream releases from my throat. Fear pumps through my veins like poison as he drags me across the dirty floor and to the middle of the room. My hand curls around his wrist, desperate to pull myself up to relieve the sharp pain spreading throughout my scalp.

"Ungrateful bitch," he spits, shoving my head away. My temple knocks onto the cement floor. Stars burst across my vision, leaving trails of black spots in their wake. My face is then pushed to the ground with one hand while he tears at my pants with the other.

"What I really should've done," he starts, his breath heaving with the effort of pulling my pants down my kicking legs. "Is push your mother down the fucking stairs when I got her pregnant with you."

"Yeah?" I shout, hysteria starting to possess my body. "I wish you fucking would've, too, Billy! I wish you would've, too. At least then I would've never known a vile, pathetic man like you!"

"Shut up!" he roars, stopping his goal in order to punch me once in the back of the head. Stars explode in my eyes, and without my permission, my body slackens. Once I do, Billy finally gets my pants down. The cool air hits my backside, and something about that feeling makes my skin crawl. That was always when I knew it was going to get ugly while growing up. Once I felt my pants slip down my legs, my safety net was gone, and what came after would always hurt.

The fight in me rejuvenated, I wriggle hard, bucking to and fro but to no avail. His weight comes down on top of me, pinning me in place. I feel his hardness pressing into my bare backside, the zipper painfully rubbing against my skin.

He shoves a hand between our bodies, quickly unbuttoning and unzipping his pants in a matter of seconds. I gag when I feel flesh on flesh.

"You're my *father*, and you're going to *rape* me?!" I scream, outraged and disturbed by his lack of morals.

I still don't want to believe he's my father. But deep in my bones, I know Barbie and him aren't lying. Little bits and pieces of memories flash through my head. Barbie spitting on me when I smiled at my worn teddy bear, telling me I smile just like Billy does. Or when I pushed another kid down for sticking his hand up my dress, cracking his head open, followed by her snide comment telling me I'm just like my father. Words that never held enough weight at the time but suddenly feel like a ton of bricks now.

Another punch to the back of the head is my answer. He doesn't care that I'm his blood. Billy raping me was never about attraction or desire. It was always about power. About using fear to keep me in line. This time is no different.

Before, I'd stay quiet and let Billy defile my body. The harder I fought him in the past, the harder he fucked me. Even knowing that, I don't stay quiet this time. I don't stay still or docile.

No. Pent up rage is exploding from me, eviscerating any semblance of strength I had left inside of me. I scream when he enters me. And I continue to scream long after he finds his release. I scream and scream until my throat is raw and the cellar door is locked behind him.

Even when my voice gives out, the screaming continues to resonate through my head until all five of my senses are consumed by my pain.

DAYS PASS BEFORE BILLY visits me again. Wrapped food and a bottle of water had been thrown down the steps before the door slammed behind him—three times a day for the past three days. I refused to touch any of it. Part of me dared to, just hoping that he poisoned the food so I could let my miserable existence fade. But that's not Billy's style. He'd rather let me suffer and agonize, sweating over the prospect of him murdering me. All I'm doing is anticipating it.

I lay on my stomach next to the cot, face smashed against the cool cement floor. A stream of drool stems from my mouth, pooling beneath my cheek and pruning my skin. I don't care enough to wipe it away. I don't care enough to do anything. Right now, he's ignoring me and letting me rot in this dank basement to be left alone with my thoughts. Bastard knows what he's doing too because fuck, if my thoughts aren't spiraling down.

I don't want to live anymore.

I don't want to exist.

To *be*.

If there were anything to kill myself with in this basement, I would've done it already. And he knows that, too. He knows it and is dragging out the torture. That's why he took the wooden chair away. He must've seen me eyeing it, already planning on breaking the chair and using the sharp end of the wood to cut my wrists. He walked away with that chair in his damn hand.

I tried to crack wood off the wooden steps, but I had nothing to use, and my body was too weak to even get a splinter.

What point is there in life anyways? Amelia has her own family, and though I know she loves me dearly, she can also live without me.

There's Mako.

But he hates me.

I close my eyes tightly. I can't keep the onslaught of memories flashing through my mind, despite my desperate attempts to push them out of my head. Images of Mako flicker through my thoughts like a slideshow. Of his smile. His determined expression anytime he'd try to knock some sense into me. His sexy smirk when I said or did something he liked. And his acceptance when I told him about my sordid past.

He's done so much for me. Given up so much. Risked *everything* for me. And I couldn't open my mouth and give him one piece of information that could've changed everything. He could've caught Billy, and I'd never be in this stupid fucking situation. Once again, I got myself here.

I was too selfish. Too weak. Too scared. All I could consider is that Billy would come for me if I snitched.

Look where that got you, dumb bitch.

I could laugh at the irony.

A stream of light shines on my body before I hear the groan of wooden steps beneath his weight. I clamp my lids shut, too tired and weak to lift a hand to block the light. Each step feels like a thud of my heart.

"You look pathetic," he sneers, his fancy black shoes appearing in my line of vision. I don't move, hoping, *praying*, he kicks out that shoe just one time, hard enough to knock me out completely. Once I'm out, he can keep kicking for all I care.

His shoe can snuff my life out like he does to his cigarettes.

"I *am* pathetic," I correct weakly, sucking in my lips to stop the stream of drool.

"No fight? No will to live? How boring." A wad of spit lands on my cheek. I recoil, causing every ache in my body to flare to life.

See, this is why I stayed still. The cement numbed my pain as long as I didn't move.

With an angry swipe, I fling the spit off my cheek. Asshole.

"I'd rather not trade diseases with you," I mutter snidely. He laughs. At my words. At my anger. Everything about this situation is funny to him.

"Ryan was right about you. You're so easy to kick down, it's boring." The breath in my lungs seizes.

"What did you say?" I whisper.

"We became good friends, him and I. He was practically frothing at the mouth to have a drug lord on speed dial. So desperate, in fact, that he made a deal with me. He wanted my connections. The little boy wanted to play with the big boys and start dipping his hands in my operations. And guess what his collateral was?" He leans in closer. "You," he rasps.

A sob breaks free from my throat. His words, his *truth*, it hurts. I was always expendable to Ryan. He'd trap another girl in no time once I was gone.

"He was willing to trade you to the Ghost Killer if it meant moving up in the world. I was so happy to oblige." An evil laugh trickles from his throat. "You know what the best part is? He didn't know I already owned you."

His foot kicks out, but not where I need it. It lands right in my ribs, sending shockwaves of pain throughout my body. I roll from the kick, my arms lolling out sloppily as if he just heaved over a drunk person.

My tormenter's face appears above me, sneering down at me like I'm dirt. "Can you tell me apart from the rest of the dirt on the floor, or do I blend in?" I tack on a little grin for extra measure. From this position, his foot will hit my temple and knock me out quicker.

His lip curls, and just for a second, I imagine his foot lifting up and coming down on me, filling my vision with blackness.

It doesn't, though. He just shakes his head at me and sighs pitifully. That sound makes me angrier than anything. Pity. He could've said or done anything else to me, and I wouldn't have batted an eye. But pity makes my skin crawl.

I growl. "What the fuck are you waiting for, old man? Didn't make a big enough impression scattering your little Ghosts around, so you gotta come pick on your *daughter*?" I spit the word at him with all the disgust I can muster.

He smirks at me. "You always were a daddy's girl."

Time stills, just for a moment as the words wash over me. And then I'm up, screaming and clawing at him with unpracticed movements. But I don't care. The white-hot rage overwhelms my senses until all I am is just *rage*.

I *hate* him. I hate him so much. It's all I can feel. The hate growing inside of me like a tumor, so deep, it'd be impossible to cut out without bleeding me dry.

His laughter filters through, even as my nails make contact and rake across his dried-up skin. Even as blood pools from the scratches and leaks down his face and neck. With one backhand swipe, he knocks me flat on my ass. I hit hard. My tailbone takes the brunt of my weight before my head crashes down next, bouncing off the floor like a rubber ball.

I accept every bit of the pain that follows suit. Even as it blinds me, rendering me completely invalid and useless, I accept it. I welcome it with open fucking arms. If all I can feel is physical pain, maybe I won't feel the proverbial claws ripping apart my mentality.

Tears track down my cheeks. Normally, I'd wipe them away before they could even think of falling. Showing weakness in front of Billy is the same as willingly opening your legs for him. Either way, he'll be forcing himself inside of you, whether it's with his pain or his dick. Or maybe even both.

This time, I let them fall. I just don't care anymore.

A clatter of metal rings throughout the room and into my skull. Just barely, I'm able to lift my head enough to see the tray of food. An apple rolls off the tray and into a dark corner to join the spiders, a ham sandwich, a fruit cup, and a small water bottle. Nothing that would require utensils, of course. Though I suppose it's a pretty nutritious meal for a prisoner.

"Eat up," he chirps before walking back up the stairs, whistling a low tune as he does.

For the longest time, I stare at that food. I stare until more tears form in my eyes, blurring everything into one blob, and eventually until everything takes shape again and my eyes dry completely.

I don't stop staring, not for a long while.

I SCARFED DOWN THE food and water, pacing myself enough, so I didn't get sick. I did the same for the next several meals. I can't be sure exactly when I decided to escape. It feels like I've always known I would, even when I was deluding myself with the prospect of death. This man has ruled my entire life. And when I finally got a taste of freedom, it was snatched away by another abusive prick. I've never actually gotten much of a chance to rule my own life. Forge my own path. Decide my own future. All of those things were constantly taken out of my hands.

I refused to let Ryan have the privilege any longer, so I'll be damned if I let Billy have it, either.

The groan of wood beneath heavy weight immediately sets my heart into overdrive. Adrenaline surges, leaving my hands shaky. Billy will be coming down to talk to a completely different girl than what he left three days ago. He would throw the food down the stairwell and slam the door behind him. Three meals, three rotations. Three days. The same amount of time he made me wait last time. Which means I've been down here for at least a week.

I've been waiting for another moment with him, and now that it's here, I'm not sure I'm ready.

But I don't think I'll ever be quite ready. Standing up to Billy is something I've never successfully achieved before. Anytime I'd try, I'd get kicked down and I was always too weak—too scared—to get back up and try again. In efforts to conserve my life, I just ended up handing it over to him on a silver platter.

"Are you going to let me shower?" I ask calmly, before he can utter a word to me. He looks down at me, his face arranged in his usual blank state.

It takes him a moment before he responds. "Do you think you deserve a shower?"

I hate Billy's mind games. "Yes," I answer confidently. Not because I've been a quote-on-quote *good girl*, but because I'm a human fucking being, and I deserve basic rights like using a fucking shower.

He smirks at my tone. "Do you, now? And why's that?"

I lick my lips, aiming for a new tactic. "Because I'm your daughter."

His head tips back, and a full-bellied laugh sounds from his throat. The sound irks me, but I force the tension to leave my body. If I snap at him in anger, it'll just make it worse. And I *need* to get out of this basement.

"Can I watch?" he asks, a smarmy smile on his face.

With all the control I can muster, I force my face to stay relaxed, shrug my shoulders and say, "Sure."

Sure, dad, you can watch me shower. That's not fucking repulsive or anything.

His blue eyes glide over me, calculating and shining with mirth. This is another game to him, and it seems like I've been lucky enough to catch him in a good mood. When Billy's in a good mood, he loves to play games.

He nods his head once, the small grin still on his face. "Let's go then. Daughter."

BILLY TURNS THE SHOWER water on for me, adjusting it until he's satisfied with the temperature. I'm not sure if it makes him feel as if he's taking care of me, I don't really care either way. Him taking me to the shower was my only excuse for getting out of the basement. He gave me a bucket and a roll of paper-thin toilet paper to take care of business and threw more food at me.

What else could a girl ask for other than a nice hot shower?

My eyes tracked over every inch of the house as he led me to the bathroom. I'm in some type of trap house. In the tiny living room, beer bottles and needles were scattered across the coffee table, boarded-up windows, stained brown carpet, and rotted curtains that reeked of mothballs. The kitchen looked almost identical to Barbie's, purely based on the gunk caked into the cheap, cracking linoleum floors, moldy fridge, and more needles on the table. Down a short hallway, and into the bathroom is where my fancy shower awaits.

It's just as dirty as the rest of the house.

I don't actually plan on getting in that disease-infested thing. Billy can hand over all the soap he wants, and I'd still come out the other side smelling like must. He shoos me further into the bathroom, closes the door behind me, and locks it. Sidling past me, he holds the plastic curtain open for me, silently prompting me to undress and get in. A nervous sweat breaks out across my skin as his face darkens. Shadows are pressing in around him, and the cold, detached look he gives me has the temperature dropping in the room by several degrees.

"Get in the fucking shower, River."

Twenty-Seven

Mako

ONE WEEK AGO

WHERE THE FUCK IS SHE?

The same mantra has been running through my mind from the moment Amelia told me River is missing. Even now, only an hour after watching River's kidnapping, I'm banging my fist on Barbie's door, I'm still chanting the same words. I dropped Amelia off at her house, despite her incredibly angry protests. Like hell am I allowing a pregnant woman to step foot inside this house—this *town*—where Billy could easily show up. I don't need to meet her husband to know that he'd murder me. And I'd let him.

"What, what, *what, I'm fucking coming!*" Barbie shouts from the other side of the door, her attitude increasing by the word. River's mother flings open the door, hellfire that she is, with no regard to who could be banging on her door late in the evening.

I'll give it to her, this woman has balls of fucking steel. Too bad I'm going to crush them in my fist if she doesn't tell me what the fuck I need to know.

Both brows shoot to her hairline when she sees me. One slow perusal consisting of her dead eyes sweeping my body from head to toe and a salacious grin later, and I'm ready to knock her the fuck out. Same shit she did the first time I met her, and it still gives me the creeps.

"Well, how can I help you, suga?" she says with what's supposed to be a charming grin. She leans against the door, getting comfortable.

"Billy kidnapped your daughter. Let me in now," I say, getting straight to the point. Her spine snaps straight, and what looks like concern flashes across her eyes for a brief second before a blank mask takes over once more.

She opens the door without another word, woodenly turning around and leading me to the kitchen. The smell of mold, mothballs and something fishy hits first, poking at my gag reflex dangerously. I have to clench my teeth to keep the disgust from showing on my face. I don't bother taking a close inventory of her living space—I'd rather not see something I can't *unsee* like I did last time. Big mistake. Last time I was here, I took note of the exit points. Now, I take great care to listen for sounds of anyone else in the house.

"So, when was she taken?" Barbie asks, like she's striking up a conversation about the fucking weather.

"Last night," I answer. She sits at the table, cluttered with paraphernalia of all sorts. I could easily arrest this woman, but it'd only be a waste of time. It already feels like the walls are closing in around me as each second ticks by, and she's still in the hands of that psychopath.

Is he hurting her? Did he already kill her?

I shake my head. I can't think like that. Not now, or I'll completely lose it.

"Do you know where he could've taken her?" I ask. I take a single step into the kitchen, crowding the entranceway.

Barbie lights a cigarette, inhales deeply, her cheeks hollowing out as she does. A low growl reverberates from my chest and up my throat. More seconds go by.

"I don't," she says finally before taking another drag. I cross my arms across my chest, needing to do something with them or else my hands will end up wrapped around Barbie's neck before I can stop myself.

"You've been Billy's bitch for half your life, and you don't know where he could be?" I push. It's a guess how long Barbie has known Billy, but from the haggardness in her decrepit body, it's not hard to see that a soul-sucking demon like Billy has been in her life for too many years.

She laughs, the sound hollow and weak. "Do you really think I'd *want* to know? The more I know, the more of a liability I am and less of a chance I have of surviving. I purposely stayed far out of Billy's business."

Surviving. Not living, but *surviving*. That's all Barbie's been doing, and it's all River has ever known. Pity forms in the pit of my stomach for River's mother. I don't feel bad for her situation, not when she's been a terrible mother to River, but a part of me understands why Barbie has been. She's been chained to a monster. And when you bring a child into that type of situation, sometimes it's safer to make them hate you. Because if they hate you, they won't grieve when you ultimately die. And if you refuse to attach to the person you brought into this world, it won't hurt so bad when they leave you with your shackles while they go off to find a better life. Or in this case, if they die first.

It's no excuse. No justification. But it's Barbie's logic.

"I think you know more than you ever let on," I guess, cocking a brow. River has said before that Barbie mastered the ability to obtain information from her clients. She also mentioned that Billy would rant to Barbie in his crazed states, back when he was killing people the first time he got hooked on meth. Back when he killed my father. I'm sure all kinds of shit came out of his mouth in those moments—shit he more than likely doesn't remember saying. The breath in Barbie's lungs attests to that.

She's street smart—even I can see that. Barbie may have made it look like she wasn't listening and gleaning info from Billy, but that doesn't mean she wasn't. She's too smart to purposely stay clueless, especially when dealing with someone like him.

I'm becoming desperate. If Barbie doesn't tell me *anything*, then I'm left with nothing. I'd have to start from scratch. Track down the people affiliated with Billy, find out where his stomping grounds are, and follow the fucker wherever he goes.

The washed-up woman flicks her cigarette before inhaling once more. Her hands are trembling, and she's sucking on that thing so deeply that it's obvious I'm right.

"What do you know, Barbie?" I demand through gritted teeth. When she doesn't answer, I stalk towards her, slam a hand on the table—avoiding the needles—and put my face right into hers. Her eyes widen into round discs as she inhales sharply, stunned by my sudden proximity.

"I swear to fucking god, Barbie, if you don't start talking, I will make all the years of suffering alongside Billy look like a fucking pipe dream. Put that cigarette in your mouth one more fucking time without answering my goddamn question, and you'll be swallowing the wrong end. Now. Where. Is. She?"

I stare straight into her dead eyes, now infused with the fear she's been lacking since I told her that her daughter had been kidnapped by one of the most dangerous men in the country. Heavy breaths fall from her cracked lips, her chest pumping deeply.

"I… I'm being honest when I say I don't know where he took her. But I do know that he conducts some of his… operations at Hawk's downtown.

He's good for showing up there a few times a week. That's the only information I have. I meant it when I said I would stay out of his business."

Liar. But I'll take the little information she gave. Better than fucking nothing, I guess.

Without breaking eye contact, I slowly pull away. Her hand continues to tremble as she ashes the cigarette and then, ever so gently, brings it to her lips.

"I'm going to find River. Alive. And then I'm going to take her home and give her the life she deserves. But you will never see her again. So, if you give any fucks about your daughter, then take comfort in the fact that she will live like a fucking queen while you rot here and waste away."

She blows out a cloud of smoke and ashes her cigarette. She doesn't look affected by my words, but she does bring her gaze to mine, an unnamed emotion glittering in the depths of her dead eyes.

"Thank you."

She stands, drops the cigarette butt into a soda can, the cherry extinguishing in whatever liquid is in there. And then calmly walks past me and disappears down a hallway, shutting a door gently behind her.

Unsettled by her reaction, I turn towards the exit, push open the crooked door and slam it behind me. About a hundred feet away, right outside her house is the river where River was born. It's murky and lifeless, just like the rest of this town.

The complete opposite of the woman named after this body of water.

Because if River *is* as lifeless as the water before me, I will take great pleasure ripping Billy apart piece by fucking piece.

HAWK'S RESTAURANT IS PROBABLY the nicest building I've come across in Shallow Hill yet. Which is pretty fucking sad, considering it looks like the building is starting to collapse in on itself. A twenty-four-hour Waffle House sits across the street, looking just as pathetic as its competition. I parked in the very back of the parking lot, closest to the street and in direct view of Hawk's. The lack of foot traffic and the window spanning the front of the building provides me with a perfect view inside. Though, I have to concentrate to see past the handprints and thin layer of grime coating the window.

If Billy is inside, storming in the restaurant like a Hellion is nipping at my ass wouldn't get me anywhere except shot. All I'm waiting on is a warrant for Billy.

Billy knows my face. He'd only been giving me false leads and attempting to fuck with my case. And he would rather attempt homicide in front of Shallow Hill residents dining than let me cart his ass off to prison. After all, he owns Shallow Hill and if he succeeded in shooting me dead, no one would tell a soul. They'd probably even offer to help him hide my body.

My fist curls tight, my knuckles bleaching white. It takes all my strength not to send them flying through the windshield. My knee bounces, restless energy coursing through me. More seconds go by. Minutes. Hours. Until eventually, the restaurant closes and the lights go out. I've seen every type of person go in and out of that restaurant. Sex workers, pimps, drug users and dealers, and even some average joes who look like they work a nine-to-five job.

So many faces, but none that I need to see.

I throw my head back on my headrest and release a harsh breath.

I need to go home and catch a few hours of sleep before I come back out. By then, I'll have my warrant. Because when I do, I will hunt for my girl in every house in this shitty town if I have to.

"HAVE YOU GOTTEN ANY sleep?" Amar asks from beside me.

My fingers tap on my thigh as I continue to stare at the restaurant. It's only ten in the morning, and it's been a week since River was taken. A week of her going through god-knows-what kind of abuse at the hands of a walking dead man. He's been evasive. No leads. No tags. Nothing. I refrained from banging on random doors. Only because I know Billy runs this town, and if word gets out that a detective is looking for him or River, he would go into hiding like a groundhog that just saw his shadow.

Amelia reported River missing, and I let my sergeant know my suspicions of who the Ghost Killer is and showed him the video of River being kidnapped. Finding River isn't a solo job; I have several undercover cops patrolling every block in Shallow Hill, keeping themselves elusive. I've no idea how much Billy knows about my relationship with River, or if he knows we have one at all. The less Billy suspects about any cops coming for him, the more comfortable he'll feel walking outside and showing his face around town.

I got a warrant, which allowed us to search any of Billy's property. He owns one house in Shallow Hill under Benedict Davis. It was completely barren, devoid of any signs that it's being used. I'm sure he owns property under a false alias, but that does me no good when I don't know the names he's using.

Amar sits next to me, watching Hawk's closely, waiting for Billy to appear. Amar showed up a few hours ago, walking into the restaurant himself, questioning the owner, and eventually getting the stubborn man to admit Billy frequents the restaurant often, with only a single nod. He refused to say anything more than that, and Amar let him be for now.

After going through the surveillance at Ryan's house again, we caught a black SUV parked behind the house on one of the cameras, where Billy eventually dragged River into. With a partial license plate, we were able to track down the car and confirm its registration to Benedict Davis. We tagged the make, model, and license plate across the board. Anytime the street cams tag the car, we'll get an immediate alert as to where and when.

"Mako?" Amar pushes. I glance at him for a second before my eyes involuntarily slide back to Hawk's.

"Barely," I admit. Amar doesn't say anything for a moment. I know he won't berate me. Not when he'd be doing the same exact thing had his wife ever gotten kidnapped.

"He's going to show up." While I appreciate his encouraging words, they do nothing to make me feel better. I won't be able to breathe properly until I have River in my arms, alive and safe. And if there's one hair out of place on her pretty little head, I'm going to lose my shit.

"Am I going to be held accountable for what I do to him when I find him?" I ask. I'm not asking because I'm worried, nor is his answer going to change anything. I'm asking to get an idea of where Amar's head is.

He's silent for a few moments. "As long as no one else is around... no. No, you won't be." If Amar were anything but a man in love, I don't know if he'd feel the same way. I've never been more grateful for his wife in my entire life. "She's going to be okay, man. She's a tough girl."

That, I know. River McAllister is perfectly capable of grabbing her prey by the throat and tearing them to pieces. She's the strongest fucking person I know, and no matter what Billy puts her through, my girl will come out the other side stronger than before.

I drag my eyes to his, shooting him a brief look of gratitude before turning my focus back to Hawk's. Right as I do, my phone buzzes in the cupholder next to me. Snatching it up, I look to see that we got a hit. Billy's car is down the road, heading towards Hawk's. I angle the phone to Amar, showing him the alert. A slow, sinister smile builds on his face, matching the one on my face.

We got him.

"What's the plan?"

"We're going to wait until he leaves and then tail him." Adrenaline releases into my bloodstream steadily. He's here. And he's going to lead me back to where I need to be. I'm so fucking close, I can taste the bloodshed on my tongue.

And fuck, does it taste sweet.

"HE'S LEAVING," I SAY aloud, perking up from my hunched-over position. Billy parked his car in the back, hidden away from street view. It took a few drive-by's, but Amar and I managed to find a little alleyway to park in, close enough to get an unobscured view but far enough away that Billy shouldn't notice us.

Billy revs his engine and takes off down the street. I wait until he makes a turn until I pull out behind him.

Eventually, he turns into a trailer park—Towner's Park. The trailers are placed sporadically, each house sporting a different design of rust and rot in the paneling. Overgrown, brittle grass licks at the sides of the trailers, with more rusted items cluttering the beds of grass. Cars, trinkets, kid toys. Everything about this place looks run down and beaten.

Five minutes. River was five minutes away from me the entire time.

Ahead of me, Billy speeds up and whips around a corner. Not wanting to seem obvious, I force myself to keep the same pace. Turns out, this park is more elaborate than I gave credit for. Once I turn down the road, Billy's car is no longer in sight. Various routes and dead ends break off from the street.

"Fuck me," I spit, stepping on the gas harder. I no longer care if Billy sees me coming. The last thing the fucker will see is my headlights before he turns into a mangled mess beneath my tires if I have it my way.

"Do you see him?" I bark, my voice nearly rising hysterically. My heart is pounding so hard, it's all I can hear. I barely hear the words come out of Amar's mouth.

"He can't be too far. Turn here," he directs.

I follow his directions a little too eagerly, jerking the car roughly to the left and squealing the tires. I speed past several homes, searching down every side road, desperate to find even a glimpse of Billy's car. In the streets or parked by any of the homes. But his car has entirely vanished. The tension in my body rises until all my body can process is unfiltered hysteria.

"FUCK!" I roar, banging my fist on the steering wheel several times, causing the car to swerve. Amar grabs my hand before I put my first through the wheel and engage the airbag or run us straight into a trailer. Whichever comes first. Straightening the car, I force myself to calm down as I take more turns, getting lost in the maze of this shitty-ass trailer park.

"Turn here," Amar says again, his voice barely penetrating the blood rushing through my ears. I follow his directions and will myself to calm down. Losing my shit isn't going to find her any faster. I need to fucking focus.

I'm searching every yard and driveway, my eyes sweeping one side of the road while Amar inspects the other side. For another hundred feet, I don't see anything. Just as I'm casting my eyes forward to see which way to turn, I notice off in the distance a lone, dilapidated house. It doesn't look like it's part of the trailer park, but it appears to be on the land. I see a car poking out from behind the house, but it's not revealed enough for me to tell if it's Billy's car or not.

"Do you see that?" I ask. Amar directs his eyes towards where my finger is pointing.

"Let's check it out."

I'm already driving towards the house before Amar can say so. Billy is not anywhere in this park. What other reason would he have to go through here? A gut feeling settles in my stomach. I just know this is where River is. I can feel it.

My hands threaten to tremble, but I force them steady. The adrenaline is becoming more potent in my bloodstream as I drive up towards the house. I see a flash of movement through one of the first-floor windows. The movement was too quick, and I hadn't been close enough to make out who it was, to be sure, but it looked like a flash of black hair.

My car crests the driveway, and Billy's car comes into view. My foot is slamming on the brakes and just barely do I shift the car into park before the door is open and my ass is off the seat. I round my car and charge towards the front door, just as said door is flung open and my girl comes barreling through, her eyes wide with panic.

"River!" Her eyes fix on me, and when they do, tears flood them. She nearly tackles me, throwing all her weight into my body.

"Mako! Watch out!" The last thing I see is the barrel of a gun being pointed directly at my head.

Twenty-Eight
River

THE SHOT FIRES, A loud, abrasive sound echoing. I feel Mako jerk beneath me, right before we both topple to the ground. Another shot rings out. I squeeze my eyes shut tight, waiting to feel the burn in my back, but all I feel is Mako's unmoving weight beneath me.

"Don't move another fucking inch!" a voice screams from behind me. I turn my head and see Mako's partner pointing a gun at Billy, with the latter pointing his right back, holding onto his bloody shoulder.

Whipping my head back around, I lift up and inspect Mako. Blood is pooling beneath him, but his eyes are open and lively, and his teeth gritted in pain.

"Mako! Are you okay? Please tell me you're okay," I say, the words spilling out of my mouth as I carefully scramble off of him. He wheezes from the movement.

"I'm fine," he grits.

Liar. He's not. He's been shot and is bleeding.

"Where are you shot?" I ask. He's wearing a black shirt, which is concealing the bullet wound too well for my panicked eyes. All I can see is blood. Blood everywhere.

"My chest," he gasps.

No, no, no. Before I can raise my hands to apply pressure, he's lifting himself up. A long groan hurdles past his tightened lips.

"Stop it!" I gasp, attempting to push him back down. He evades me, though, and is on his feet before I can process that this man has just been shot in the chest and is *standing up.* And not just that, but lifting his own gun and pointing it at Billy.

Billy is also bleeding, his injured arm dangling and now holding the gun with his left hand. Amar must've shot in retaliation once Billy shot off his round.

Billy dares to take his eyes from Amar, watching Mako rise and point a gun at him with an evil smile on his face. "Hurts like a bitch, doesn't it?" he taunts from the porch.

I growl, charging back towards my captor, but Mako's free arm scoops around my waist and shoves me behind him. I'd send a fist into his back in defiance if a bullet didn't just pass through it. Or did it?

Oh, God, it could be lodged in there for all I know.

"I know, baby, you don't need me to save you," Mako placates, his eyes still on Billy. "I'm only going to murder him, that's all."

Billy tips his head back and laughs at Mako's words.

"You think you can kill a god?" he asks, his hazel eyes bright with excitement and pure incarnate evil. He's enjoying this stand-off. Even being completely outnumbered and already shot, he's getting a sick pleasure out of it. Billy always did love the thrill of his life hanging precariously close on the edge of death.

I step aside, still keeping the majority of my body behind Mako's, only if it means to keep him from stressing further. "You're not a god, Billy. You're just a washed-up old man that has *no* loyalty. That's why you keep killing everyone, right? You can't trust a single soul in this world because everyone despises you." I spit the words with every ounce of hatred I can.

Billy's lip curls. My words eat at him because he knows it's true. The drugs have crippled what little sanity he had left. He's too paranoid now. Too nervous. That's why he inserted himself into Mako's investigation. He thought if he could pull strings on the inside as well, no one would catch onto him. The last thing he expected was for me to have a relationship with a detective and get close enough to spill the truth. Billy has killed so many people. Hurt so many families. He has an enemy within ten feet of him at all times, and he fucking knows it.

"I gave you life, bitch. I *will* take it away," he growls. I laugh at his words. At his audacity to think that killing me is the worst possible thing he could do to me. He's already done his worst. He's already ruined me for life. I'll never be normal because of him. Killing me would be a mercy.

"The fuck you will," Mako intervenes before I can say anything else. In one quick movement, Mako flips the gun in the air, catching hold of it by the barrel, lifts his arm, and throws the gun directly at Billy's head. His aim strikes true, the butt of the gun smacking Billy directly in the forehead before he can process what's happening.

The moment the gun left Mako's hand, he charged towards Billy, seemingly confident the gun would hit. Billy's head knocks back, and he falls to the ground.

"Fuck!" Billy shouts, his hand whipping to head, now spilling blood profusely from where he was hit. "You motherfucki—" He doesn't get to finish his sentence. Mako's upon him, lifting Billy up despite his own gunshot wound.

"Mako! Be careful, you idiot!" I shout, my legs finally unlocking and carrying me towards the two. Mako ignores me and drags Billy back inside the house. My legs falter. I don't want to go back inside that house. I worked so hard to come out of it.

Amar runs up to me. "River, please go sit in the car. I'll make sure Mako is okay." I don't look at him. Not when Mako disappears around the corner, dragging a fighting Billy into the kitchen and out of view.

"I… I can't leave him alone," I say. Yet, my legs still won't move. Why won't they fucking move? Why *now* does my body decide to process the trauma?

Move, River.

"Sweetheart, I got him. Just go sit inside the car." The end of Amar's sentence is drowned out by a loud scream, filled with agony. It sounded like Billy.

"No," I say, the sound finally spurring me into action. Mako didn't run away when I got my revenge on Ryan. I'm not going to do the same to him. Plus, it's only fair I get a few of my own punches in before Billy meets his death. Billy was my abuser far longer than Ryan ever was and has done much worse to me over the years. I want in on this, too.

I scramble into the house, fighting the chill that wants to overtake my body at being back inside. It took months before I could walk inside Barbie's house without wanting to vomit and have a mental breakdown.

I just need to remind myself—I'm safe now. Mako is here. Amar is here. Billy is going to die, whether he wants to or not. I'm *safe*.

Just as I'm rushing into the kitchen, I see a knife plunge into Billy's chest. Mako is bleeding profusely and looking more ashen by the second. He's not doing good, and that knowledge instantly takes anything else I'm feeling and tosses it into flames. All I can think about is Mako's declining health.

"Amar, take him to the hospital."

"Fuck that—"

"—I'd be glad to." Amar and Mako both speak at the same time. "But I'm not leaving you alone with him. I'm taking Mako to the car, and I'm coming right back."

I side-eye Amar, still wary of where his morals stand when it comes to upholding the law. Something tells me he's not straight-laced and was more than willing to let Mako do what he wanted. But I'm not so sure he'd do the same for me.

"I'm fine, I got this handled," Mako argues. He sways.

"You're going to the hospital, man. You've lost too much blood," Amar says, rushing towards him and forcing Mako's heavy arm around his shoulders. The fact that he doesn't fight any further only cements my worry.

With one last passing glance, Amar says, "I'll be back."

I watch Amar nearly drag Mako's body out of the house. Billy's groans drown out Mako's grunts of pain.

Focusing my attention back to the bleeding, groaning monster before me, I turn my worry over Mako's possible death into blinding rage. If Mako dies... if Billy takes the *one* man in my life that has *ever* given a shit about me—and I mean *actually* cares about me—I won't survive it. Billy will have succeeded in completely breaking me, just like he always wanted.

I walk back out on the porch and find Mako's forgotten gun lying on the rotted wood. Picking it up, I turn the gun around, reveling in the weight in my hands. I've never shot a gun before. Never felt the mixture of trepidation and power that nestles deep inside you when holding a gun. I can understand why people use guns. Such a tiny thing has the power to take a life in a matter of seconds.

Loud clattering draws my attention back inside the house. Having fitted

Mako in the car, Amar rushes in with me, finding a toppled chair next to Billy. He must've tried to use it as leverage to lift himself up. The knife is still protruding from his chest, rivulets of blood streaming out of the wound and onto the floor. He tries to get up again but slips on the blood.

"Get over here and help me, you fucking bitch!" he screams, spittle flying from his lips.

I stare at him.

"What the fuck do you think you're doing, just standing there? Help me!" His bloodshot eyes are wide with pain and rage. I want to stare into his eyes as I take his life. I want to watch the life fade from them when I do.

Slowly, I walk over to my father's sprawled form lying on the ground, careful not to slip on his blood.

"Amar, please leave," I whisper.

"Do what you need to do, but I'm not leaving you alone."

I turn my head to the side, studying him closely. When he sees my look, he repeats himself, "*Do* what you need to *do*."

I smile and turn back to Billy.

"You're pathetic," I say calmly. I crouch down, the gun dangling between my knees as I study him. "You've lived your whole life as the monster. Desperate to be the meanest so no one can hurt you. Tell me, Billy. Are you hurt?" I pause and rip the knife out of his chest. His screams send warm shivers down my spine. "Do you feel the pain now?" I taunt as I plunge my thumb into the knife wound Mako inflicted.

Billy screams intensify, his hands wrapping around my wrist tightly. He could snap it if he wanted to, but his grip is too weak. He's losing blood, and if I don't hurry, he'll die from his injuries before I get my chance. If I don't hurry, *Mako* will die, too. And that just won't do.

"You may kill me, River. But I'll never die. I'll be inside you the rest of your life, causing you pain. You'll never be able to let me go." He looks manic with his crazed eyes and bloody teeth.

I smile.

"That may be true. But it'll be easy not to feel pain when I have the sweet memory of being the last thing you see before you die."

He snarls, opening his mouth to spew more venom. I don't hesitate. I lift the gun to his forehead and lock my eyes onto his.

And I pull the trigger.

His head jerks backwards, blood and brain matter splattering across the tile. His body slumps, and everything fades to silence following the ring of the gunshot.

Pure, utter silence.

Something I've never had the pleasure of experiencing when in Billy's presence. It feels… nice. Good. I drop my butt on the ground, not minding that I'm sitting in a pool of blood. The gun clatters next to me.

And I stare at Billy's dead body, and just smile.

I SHOOT UP FROM THE hard, plastic chair and rush towards Amar.

"How is he?" I ask Amar, my ass having long grown numb from the uncomfortable hospital chair. I've been sitting here for hours on end, just waiting to hear anything. I'll gladly give up all feeling in my ass if it means Mako will be okay.

"He's stable," he answers, his eyes sparkling with relief, despite the exhaustion etched into every wrinkle on his face. Immediate relief assaults me, nearly stealing my breath. Slowly, the immense amount of pressure sitting on my chest starts to ease.

Amar had rushed us to the hospital and got Mako admitted into the ICU. During the drive, I prayed. I prayed that I didn't take too long to kill Billy. I prayed that the bullet didn't hit anything vital. I just prayed. While I did, Amar called in the death to his boss, explaining the story he told me right before the cops arrived.

Mako and Amar watched Billy. Followed him here. And they basically told most of the truth, with a few different details. I managed to escape myself, running out of the house just as they arrived. Billy immediately opened fire, shooting Mako once in the chest. Amar returned fire and shot back. Billy ran into the house, and Mako followed while Amar held me back from entering the house. There, Billy came at Mako with a knife, in which Mako got ahold of the weapon and stabbed Billy with it. During the scuffle, Mako was able to overpower Billy and then shoot him dead.

Mako got the glory of killing Billy, but I couldn't care less. I don't care what the cops believed happened at all. A complete stranger could've gotten the glory for all I care, because I will go to sleep peacefully at night knowing the truth. I took Billy's life from him.

"He had a collapsed lung and needed surgery. Had to get a blood transfusion 'cause he lost so much blood. But luckily, the surgery was successful. He's going to be okay," Amar continues, pulling my attention back towards him. I nod, wiping the nervous sweat on my hands on my jeans. I was able to wash my hands and face off in the hospital bathroom, but there isn't much I can do about my clothes. Every passerby has looked at me like I'm a lunatic.

I suppose I am one.

"Can I see him?" I ask, standing up.

"Yeah, you can see him. He just woke up from surgery. There's gonna be a couple of cops here that are going to want to take your statement, though."

I nod, another nervous sweat breaking out across my forehead. Speaking to a cop always makes you feel like you did something wrong, even if you didn't. And well, in this case, I think murdering someone would be classified as *wrong*.

Noting my nervous energy, he says, "Just stick to the story, and you'll be fine. It's just protocol."

Stick to the story, River. Yeah, as if cops don't ask the same question five hundred times just to see if you change your story.

"Oh, and Julie and Matt are on their way."

I don't say anything in response. I'm not ready to face them yet. Especially, least of all Matt. I might be liable to kill him, too.

Brushing past him, I speed walk towards Mako's room. Anxious to see him, yet incredibly nervous. The last time we spoke, he was done with me. I had information that he'd been searching for for a long time. And I kept it from him for entirely selfish reasons. I didn't blame Mako if he wanted to cut ties with me. At this point, I've been nothing but a headache to him.

Timidly, I walk into the room. It feels wrong. Nothing about me has ever been timid. Not until I met Ryan. Forcing my spine to straighten, I walk around the corner and see Mako lying in the hospital bed, staring mindlessly at the television screen. He's a large man, but even he looks small in the hospital bed. Hooked up to IVs and wires, with pale skin and dark circles under his eyes. The sight nearly brings me to tears.

I glance up, noting some cooking show that's on. By the time my eyes drift back to him, his grass-green eyes are already pinned on me, holding me in place. I can't move now. I can hardly breathe from the intensity of his stare.

"Teasing yourself with all the things you can't eat?" I ask, proud of how well I kept my voice steady.

A slight grin slides on his face. That minor movement gives me a tiny amount of comfort, though. Maybe this conversation won't be as hostile as I assumed it would be.

"Teasing? Please, I'm getting gourmet food here," he jokes. I offer a small smile and sidle further into the room.

I clear my throat. "I'm sorry you got shot, Mako."

He quirks a brow. "What part of me getting shot was your fault?"

"The fact that you were there at all? I know you came looking for me, and I appreciate that. But none of that should've happened."

Mako just stares, the intensity in his stare increasing.

"It wasn't all about you, you know?" I flinch, shame filling my pores. *Stupid, River.*

Once again, being selfish and assuming Mako was coming there purely because of me. Of course, Mako had to come looking for Billy. Not only was he the Ghost Killer, but he was holding someone captive. He would've come looking regardless.

"I know, that was stup—"

"Billy killed my father. My real father," he cuts in. I snap my mouth shut, startled by the information. "He was Billy's first signature victim. Carved 'Ghost' into his chest and shot him once in the head. Assuming my father was betraying him or something, I'm guessing. Who really knows why. My need to find the Ghost Killer was because I wanted to avenge my father's death. He wasn't a great man, but he didn't deserve what happened to him."

I nod slowly. "I'm sorry," I whisper.

"But then you came along. And it turns out you had a close connection with the Ghost Killer. The same man who murdered my father was also actively abusing my girl." My heart drops when he says *my girl*. "I was

397

always meant to find Billy, River. But the original plan was to find him and put his ass in prison for the rest of his miserable life. Not attempt to murder him. That—that *was* about you. He stole you away from me and hurt you in god knows what ways." He closes his eyes, seemingly losing a bit of control. After a moment, he speaks again. "That was far more personal than what he did to my father. And I wanted him to die for it."

I'm not sure when tears started tracking down my face, but by the time he's finished, I'm wiping them away profusely.

"You're not angry with me anymore?" I question, glancing at him through blurry eyes. A sad smile teases his lips.

"Not anymore. You hid the truth because Billy scared you. Obviously, you had good reason to be afraid of him. The only thing I hate is that you didn't feel safe enough around me to trust me with that information."

My head is shaking before he finishes his last sentence. I rush to him, carefully sitting on the edge of the bed next to him.

"That wasn't the issue, Mako. I did—*do*—feel safe with you. I wasn't only scared for my own life, I was scared for yours, too. I guess… I guess I just feared Billy more."

He nods and grabs my hand. I can't look away from the way his massive hand completely engulfs mine. I feel so small compared to Mako, but it makes me feel secure instead of it intimidating me.

"He terrorized you your entire life, along with many other men, including my brother. You've only known me for a short period of time. I can't expect your fear and lack of faith in the male population to override the protection I tried to give you. If anyone should be apologizing, it should be me. I tried hard to protect you, and I failed. I'm so sorry for that." His voice cracks on the last word. More tears flood my eyes, and I'm once more shaking my head.

"Please don't ever apologize for that. Billy was always going to find me, Mako," I parrot, stealing his similar words from earlier. "I made it impossible for you because I wanted to save myself. That's important to me."

"River, I know you can save yourself. But just because you can, doesn't mean you always have to. You're incredibly strong, and I admire you for it, but that doesn't mean I'm going to let you walk through this world alone. You're no damsel in distress, but I'll be damned if I don't have my girl's back while she kicks ass, you understand?"

Unfiltered love fills my chest so tight, it feels as if my heart is a balloon pumped full of helium. I can't describe the overwhelming feeling that's taking my soul and ripping it apart, making room for the man next to me. That's the only way I can describe it. Two souls coming together, entwining deep until there is no end to him or me.

"I love you, Mako. I'm sorry I didn't say it sooner. But I love you so much."

A cocky smirk adorns his face, and before I can smack it off, he wraps his hand around the back of my neck and pulls me to him, effectively distracting me with his plump lips. Lightning explodes, skating across our connected lips.

Finally, I found a home.

Twenty-Nine

River

THE KNIFE IN MY HAND trembles. I'm not okay at this moment. My eyes bore into the tomato I was chopping, the red juices dripping off the serrated edge. I was fine, and then the red juice slowly turned into blood.

A hand slides across my body. My mind spirals. I feel Billy's hand. Ryan's. All of the men that took from me were all morphing into one. The hand grips my hip and turns me around. Instinctively, my hand whips up—the one holding the butcher knife—and snaps to his neck.

He stills. Green eyes penetrate, the familiarity swirling in the darkness that has invaded my mind. Clarity comes rushing back and the world comes into focus once more. Mako is staring at me intensely, his face arranged carefully into a blank slate. A trickle of blood leaks from the point of the knife digging into his skin.

"Oh my God," I rush out, the knife slipping from my grasp. He catches it before it falls and gets stabbed on the way down. My hands fly over my face, and embarrassment floods my pores. "I am so. Fucking. Sorry, Mako." My hands muffle my voice, but I know he heard me just fine.

I'm absolutely horrified. I almost killed him. I actually almost killed him.

I hear the knife clatter on the countertop behind me. And then it sounds like the cutting board is being slid down the counter, away from us. One hard tug and my hands fly away from my face. The suddenness of it forces a gasp from my throat, and my hands fall easily.

His hands grip both my hips and in one swoop, he lifts me up and sets me on the countertop. He arranges me, so my body is sitting on the catty corner, where the two counters meet.

"Mako! Careful!" I admonish, wary of his gunshot wound. He's mostly healed, but he's still not one hundred percent yet. He's not allowed to lift heavy things, and I'm pretty sure the doctor would categorize me as a heavy object.

He still hasn't spoken a single word. Oh, God. He's probably going to kick me out now. I almost just sliced his neck open. And what's worse, is I'm actually capable of it.

"What triggered you?" he asks finally, cupping a finger under my chin and jerking my chin up. My tear-filled eyes meet his steady greens.

"The knife," I admit reluctantly.

"Why?"

I try to look away, but he jerks my chin back to him again. "Because the last time I used one, I hurt someone with it. It feels like I'm holding a weapon in my hands now, not something to cut tomatoes with."

"Would it help if the knife became something different than a weapon?"

My brows pucker with confusion. "What do you mean? I thought that's what I was doing by cutting tomatoes…" My voice trails off when he grabs the knife with one hand, and pulls out the collar of my shirt with the other, cutting the fabric down the middle.

"Mako," I gasp, stunned. The tip of the knife grazes my skin. Not enough to break the skin, but enough to leave a dull sting. When I glance up at him, his eyes are concentrating hard on the knife. He's grazing me on purpose.

My heart rate escalates, accelerating my breath along with it. My shirt falls off my shoulders and down my arms. He cuts my bra next—I *liked* that bra—and then my shorts and panties. By the time he's done, my naked body is adorned in scraps of fabric.

"What are you doing?" I whisper, the tip of my tongue darting out to wet my dry lips. He ignores me then grabs my ankles and spreads them, setting each foot on either counter. Next, he bundles up all the scraps and throws them behind him. Distractedly, I watch them all flutter to the ground.

"Reclaiming what a knife means to you."

My eyes snap back to his. He steps into my space. Electric shivers run down my spine when the rough texture of his jeans rubs across my bare pussy, eliciting a sharp gasp from my throat.

"Mako…" He deliberately rotates his hips, making sure the zipper skates across my clit. His breath warms my neck as his body presses further into mine, heating me up from the inside out. His lips glide up my neck and to my ear, tickling the tiny hairs on my ear.

"Do you trust me?" he asks, his deep ocean voice low and husky.

No, because in this moment, I'm the closest I've ever been to heaven, and I'm not ready to die yet.

"Yes," I whisper only because I'm more scared of him stopping.

My nerves intensify when I see his hand grip the knife, not by the handle, but by the blade. I'm tempted to open my mouth and tell him not to cut himself, but something tells me he wouldn't mind so much. I keep my mouth firmly shut, even when he lifts the knife and glides the handle lightly across my abdomen. My stomach clenches in response, equally terrified and anxious to see what he's going to do.

The handle trails further down my stomach until he reaches my pussy. The minute Mako started undressing me, my core flooded with juices. But now that he's dangerously close to my most sensitive area with a knife... *god*, I'm soaked.

My breathing escalates when he circles my tight bud with the handle. I'm not proud of the squeak that escapes my mouth, nor the way my legs tremble. His wicked, satisfied smirk slides across his face, and if I weren't so distracted, I'd do something about it.

Involuntarily, my eyes drift shut as I get lost in the sensation—just the right amount of pressure. The coil in my stomach is already dangerously tight. The pressure lifts from my clit and reappears right at my opening.

My eyes snap open. "Mako," I warn, my tone filled with trepidation. He lifts his eyes from his task, ensnaring mine in a heated dance.

"You said you trusted me," he reminds me, the wickedness still present on his face.

I gasp when the tip of the handle slides past my lips and enters inside me. He doesn't push any further, waiting for me to protest or tell him not to stop; I don't know what he wants. Too many thoughts and emotions are swirling through my body like a cyclone.

I couldn't tell you my left hand from my right at this moment.

Licking my lips nervously, I give a subtle nod. I'm not capable of anything more than that. In one swoop, he pushes the handle all the way to the hilt, careful to keep the sharp metal away from my skin. My mouth falls open, no sounds escaping when my throat has completely closed.

A moan breaks through when he draws the knife out and then back in again. "Mako," I groan loudly, no longer embarrassed by the wanton noises spilling from my tongue.

"That's it, baby," he urges when my hips begin to rotate. He keeps the same, steady pace. It becomes agonizing, and soon, desperate mewls are following the moans. My hips rotate more insistently, my body begging for more.

"What do you need?" he questions, refusing to quicken his pace.

"More," I whine, jerking my hips forward.

"Tell me what you want," he demands, still not giving in to my body's pleas.

"Lick me," I whisper urgently. I nearly scream from frustration when I feel his tongue dart out, licking my neck. Normally, I wouldn't complain, but not when I need his tongue on my pussy instead.

"Mako!" I bark, knowing damn well he knew precisely what I meant.

"Yes?" he asks innocently.

"Lick. My. Pussy," I growl, my hand sliding into his hair roughly and tugging hard. I feel the smile against my neck.

"Good girl," he praises. He kisses my neck softly before he trails those kisses down my chest. Stopping at my breast, he wraps his hot mouth around my nipple. My head falls back, and my hips start rotating once more as he continues to plunge the knife inside me.

He pulls another gasp from me when his teeth replace his tongue, and he bites down on my nipple. Hot pinpricks sluice through my nerves, nearly making me scream from the intensifying pain. But more potent than the sharp pain is the waves of pleasure rolling through my body. They blend together until I can't tell them apart.

With a pop, he releases my nipple. Kissing the sensitive area first, he continues his path past my breasts, to my stomach, and finally, down to my drenched pussy.

He kneels before me, the knife firmly inside of me. When he looks up at me, his eyes darken to moss green, and I nearly come right then and there. Seeing Mako kneel before me like a knight would a princess, I question why I never wanted him to save me.

Keeping eye contact, he slowly leans forward and darts his tongue out to swipe at my clit. The small amount of contact sends my eyes rolling to the back of my head. Before they can find Mako's eyes again, he's growling and shoving his mouth on my core. I can't stop the loud moan that bursts from my lips and echoes in the kitchen. Not when his tongue is so hot and sharp against my bud.

He groans against me, sending delicious vibrations throughout my pussy. The only thing I can think to do is shove my hand through his soft hair and ride his mouth, careful of the knife still plunging inside me. The coil in my stomach tightens further and further. My stomach clenched as the orgasm crests. My body stills, making the fall over the edge that much sharper.

The coil snaps, and I let loose. Pure euphoria overcomes my body. It feels as if my soul lifts from my physical body. The screams coming from my mouth sound so far away, like I'm drifting above them as the waves of ecstasy wash over me.

Distractedly, I feel the knife slip out and Mako pull away. My half-lidded eyes barely register Mako standing and slipping down his own jeans. The only thing that pulls me back down to earth is the feel of Mako's cock jutting out against my core.

The view has my eyes widening once more. I don't think I'll ever get used to the sight of him. Incredibly thick, with a length that's undoubtedly not natural. Mako's cock is intimidating and mouth-watering, and right now, it looks furious.

He wraps his arms underneath my legs and pulls me forward. My hands grip either side of the counter, steadying my body as he lines himself up.

My brow wrinkles when I feel something wet against my thigh.

I look over and notice an ample amount of blood coasting down my thigh, trailing from Mako's hand.

"Oh my god," I say. He lifts said hand and jerks my face towards his, not giving a damn that he's covering me in his blood.

"Does it bother you?" he asks, his voice and face cast in a serious tone.

It takes me a second to respond. Does his blood bother me? Not in the sense he thinks. I don't like the thought of him hurting. But am I appalled by it? Turned off? No, none of those things. Furthermore, I get a feeling that Mako deliberately made himself bleed. I eye the tiny trail of dried blood on his neck. He didn't even flinch when I did that. My eyes travel back to his. They're fiery pits of lava spitting their need at me. The last thing Mako is feeling is *hurt*.

I bite my lip and shake my head no.

He doesn't need to hear anything else. Tugging his plump lip between his own teeth, he lines himself up and plunges his cock deep into my pussy in one thrust.

"Oh my—fuck, Mako!" My head thumps against the cabinet. I feel so impossibly full.

Much like his ministrations with the knife, he glides out slowly before filling me all at once again. Intense pleasure shoots up my spine, causing my body to arch.

He leans forward, pressing his body into mine and thrusting his hips in sharp little jabs. His lips find my ear, giving it a sharp nip.

"Say it again." The growled words radiate through my ear, down my spine, and straight to where we're connected.

"Mako," I grit hoarsely, the name punctuated by a sharp gasp when his cock slides deep inside me. I squeeze my eyes shut, desperate to come but just as desperate for the moment to never end.

His hands slide down my thighs, one hand leaving a trail of blood. The sight sends a spike of pleasure to my core. Something about the wrongness of it turns me on that much more. Gripping my hips, he forces my body towards him as he begins to drive into me fast and hard.

His grunts join my loud screams, the pitch of our voices and the joining of our bodies becoming a deafening crescendo. The familiar tightening in my stomach warns me of the orgasm that's undoubtedly going to devastate me.

"Fuck, River, I need to fill you up. Come on my cock, now," he demands harshly. Just as simple as stroking a key on a piano, his demand has immediate results. The coil snaps, and I fall over the edge once more.

I can't breathe. My eyes roll and my body convulses around him. Mako's loud grunt is my only warning before he slams inside me a few more times and then stills. Hot spurts of cum fill me up, so much of it that it leaks past his dick.

"Fuuuuck, River," he groans, long and hard.

Our breathing is heavy and choppy. It feels like all the bones from my body have been extracted, making me feel like a melting skin bag.

"I think that worked. Knives are my new favorite thing."

"THE GHOST KILLER'S MOST *recent victim, River McAllister, rebuilding her life after her tragic kidnapping.*"

Red bleeds into my vision. *Victim.* That's what I'm known for. Not someone who survived. Just someone who was victimized. I crumple the paper in my fist and throw the stupid newspaper across the living room.

Mako's eyes turn to me, a brow raised in question.

"Who even reads the goddamn newspaper anymore?" I mutter, my cheeks flushing red with lingering anger and embarrassment.

"Apparently, you," he states bluntly.

I sniff. "Well, not anymore."

"You're still reading those articles?"

"They're everywhere!" I explode, tossing my hands in the air with frustration. "The Ghost Killer's victim does this, the victim does that. When are they going to stop referring to me as a victim and not a goddamn survivor?"

Mako opens his mouth to speak, but I cut him off. "Matter of fact, when are they just going to leave me the fuck alone? Whether I'm a victim or a survivor, reminding me of my trauma isn't healing for me!"

The investigation was closed fairly quickly after Billy's death. With Amar and Mako's statement supporting mine, they deemed the case closed. The Ghost Killer was officially off the streets, and that's all they really cared about anyway.

I decided it was best to get myself into therapy. It'd be awfully hypocritical of me to become a therapist but refuse the service for myself. It's been helping, but I'll never be able to talk about the real truth. What I did to Ryan and Billy, and how I killed them so callously. Only a few people know the truth, but Mako is the only one who truly knows the details of what happened on both of those days. It's something that's deepened our connection tremendously.

Some nights, we stay up until dawn, talking through my feelings and thoughts on the matter while he just listens. I've already concluded I'm not entirely sane due to the years of abuse and trauma. Certain things are triggering for me, even something as small as Mako raising his hands towards my face.

I've also concluded Mako isn't sane, either. Purely because he's okay with staying with a lunatic like me. He loves my crazy, and accepts every single part of me, including the dark, murderous side. Even now, I haven't fully accepted that yet. There's a small part of me that's waiting for Mako to turn on me and become a familiar monster. But every day, he proves he's the furthest thing from a monster, and more like the knight in shining armor I never wanted him to be.

Mako sets down his phone and scoots across the couch until he's huddled around me.

"I can't tell you why they choose to see you as a victim and not a survivor, and I can't tell you why they choose to see you as a story and not a person, but what I can tell you is the people who matter *do* see you as those things. You're right that it's not healing for you, so maybe it's best you just stop reading the articles."

I sigh, my shoulders drooping.

"I just want the rest of the world to move on like I'm trying to do. I don't want to be known as Ryan Fitzgerald's late girlfriend anymore. Or the Ghost Killer's victim. I just want to be *me,* and the rest of the world goes back to not knowing who I am."

He turns my body and scoops me up under my butt, and settles me onto his lap. My legs circle around his waist. Calmness washes over my body and mind with his presence enveloping me. As much as my inner badass hates to admit it, this is where I feel safest. In Mako's arms.

My existence was so bleak before he came into my life. I was constantly surrounded by the evil of the world that sucked all the good things out of life and left me with nothing but the will to die. Now, I have all those things back. All the good things. Hope. Love. Safety. A real future. And the will to live. Mako handed those things back to me like he was picking them out of the Lost and Found bin and handing them back to their rightful owner.

"It's impossible for people to forget about you, baby. All you can do is show them who you are. What they take from it is no concern to you. Other people's thoughts and opinions won't change you."

I lean in and place a soft kiss on his lips.

"Thank you," I whisper.

"For what?"

"For reminding me of who I am."

I'm worthy. I'm strong. I'm independent. And I'm a survivor.

Epilogue
River

"I THINK IT'S TOO soon for this," I say, my eyes locked on Bilby as I pet him. He glances at me and jumps away. I think he just showed me his disagreement.

He's recovered from the stint with Ryan. Mako and him have taken to each other. Constantly cuddling and butting heads. I think I'm Bilby's second favorite now. It's as annoying as it is cute.

"What is?" he asks.

I flick my pointer finger between myself and the living room.

"Staying here every night. Leaving clothes here. I'm practically living here now. I'm pretty sure it's too soon. Are we even boyfriend and girlfriend? You never asked me, you know. You never asked me to move in, either. Are these things that we're supposed to just assume, but never speak about? Are we not going to have an anniver—"

"Baby, please shut up," he orders softly, his deep voice lower than usual. The sound has my core clenching with need. God, what his voice can do to me alone is wholly unnatural. And after the knife incident a couple of months ago, my body has been even more reactive to him than it was before. Mako's kinkiness has opened a whole new door of desire for me.

My lips snap shut, tightening into a straight line. I'm nervous. I don't know why I'm nervous, though.

Mako walks towards me. Or rather, he *prowls* towards me. He looks like a tiger stalking prey the way he approaches me. My breath catches and my nerves light up like fireworks. When Mako Fitzgerald turns all of his attention to me, I come alive.

"Do you want to be my girlfriend?" he asks, but not in the typical high school way, but rather, asking me what I want. He pulls my body to the edge of the couch and crouches before me, settling his hands on my bare thighs. Goosebumps rise across my skin from the slide of his flesh on mine. I'm too enraptured by him to be embarrassed by my reaction.

He's always giving me a choice and always coercing me to voice my opinion and stand up for what I want. I've had my free will and voice stolen from me since I could remember. Billy was the first, like a child ripping a voice box out of a doll. No one has ever let me have it back until Mako. It feels like breaking in new boots—it hurts and it's uncomfortable, but once I'm used to it, I'll feel secure and comfortable standing up for myself. Especially knowing that I'll no longer get a slap to the face—or worse—because I decide to speak up.

"Yes," I say finally. Mako doesn't look surprised by my answer. I suppose putting a label on it doesn't really change things between us. In these past two months, Mako and I have moved beyond just boyfriend and girlfriend anyway.

"Do you want to be here every night?" he asks again, his emerald green eyes growing more intense.

A single nod. "Yes," I whisper.

"And if it becomes too much for you, then you're welcome to leave," he states bluntly. I don't take offense. It's exactly what I need to hear. "But I'll admit, I won't ever want you to."

"Are you going to try and convince me to stay?"

"Yes," he murmurs, sliding his hands up towards my shorts. My breath catches in my throat. "In the hopes, you'll pull a knife on me again."

I roll my eyes, a small smile cracking my face. His words have their desired effect, nonetheless, causing my blood to heat despite my efforts to stay cool. I'm never cool when it comes to Mako, though. His presence eats up any semblance of control I possess and feasts on it like a starving man. I'm unhinged around him, and I've never felt so fucking good.

"Maybe I should try to leave then," I say around a gasp when he bends down to place a chaste but electrifying kiss on my knee.

"Or maybe you could stay." My attention is pulled away from his magnetic eyes when I feel something cool sliding on my ring finger. A gasp lodges in my throat when I look over and see a beautiful princess cut diamond ring nestled on my finger. My eyes widen and snap back to Mako's. His eyes ensnare mine as he leans down and places another chaste kiss on my knee. "Maybe just for a little while?"

"I SWEAR ON ALL THAT is holy, I am so divorcing you, David. When this baby is out of me, it's over," Amelia seethes on her hospital bed. "This is all your fault. You insist on getting me knocked up, and now I'm—ahhhhhh!" Her tirade is cut off by another contraction. She bares her clenched teeth, her face turning red from the pain.

David just sits there calmly and takes it. We both know Amelia doesn't mean a damn thing that's coming out of her mouth. She was feeling him up on the ride to the hospital before the contractions started getting more intense and closer together.

She went from lovingly stroking his dick to wanting to rip it off in a matter of minutes. After Amelia was admitted and settling in, her threats started. I cracked up when David subtly angled his lower half away from her.

She went into labor pretty quick. Alison, Mako, and I were visiting them, drinking wine—sans Amelia— and eating tacos when her water broke. Alison and I hitched a ride with David and Amelia, so we could try our best to comfort her while Mako followed behind us. He and Alison were staying outside of the room since Amelia screamed she didn't want Mako seeing her clam and to get out—her words, not mine. Mako looked like he was just told he won the lottery and high-tailed it out of the room. Alison blushed and followed after, apparently not wanting to see Amelia's clam, either.

"You're crowning. I'm going to have you start pushing in a minute," the nurse announces. Amelia's doctor comes rushing into the room a second later, already scrubbed in.

"Are we ready to meet a beautiful baby?" the doctor asks excitedly and smiles wide, her straight, white teeth a stark contrast to her deep brown skin. Dr. Ivy Jackson is one of the best-renowned doctors in the country, and Amelia refuses to let anyone else touch her during the delivery. I'm pretty sure if Dr. Jackson had not been able to deliver Amelia's baby, she would've tried to plug herself up in stubbornness.

"Doc, get this alien out of me," Amelia whines, sweat gleaming across her forehead. Dr. Jackson laughs and settles down between Amelia's legs.

"Don't you worry, baby, this sweet little boy is going to be out soon, and you won't feel anything else but love. I promise you that."

Before Amelia can come up with a response, she's screaming again.

"Start pushing," Dr. Jackson orders. I can only assume Amelia's listening based on her purple contorted face and the intensified screams coming out of her mouth. David holds her hand, not looking the least bit bothered by the fact that Amelia is currently crushing it. No, he's too busy staring down between Amelia's legs in wonder.

A couple of minutes later, tiny screams replace Amelia's. Tears are already streaming down my face by the time Dr. Jackson places the baby in Amelia's waiting arms.

An indescribable love shines on her and David's faces as they stare down at the new love of their lives.

"Hi, baby Beckham," I say hoarsely, tears clogging in my throat. I sniffle and coo over his cute, little squished face.

Amelia glances at David before smiling up at me.

"Beckham River," Amelia says. I stop cooing and stare down at Amelia in shock. "River is his middle name. And David and I would be really honored if you'd be his godmother."

A sob bursts from my throat. I slap a hand over my mouth and nod my head, overwhelmed by my love for my two friends and their baby.

Beckham is pulled from Amelia, and in a matter of seconds, exhaustion takes over her face. She settles back down while David goes to have his own time with Beckham.

"I love you, River," Amelia says tiredly.

I grab my best friend's hand. "I love you, too, Amelia."

EIGHT MONTHS LATER

"I'M SO HAPPY TO SEE you two together," Julie gushes, her clasped hands under her chin as she gazes at Mako and my conjoined hands with excitement.

A little over the top, Julie.

We decided it was time to come over for dinner. It's just us three now. A vast difference from the last time I was here, over a year ago now. The Ghost Killer didn't truly kill Ryan, nor did Matt ever suffer any real consequences for his actions—other than losing his wife and adopted son—but they're both still ghosts to us. Neither of them is here, but we can feel their presence anyway.

I finish chewing the best apple pie ever, and smile wide at her, appreciative of her acceptance more than she'll ever know. And I appreciate this delicious apple pie, too.

I made Mako wait to announce our engagement after he slipped that ring on my finger over eight months ago. I felt it was proper, considering it hadn't even been a year since Ryan's death and I'd already moved on from him. And Julie was still recovering from her recent divorce with Matt, to top it off. This woman has been through a lot in the past year. Too much. So, I think had I moved on with anyone else, Julie might not have been so excited. Not that I would've ever seen her again anyway.

Mako confessed what he knew about Matt the day his parents visited him in the hospital—lying in a hospital bed, recovering from a gunshot wound. Mako blames the morphine for letting it slip when he did, but he doesn't have regrets. Julie, of course, went into denial. But eventually, Matt admitted he did touch Ryan.

It was a whirlwind of drama after that. Julie wanted Matt to go to prison, but there was no proof. Ryan is dead. The only downside of that fact, I guess. So, Matt got away with it. He claims he never touched any other boy—only Ryan. Mako and I will never know if that's true, but I have a feeling Mako is going to be keeping a close eye on Matt for as long as he lives.

Mako is healing from that blow, too. I, at least, had the luxury of knowing my mother was a piece of shit from the start. Mako was lied to his entire life, believing Matt to be an amazing father and respectable guy. He's still coming to terms with it, but he's getting better.

He still has Julie. We both do.

About three months after the incident with Billy, Mako was promoted to Sergeant. At his ceremony, I finally faced Mako's mother. After a heartfelt apology—which I truly meant in my soul, because despite Ryan being an abuser, it's not easy for anyone to bury their child—she forgave me immediately. She assumed I was too distraught by Ryan's death to come around, and I obviously had a good excuse for not attending the funeral.

Mako and I didn't announce that we were together that day—I slid the ring off my finger before facing her. However, when Mako's ceremony ended, and he came to stand beside me, I could see in Julie's dark-rimmed eyes a spark of hope.

We felt today was finally the day to announce our engagement. We told Julie that our connection blossomed when he saved me from the Ghost Killer. It was easy to spin a love story from the knight who saved the princess from the dragon's lair. Mako's mother gobbled the story up and had said it was only natural that we would be drawn to each other.

"I just know Ryan would love you two together," she continues. My smile falters, and it takes an immense amount of strength to keep it on my face.

"Mom," Mako admonishes. "Don't make it weird."

Way over the top, Julie.

She waves her hand, nonplussed by her words. Bringing up Ryan is still… touchy. Julie is still grieving, and sometimes even saying his name will have her bursting into tears. Every time I witness her pain, guilt lodges deep inside of me.

I'm not a sociopath. She's living with a hole in her chest every day because I murdered her son. Did he deserve it? Absolutely. But Julie? She didn't deserve anything that came her way. I wish there were a way I could take away her pain without taking back my actions, but we're living far from a perfect world.

"It's okay," I say lightly. "I think he would've been happy, too."

Mako squeezes my hand in response. Ryan would've been livid. But the good thing about that is Ryan's dead.

TWO YEARS LATER

"OH, FUCK."

"What?"

"Ohhhh, fuck," I groan. My husband bursts into the bathroom, nothing but basketball shorts on, nearly toppling over me in his pursuit to save me from… I don't know what he thought he needed to save me from.

He stops short, inspects my perfectly intact body and then looks back at me again with confusion. I inspect his body in return, momentarily distracted from his crisis when I get a good look at his six-pack abs and tattoos covering both arms.

I'll never get used to how delicious he is.

"What?" he asks again, drawing me back to reality.

"This!" I exclaim, shoving the stick in his hands.

He looks down at it with a mixture of shock, awe, and horror. Somehow, all three of those emotions are equally prominent on his beautiful face. I'm still feeling those same emotions myself.

Pregnant.

A few years ago, I looked down at a pregnancy test and felt like my life was possibly ending. I was in an abusive relationship with an evil man who was trying to trap me. He drugged me with antibiotics so my birth control would be ineffective, so that I could never leave him. Luckily, the test came back negative.

Now, my husband looks up at me with just one emotion. Love.

We weren't planning on having a baby for another few years. Children were something we openly discussed and agreed on, but neither of us has been quite ready to take that next step. We've been enjoying our time together a bit too much and have been content staying selfish for the meantime just being together.

Plus, Beckham has kept both of us teetering away from that edge, too. Amelia and David's kid is quite a handful. He stays with Mako and me twice a month, and by the time Amelia comes to pick him up, we have a handful of new gray hairs sprouting and dark circles under our eyes. And every single time, Amelia drives away cackling.

After everything came out about Ryan, and I admitted to Amelia that Alison is not an evil, sabotaging bitch like I led her to believe, Alison found herself thrown into our little family. She's considered Auntie Ali to Beckham and probably just as traumatized as Mako and I are after she babysits him.

And now, Mako and I no longer have an option to be selfish.

Because we're having a fucking baby.

"How do you feel?" he whispers, his hands sliding around my waist and pulling me close. I look down at where our chests meet. In about eight months, a big round belly is going to prevent us from getting this close because there's going to be a full-grown baby between us.

"I'm scared. Terrified, actually."

He nods his head, the same sentiment written on his face.

"I'm scared, too. This is sooner than we expected, but I'm ready for it."

I stare into his eyes, trying to find any hint of a lie. Some indication that he's dreading the idea of having a kid with me. But all I can find is devotion.

My chest fills with warmth. "As long as you're by my side, I'm ready too."

He smiles wide, showcasing his straight white teeth and causing the skin to crinkle around his eyes. Mako has the most beautiful fucking smile I've ever seen. It's so goddamn genuine. Every time I see it, it feels like staring straight at the sun. It's beautiful.

I like that word now. Mako has put a new meaning to it just like he's put a new meaning to life.

My eyes settle on the scar from his gunshot wound. It's a constant reminder of how much Mako has done for me. Sacrificed for me. From showing up in my life and trying to get me to see the light and help me, to covering up his brother's murder for me, and then saving me from Billy and getting shot in the process.

Mako owed me absolutely nothing when we first met. I was just another fly in his brother's spider web. Just like Alison had been. He was the only one who knew the true nature of Ryan Fitzgerald. And instead of letting the flies be eaten alive, Mako went out of his way to untangle the web we were weaved in and help us to get away. I owe my life to this man. To this day, Alison shares the same sentiment.

"Do you think I'll be a good mother?"

"I think you were shown the perfect example of what a mother shouldn't be. I think you'll be perfect."

My shoulders drop with relief. Mako's right. Barbie did everything wrong with me, which is exactly why I haven't seen her since I gifted her the house in Shallow River. Barbie didn't deserve any part of the gift, but I wanted to cut all ties with her. What happens to her and that house is no longer a concern to me.

Mako admitted he went to see her when Billy first took me. He never said what he told her, but by the way Barbie looked at Mako with reluctant respect and maybe a slight bitterness. I imagine he did the equivalent of running her through with a truck and then reversing back over her.

"You're going to be such a great dad, too. If we have a girl, I know she'll be a virgin until she's thirty."

He laughs. The sound fills me with so much happiness. "Nah. I refuse to be one of those dads that try to control their daughter's sex life. I always thought it was creepy when guys do that. The only thing I have the right to do is show her the right way a man treats his woman, and she'll learn that from watching us together. And I can only hope she'll be honest with us, so we can make sure she knows if she's being treated right."

Unexpected tears spring to my eyes. I didn't realize how much I needed to hear what type of parent Mako plans to be. But knowing that he'll be so fucking good to our kid is causing all sorts of emotions to rise within me. So much fucking love and happiness. And definitely a whole lot of horniness.

He smiles at my reaction. My cheeks flush red with embarrassment. I'm not normally a crier.

"Hormones," I mumble.

I stifle his laugh with a kiss, shutting him up quickly. I'm so ready to live the rest of my life with this man. And the best part is we're only just getting started. I pull away and rub a hand across my stomach.

"I already know what I want to name her if it's a girl."

"What's that, baby?"

I smile, looking down at my flat stomach. I'm already excited to see my belly grow.

"Camilla. I want to name her Camilla."

He gives me a wide smile. "That's beautiful."

THE END

More Books by the Author

Acknowledgments

I'm not sure where to begin with this one. This story is personal to me. It was therapeutic. It was my version of revenge against the men who continuously escape justice and prey on women. And although there's nothing that will ever fix the pain put upon women since the dawn of time, this is my form of justice.

And to the men who are suffering from abuse, I also stand with you. *No one* deserves to feel this pain.

I guess first and foremost, I'd like to thank *you*. For reading this book. For suffering through the darkness alongside River. For being strong. And for not judging a girl who has suffered an immeasurable amount of pain and handled it the only way she knew how.

Secondly, I'd like to thank my beta readers for helping this story come together. To Micheala Knight, Jessica Brown, Melissa Morris, and of course my mother, Lisa.

A huge thank you to my editors, Sarah Lamb and Angie Hazen. No one has believed in this story quite like you, and I'm incredibly thankful for you.

And I can't forget my River Sister, Chelsea, for making the interior look stunning.

Last but not least, thank you to Leila, my beautiful and too-humble cover designer that really made this book beautiful again.

About the Author

H. D. Carlton is an International and USA Today Bestselling author. She lives in Oregon with her husband, Bigfoot, two dogs, and cat. When she's not bathing in the tears of her readers, she's watching paranormal shows and wishing she was a mermaid. Her favorite characters are of the morally gray variety and believes that everyone should check their sanity at the door before diving into her stories.

Learn more about H. D. Carlton on hdcarlton.com. Join her newsletter to receive updates, teasers, giveaways, and special deals.

Facebook | Twitter | Instagram | Goodreads